BESTIARII
BOOK ONE OF
THE ECHOES OF PANGAEA

James Tarr

Theogony Books
Coinjock, NC

Chris Kennedy/Theogony Books
1097 Waterlily Rd.
Coinjock, NC 27923
https://chriskennedypublishing.com/

Publisher's Note: This is a work of fiction. Names, characters, places, and incidents are a product of the author's imagination. Locales and public names are sometimes used for atmospheric purposes. Any resemblance to actual people, living or dead, or to businesses, companies, events, institutions, or locales is completely coincidental.

Cover Design by Shezaad Sudar.

Ordering Information:
Quantity sales. Special discounts are available on quantity purchases by corporations, associations, and others. For details, contact the "Special Sales Department" at the address above.

Bestiarii/James Tarr -- 1st ed.
ISBN: 978-1648554421

For Andrea, who always believed.

3

Prologue

"Jesus!"

Andy never saw the pothole in the headlights, and it was so deep that when the left front tire dropped down into the chasm, his head bounced off the ceiling, even though he was wearing a seatbelt. The truck full of tools clanked and rattled like an out-of-tune wind chime.

"Slow down, Andy, you're going to give us another flat," Gabe told him. His partner was using both his hands to brace against the seat and the door...and laughing. "We're already late, it's already dark, just relax *hombre*. *'Spacio*." Gabe could speak English without even the hint of an accent, so it was weird to hear the Spanish words rolling out of his mouth as if he was one of those actors on the Mexican soap operas. They could make women sigh just twirling their *rrrrrrr*s. Not that Gabe ever tried to use it to his advantage with their *gringa* coworkers. He was hopelessly, truly, annoyingly in love with his wife.

"I hate being late. I just want to get there, you know?" Andy peered out the windshield at the road disappearing into the dark in front of them.

They'd blown out the rear tire on a piece of rebar jutting from a chunk of concrete. The chunk had somehow found its way into the middle of the dirt road they'd been hustling down, forty kilometers from anywhere. *So where the hell had the chunk of concrete come from?* That's what Andy wanted to know.

They'd been running late before the flat, and it had been half an hour's work just getting the lug nuts off. The lug nuts had been rusted tight, and both of them had nearly busted their backs and bent the wrench loosening them. By the time they were done, the sun was big and orange on the horizon. Andy cursed the tire again. One hundred and fifty years since the invention of the automobile, and they were still riding around on rubber balloons filled with air. There had to be a better way.

"*Sí, pero* Hybridge knows where we are. We aren't due back for two days, and we will catch up on our route tomorrow. *Relajo.*" Gabe hit the button on the dash to display their route. The GPS map popped into existence in the HUD in the low center of the windshield, automatically dimmed as the computer sensed it was dark outside. Don't want to blind the driver at night with a too-bright display. Gabe pointed at their location on the map, then at their destination. They were almost there.

"Okay." Andy rolled his window down the rest of the way and breathed the cool night air. During the day, the heat and humidity were just awful, and running the air conditioning at high with the windows up was necessary to prevent heat stroke, but once the sun sank below the hills it got downright pleasant. There were all sorts of scents on the breeze. The countryside was a living creature, with its own odor. What he smelled on the air as he drove was nothing industrial but rather farm chemicals, probably fertilizer. Farm country. Plus the hint of something green, but whether it was a crop or something wild he had no idea. When he went to work, he was surrounded by much more familiar smells—oil and the weirdly comforting aroma of heated metal.

Stocky and, even after three years of this heat, still committed to wearing a beard, Andrew Brady was forty-three years old and divorced. He'd worked for two oil companies on three continents before coming to Hybridge. He'd been in the industry for eighteen years and was good at his job. The Mexican heat had helped him drop a few pounds, and he tended to keep his black beard trimmed a lot closer to his face than when he'd been in Ukraine, but he'd found that the job was the job, pipelines were pipelines. Location was pretty much immaterial.

Married and widowed young, Gabriel Alvarez had raised two children while working an office job for Hybridge. A few years earlier, about the same time he shipped his youngest off to college, he'd met and married a fiery Latina five years his junior. She'd seen that the office life was beginning to chafe him, and even though his practical skills as a mechanical engineer were a little rusty, encouraged him to apply for a field position. He'd gotten the position and couldn't be happier. He was actually surprised how easy it had been to get a field position. He'd assumed that because Hybridge paid a field bonus there'd be serious competition for the positions, but apparently not. Even though he was on the road a lot, his wife didn't mind, because when he was home, he was all hers.

They'd just spent two days driving through the southern end of the Sierra Madre Oriental mountain range, but in front of them now it was flat land all the way to the Gulf of Mexico. Almost empty, as so many of their routes were. Gabe peered out the windshield and shook his head. So much of his country seemed simply to have been abandoned. Some days it was hard to believe the nation was at war, had been in open civil war for close to twenty years. He'd never seen any fighting, but then again he spent his days driving around the back roads. The combat—which he'd only ever seen on TV— seemed centered on the cities. He supposed there was nothing to fight over in the country.

"We could be anywhere," Gabe said, staring out the windshield at the blackness beyond the headlights. "Or anywhen, you know? The eighteen hundreds. Or forty years ago, before the war."

Andy nodded. The only thing Andy Brady had ever seen of the war was the occasional troop truck. That and military roadblocks on some of the major roads, and the inconvenient and annoying security measures around Hybridge's refineries. The military never seemed to give Hybridge employees any hassle, probably because of the tight relationship Hybridge had with Pemex, the state-run petroleum company which controlled all oil drilling and exploration in the country. Hybridge officially was a subcontractor, but the relationship often seemed much closer to that of equals, as far as Andy had observed. He tried not to get involved in the politics; he was there to do a job.

They were heading for Pump Station 23, several miles southeast of Chicontepec, and southwest of a spot on the map labeled Corral Falso. About 150 miles northeast of Mexico City in a poor rural area. But weren't they all? He didn't know if Corral Falso was a small town or what. He'd never seen it; all he knew was that it was a lot easier getting to the pumping station in daylight. Or at least a lot easier to avoid the biggest holes in the road. Rural road maintenance was a distant priority when you were fighting a protracted civil war, apparently.

HCBCM—Hybridge Chicontepec Basin Central Monitoring, what he and everybody else called HyBacon—had been receiving some twitchy readings from a sensor at the crude oil pumping station. They didn't think there was a problem with the pump, just the sensor. He and Gabe had not one but two replacement sensors, and all the hand and power tools and diagnostic devices they would need to fix whatever the problem was.

While the battered truck and dusty uniforms weren't exactly impressive, both he and Gabe were mechanical engineers, undoubtedly the most highly educated and paid people in any of the rural towns they drove through to do their jobs. After Station 23, they had to head another 62 kilometers down the line to Station 24 and perform the semi-annual inspection of the electrical system.

"Looks like we're going to be spending the night at 23. If I remember correctly there's a worker's bunkroom, couple of cots and a sink, maybe a shower. Definitely drinking water." They spent so much time running the pipeline, on their own and in the middle of nowhere, that they kept the truck stocked with food and water, just in case. You could never be too careful. There was also a pistol in a hidden compartment under the seat, but they didn't talk about that. Ever. So far, neither one of them had even had to think about grabbing it. They'd heard rumors that not all the field teams had been so lucky. Officially only Hybridge Security officers were allowed to be armed, but HyBacon middle management had an unofficial motto— what happens in the field stays in the field.

"Ay, that's why we make the *mucho dinero*."

"Yeah," Andy said drily.

"Do not worry, they know where we are before we get there," Gabe told him cheerfully, banging a hand on the work truck's dash.

All the Hybridge vehicles were equipped with GPS trackers and emergency beacons.

Andy looked out the truck to either side. Couldn't see anything, even with the windows down. His headlights were the only lights from the truck's hood to the horizon. Above the horizon was a different story. No moon, but the stars were amazingly bright. Three years down here, and he still couldn't get used to how bright the stars were. How many he could see. He found himself staring up at them late at night. If you really understood the vastness of space, of man's tiny bit of real estate in the cosmos, it could mess with your head. Some people let it make them feel insignificant. Andy, on the other hand, thought it had to be a sure sign there was a God. Knowing all that man knew about the stars, the size of the universe up there, how could there not be a God?

They came around a low hill on the rutted road. Far beyond the reach of the LED headlights they saw the red and white lights of the pumping station, shining like a beacon in the night. Pumping stations weren't that big, and Hybridge liked to advertise that they built them to "minimize the visual impact" on the surrounding area, whatever the hell that meant. Not that there was anyone around here to see this one.

Pumping Station 23 resembled most of the others where space wasn't a concern. Located on just under two acres, there were some pipes above ground, a lot more below. There were two plain buildings which could have been oversize aluminum-sided tool sheds, one which housed the electric motors and the other which contained the control and monitoring room, as well as the living quarters. In the old days, a technician lived on site, but technology had done away with that. Now computers and simple robots did a lot of the adjustments and maintenance at the station. The robots were mostly autonomous, but were equipped with cameras and could be remotely controlled if necessary. Still, sometimes an actual human being was required.

The purpose of the pumping stations was simple, and the basic design had been around for over a hundred years. As the product—in this case crude oil—flowed through the pipeline, variables such as elevation change, fluid friction, and the delivery point changed the pressure along the pipe, not to mention the speed the product was moving. At the pipeline's origin and intermediate locations, pumps increased the pressure in order to achieve the desired flow rate. The pressure along the pipeline between stations dropped progressively from the discharge point of one station to the suction of the next station due to the friction of the product flowing in the line. Pumps were driven by electric motors and located at stations with variable spacing along the route depending on terrain and pipeline diameter. Most of the pumping stations along the Chicontepec pipeline were about 60 kilometers—roughly 36 miles—apart.

The station grounds were enclosed by a chain link fence topped with razor wire. As the truck pulled up to the gate, security lights popped on and blinded Andy. Squinting, he punched the code into the terminal and waved his magnetic ID badge across the scanner. As the wheeled gate slowly rolled open, he looked over what he could see of the station grounds. White gravel and dark green weeds between the tan buildings, the familiar and somehow comforting throbbing hum of working machinery. Fat pipes and plain industrial buildings, plus a short radio tower, a relic of the days before satellite communications. In the spotlights, the buildings seemed sheer white, the shadows between them impenetrable.

"Central, this is Bravo 4, we've arrived at Station 23," Gabe called out on the radio.

"Roger Bravo 4," came the bored voice from whatever HyBacon technician happened to be monitoring the radio.

Andy idled the truck right inside the perimeter until the gate closed behind them, then rolled forward to the gravel parking area in front of the building housing the control room and sleeping quarters. "Let's spin up and dust off the diagnostic monitors inside the control room, then head out and check the sensor," Andy said. He had slightly more seniority than Gabe, and also tended to take charge. Gabe had a tendency to sit back and wait to be told what to do. It was an almost perfect match-up, and Andy wasn't convinced it hadn't been deliberate, planned by some Hybridge personnel psychologist who'd matched their profiles sitting in his office in New York. Actually, he'd probably been sipping coffee and staring out the window as his computer software did the matching.

Gabe punched in the code to unlock the middle compartment in the back of the truck and pulled out the bag of his personal tools and a backpack containing spare clothes and toiletries. Company equipment was one thing, and Hybridge usually got them anything they needed, but any mechanical engineer worth his salt, with any time in the field, amassed a personal collection of tools absolutely indispensable to the job. Items that ensured that they would be able to do the task required, no matter what.

Scuffed work boots crunching across the gravel, Gabe climbed the three steps to the door of the control building, punched in his personal access code, then swiped his ID. The door clicked, and he pushed it open with a foot, then set the backpack down to keep it propped open. He was surprised to see the lights inside the small building already on—normally they were motion activated, to save energy. Maybe the light switch sensor had been clicked from Auto to Manual. He—

Gabe stopped short, staring. "Uh, Andy?" He heard Andy coming up the steps behind him, and Gabe moved half a step to the side. Andy made it one step into the room before he froze.

"About bloody time you nobs arrived," the man in front of them said cheerfully. "We were worried you were going to show up in the middle of the fireworks."

"Ummmm," Andy started to say, then stopped. The one thing he hadn't been expecting to see inside the small control building was six men in full combat gear, weapons slung, one of them speaking with a British accent. "Uh, can I help you gentlemen?" he finally asked.

"Andy…" Gabe said quietly. Andy saw that his partner was looking out the open door, and turned to see two more soldiers had appeared silently behind them on the gravel.

The man who'd spoken broke out with a friendly laugh. "That's the spirit. No, but we can help you," he informed Andy. "Come on in and shut the door, and we'll tell you why your control room is full of sweaty heathens."

"Screw you O'Malley, I'm a Baptist," one of the other soldiers said with an American southern twang. A few laughed. Andy saw one soldier had a rugged-looking laptop computer opened on a desk and plugged into the power supply. The soldier's hands were moving rapidly over the keyboard, but Andy couldn't see the screen.

The two soldiers coming up the steps forced Gabe and Andy into the building whether they wanted to be in there or not. Once everyone was in and the door shut, O'Malley, who appeared to be the leader, began explaining.

"Sergeant Seamus O'Malley and guests, of Raven PMC," he said, sweeping an arm to include everyone in the room. "We're here because you've got a squad of FRAP on their way here now to blow up your precious pump station."

"What?" The *Fraternidad Progresista para un Mexico Nuevo*—Enlightened Brotherhood for a New Mexico—were the communist guerrillas who had been fighting the Mexican government for the better part of two decades. Depending on who you asked, they were either about to win the war or fade into obscurity.

O'Malley cocked an eyebrow at him. "You do know there's a war on?"

"Well, yes, but, *this* pumping station?"

O'Malley shrugged. "Why not? They hate America, hate the Mexican government, hate capitalism, and hate oil—at least until they're in charge of the profits, then they'll love it. If they blow the pipeline itself, the pump stations on either end of the leak automatically shut down, and all chaps like you have to do is come back in and replace a section of pipeline. Or so I've been told. What happens if they take out an entire pumping station? Wouldn't it be harder to repair, put the pipeline out of operation for a much longer time?"

"Um, well, if they completely succeed in destroying the motors, yes," Andy said, his head still spinning. "We have replacement pump motors they can bring in by truck, but best case scenario is it would still take weeks to get back online. But they'd need a lot of explosives to destroy the motors; they're pretty damn big. And they'd have to destroy all of them."

"However much they need, they've got that and more. Carter, where are they? We've got to get into position before they're in visual."

The soldier with the laptop computer looked up. "About fifteen hundred meters out. Coming in from zero-one-five magnetic. There's a small rise about two hundred meters out, so the facility won't be in view until they top that."

"Let me see."

The soldier spun the computer so his commander could see the screen, and Andy saw a handful of oddly-shaped bright green objects moving vaguely across a darker background.

"Real time satellite imagery," O'Malley explained to the engineer.

Andy's eyes finally figured out what he was looking at. Half a dozen people on foot, walking, seen from almost directly overhead. "Why are they walking?" he asked. "Why don't they just drive up here and smash through the gate?"

O'Malley smiled. "Because a bridge is out. They could either park and walk a bit over a mile, or drive an extra twenty klicks— kilometers—in a big circle to come in from the other direction. Through a small village, where they risk one of the locals making a call and ratting them out to the military. Better just to walk." The soldier with the laptop pulled it back toward himself and began hitting buttons again.

"Oh. Lucky for you, I guess."

"Luck didn't have a damn thing to do with that bridge being out," one of the other soldiers said grimly.

"Control the battlefield," another one of the strangers said.

"Okay, cut the chatter, time to head out," O'Malley announced. "Remember, these buildings and the pipes are the only things that provide any real cover out here. Beyond the fenceline there's nothing that will stop a bullet shy of your noggin. They won't be expecting any resistance, and I don't want them seeing or hearing anything until we go loud. They'll probably bunch up as they start to come through the fence, and that's when—

"Boss, you're going to want to take a look at this," the computer operator said in surprise. He spun in his chair so he could work the keyboard while showing them the screen. He pointed at the small bright green figures of walking men, foreshortened. "Okay, here are the tangos, we've got six bogies now just over one klick out. Coming in from bearing zero-one-five. They are on foot and at a walking pace. Two to plant, four to cover. Probably."

"Aye, but what do you want me to look at?"

The man hit some buttons and the view pulled back. The walking men shrunk until they were tiny green dots at the top right of the screen. At the bottom left of the screen he saw the pump station appear. The terrorists were coming in from the north-northeast, cross country. The soldier operating the laptop didn't say anything, he simply pointed at the top left of the screen. O'Malley squinted, then bent down until his face was a foot from the computer. Andy had seen more green dots. More men?

"Let me zoom in on that for you," the soldier said. A few taps of the keys and the satellite did just that. Andy moved a step closer and peered over O'Malley's shoulder. He saw a lot more green figures, maybe twenty in all, and they weren't walking men. They were heading southeast.

"Is that thermal?" O'Malley asked.

The soldier shook his head. By then the rest of the troops were clustered behind them, trying to see the screen. "No, I tried that. They don't show up on thermal nearly well enough. Not enough heat differential. This is straight amplified visible light." The man hit a couple of keys, and suddenly the entire screen shifted color to variations of red. "That's thermal, see?" The moving shapes all but disappeared against the background color. He flipped back to night vision and the bright green figures popped back out. Andy moved his head closer to the display. The shapes…they definitely weren't human.

"They're on an intercept course," one of the other soldiers observed. "Farther out, but moving quicker…."

"They can't see that far, can they?" someone else asked.

"Smell. Wind's running almost directly east to west."

"Ah."

Andy looked back to see Gabe standing quietly in the corner, looking worried. Andy gave him a look, but Gabe only shrugged. Andy turned back to O'Malley. "I'm confused. Why don't they show up on thermal?"

"Boss, if we're going to set up, we need to do it now," someone said.

O'Malley nodded. "Right-o. Go, set up in your spots, but do not engage anyone unless they get inside the fence. We may not have to do anything tonight. Pay attention to your comms. I will be watching the eye in the sky from in here, and if I say pull back indoors, you do it, and do not waste one second about it. That fence out there won't stop anything past a drooling toddler, and sure as hell won't stop any beasties from smelling you."

The men pulled on their helmets as they headed for the door. Andy knew from reading that the full-face visors with their HUDs would stop most rifle bullets, but he imagined the impact would shock the hell out of a person's neck. Still, whiplash was better than a bullet in the face.

O'Malley and the computer operator stayed in the building, and with the other soldiers gone, the small room didn't seem nearly as cramped. O'Malley wasn't that tall, Andy saw, barely six feet in his boots, but he definitely had an air of command about him. Gabe moved to the door and made sure it had latched behind the last man.

O'Malley put his helmet on but retracted the visor. The other soldier did the same. "Check in when you get into your positions," he said into his helmet's built-in microphone.

Andy was sweating, and had to keep blinking his eyes to unblur the image on the computer screen. After less than a minute, O'Malley said, "Roger, everybody is in position. Hold."

A few minutes later, the soldier operating the computer announced, "Five hundred meters." O'Malley relayed that over the comm.

"Did they know we were going to be here?" Andy asked suddenly.

O'Malley seemed to consider the question before answering. "I doubt it. But when they found you here, they'd have killed you. No question. Just bad luck for you."

On the computer screen the two fuzzy green dots converged on the pump station, until they nearly blurred together. The operator zoomed in, and suddenly the wavy smudges were individual dots again. The guerrillas had circled around a bit and were coming at the station from the east, and moving more slowly. "They're getting close to the rise. 'Bout two hundred meters out. Confirm, six tangos."

"Six tangos, two hundred meters due east," O'Malley said into his mike. "Stand fast, they're about to have company."

"I count twenty-one in the other group," the other soldier said. The second group was almost directly north of the guerrillas. The dots were moving quickly, quicker than the guerrillas. As Andy watched he saw the mystery group dissolve, its members flowing out and around the guerrillas at a distance, forming a circle. When they had surrounded the guerrillas, who seemed to have paused in a group on top of the small rise, the smaller dots suddenly shot inward at blinding speed.

Andy couldn't tear his eyes away from the horror on the screen. Even though the resolution didn't show details, he could see with his mind's eye what was happening. He could *feel* what was happening; it was primal, primordial. Faintly, so faintly beyond the steel walls and the humming machinery he could almost believe he imagined it, there were bursts of automatic weapons fire and screams. Both were brief. He glanced over at his co-worker and saw Gabe cross himself, his face pale.

"Can bloody see in the dark like its daylight," O'Malley muttered. He studied the real-time satellite footage on the computer screen for another minute, then said into his microphone, "Gentlemen, that's it, our job here is done. The dinner bell has been rung, but good. All of our guests were invited. Pull back to my location. I think we'll be sleeping in here tonight; too much fresh blood out there. We'll pick up their gear and check for intel in the morning, provided nothing bigger has shown up."

"How'd you get here?" Gabe asked him, the first thing he'd said since walking into the building.

"Two vehicles, concealed in a wide spot in an irrigation ditch about a kilometer west of here," O'Malley told him. "I'm guessing you drove right by them."

"What was that?" Andy blurted out, still staring at the screen. He couldn't look away.

O'Malley looked at the screen again. "You mean what species? Who knows if anyone has a complete list of what's out there." He squinted. "Hmm. Could be Syntax just from the pack size. I don't think we have the resolution in this satellite to det—"

"No," Andy said firmly, "what was that? What attacked those men? Was it a pack of dogs or wolves or something?" He couldn't imagine what else it could be, from the size the dots on the screen. They'd been travelling in a pack, but this was too far south for wolves, wasn't it? And what kind of feral dogs would attack a group of armed men? Twenty-one seemed a huge pack.

The soldier operating the computer looked at O'Malley, and O'Malley in turn looked at Andy. "Don't they tell you blokes anything before they send you out here?" O'Malley asked in shock. He looked at the other soldier in disbelief. "Unbelievable."

* * * * *

Chapter One

The Scout hit so many potholes at once it bounced sideways, and the driver had to take his foot off the gas, stifling a curse. At one point, the two-lane road had been paved, but after years, maybe decades, of neglect, it could have been in a video of the original moon landing. It certainly was dusty enough, although it was the red-brown of Texas, not gray moon dust. Nothing on either side but land that had once been farmers' fields. Now the only crop the land held was weeds, and most of them were dead in the heat.

"I don't care what the board thinks," Roger Rudd said, frowning past the steering wheel.

The disembodied voice of his assistant Jamie echoed around the vehicle. "Yes you do."

Roger huffed. "Okay, I do, but they're wrong." He looked out the windshield at a whole lot of nothing. "That country is way too unstable to be building a new hotel. Their economy is nothing but ultra-rich versus dirt poor, and the countryside is filled with rebels just itching to attack *something*. Like a luxury hotel. It's a civil war waiting to happen."

"The board—you've read the report they commissioned. They see the low cost of labor, they see a country full of idle rich, a regional transportation hub—"

He cut Jamie off. "Have any of them even been to Malaysia in the past five years? Or Kuala Lumpur? Or are they just reading the reports they commissioned?" He heard Jamie sigh.

"I don't know."

"Well, I've been there. You know I have; you're in charge of my schedule. And even with a board, it's still my company, and I'm not going to spend tens of millions of dollars in what I think is a bad investment. On what I think is only going to become a target for the rebels. It'd be like hanging a piñata in their faces. I've listened to the board, and, God bless them, for a bunch of smart people, they don't seem to have a clue. They actually believe the unemployment numbers *our* government's giving out. We haven't had real single digit unemployment in this country since that actor was President, what's his name. Reagan. And that was over seventy years ago."

Jamie sighed again. There was no use arguing with his boss when he was in this mood. "How long are you gone this time?"

"Four days." Roger glanced over at his son, then back out at the road. "And I'm not going to be reachable; don't try to call."

"Sir, we've got that big meeting about the San Francisco project two days after you get back. I think we're going to need to talk with the engineers...."

"We can do that when I get back. I'm serious Jamie, no calls. Or call all you want; it won't matter. I'm leaving my palmpad in the car. See you in four."

Roger hit the Call End button on the steering wheel and looked over at his son. "Sorry about that," he said.

Mike shrugged. It wasn't as if he hadn't listened to his father make a thousand business calls.

"No, I'm serious," Roger insisted. "This trip is just for the two of us. I'm going to leave the palm in the Scout. Honest. No calls, no checking emails, no videoconferencing, nothing. Okay?"

Mike looked at him, wondering if his father was actually serious. Had he ever seen his father without a palm? He tried to remember. After a few seconds he nodded. "Okay."

The GPS 3D display on—or rather just above—the dash indicated they were approaching La Grulla, but it soon became apparent that the town existed in name only. One main intersection populated with abandoned and listing small commercial buildings, and a few sidestreets, heading to nowhere.

Mike squinted at the GPS map of the town, which for some reason was remarkably detailed. "Solizes, San Vicente, Longoria…how many cemeteries does one tiny town need? One tiny abandoned town."

The very openness of the land itself seemed alien to him. Mike was born and raised in Houston. Nearly four million people, skyscrapers everywhere, and he'd lived at or near the top of one of them as long as he could remember. Even on those rare occasions his father had taken him on business trips—er, vacations—it had been to other cities. Tokyo, New York, Moscow. Tall buildings, lots of people. He'd only ever seen country like what was passing outside the windows in movies.

His father glanced briefly at the color map which moved with their progress, then back at the heaved and pockmarked road. Even though the Scout was four-wheel drive and advertised as off-road capable, this was the closest it had ever been to driving on actual dirt, and he didn't want to damage it. As good as it was, the holo-map didn't quite match the reality in front of them. They were so deep into the middle of nowhere that the Auto-Drive computer didn't even register there was a road beneath them to navigate. "People have been living in this area for thousands of years. And dying. One day there'll be people living all over here again."

"You really think so?" Mike looked out the dusty windows as they rolled through what used to be La Grulla. He rolled down the window, and the leather and new car smell was replaced with swirling fine particles that smelled of dust and ancient horse manure.

Roger Rudd looked at his son. Seventeen years old, almost eighteen…and it felt like he'd only been born yesterday. It seemed impossible. Where had the time gone? But it had disappeared, leaving nothing in its wake but more fat and wrinkles and gray hair for him, and a son who overnight had gone from waist high to an inch taller than Roger.

Michael had been in his life for seventeen years. Seventeen! You'd think he'd have some clue about what was going on in his son's head, at least some of the time, but his son was a complete mystery to him. A near stranger. But hopefully not forever. Roger nodded at the question. "Sure. Everything works in cycles." He kept his eyes on his son another second, then looked back at the road, if you wanted to call it that.

Mike grunted and slid his window back up. La Grulla didn't smell any better or worse than Houston, just different. He pulled his palm out of his pocket and tapped the GPS button. Like everything his dad had bought for him, it was top of the line—a Sirion E7 DataPalm with 20G LTE speeds, at least in the city. Sirion had been the market segment leader for so long their trademarked name had become synonymous with the type of device—palmpad. Like Kleenex, he supposed.

The road map displayed on the screen in less than three seconds, with their position indicated by a blue arrow. Mike checked it against the GPS unit on the dash. "You sure we're going in the right direction? There's absolutely nothing on the map between the town and the Rio Grande." The device's display showed him it was only getting one bar of 6G service, the practical equivalent of being on a deserted island. He could get 10G in the lowest level of the underground parking garage of their apartment building.

Mike switched on the palm's 20MP camera and took a few photos of the nothing passing outside the window, then the device buzzed in his hand. A text from his buddy Brad: DUDE, WHERE ARE YOU? WANNA JUMP ON THE BOX AND PLAY A LITTLE MAN O WAR?

Mike didn't want to talk-to-text because his father was next to him, so he typed with his thumbs: VACATION W MY DAD, REMEMBER? GONE FOR FEW DAYS

There was a few seconds pause, then Brad replied, SERIOUSLY? GOOD LUCK. HIT ME WHEN YOU GET BACK AND TELL ME HOW BAD IT WAS. Mike snorted.

La Grulla was set above a southward bulge of the Rio Grande nearly two miles wide. The river was about a mile beyond the town. A few hundred yards past the last building in town they passed a new-looking concrete road coming in from the left. It wasn't on the GPS map but it glared white under the hot Texas sun. Not long after the mystery connecting road they saw the fence and the gate. Like everything else, the fence and gate were dusty, but they didn't look old.

"See? Have a little faith." As Roger took his foot off the accelerator and let the Scout coast. Both he and his son peered out the windshield as a black shape rose up in the middle distance. With a throbbing hum it headed off southwest.

"Was that a Hydra?" Mike asked in disbelief. He thought he'd seen the distinctive beak-shaped nose of the legendary military jumpjet, but the swirling dust made it hard to be sure.

"I don't know, maybe," Roger said as he keyed the window down and pulled up before the tall gate.

"This is an airport?" Mike asked him in confusion. Past the double rows of chainlink fence, both of which were topped with razor wire, was a berm fuzzy with brown grass. Past that were the tops of some low buildings, but nothing else was visible.

The building next the gate was the size of a contractor's trailer. The aluminum siding rattled in the breeze and looked more than a bit weather beaten. The small porch in the front sagged in one corner and was covered in Astroturf that had faded to a color closer to tan than its original green.

The door opened, and three men stepped out. The men were dressed in the new optically reflective camouflage pattern uniform Mike'd read about in Popular Mechanics. The fabric reflected, to varying degrees, the colors of the objects around it, and came complete with integral armor plates. He also recognized their weapons as M7 carbines, current military issue, mounting hybrid optics. He looked left and right; the fence in front of him ran in each direction in a laser-straight line until it faded into the landscape. Had to be at least half a mile.

One man approached the driver's door of the Scout while the other two spread out. *To get better fields of fire on us if we try something*, Mike thought to himself, eyeing their carbines. He'd read enough war novels, played enough video games to know that much. He wasn't scared, but he was surprised, almost shocked to see them here, twenty miles past the middle of nowhere. Not that he and his father could appear much of a threat to anyone, a fat middle-aged guy and a teenager riding around in a new, overpriced, cream-colored SUV.

"Shut your vehicle off, stay inside, and refrain from making any sudden movements," the man closest to Roger's window told him in a flat voice. "IDs and reason for visit." The man was deeply tanned and wore his combat kit like he'd been born in it.

Roger had been out of the Air Force for over thirty years but he knew professional soldiers when he saw them. These weren't minimum wage flunkies, and they damn sure weren't draftees. The uniforms appeared to be current military issue, but he didn't see any insignia on their shoulders or anywhere on their persons, not even an American flag. Or a nametag. There were no signs anywhere indicating what kind of facility this was.

Roger stuck his hand out at his son even as he dug out his own wallet. "What the hell is this place?" Mike murmured, so softly only his father could hear him, but dug out his ID and put it in his father's hand.

Roger handed their two IDs over to the man and told him, "We're here for PSI. Our contact is Aarne Anders."

The man grunted and swiped both IDs through the armored palmpad hanging off his webgear. He studied the readout briefly, then held the pad out to Roger. "Press your thumb on the box."

Roger pressed his thumb against the screen inside the virtual rectangle, and he saw a flash and heard a beep as his fingerprint was scanned. The man then reached a little deeper into the car, and Mike, stretching across his father, had his thumb scanned as well. The man studied his pad for a second, then pressed a finger to the radiobud hanging on his ear. He turned away as he started talking, and Roger didn't catch any of it.

He glanced at his son, who was looking around excitedly. The other two soldiers were at their one and nine o'clock positions, and kept their hands lightly on the grips of their carbines as they waited for the word. Their deep tans made it hard to tell, but Roger put them in their late twenties or early thirties, old enough to have seen quite a bit of combat what with the state of the world. After about thirty seconds, the lead soldier turned back toward them, and the last word of his end of the conversation was audible. "Roger."

"Yes?" Roger said, then felt stupid. The man had been acknowledging someone else, not saying his name.

The man ignored the misstep and instead asked, "What's in the vehicle?"

"Two rifles, a handgun, ammunition, spare clothing and other personal effects including electronics," Roger told him. "Palmpads." He hoped to God that the firearms wouldn't cause any problems. He was supposed to have been cleared to bring them into this facility and beyond, but you never knew. He'd been told there would be a 'security presence,' but he'd been expecting a small private airstrip in the middle of nowhere. This facility was anything but small or private. "I have the serial numbers of the weapons if you need them."

"Any explosives or biological agents?"

"No sir."

"Stand by while we scan your vehicle. Do not move." No threats, no profanity. He kept his voice even, and he never even put a hand on the carbine slung across his chest, but Roger had the impression the man wouldn't hesitate to kill them both and burn their corpses if necessary.

Roger waited, but nothing happened. After a few seconds, he opened his mouth to ask a question, then remembered that the rectangle of road directly in front of the gate, on which his vehicle now sat, had been unexpectedly clear of the blowing dusty dirt that was everywhere. *The scanner's underneath us.* His eyes strayed to the fence stretching out in front of them. The fence was only the visible security, he realized. The first layer. There had to be a lot more. Sensors, cameras, drones, maybe even mines.

"You are clear," the soldier told them after another thirty seconds. He returned their IDs then gave them two clip-on badges which he pulled out of a cargo pocket on his thigh. The badges were completely unmarked except for the word VISITOR on the front and a magnetic strip down the back. "Proceed directly through the gate. Follow the green line until it reaches a parking lot. You will be met at that building. Do not stop before then and do not deviate. Don't sightsee. Follow the green line. Am I understood?"

"Yes sir," Roger told him. He noticed that the other two soldiers had migrated back to the front of the trailer, and then the gate before him began to roll open.

Mike waited until his father rolled up his window and had driven through the gate before the words burst forth. "Dad, jeez. Where are we going? I thought this was going to be a hunting trip." He was practically bouncing in his seat.

Roger was more than a little intimidated by their unexpected surroundings, but showed his son a smile. "Who said it wasn't?"

"Hunting at a military base? At a secret military base?" It had to be secret because there were no signs, and the soldiers weren't wearing any insignia. "And don't tell me it's abandoned. In the three minutes we were at the gate two helicopters and a cargo plane took off," Mike said, his words coming out so fast they were falling over each other, "and another helicopter landed. I think it was a Copperhead," he told his father, naming the top-of-the-line U.S. attack helicopter.

"Hmmm," Roger said, faking indifference but smiling on the inside. They hadn't even gotten on the plane, hadn't even loaded their rifles, and already the PSI people were living up to their reputation. *This is going to be great*, he thought. But then again, for what he had paid, it had better be. Behind them, in his rearview, he saw a long line of military heavy-hauler trucks pulling up to the guardhouse.

Past the gate and a slow S-curve through a double row of earthen berms, the road straightened and stretched before them for at least half a mile. There were low pre-fab buildings scattered about looking like dice tossed by giants. Roger saw metal storage containers by the thousands, and heavy trucks and tractor trailers parked everywhere. Pickup trucks and a few personal cars were here and there, usually tucked behind the buildings. As he watched, a fat cargo plane lumbered into the sky with a bright flare of light. The rocket-assisted take-off was the only way the heavily-loaded transports could get airborne before the runway disappeared.

"What are those?" Roger asked his son, nodding out the windshield. Like most teenage boys, Michael had some knowledge of and interest in all things military. God knows he played enough army shoot-em-up video games. There were a number of balloon-tired vehicles sporting desert camouflage moving around in front of them.

"Those are Spartans," Michael told him in awe. "Light armored vehicles. Gun turret up top, runflat tires, holds up to eight people. Their armor will stop bullets, but not rockets." He'd never seen one in person. They looked even cooler in person.

"You know a lot about them," Roger observed, surprised at the amount of detail coming from his son.

"I asked for one for my twelfth birthday," Mike told him. "You got me an RC one instead of the real thing. Don't you remember how mad I was?"

"Twelve?" Roger shook his head. He couldn't remember the birthday at all.

His son smiled ruefully. "I knew you had money, but I didn't quite grasp how expensive the real things were." They sat in silence as the Scout coasted down the road, following the green line painted down the middle of their lane.

"I'm glad we're doing this," Mike said finally. The great Roger Rudd, founder and CEO of the Pearl Sapphire hotel chain, wasn't a bad guy and wasn't a bad father. He was just never around. And when he was, he was on his palmpad, taking calls, reading notes, working, working, working. Michael's mother had died from cancer when he was five, and neither of the men in her life had known how to deal with the loss. Michael pulled into himself, and his father had buried himself in work. Roger was on replacement wife number…three, was it? Each successive one seemed twice as pretty and half as smart as the previous one. His current stepmother, Bianca, was only twelve years older than Mike, and seemed nearly as plastic as a Barbie doll. She spent all of her time at the spa and shopping, and couldn't talk about politics or current events without giggling, and even then she could only last about thirty seconds. She was nice, and Mike didn't dislike her, but she was about as useful to him as an uncomfortable piece of furniture. His friends liked staring at her cartoonishly big gravity-defying chest when they were over, and he couldn't say he hadn't done the same, but knowing his dad and her....

He sighed. Couldn't his dad do better than a vacuous former model? The man was a self-made millionaire. Multi-millionaire, he was pretty sure. Not that Mike knew him, not really...or at least, not as a father. He was just the old guy he lived with.

Mike didn't hate his father. His dad had never been a jerk; he simply didn't know him. Roger Rudd was a stranger Mike happened to be related to. Well, not a stranger, but sure not family. At least, not as close as family were supposed to be. Mike was pretty sure his father felt the same way about him, and that's why he'd sprung this surprise hunting trip on him the week after Mike graduated from high school. Father/son time, male bonding, whatever.

His dad didn't know Mike, either. They never had those fabled father/son talks. His dad could barely remember the names of his two closest friends, Brad and Jerdy. His dad had no clue Mike was currently on the outs with his sort-of girlfriend, Carrie. His dad had met her, but whether he even remembered her name wasn't a bet Mike would want to take.

His dad was so busy making sure Mike applied to the right colleges that he never once asked Mike if he wanted to go or had any clue what he wanted to major in. He did want to go to college, as much to get away from home as anything else, but didn't have any clue what he wanted to study. It would have been nice to talk about it with his dad, but he was always so busy, so...unapproachable.

The street began to branch left and right, and they followed the green line to the right on the third fork in the road. It led to a small, low building squatting in front of an empty helipad. Standing at the curb was a cheerful older man with ginger hair in a tan three-piece suit. He gave a little wave at them and waited as Roger picked a spot in the empty lot and parked.

Mike cracked the door and got out, but it wasn't until he'd shut the door on the last dregs of air-conditioned goodness that the heat and humidity hit him. Oh my GOD. It felt as if someone had microwaved a wet blanket and wrapped it around his head.

"Mr. Anders, I presume?" Roger said, stepping forward. Before he'd taken two steps sweat beads had popped out on his forehead.

"Yes, oh yes indeedy," Anders beamed at them. He shook Roger's hand, then Mike's, pumping it quickly. He spread his hands, indicating the empty parking lot and the small unmarked building behind him. "Welcome to PaleoSafari, Incorporated, such as it is."

Mike's eyebrows went up. "PaleoSafari?" he said.

Roger turned to his son. "I may not have remembered that you wanted a Spartan, but I damn sure remember how much you've always loved dinosaurs. Happy Graduation, Michael."

* * * * *

Chapter Two

Anders looked the two Rudds up and down and beamed like a new father. "Welcome welcome welcome!" He peered at Mike closely. "You're a good-looking young man," he said. "You must make your father very proud."

"He sure does," Roger said. Mike made a face.

Anders' eyes flicked back and forth. The elder Rudd was thick, with a bit of a gut and heavy features, but there was some resemblance between the two around the eyes. They both sported dark hair and big white teeth. The boy was over six feet tall, with that innate effortless thinness that most males begin to lose shortly after high school.

Anders looked at the father and saw him perspiring freely in the Texas heat. "How about we go inside for a bit while we wait for your ride?" Anders asked. "It's a tad cooler." He waved them to follow and started up the concrete walk to the building. Everything was shades of brown—the sidewalk was lined with brown grass, and the building was tan. Anders' khaki suit was almost camouflage.

"It's an oven out here," Roger said. "I can't believe you're wearing that."

Anders looked down at himself and touched the vest as they walked. "It's all what you're used to, I suppose," he said. "I've spent so much of my life in the equatorial regions that a little heat doesn't bother me anymore."

"A little heat?" Roger said. He could feel the sweat trickling down his spine as Anders opened the steel door for them. He could feel the frosty air on his legs first as he followed Michael inside. "It's pushing a hundred. Will it be okay to leave our gear in the vehicle?"

Entering into the dim room felt like stepping into a walk-in cooler after the heat outside. The building was square and almost bare. A large classroom took up most of the space, with long tables and chairs lined up facing a podium. There were a number of posters on the walls, mostly generic military admonishments about safety. *After You Pull The Pin, Mr. Grenade Is NOT Your Friend.*

"The Libyans would call this a nice spring day," Anders said cheerfully. "Although it would be a bit moist for them. Your equipment will be just fine left in your auto. We don't have much problem with crime here, as you can imagine. Beverage? I'm not sure exactly how long we'll have to wait."

The empty classroom in front of them ran to the edges of the building to the left. To the right was a short hallway with several doors. "Do you have Coke?" Roger asked him.

One of the hallway doors led to a small room which contained two vending machines, one for snacks and the other for drinks. "How much are they?" Roger asked, reaching for his pocket.

Anders hit the Coke button, and they heard the mechanical hum and then the thud of the plastic bottle hitting the dispensing door at the bottom of the unit. "For clients? Free. I think I've taken enough of your money," Anders said with a smile. "And you?" he asked Mike.

Mike just extended his hand a few more inches and hit the button himself for some vitamin-infused water. Anders retrieved it for him, then handed it to Mike as he ushered the two of them next door into a small office. A small sign on the door read PSI, but that was it.

The office itself was small, barely eight by ten feet. There was a modest desk, with a padded leather chair behind it and two more in front. There were a few books on a shelf behind the desk, and a piece of tech that Mike didn't recognize. He thought it might be a satellite vidphone, but he'd never seen anything like it—it looked military. Across from the desk was a large topographical map of Mexico, including bits of the United States to the north and Guatemala and Belize to the south.

"How about some brochures?" Anders said, digging around in a drawer. He pulled out two and handed them to the men. Mike stared at his.

"What are we going to be doing?" Mike said. *PaleoSafari? There really was such a thing?*

Anders looked at Roger and raised his eyebrows.

"It's a graduation present," Roger explained. "I sort of sprung it on him, a surprise."

"Well!" Anders said, nearly jumping with excitement in his seat and clapping his hands together. He reminded Mike of a hyper young Santa Claus. "Your father really must love you, because you're going to get to do something few people on the planet have ever done."

Mike looked up from the brochure, which he'd read nearly all the way through. It was surprisingly vague. "Which is what, exactly?" He was afraid his father had been scammed by a con artist.

"Ooh, I can tell a little history lesson will help you, young Mr. Rudd," Anders said. He jumped up from behind the desk and came around to the front, where he perched. "How old are you?"

"Seventeen."

"Seventeen...." Anders drifted off in thought, thinking of his seventeenth year. He'd been in combat in what had been Libya and Chad before the Caliphate, after having enlisted with his father's permission at sixteen. But that was two occupations and three wars past. "You're aware of the advances in genetics that began happening forty years or so ago?"

"Um, which advances are you talking about?" Forty years ago was ancient history. Mike had taken a few science classes in high school but hadn't excelled. He'd forgotten most of what he'd learned. Even now, with a diploma, he still didn't know what he wanted to do for a career. His father never pushed him one way or the other, but Mike knew getting a business degree would make his father happy.

"Not cloning, of course, they've been doing that since the twentieth century I believe. I'm talking about the human genome. DNA, unlocking and being able to read DNA. And replicate it, of course. The first huge breakthrough was successfully growing human skin in a lab. Then other organs. Lungs, hearts, kidneys; whatever was needed for the transplant. Within ten years, the need for organ donations almost disappeared."

"Sure," Mike said. There'd been lab-grown organs for as long as he could remember. One of the girls he went to grade school with had been in a bad car accident and needed a new liver. She'd only missed a few weeks of school.

"There were many other more substantive scientific and medical achievements, but the next one that captured the public interest was when GenVen announced they'd brought an extinct species back to life—in this case a dodo. That dodo started an explosion, almost a race between all the genetics companies, to resurrect extinct species. Law at the time was murky, but their thinking was that, if the species was extinct, whatever they created they could patent as a proprietary biological. The DNA samples of the creature were never perfect, and the boys in the labs always had to tinker a bit to get a proper finished product, so getting patents turned out to be easy."

"I thought the saber-tooth tiger was the first extinct animal brought back," Roger said.

"No," Anders corrected him. "But it was the animal that sparked everyone's imaginations. Nobody cared about the dodo, but as soon as there was video of a living breathing smilodon walking around, suddenly the race was on. And everyone now knows where the finish line was."

"With dinosaurs," Mike said.

"Exactly." Anders looked at Roger Rudd, and then to his son. "Your father is, I'm sure, old enough to remember that there was a huge amount of controversy when the first 'dinosaurs' were unveiled. The truth is, while to the eye they were dinosaurs, the scientists had to patch so many holes in their DNA with material from other animals that genetically they were anything but true dinosaurs. The scientific community was aghast at what these mercenaries working for the bio-gen companies had done. 'Frankenstein's Monsters' they called them. 'A latrine full of DNA' I think is my favorite quote from the press. Delightful. As for the public outrage…."

"There was none," Roger said. "Nobody cared about their pedigree. They were dinosaurs. Dinosaurs, walking around." He'd been in college at the time, and remembered seeing it on the news. Some female reporter, petting a real live baby triceratops, no special effects.

It was like being a kid again, Christmas and his birthday all wrapped up into one. It was magical.

"Right," Anders agreed. "But creating them was expensive as hell. Lots of trial and error for everyone involved. Science for science's sake doesn't pay much, if anything. But you know what does? Entertainment. Enter the dinosaur theme park. Just like in those movies."

Roger Rudd smiled. "Those didn't work out so well in the long run. And not because the dinos escaped."

Anders smiled back and shrugged. "Right. Zoos have been successfully restraining dangerous animals, like lions, for centuries. I think in the end the problem was location. The only countries in the world willing to risk living breathing dinosaurs walking around, even behind giant walls, were the ones in dire need of cash. And countries in desperate financial situations generally aren't stable."

"The park in Japan is still open, isn't it?" Mike said. He couldn't remember what it was called. Dinosaurland or something stupid like that, once you translated it into English. His father had been supposed to take him there years ago, but that trip had never happened for one reason or another.

"Yes, if you've got the money. The #1 Vacation Spot for Billionaires, I believe Forbes called it. I think I read that the average two-day visit to the park costs a million dollars. The one in Indonesia is still operating as well. There never were nearly as many dinosaur parks as people expected, simply because of the cost involved. First, no dinosaurs exist in the wild, so you have to grow them yourself, which takes not just money but time, which is, as they like to say, money. Unsurprisingly, all the dinosaur DNA is patented. If you're not the company that owns the patent, on top of the cost of building a park you've got all the DNA user fees and royalty costs. Those bio-gen companies had to make all their money back somehow. Usually, they formed a partnership with an entertainment conglomerate. Even so, at the height of the craze, there were only half a dozen such parks around the world. We're here," he swung his arm around the room, "because of Pangaea."

The swinging arm stopped, pointed, and he took a step forward between them to stab it at the map of Mexico. Both Roger and Mike turned around to see what he was touching with his finger. Anders tapped a small green blob near the east coast of Mexico. The closest city, not too far to the north, was Ciudad Victoria. "*Reserva de la Biosfera el Cielo*" he said, the Spanish rolling off his tongue with ease. "Where Pangaea was—and still is—located, and near where you'll begin your hunt."

Mike blinked. So it was true, they were going to be hunting dinosaurs? It was unbelievable. "This sure seems like a scam to me," Mike said suddenly, waving the brochure around.

Anders stopped and looked at him. A hint of a smile touched his lips. "Yes?"

"This brochure is about as vague as it could be without being blank. You could be real estate agents or adventure travel guides; there's no way to tell what you're selling from this. Just a lot of pretty pictures of Mexican hills. 'The complete paleo experience'? What the hell is that even supposed to mean?"

"Exactly. That brochure is deliberately vague, with a misleading photo," Anders assured him. "Similar to an online dating profile." Roger snorted.

"What?" Mike had been expecting him to deny it, or argue. "Why?"

"It is legal to book hunts in Mexico of recognized game animals. Legal for U.S. citizens to enter the country with firearms to hunt, as long as they have all the proper paperwork and licenses. You two are hunting white-tail deer. I know, because it says so right here on your hunting licenses." He produced some documents from a desk drawer. Mike was surprised to see that the documents weren't digital, but honest old-fashioned paper. "It's also listed on your permits for bringing firearms into the country.

"According to the Mexican authorities, when the communist guerrillas attacked the park eighteen years ago, they killed off all the animals. None were released into the wild. They made sure to tell everyone that. There was no danger to the public. Those not killed were recovered in their enclosures or put down by park staff."

"Right," Mike said slowly. That was pretty much what he remembered from his history text. Something similar had happened to the park in Russia.

"So if we advertise that we sell guided hunts of dinosaurs, we could be charged with fraud. Selling hunts for animals that officially don't exist in this country. Therefore, all of our advertising has to be vague, and in general we get business through word of mouth. That is not to say that the authorities—on both sides—don't know what we're doing. They very definitely do. A significant percentage of your hunting fees goes to…well, let me be short and just call them what they are, bribes. The cost of doing business. As long as we're discreet about what we do, and the right palms get greased, everybody is happy."

"I'm confused," Mike said. "So the dinosaurs didn't all die?"

Anders smiled like a kind uncle. "Would it surprise you to learn that governments sometimes lie to people? Even their own citizens?"

"Well, uh, no."

"The reality of the situation was far different from the reports that the Mexican government—and then our own—put out. The Mexican government still hadn't been taking the guerillas seriously, even though they'd planned a few ambushes and organized attacks that had done real damage. Most of the early fighting was just north of Mexico City, which is hundreds of miles south of us if you don't know your Mexican geography. Attacking Pangaea was a completely unexpected move, but it shouldn't have been. Communists hate capitalists, and what better example of capitalism run amok than a dinosaur theme park run by an American company on Mexican soil, catering to the rich? The park had a few security guards, who apparently gave a good accounting of themselves, but they were no match for a military-style raid. The guerrillas killed most of the staff and all the visitors who couldn't get away, then they set off bombs which destroyed most the administrative building and offices. The official story was that they also killed all of the animals in the park, but that park was huge, miles and miles across. It would take them days to track down all the animals. And why would they? No, instead, to spread as much panic as possible—for they are terrorists as much as they are anything else—they planted charges on a lot of the exterior habitat walls. Shot others with rockets. Terrorists always love chaos.

"The Mexican authorities didn't believe the stories at first, and then they didn't believe the attack had been as bad as it was. When they were finally convinced of the facts of the situation, the orders went out. Six days after the attack, the Mexican Army finally arrived at the scene in force."

"Six days?"

"Yes. Efficient and speedy and professional as always. And they discovered that eighty percent of the habitats had their external walls breached by explosives, and the power to all the internal, electrified fences had been down since the attack. They found dead animals, and a few still wandering around. They killed them so they'd have a few carcasses to show off, but the fact of the matter is a large number of animals escaped. Just how much of the park's animal population made it out nobody knows."

"How do you know any of them were even able to survive in the wild?" Mike asked him. "They were living in a controlled environment."

"No, they were living in a *contained* environment. To 'make' the external habitats, mostly all the park designers did was wall off huge sections of the Cielo Biosphere. That's why they chose that location, because environmentally it had everything they needed. If any animals got out, the landscape they encountered would be identical to what they were already used to, minus the moats and electrified fences and such. And you know what animals that don't die do, as often as they can?"

"What?"

"Breed. Well, breed, eat, shit, and wander about. There have been sightings as far north as Corpus Christi, and as far west as Guadalajara. No one can quite agree on what their actual reproductive capacity might be. Some geneticists still want to argue that they shouldn't even be able to breed in the wild, or at all, because of their mixed DNA, but of course they've been proven completely wrong."

"There are dinosaurs in the U.S.?"

"Even with all the terrorist attacks of twenty years ago, Congress still couldn't complete the border fence. So yes. Wild animals have no concept of international boundaries or safe sex. The scoundrels."

"Why hasn't the army hunted them all down?"

"What army? The Mexican army? Twenty years ago, they found themselves in the middle of a war they were ill-prepared for, riddled by greed, corruption, and incompetence, and now they are but a shell of what they once were. The whole country is a house of cards propped up by the United States."

"What do you mean?" Mike had heard it was bad, but surely it couldn't be that bad. "They don't even talk about the war on the news, except for politicians promising not to send any U.S. troops to fight in it. Wouldn't they send troops if it was that bad?"

Roger told his son, "The politicians in vogue at the moment keep repeating that they won't pay to fight another country's war when we're still struggling on the rim of another depression, but the facts are quite different. We've officially pulled out of Mexico's civil war, but no matter what they say publicly about non-intervention and not providing military assistance, there's no way in hell the U.S. government can allow the communist guerrillas to win in Mexico. The border is too big and porous, and they'd bring their communist revolution here in a heartbeat. Or widescale combat and chaos. And everybody in Congress knows it."

Anders smiled at Mike. "We haven't had any active duty U.S. soldiers fighting in Mexico for years—that much is true—but did you happen to notice the base driving in? We've been helping the Mexican army through the use of a private military corporation, and depending on whom you ask, the corporate contractors are now shouldering thirty percent of the entire war effort, or eighty. Mexican death tolls for the war over the last twenty years range from a low of one million all the way to twelve million. I think the higher number is more accurate. For a country with a population that started around 120 million. That's three times the casualty rate we had in our own civil war, and we lost more people in the Civil War than in all our other wars combined. But your Senators and Congressmen can, without lying, say that there are no U.S. soldiers in combat in Mexico."

"Contractors. As in mercenaries."

"All soldiers get paid to fight, and while some of these gentlemen would probably fight for anybody who gave them a check, many more are just happy that they can continue to serve their country, and would slap an American flag on their fatigues if it was allowed. They are doing the job American soldiers should be doing, if only our politicians weren't spineless."

"So wait, we're heading down to Mexico to hunt? We're heading into a country at war? How can that be safe?"

"Oh, you needn't worry," Anders told him. "You'll be in no danger. All the fighting is far south and west of where you'll be. It's a big country, and terrorists only care about cities. Plus, you'll be doing most of your scouting in an armored vehicle."

"Are you going to be our guide?" Roger asked him.

"Oh no, I'm just an old repatriated expatriate," Anders said with a laugh. "I've had a number of jobs in my life, but professional hunting guide is not one of them. No, your PH will be Peter Hein. You'll be flown from here down to Victoria Base, which is the military compound closest to Pangaea. It's a joint installation—Mexican army and Raven contractors. From there you'll head out in armored vehicles with Peter. He knows that whole area and knows where all the game trails are. It should be quite the adventure."

"I still can't believe there are still dinosaurs alive after twenty years," Mike said. "Why wouldn't they have been shot by the people who live in the area? Farmers or whoever. Like they'd shoot—what is it they'd have around here? Foxes? Coyotes?"

Anders blinked several times, then cocked his head at the young man. "Do a lot of hunting with your father?" he asked.

"Not really," he admitted.

"We went duck hunting last year," Roger said. "And we planned to go hog hunting in Texas, but that hasn't worked out yet." Roger honestly was at a loss, coming up with ways to spend time with his son at home, much less on vacation. They didn't seem to be interested in any of the same things. A client had offered him the duck hunt last year, and on a whim, he'd asked if he could bring his son. Much to his surprise, when he asked Mike, his son had accepted. And they'd had a great time. He'd taken Mike shooting a few times when he was younger and taught him gun safety, but they weren't exactly "hunters." The duck hunting trip had been great because they'd had three days alone in the duck blind together, with no voice or data service, and had actually talked, like people. They'd connected, at least for a time. Roger was hoping the same thing would happen on this trip. When he'd made a point of thanking the client for the trip, the man in confidence had told him about PaleoSafari, Inc. Roger spent enough time outside of the country to realize how bad things were, and how many lies his—hell, *all* the governments were telling their people, so he didn't immediately dismiss the man's story as fantasy. Some discreet research on his part had turned up evidence that quite a few of his wealthier customers had been clients of PaleoSafari. And all the unbelievable stories seemed to be true.

"Hmm," Anders said. "Well, I'm sure the locals have been killing their share of the animals, but that area of Mexico was some of the most sparsely populated in the country *before* the war started. Civil war does a lot of things to a country, but increasing the birth rate isn't one of them. Do you know that twenty-five percent of Mexico's population had immigrated, mostly illegally, to the U.S. by 2015? And that was without a war. When you add up the death toll from the war and the people fleeing it Mexico has lost over half its population.

"The Sierra Madre Orientals and parts east were pretty much barren of people; that's why Pangaea was sited there. And that explains how it continued to operate smoothly for over two years, even though the south end of the country was literally on fire. Poor timing, that. It took them four years to build the park, and they weren't going to walk away from it merely because there was some fighting hundreds of miles away, fighting that the Mexican government kept saying was between rival drug cartels. And apart from the attack on Pangaea, that area of Mexico has nearly been ignored by the terrorists. That's why you don't need to worry about the war. There's nothing to fight over in that area. It's a ghost town."

"Have you ever, you know, hunted them?" Mike asked.

"Terrorists? Or dinosaurs?"

"Ummm." The question surprised Mike. "Uh, dinosaurs."

Anders smiled. "No. I can't afford the experience I sell, unfortunately; I'm simply a facilitator. Well, actually, I have killed a crocodile," he admitted. "They and alligators are basically unchanged since the Jurassic, so in effect they are dinosaurs walking the earth. Tasted a bit like chicken, if I must admit. And it's about the same color. You eat the tail meat."

"Really?" Roger said, surprised. Looking at a croc or gator, the last thing he'd expect was that they tasted like chicken.

"Well, honestly, the crocodile has been on the planet longer than the chicken, so to be accurate, chicken tastes like crocodile."

They became aware of a steadily growing roar, and Anders raised his eyes to the ceiling. "I believe that is your ride," he said, but made no move to get up.

"Should we head out there?" Roger asked.

"We've got some time. They always want to grab a few things for resupply," Anders said. "And the wind and the noise and the dust." He waved a hand around his head. But then he looked at Mike. "But the boy might find it interesting. Spent much time around helicopters?"

"We're riding in a helicopter?" Mike said in excitement and disbelief. "Where is it?"

"The landing pad's around the back of this building. I'd stay back from the pad…" he started to say, but Mike was already out the door.

"C'mon, dad!" Mike yelled from the hallway.

Roger looked at Anders, and the two men smiled at each other.

* * * * *

Chapter Three

The heat hit him like running face first into a heavy punching bag in the middle of a hot sweaty gym. Mike pushed through it and ran around the back of the low building.

The helicopter's blades were still turning, and he was buffeted by hot wind as he rounded the corner of the building. He'd never ridden in a helicopter, and with all the high-tech hardware he'd been seeing on the base Mike was wondering what they'd be riding in. A Copperhead? No, they were attack helicopters; no room for passengers. A Krait? For an attack helicopter they had the ability to transport a lot of weight, but they were still brand new.

He stopped on the sidewalk near the building and held up a hand to block the grit. He was surprised at how much wind the chopper blades were throwing at him, it never looked that strong in the movies he'd seen. The helicopter on the concrete pad was big, a lot bigger in person than he expected. Way up there, in the sky, they looked tiny, but standing fifty feet away, the thing made his father's Scout seem a toy.

Behind the glass he could see the helmeted pilot and co-pilot flipping switches and pressing buttons as they powered down the aircraft. The rear door slid open, and a contractor wearing a full military field uniform complete with armor plates climbed out. As Mike watched, the soldier's uniform change from a mottled dark color to more of a tan as it began reflecting the colors surrounding it.

"That is so cool," he murmured. He'd seen it hundreds of times before, in his video games, but this was *real.* The soldier pulled off his helmet and set it on the floor of the chopper, leaned forward to say something to the pilot, then began walking toward Mike. Short sandy hair, almost stubble, with a bored look on his face, squinting against the bright glare. He wasn't carrying a rifle, but Mike saw he had a pistol on his hip, slung low, gunfighter style. Just inside the rear door of the chopper on a sliding mount was the gleaming silver shape of a mini-gun, an electric Gatling gun that could pump out fifty bullets a second. There was another soldier in the back of the helicopter, and Mike watched him lie down on his back on the floor, still wearing his helmet.

"PSI? Twenty minutes," the soldier said as he walked past Mike, who belatedly nodded. Blinking, Mike turned to watch him go, surprised that the man in his boots had been an inch shorter than him. He'd thought soldiers were all big huge guys. Past the soldier, he saw his father walking up.

Roger stared at the helicopter squatting on the helipad. "What a piece of junk," he said incredulously. He stood next to his son and frowned. The Blackhawk looked to have been repainted six times, and Roger could see patched bullet holes in the fuselage and scorch marks. The thing had to be older than Mike. For that matter, he didn't know Blackhawks were even still in service with the U.S. military. "Anders can't expect us to ride in *that*. With what I paid? I'm going to go talk to him."

"Dad. Dad!" Mike had to almost yell to be heard over the sound of the helicopter, even though the engines were powering down. Roger turned from where he'd been stomping off to give Anders a piece of his mind. "It's fine. It's cool. They flew it here, so it must run, right?" When his dad started throwing his weight around Mike didn't like to be anywhere near him.

Roger opened his mouth to argue, then saw the look on his son's face. He stopped, took a deep breath, and nodded. Vacation, they were on vacation. Father/son bonding time. If only shutting off the CEO part of his personality was that easy. "Yeah? You think so? You think it looks cool?"

"Are you kidding me? Look at all the guns and rockets. Are those patched bulletholes? That's awesome!" The Blackhawk looked like it had been through four wars. Mike grabbed his palmpad out of his pocket to take a photo.

"No, no pictures," Roger told him quickly. "Not here. This base is secret, remember?"

"Oh, yeah, right," Mike said, chagrinned. He put away his palm, but he quickly perked up. They were on a secret base, about to fly off in a helicopter—*this was so awesome!* "Should we get our stuff?"

"What did the soldier say? Twenty minutes?" Roger mopped at the sweat beads popping out on his forehead. He didn't want to be outside any longer than absolutely necessary. The Blackhawk had to have air conditioning, right? To keep the electronics from overheating? "Let's check with Anders."

Inside, the cheerful Anders was back behind his desk. He beamed at Mike. "Ready to head out on your adventure?"

"That helicopter we're supposed to ride in seems a bit long in the tooth," Roger began.

"*Daaad,*" Mike complained.

"I'm not surprised," Anders responded. "Is it one of the Blackhawks? All the newer cargo helicopters are down in southern and central Mexico, where the fighting is." His lips twisted into a wry smile. "One of the problems with fighting a secret war is—and always has been—funding. Too much and people might notice, start asking questions. Too little and why bother? Don't worry. New helicopters cost tens of millions of dollars and are a hard expense to hide, but mechanics are a lot cheaper, and we've got excellent ones. Whatever you'll be flying in, it's mechanically sound."

"Give or take a bullet hole or two," Roger grumbled. He held up a hand as Mike was about to complain about his complaining. "One of the crew said we had twenty minutes. Should we load our gear? Or wait?"

Anders glanced over at the boy, practically bouncing with excitement. "It wouldn't be a bad idea to get your gear and take it out to the bird, but before you do that I'd recommend a stop at the men's room down the hall. Sitting in a vibrating metal can while badly needing to urinate is quite an effective torture technique, and I wouldn't want your PaleoSafari experience to start out like *that*." He aimed a pointed look at Roger. Roger, who had noticed that his trips to the bathroom were taking longer and longer, nodded. First stop on the PaleoSafari Inc. tour—the urinal.

When researching PSI, Roger had been assured that food and lodging would be taken care of, and the only supplies he and his son needed to bring were their firearms, clothing, and any toiletries and personal items they might need. It felt strange to be travelling so light; usually he had a rack of fresh suits with him and often Jamie.

"Do they have electrified tents or what?" Mike asked him as they unloaded their gear from the back of the Scout. "To keep the animals away when we're out in the field."

"Electrified tents?" Where did kids come up with these ideas? "No, we'll be driving around in some sort of armored vehicle, and if we spend the night outside of the base I imagine we'll be sleeping in the vehicle. But I guess we'll find out when we get there."

Roger stared at the rifle case in the back of the Scout. He'd done a lot of research. The common perception was that all dinosaurs were huge, but the reality was that most of the creatures wandering the planet during the dinosaur era were the size of dogs and horses.

A good percentage of the species grown for Pangaea had been on the small side as well. That said, Roger hadn't paid PSI such a princely sum to hunt scaly dogs, and when it came to dropping animals so big they made elephants seem small and friendly, he didn't want to show up undergunned. Since the animals were in the wild and free there was no guarantee which species they'd encounter, if any, but what was that phrase he'd heard once? Oh yeah, *Overkill is underrated.* He grunted once as he lifted the case out of the cargo compartment, then again even louder as he lifted the canvas pack containing the cleaning kit and ammo for all the guns, convinced it weighed more than the big rifle case.

"You need me to grab that?" Mike asked him.

"No, but grab the other pack, with our clothes and stuff," Roger told his son.

Treading heavily under all the weight of their gear, they made their way to the helicopter sitting idle on the pad. The rotors had finally stopped moving.

"Where should we put this?" Roger called out to the black pilot, or co-pilot—whoever was the right stick on the bird. He thought back to his time in the military—this guy would be the pilot in a helicopter, as the co-pilot was on the left. The co-pilot in the left seat appeared to be asleep, his helmeted head tilted back. One of the contractors lay on the floor in the back of the Blackhawk in full kit, including helmet, tinted visor down, apparently asleep as well. He didn't move as Roger spoke.

Danny Hansen, the pilot, looked over his shoulder at Roger. "We'll stow it for you," he said. He'd learned to fly rotary wing aircraft in the Air Force and spent eight years there before getting a job flying cargo for FedEx. After helicopters, planes were easy. His civilian job had paid well, but mostly involved sitting while the fully automated planes took off and landed themselves. The only reason there were human pilots on board was to keep the insurance rates down, which seemed backwards to him—if an unmanned cargo drone crashed, all you lost was the plane and cargo. The new autopilot systems were as good or better than any human pilot and didn't leave behind grieving family members in the event of a crash, but apparently the insurance companies considered a human crew extra insurance against a crash.

Two years of riding passenger in an airborne cargo bus, and he was ready to do something else. Anything else. Raven had offered an obscene amount of money, and the job was anything but boring. He looked over his other shoulder at the man prostrate on the floor. "Seamus! Wake up! Time to play tour guide."

The man on the floor of the helicopter reached a hand to his helmet and hit the button to flip the visor up. "That wasn't twenty minutes, was it? I barely nodded off." Still on the floor, he turned his head and looked over at father and son. "Good morning gents. Ready to go tooth and claw with some beasties?"

Roger was surprised at the man's Irish or English or Australian accent—it was hard to pin down—but then he remembered that Raven hired former soldiers from the armies of allies as well as G.I. Joes. "If we end up going tooth and claw with 'beasties' I'm guessing something went horribly wrong," Roger said drily. "That's why we brought rifles. And a pistol."

The soldier laughed and climbed to his feet, poly-ceramic armor plates creaking. "Aye," he agreed. Then he looked Mike in the eye and winked. "But what a story to tell your children and grandchildren. And you might even be able to wrangle a refund out of ol' Aarne." He jumped off the helicopter, and bowed as low as his armor would allow. He twirled his hands with a flourish. "Welcome to the PaleoSafari taxicab. Keep your arms and legs inside at all times, don't piss in the back, and always remember, tipping your pilot is not only allowed but encouraged—provided he doesn't crash the bloody thing and smear us all across the landscape."

Mike grinned—he liked this Seamus. Again, he was surprised to see that this soldier/mercenary/whatever was of normal human proportions. After years of only seeing actor portrayals of such men in movies and video games, doing superhuman deeds, Mike naturally thought they'd be superhuman sized. This guy with the cool accent had a compact body and showed deep dimples when he smiled—not exactly the stone-faced war machine Mike had been expecting.

"Screw you, O'Malley," the co-pilot said reflexively, waking up. Chris Delian had retired as a captain out of the Air Force and had more experience and seniority with Raven than Hansen, but company policy was to switch off as often as possible to keep the pilot fresh. He lifted his helmet off the headrest and worked his neck back and forth.

"Absolutely," Seamus said. He looked down at the packs and rifle cases. "Right-o, let's get this stowed, and we'll be on our way." He pulled off his helmet and set it aside, revealing a short brush of black hair starting to turn to gray at the temples.

Quickly and efficiently, O'Malley stored their gear in compartments at the rear of the helicopter behind the passenger compartment. "Don't climb in yet," he told Roger, who'd been looking like he wanted to do just that. "Waiting on a few more supplies."

Roger nodded, and the two men stared at each other. Roger was sweating heavily in the heat, and he was wearing nothing more than a polo shirt and khakis. O'Malley had on a full field uniform with plate armor. The soldier seemed to know exactly what he was thinking. "You get used to the heat," he told Roger. Roger nodded, and Seamus added neutrally, "Of course, it helps to be in trim."

Roger looked at the man's lean build, then down at his own gut. A few dozen extra pounds weren't a handicap in the boardroom but wandering around Mexico on a hunting trip…he'd been meaning to get into shape for months, for his own health, but never seemed to find the time.

"There he is," Seamus said, and Roger turned to see a small flat-bed truck pulling into the parking lot. It gently hopped the curb and rolled to a stop near the helicopter, and the soldier who'd first stepped out of the helicopter climbed out of the passenger seat. The driver wore dark coveralls and looked bored.

"Did you get it all?" Seamus asked the other contractor. Johnny Corey was young compared to Seamus, having just turned twenty-five, but he'd joined Raven after doing two combat tours with the Marines. When he smiled, he showed big white teeth.

"Water bottles, Gatorade powder, nuts and protein bars, but they haven't had pudding cups in weeks. No butterscotch for you."

"Bugger," Seamus cursed.

The two men quickly transferred boxes and several shrink-wrapped flats of plastic water bottles into the back of the helicopter and strapped them down. As they were doing that, the pilot and co-pilot started going through their pre-flight checklist. Anders walked up.

"Peter Hein, your PH—" Anders stopped and cocked his head. "I never realized his initials were PH as well," he said almost to himself. "Anyway, your professional hunter will meet you when you land at Victoria Base and see you to your quarters. I imagine you'll head out this afternoon for a brief hunt, but that's really up to Peter; he knows what the local fauna's been up to. Good man, he'll take care of you." He held out a hand, and Roger shook it.

"How long's the helicopter ride?' Mike asked him over the rising sound of the engines. He looked up at the rotor blades starting to turn.

"Shouldn't be more than an hour or two. Good luck, young man. And good hunting!" He shook Mike's hand and then backed away from the helicopter, keeping his head low and away from the spinning blades.

"Pick a seat, strap yourselves in, and put on a headset," Seamus told them, then he pulled his rifle off the floor and hooked it to the front of his uniform with a sling.

Mike watched the contractor shrugging into his rifle, then ran his eyes over the helicopter. He again was surprised at how noisy and windy a real helicopter was. And how rattly.

"Well?" Roger asked his son.

Mike turned to him, practically vibrating with excitement. "This is awesome!" he shouted over the sound of the engines. He jumped up into the helicopter, then helped his father up. There were two benches constructed of tubular steel and canvas running the width of the aircraft, one facing forward, one aft. Mike went all the way to the right side of the bird and sat facing forward. Roger took the left side of the bench seat, with room between them for at least two more people. The seat had a traditional seatbelt, and Mike quickly put it on and made sure it was tight. He assumed they would close the sliding doors on either side of the helicopter before taking off; he was practically hanging out of the thing. Once settled in his seat, Mike stared at the mini-gun on its pedestal, resembling nothing so much as a gleaming killer robot. At the moment, it was aimed down at the ground, almost as if it was hibernating.

"You can look, but don't touch," Seamus yelled into his ear, making Mike jump. Seamus grinned and jumped up into the bird. He sat behind the pilot, in front of Mike, facing to the rear. There were six inches between their knees. "Strap yourselves in, then put on the headsets," he told father and son again, pointing above their heads. Then he saw Mike was already belted in, and gave it a tug to make sure it was tight. Wouldn't do to lose a paying customer out the door at fifteen hundred feet. He then pulled on his helmet, leaving the visor up.

Roger looked around. There were several sets of headsets with adjustable microphones on the wall behind them. Roger and Mike each grabbed one as soon as they were strapped into their seats. The earmuffs blocked out most of the sound of the helicopter, but the vibration was still impressive. The ceiling was low above their heads.

Roger bent his microphone down. "Can you hear me?" he asked his son.

"We can all hear you," Roger heard in his ear in clipped, electronically processed tones. Seamus' accent was unmistakable, and Roger looked over to see the man nodding at him.

Mike moved his microphone down. "Yeah, dad, I can hear you," he said excitedly. The other soldier hopped up into the helicopter, grabbed a carbine from the back, and strapped it to the front of his body before sitting down across from Roger, next to the mini-gun.

"All aboard," Corey told the pilot after he hooked his helmet to the intercom. Mike noticed that his M7 carbine sported an underbarrel grenade launcher. Awesome!

Mike was in heaven already—soldiers with rifles, riding in a Blackhawk helicopter with a mini-gun...even if they never saw a dinosaur, it was already the best vacation *ever*. He looked around, eyes wide, as the engines grew louder and louder, and the helicopter shook like a carnival ride. After forever, he finally felt some pressure in his butt and looked out the open sliding door to see them lifting away from the landing pad. He felt a little nervous with the door open and re-checked his seatbelt. It was as tight as he could get it.

"So, what? Totally boring so far, right?" Roger said. He had to fight the urge to yell over the noise and instead talk normally into the microphone. While he flew several times a year in private jets, it had been years since he'd been in a helicopter, and he'd forgotten how noisy the damn things were. Mike turned to him and the two of them shared a big grin, then his son looked back out the open door. They were already several hundred feet in the air, and in a blink of an eye they were across the curving Rio Grande.

The helicopter banked right and, as it climbed, it crossed directly over the small town of Valadeces, following the Nuevo Laredo-Reynosa freeway. Father and son stared left and right, enjoying the strange experience. Gradually, the town faded behind them, and there wasn't much to see out either side of the aircraft beyond empty countryside, more brown than green.

"This looks just like in Man O'War," Mike said, looking around the interior of the helicopter. He'd heard they'd 3D modeled all the weapons and vehicles in the game after their actual real-life counterparts, but he was surprised how close the interior of the helicopter in the game was to the old Blackhawk mission in the first Man O'War franchise.

"Just like what? Is that one of your video games?" Roger asked. He shook his head. Boys.

"I'm guessing you see the real thing's a mite noisier," Seamus said drily.

"A lot shakier, too," Roger said with a frown.

"Well, if it's not vibrating, then the engines have quit working, and we've got a whole other set of problems," Seamus said brightly.

"Way to sweet-talk the tourists, Seamus," Delian said from the co-pilot's seat.

After about five minutes, Roger saw a big green lake coming up ahead. He blinked, and frowned. "Why are we heading west?" he said into his mike, looking at Seamus. "Isn't Victoria Base due south of here?"

The soldier nodded. "Yes, but FRAP has eyes in Valadeces, we assume logging every aircraft that comes and goes, including type and direction. We do what we can to make their job more difficult."

The lake was about ten miles wide, and the helicopter stayed barely five hundred feet above it as it crossed. The land was noticeably greener around the lake. Mike stared down at the surface of the water and could see small waves. In the distance there was a small boat, with one figure inside it who looked up at the sound of the heli. He fought the urge to wave. The shoreline was markedly uneven. "Is that a reservoir?" he asked. He looked around the helicopter, but only Seamus was looking at him. He pointed out the window. "I'm looking at the shoreline and it doesn't look natural, it looks like what happens when you build a dam. The valley floods back along the length of the river."

The Raven contractor shrugged. "Don't have a clue," Seamus admitted.

"You're a smart kid," Mike heard in his headset, and looked over to see the other contractor looking at him. He had the visor of his helmet up so Mike could see his face. "We call it Sugar Lake. I can't remember what the Mexicans call it, but there's a dam upstream and one downstream to keep it full and the levels consistent. Great bass fishing there."

"Corey, you go fishing?" Seamus said in surprise. "In Mexico? You don't spend enough time there as it is?"

"Where the hell else am I going to go bass fishing around here? It's only half an hour drive from the border. A few of us head out on our days off. Hardly anybody lives in the area, and I'm not worried about the FRAP coming out after a few Yankee fishermen." *Who happen to bring their rifles with them, just in case*, he didn't add.

"A bloody waste of time, you ask me."

"What, fishing? We do it to relax. You can only sit around the base on your days off for so long, and there's nothing to do in McAllen—no gambling, no women, just drinking. And I can do that cheaper on base. What the hell does a Brit know about fishing anyway?"

"What? Are you serious, mate? We live on a bloody big island. Which means it's surrounded by water. Ever hear of 'the British Isles?' The English Channel isn't a station on the telly."

"If you're surrounded by so much water, filled with delicious seafood, explain to me why so many traditional British meals taste like ass," Corey countered. "You don't even know how to refrigerate beer properly." They began throwing good-natured insults back and forth.

Mike smiled and listened to the two men, who obviously knew each other well. Idly, his eyes wandered over Seamus' helmet, down his plate armor, and fixed on his rifle. It had a tan camo pattern which looked to have been spray-painted on by hand. M7 carbines, with their hi-tech polymer shells, had their digital camo patterns molded in. Seamus' rifle obviously wasn't an M7, and while it looked vaguely familiar from all the video games he'd played, Mike couldn't identify it. While it wasn't much longer than an M7, it looked beefier, and the magazine was noticeably fatter.

"America doesn't corrupt food, we make it better," Corey insisted. "Like pizza. English food sucks so much even the names of the dishes sound horrible. Spotted dick? Seriously? And what was that traditional British dish you said you liked?"

Seamus sighed. "Faggots."

The young American contractor threw up his hands. "I rest my damn case."

As the men continued their banter, the helicopter finished crossing the lake. After about a minute, it banked hard left, began climbing, and increased speed. The buffeting wind inside the cabin got violent. Seamus and Corey reached over and slid the doors most of the way shut, leaving a six-inch gap for airflow.

"How fast are we going?" Mike asked, looking out the windows. Even after accelerating they didn't seem to be flying that fast.

"A hundred and twenty knots," Hansen said in his headphones. The pilot glanced back at them. "The bird'll do better than that, but there's no reason to push it on these shuttle runs."

"So now we're heading to Victoria Base?" Roger asked. From the sun it appeared they were heading south or southwest.

Seamus smiled. "Not quite. We have to make a stop first."

"A stop? Where?"

Seamus smiled. "The north side of China."

The country beneath them was brown and green, a lot of it cut into the rectangles of farmers' fields. This time of year, about the only green to be seen was along the few rivers and in the occasional fields where crops were planted. The air was a little cooler up where they were flying, and between that and the wind swirling around the cabin, Roger finally stopped sweating. Almost. About fifteen minutes later, off the nose of the helicopter another body of water came into view on the right. "Another lake?" Roger asked.

Mike saw where he was looking and squinted. "Another reservoir," he said confidently. More altitude made it easier to spot. He looked at Corey. "Right?"

The sandy-haired soldier nodded. "Right. That's where the other dam is, that helps keep the water level steady in Sugar Lake. That's Knife Lake—*El Cuchillo*," he said, rolling the Spanish pronunciation off his tongue.

Before the reservoir a major road cut left to right, and Mike saw the checkerboard of streets in a few small towns between the road and the water. The helicopter banked gently left, heading to the outskirts of a small town near El Cuchillo.

"China Control, this is Sierra Bravo Six," Hansen said into his radio. "We are two minutes out. Permission to land?"

"Sierra Bravo Six, China Control," a bored voice came back. "Permission granted, Condition Green. Your cargo is here and more than ready to be picked up."

"Roger that."

"The town's called China," Corey told the passengers. "Although here it's pronounced '*Cheena*' by the locals. We've got a small supply post; have to pick up a few things we need."

"And some we don't," the co-pilot added in their ears. Seamus and Corey glanced at each other, and Corey shrugged.

China stretched for the better part of a mile between the shore of Knife Lake and the San Juan river. At one point, its population had been close to 10,000, but after decades of civil war, and being so close to the refuge of the U.S. border, more than half the residents had vanished. What was left of the town was a struggling shell of its old self.

"That's where we're headed, that island right there," Corey told them, pointing. In the middle of the wide river which ran west to east from Knife Lake, just above downtown China, was a teardrop-shaped island. Not quite a mile long, it was ringed by a double line of tall fences. There wasn't a whole lot to see on the island other than a wide runway and a few scattered buildings at the west tip. The rest of the flat land was covered by low struggling grass and the occasional bush, although trees lined the edge of the island along the river, outside the fence line.

"No bridges, and nobody was using the island for anything other than racing motorcycles, so Raven was able to get the land for a steal," Mike heard the pilot say.

Mike spotted a fuel tanker truck between two buildings. "How'd you get the trucks on the island if there's no bridges?" he asked.

"Well, the bloody engineering corps loves to build bridges, don't they," Seamus said. "Not as much as blowing them up of course. They put in a floating bridge at one end of the island when they were building the place, for the heavy trucks. Supposed to be temporary, but it's been there at least five years now."

"We've got a few passengers to pick up, and we'll top off the tanks too," the co-pilot said.

Hansen aimed the bird for one of the helipads near a large hangar at the west end of the island. "How long are we going to be here?" Roger asked. He'd peed before getting on the bird and yet he already had to go again. Even after sweating so much. It had to be the vibration.

"No more than an hour," the pilot told them. "Probably less. So don't go far. Not that there's anywhere to go, but I don't want to wait on you or have to go searching for your tourist ass. Got it?"

* * * * *

Chapter Four

The helicopter settled down in the center of the concrete pad with a light thump, and Seamus and Corey slid open the doors on either side. Seamus pulled his helmet off.

"Keep your head down whenever you're getting in or out of a helicopter with moving rotors," Seamus told the Rudds, nearly shouting to be heard over the noise. "Nobody should be tall enough to get hit by them even standing on their tippy toes, but the blades are flexible, shit happens, and you're not wearing brain tins." He rapped his knuckles on his helmet. "Got it?"

Mike nodded vigorously. The two contractors climbed out either side of the aircraft and remained hunched over until they were off the helipad. Mike unbuckled himself from the seat and looked around. Apart from half a dozen unmarked buildings and a few military trucks, there wasn't much to see, but he still wasn't going to miss the chance to walk around one of Raven's bases. He looked back at his father.

"You go, look around," Roger said. "I'm going to stretch my legs, maybe water one of those bushes out there."

Mike grinned and hopped down from the helicopter, bent almost double as the Blackhawk's rotors decelerated overhead. When he got far enough away he turned around and looked at the helicopter, having a hard time believing he'd just taken a ride in it. Beyond the helicopter was the end of the wide runway. There were beacon lights set up to either side of the concrete for its entire length, but none of them were illuminated. Past the runway, there was nothing before the distant fence line other than a small radio tower with satellite dishes all over it. Even though he couldn't see it past the trees, he could smell the river.

The ground around him was covered with knee-high grass, mostly brown, with a few scattered low green bushes here and there. The ground was flat enough for helicopters to land anywhere, although he counted six helipads nearby. The buildings were in a cluster off to the side, away from the runway in case a plane slid off the end. The runway at the small post was just a half mile long, suitable only for small observer planes and VTOL jets, but ninety percent of the aircraft in use by Raven in Mexico were helicopters.

The Blackhawk they'd arrived in was the only helicopter visible, and the island had a sleepy feel to it. Mike headed toward the buildings, feeling the sweat pop out on his skin. He saw two hangars, but it wasn't immediately clear what purpose any of the other buildings served.

* * *

Seamus' first stop was the small kitchen, and he cracked open the refrigerator. Bottles of water, sports drinks, soda, and protein bars, but no butterscotch pudding cups. Hell, no pudding at all. He grabbed a flavored water as a consolation prize and stuck his head into the small China Base control room. He realized he recognized the communications specialist. "Mornin', Charlie. Sierra Bravo Six—what are we picking up?"

The bored Raven employee sitting in front of the radar, radio, and computer equipment was dressed in gray coveralls and drinking coffee. When Seamus saw the steaming beverage, he realized the building was air-conditioned and pried his armor away from his neck, hoping some of the cool dry air would worm its way to his core.

"Seamus! Haven't seen you this far north in a while." The man looked genuinely surprised. "You're Bravo Six? Let's see…two souls and a bin full of spare parts," the man said, reading from the digital manifest on the computer monitor in front of him. He took a sip of coffee. He looked jittery, and Seamus wondered how many cups the man had already sucked down.

Seamus eyed the big skull mounted on the wall beside Charlie. He'd forgotten it was there. "Who are we picking up?"

Peering at the screen, Charlie said, "Todd, Derrick, with the 5th TST. He should be wandering around somewhere. The other, well, I'm sure you won't have any problem spotting her."

That brought Seamus up short. "*Her?*"

* * *

Mike wandered between two of the big buildings and looked over the forklift parked out of the way. He'd never seen a camouflaged forklift before. Standing in the sun, the heat rolled off the blacktop, and he could even feel it soaking through the thick soles of his boots.

The front of one of the hangars was open, and the shadows inside looked inviting. They also looked cool. He headed in that direction. Inside, out of the bright sunlight, it took a few seconds for his eyes to adjust. There was another Blackhawk parked off to one side, its engine partially dismantled, and an old, small, and brutally battered pickup truck painted four shades of green. As he peered at the weird paint job he realized that the entire truck had been painted green numerous times, but huge patches of paint of various thicknesses had peeled off. As none of the shades of green were the same, it gave the small pickup a strangely mottled appearance.

The hangar felt cool, but it was probably eighty degrees inside. It smelled of diesel and paint and hot metal. The roof was high over his head, and he saw a few small birds flitting back and forth. He also heard voices echoing from somewhere and walked a little further into the hangar. There was a small office at the rear of the building. Standing in front of it was a small group of men in camouflage uniforms. He recognized the spotted design on their fabric uniforms as the U.S. military's previous camo pattern, "Multi-Cam," and correctly assumed they were Mexican Army troops. What they were doing on the Raven base he had no idea. Then he saw the small woman in their midst.

* * *

Margarita "Tina" Echevarria looked up at the five young Mexican soldiers in a semi-circle around her and sighed, trying not to let her frustration show. She'd been dealing with unwanted advances from men—and boys—since she was eleven. Eleven! *Gracias, Mama*, she thought, for the thousandth time. She better than most knew that genetics will win out, and she'd had the curves of a mature woman—specifically her mother's—by the time she hit sixth grade, but that didn't mean she'd ever welcomed attention for something she'd literally had no control over. Everyone told her she was beautiful as well, but she'd never gone looking for attention, and as a graduate student, wanted to be taken seriously for her studies and knowledge. It hadn't been easy. She did whatever she could to "dog down," as her oldest sister referred to it, but there was only so much you could do with high cheekbones and breasts big enough for her sisters to have given them a nickname—*Las Chicas*.

"I think you look a little lonely, that's all I'm saying," the ringleader of the soldiers said to her chest. He was the oldest of the group, maybe her age, and the tallest. The rest of them looked like teenagers. Angry, horny, stupid teenagers. With rifles. The soldier's Spanish was lightly accented, and between that and his bone structure she guessed he had Mayan blood in him and came from the Yucatan peninsula. He nodded his head behind her. "The office is locked, but it's nice and dark in the back of the hangar."

"I think you look lonely enough for all of us," one of the other soldiers said, reaching out to touch her glossy back hair, which she'd pulled back into a ponytail. It was too hot to wear her hair down, but she couldn't bear to cut it. She turned her head and twisted the ponytail out of his reach. She was the first woman they'd seen on the island, ever, and the most beautiful woman most of them had ever seen in person.

That's what I get for showering, she thought to herself. *Yesterday I smelled* como un *skunk, and they wouldn't have gotten within six feet of me.* Prior to the shower, it had been close to a week since she'd been near soap or water, and had spent that week hiking through some of the harshest terrain central Mexico could offer. When Charlie had offered the use of the facilities the night before, she'd wasted no time in accepting. She'd washed herself and all her clothes in the shower outside the base's radio room, and hung her clothes out to dry while wearing a pair of gray base coveralls. She'd put her own clothes back

on that morning just in time to catch the attention of the horny soldiers.

"I'm not lonely, I'm bored," she told them. "Don't you have
work to do? Where's your Sergeant?" Her big backpack was on the
painted cement floor by her feet. She touched it with the toe of her
boot, to verify its position, but she didn't look down at it. No use
giving them any warning if she could avoid it.

"Don't you worry about him, we're all you need," the shortest
soldier said to her with an ugly sneer. She was only five foot two, and
he was barely taller than her, with bad acne. He reached a hand out
toward her chest, and she smacked it away.

"I don't think you need me. I think you can go back into that
dark corner and take care of yourself just fine, *como* you've been doing your whole life," Tina snapped at him. She was starting to get
more than a little nervous, even though it wasn't showing on her
face. The young men didn't look like they were going to go away on
their own, and they kept edging closer.

"What did you say to me, bitch?" The stunted soldier looked
ready to hit her, his face screwed up into an ugly snarl.

"Just grab this *puta* already. She thinks she doesn't want it, but
she'll be moaning our names in two minutes," the leader said, taking
a step toward her and reaching out.

With one smooth motion Tina reached down, grabbed the handle of the machete strapped to the side of her pack, and slid it from
its sheath. She cocked it above her shoulder and stared at who she
thought was the ringleader. "You want to rape me, go ahead, I won't
be able to stop you, even with this. But then you'd better kill me. I
spent four months in Guatemala on my own, and got pretty good

with a blade. I will not kill you, I will let you live, but not as a whole man."

The soldier froze, staring at the long blade of the machete. It looked dangerously sharp.

"All right gentlemen, back to work," Seamus said in fluent Spanish, striding swiftly past Mike. Completely surprised by the confrontation and having a hard time following the rapid Spanish, Mike had been unable to do more than stare at the unexpected scene in the hangar. "Aren't you our refueling crew? I think your Sergeant could probably use your help."

The soldiers turned to see the contractor stop a dozen feet away, his hand casually resting on his holstered pistol. Seamus looked from one angry face to another and smiled. Then he let the smile fall away and stared at them with dead eyes. Young they might have been, but they'd seen enough rough men to recognize someone to whom violence was no stranger.

"Nobody said anything about rape," one of the young looking soldiers said in a small voice, darting his eyes at the woman.

"Shut up," one of his buddies said to him out of the corner of his mouth.

"This *puta* has a smart mouth, *escara*," the oldest soldier said loudly, talking to Seamus but staring at her.

"Have you ever known a woman who didn't?" Seamus shrugged, and took his hand off his pistol. "*Pero esta mujer tiene un machete. Su decision, amigo.*"

With grumbling and a few more choice words, and hate-filled glances at Tina, the soldiers turned away from her and trudged toward the open hangar door. Seamus turned to watch them go, then looked back at the woman, who was giving him a strange look.

"*¿Que?*"

She shook her head, then answered him in nearly accent-less English. "Nothing. It's just that I've never heard Spanish spoken with an Irish accent before."

"Yes, the Irish tongue is a magical thing," Seamus replied, winking.

"You too?" she said, rolling her eyes. With a decisive thrust she shoved the machete back into its sheath, eyes on Seamus. "Men." She eyed his armor. "I heard a helicopter. Are you my ride?"

"That's what they tell me, Rita, if you're the woman heading to Victoria Base. I'm Sergeant O'Malley. But I'm not the pilot, just another passenger."

She lifted her big backpack with a grunt and threw it over one shoulder. As she walked toward him, Seamus eyed her and the machete strapped to the side of her pack. She'd been completely believable in her threats when the blade had been in her hand, but he knew—convincing a few green troops that you'd be happy to hack off their willies was one thing. Actually doing it…well, cutting someone with a blade took a vastly different level of conviction than using a gun. Especially going after that part of a man.

The woman stopped in front of him. "If you don't know if I'm the right woman, why are you calling me Rita?" she asked Seamus. "And I prefer Tina. Only my sister ever calls me Rita." With his accent, it came out "Reeter." She glanced at the teenager standing next to the contractor, gawking at her, then back at Seamus.

Seamus gave her his best 1000-watt smile. "I call all the *señoritas* 'Rita.' It saves on the confusion in the morning. Tequila is a bloody harsh mistress."

Tina looked like she'd eaten something sour and pushed past him, muttering "*Puerco.*" She stopped, then turned and looked over her shoulder at him. She opened her mouth, closed it, then said, "I didn't need any help."

"I didn't give you any," he replied.

Her eyebrows furrowed together, then she went clomping out the open hangar door in her big boots. Seamus grinned to himself then glanced at the boy next to him. Mike was a lost puppy drooling after the sexy woman. Even when she wasn't trying, her hips worked back and forth like a metronome. Under her shorts her legs were muscled and tan. *Madre de Dios.* He shook his head. "Don't waste your time, boyo. That one's out of your league." He clucked. "She even thinks she's out of mine."

Mike heard the words coming out of the contractor's mouth, but they were just noise to him. He was in love. Seamus got his attention with a knuckle to his forehead. "Come with me; I want to show you something."

As nonplussed as the radio operator had been to see Seamus, he was twice as surprised to see Seamus return with a teenager in tow. "Who's this?" Charlie asked, frowning. "You chaperoning a school field trip?"

"Hilarious," Seamus said. He pointed at the skull on the wall out to Mike. "Though you might appreciate seeing this," he told the boy.

Mike's eyes went wide, and he walked close to the skull. It was narrow and a foot long, not including the big armored shield. The frill was scalloped and roughly triangular in shape. The lower jaw was missing, but the snout ended in a beak. Right behind the beak was a short horn that curved backwards. "Did you shoot it?"

"No, someone found it in the field, if I remember correctly. Years ago." Seamus scratched his chin. "It's not a triceratops, there aren't three horns, but looking at that crest and the nose horn I'm guessing it's in the same family. And maybe a baby, from the size."

"A baby?" The skull and crest together were two feet long.

"Ceratops get a mite big if you let them."

"That is so cool." Mike reached out and touched the skull. The bone was slick under his fingers and the same color as his white ash bedside table. It struck him then—this wasn't a fossil, buried in rock and dirt for a millennia, turned to stone; this was an actual skull. Bone. From a living, breathing animal.

From the size of the head, he guessed the body of the creature would have been four to six feet long, not including the tail. Which, he realized, as dinosaurs went wasn't especially big. "Do you find a lot of skeletons?" he asked as he dug out his palm.

"Some. It's a rare Raven base that doesn't have one or two up on the walls."

Mike took a few photos of the skull with his palm, and stared at them admiringly.

"You come in on the Raven chopper?" the radio operator asked Mike, but the boy didn't hear him; he was busy working his palm with his thumbs.

"We should head back before they start looking for us," Seamus told him.

"Oh, okay," Mike said distractedly. He let Seamus pull him from the room. They must have had a repeater tower at the base, because he had some service for his palm, although it wasn't fast. He was trying to identify the species that the skull belonged to.

"No, seriously, who is he?" Charlie called after them, but they were gone.

* * *

Under the direction of their swearing, sweating sergeant, the Mexican troopers topped off the fuel tanks on the Blackhawk, loaded the crate of spare parts, and then retreated into the relative coolness of the hangar. While waiting to be refueled, Hansen and Delian had taken the opportunity to stretch their legs and use the toilet, then walked around the aircraft and inspected it for any cracks, bullet holes, or other worrisome new features. Finding nothing, they had their helmets back on and were seated in the cockpit. Forty-five minutes after touching down, the bird was ready to take off again, and the passengers clustered by the open door of the helicopter as the two pilots went through their pre-flight checklist.

"You look familiar," Seamus said to the man they were picking up. Derrick Todd was tall and thick, with a deep tan. His features seemed crowded together in the center of his big face. "We worked together before?"

The Irishman seemed familiar to Todd as well, especially the accent. "I've spent most of the last five years working south of Mexico City, out of Oaxaca Base." He thought for a second. "I was in León last fall trying to verify some intelligence when FRAP made their big attack."

"You were one of the boys getting buggered in the police station?" Seamus asked him. A handful of Raven contractors found themselves holed up in the León police headquarters with a few dozen cops, under attack by over a hundred guerrillas. They'd held out for thirty-two hours, running low on ammo, before reinforcements from Victoria Base could fly in. Copperhead attack helicopters rocketed the guerrilla positions up and down the street while Seamus and fifteen other contractors fast-roped onto the roof of the police building with all the ammo they could carry. After a couple hours of heavy fighting, the guerrillas still alive had faded away into the city. "That was a busy day."

Todd made a face. "It was a busy couple of days. Took you guys forever to show up."

Seamus shrugged. "I had to do my makeup and nails and powder me arse before we took off. Wouldn't do to fly off looking like a three-dollar tramp. Beauty like this can't be rushed." He gestured up and down himself like a television spokesmodel.

"Yeah, I remember you now," Todd said flatly. He shook his head and climbed up into the bird next to the electric Gatling gun. "I'll take the mini, unless somebody else is on it. I'm usually doorgunner."

Seamus held out his hand. "All yours."

Todd stowed his personal rifle, then hooked a safety cable running from an eyebolt in the ceiling to the back of the hard collar of his uniform. The cable ensured he could work the gun from side to side without fear of falling out of the helicopter, as he was sitting sideways on the bench seat and couldn't use the seatbelt.

Roger had found an excuse to spend most of the time the bird was on the ground in one of the air-conditioned buildings on the base and only reluctantly made his way to the helipad. The sun was a physical weight, pressing down on the top of his head like an iron. As uncomfortable as he was in the heat, he hadn't forgotten his manners, and he stepped aside so the young woman could climb aboard first. "After you," he said.

"Thank you," she told him. "I'm Tina."

"Roger. Nice to meet you." As she climbed up into the helicopter, Roger discreetly checked out her backside. It was as nice as her front. Her khaki shorts stretched around her heart-shaped rear and showed off trim muscular legs. Yeah, she was half his age, but he wasn't dead. Hell, his current wife wasn't much older than this little firecracker. That's why they made Bonus and all the other "male enhancement" pills. With a grunt, he climbed in after her and sat across from the contractor on the mini-gun.

Tina sat on the seat facing rearward in the middle of the helicopter and belted herself in. She'd stored her backpack in the rear of the helicopter, strapping it down herself so it didn't get banged around during the ride. She'd been hiking around some of the most remote areas of southern Mexico and Guatemala for six weeks, doing research for her biology graduate thesis, and against all of her expectations had managed to not break her expensive camera. Even though she'd completed her work and could easily get a replacement, she didn't want to take any chances with it. That camera had served her well, and they'd been through a lot together.

Corey came jogging from the nearest building as the rotors started spinning. He sat between Roger and his son, and Seamus climbed in last, sitting across from Mike once again. His rifle was lying across his lap, pointed out the open door. "Everybody buckled in?" He got nods in response. The contractor put on his helmet and hooked it to the intercom. "All passengers aboard," he told the men in the cockpit. "Ready whenever you are."

"Roger that." The pilot switched over to the radio. "China Base, this is Sierra Bravo Six. Clear to take off?"

"Sierra Bravo Six, affirmative, you are clear."

Mike felt his pulse speeding up with the rotors as the big helicopter once more strained against the air, and in just a few minutes it rose off the helipad. The bird hovered for a few seconds, then smoothly accelerated due south, steadily gaining altitude. Everyone on board finished putting on their headsets so they could talk in the cabin.

"You think you're going to need that?" Roger asked the man whose hands were on the mini-gun.

Todd glanced at the fat guy in the expensive shirt. "This far north? Probably not. But better safe than sorry."

"I think it's a monoclonius," Mike said excitedly, looking up from his palm to Seamus. "They say it gets to be six meters long. I think that's with the tail, I'm not sure." He turned to his dad, his grin huge. "They had a dinosaur skull up on the wall in there. It was amazing." Roger smiled.

Seamus shook his head. "Never heard of it," he had to admit.

"How far is it from here to Victoria Base?" Mike asked Seamus as the Blackhawk continued to climb and accelerate. He lost what little signal he had and put the palm away. The river winked by underneath them. They flew directly over the center of China, and the town seemed almost abandoned. There were few vehicles moving, and Mike saw only a handful of people on foot.

"Not quite a hundred and fifty miles, straight line. About an hour."

Mike nodded, and sat for a few minutes. Then he asked, "Why were there Mexican soldiers at a Raven base? Or was it a Mexican Army base?"

Seamus looked at the young man and thought about his answer. "Technically, we share everything. We are officially here, in this country, to help their military. At their request. This is their war, remember? The Mexican Army guards the dam at El Cuchillo against attacks, and has riverboats which patrol back and forth between the dam and the end of the island. If you'd gone behind the hangars there's a dock there. There's always a small contingent of Mex troops at China Base. As for prosecuting the war, as they say, we've found that they do a piss-poor job of just about everything and don't know sod-all about what it means to be professional soldiers. That's because their regular army is a bunch of illiterate farmers and draftees who'd rather be back bum-wrestling sheep. The blokes who have their heads on straight—their Special Forces, their mountain troops, their new airborne brigade—they are all hard-chargers. What they don't know about soldiering they make up for with enthusiasm, but there's damn few of them. If the whole army had their testicular fortitude this war would be over in six months."

"I've been hearing that for fifteen years," Tina said. Mike turned and looked at her; he'd forgotten everyone in the cabin could hear them. "The problems are much deeper here than that. They can't all be solved by shooting people and blowing things up. Corruption at every level of government, endemic poverty and illiteracy…." She waved a hand. "Our education system is horrible. Until the causes which gave rise to the *Fraternidad Progresista para un Mexico Nuevo* are addressed, there will always be conflict. And it will be just that much harder, with how badly the infrastructure has been damaged by the fighting."

"Well, that's above my pay grade," Seamus told her cheerfully. "Luckily my job is shooting people and blowing things up. Much easier than geo-politics."

"And a lot more fun," Todd added from behind the mini-gun. He ignored the evil look Tina threw his way.

"I thought the war started as fighting between rival drug cartels and just escalated," Mike said. Tina was so hot when she spoke Spanish. He'd been trying hard not to stare, but talking to her he had an excuse. The shorts, the man's button-down shirt open in front enough to show off the tank top and more than a little cleavage…which was now jiggling vigorously due to the helicopter ride…oof.

"Things are never that simple," Tina said to the boy with a frown. He was tall and skinny and looked young to her. Still in high school, probably. She looked from him to the older man who had to be his father, they looked enough alike. Nice clothes, obviously well-educated…why were they going to Victoria Base on a Raven helicopter?

Roger looked across the cabin and smiled at his son's naïveté. He knew the history. Drug cartels had been at war in Mexico on a large scale since the turn of the century, if not before. The combat wasn't one dealer shooting another, it was convoys of cartel members armed with military weapons getting ambushed by even larger groups of paramilitarily-equipped men from rival cartels. He'd read somewhere that in the first ten years of the century there had been more than one hundred thousand fatalities, even though the Mexican army had gotten involved and tried to stop the violence. And that was before the civil war had even officially started.

The global recession going on at the time didn't get any better, and it was worse in Mexico than in many areas of the world. Mexican drug cartels continued to battle each other, and while the U.S. sent some drug agents down there to help out, the conflict was otherwise mostly ignored as a "Mexican" issue. As usual, that view was short-sighted.

Whether they had begun that way or not, the leaders of the Fuerza Cartel were eventually revealed to be a bunch of communist ideologues only selling drugs to fund the revolution they wanted to start. They cared as much about killing the competition, as making money from selling drugs, and when they'd eliminated most of the competition they went directly to war with the Mexican Government. They'd already been fighting the Mexican army for years—as well as the other cartels—and their ranks were filled with combat veterans.

U.S. involvement gradually intensified over the space of ten years or so, very similar to what happened in Vietnam—first it was military advisors, then a small number of troops, and pretty soon the U.S. Army was fighting alongside the Mexicans in skirmishes across half the country. The U.S. government didn't realize what bad shape the Mexican government was in, and it was only when the Fuerza Cartel, now sporting the title *Fraternidad Progresista para un Mexico Nuevo*, came within a hair's breadth of entering Mexico City in force did the U.S. officially recognize it as a "civil war."

Sending U.S. troops to fight in Mexico had never been a popular move, and after a series of clashes designed to draw the Americans in right where they wanted them, the guerrillas set off a dirty bomb. Dirty bombs are notoriously ineffective as radiological weapons, and it only killed a few hundred soldiers and civilians, but the bomb's intent was to dishearten and dispirit America's will to fight. In that, it was very successful. Goodbye (almost overnight) U.S. military and overt action, hello Raven contractors and the covert war, which had now been dragging on well over a decade. The contractors mostly called the enemy FRAP, although the natives usually referred to them as *La Fuerza*.

"Are you some sort of political student?" Roger asked her. "I'm wondering why they're giving you a ride." He gestured around the cabin.

"Graduate student in biology. I've been out in the field for almost six weeks. It was driving my father *loco*, and he called in a favor to get me home a little sooner. What about you?"

"That's my son—" Roger began, nodding at Mike.

"We're going hunting!" Mike interjected from the far side of the cabin.

Tina glanced at him, and frowned. "Hunting?" She looked at the helicopter, and the armored soldiers, and the gleaming silver machinegun mounted in the doorway. "Hunting what?"

"Dinosaurs!" Mike said excitedly, trying to impress her. His words had the opposite effect. The string of Spanish profanity even impressed Seamus.

"What?" Mike looked around at the other faces. What'd he say that made her so upset?

She shook her head. "First off," she said, stabbing a finger at him, "those aren't dinosaurs. Do you know anything about biology? Those animals—genetically—are nowhere close to the real sauropods that roamed this planet millions of years ago."

"I take it you've never seen one of the predators in the field, stalking prey," Seamus said to her. "Apparently they didn't get your memo."

"I didn't say they weren't dangerous," she retorted. "I just said they weren't dinosaurs."

"The geneticists used actual dinosaur DNA to create them," Roger pointed out. "It's not as if they gave iguanas steroids and vitamin injections." Todd coughed out a laugh.

"Did they? Did they really? DNA only has a 520-year half-life," the young woman insisted. "And they've been extinct for what, 65 million years? *¿Mas?* I wouldn't be surprised if the corporate geneticists did nothing more than manipulate the DNA of existing animals to create those freaks. Perpetrate a complete fraud on the public, which was more than willing to pay money to see them."

Before paying any money to PSI—as the world seemed filled with people whose sole goal in life was to separate him from his money—Roger had done a huge amount of research on the subject of dinosaurs and exactly how they'd been created—or rather, re-created. The subject of dinosaur DNA wasn't so black and white even forty years ago. "I've looked into his, young lady. Back before the first dinosaur clones, or whatever you want to call them," Roger said, "most scientists were saying it couldn't be done; dinosaurs were forever extinct. That there was no dinosaur DNA anywhere on earth, no matter what the books and movies said. Many scientists were arguing that since the half-life of DNA had been shown to be 521 years—not 520—that it simply wasn't possible to recover any biological material from dinosaur fossils. However, as early as the 1990s scientists were grinding up fossilized dinosaur bones and retrieving proteins. Over thirty years ago there was a big story about how scien-

tists had discovered soft tissue, including red blood cells and colla-
gen, in dinosaur bones. All those stories about how fossilization
completely removed any and all biological matter were shown to be
in error *last century*." He took a deep breath and went on.

"Well, as you should know given your profession, one of the jobs
of protein in the body is replicating DNA. And in addition to protein, they were recovering fragments of dinosaur DNA." He held up
a hand as she opened her mouth to argue. "Yes, there are 3 billion
base pairs in DNA, however every form of life on the planet has
98% of the same DNA as humans—it's just two percent that makes
the difference between a small mouth bass, a grizzly bear, and a human. When the human genome was still a mystery to us, and computers were little more than adding machines, comparing and
analyzing all the fragmented DNA and figuring out what went where
was an impossible task. That soon was not the case. It's easy to reas-
semble a jigsaw puzzle when you're using a supercomputer." He
paused. "From everything I've read, when trying to recreate the genome of these extinct animals, they went with the source genetic
material whenever they could, and only used DNA from living animals to fill in the gaps. A scientifically comfortable middleground."

His knowledge about the subject surprised Tina, and she mentally
took a step back. Whatever else the man was, he was no idiot. But
she refused to give up her position when she'd taken a stand, something her parents had learned long ago. "Middleground? More like
muddleground. It wasn't as if they were filling gaps in the dinosaur
DNA they recovered, all they ever recovered were bits and scraps
that they plugged into the DNA of living creatures until the result
gave them the animal they were looking for. They were Franken-
steins, *todos*, every one of them."

"Frankenstein's Monster, you mean," Mike corrected her automatically. "Frankenstein was the doctor. Dr. Frankenstein." She shot him a look so dark he physically pulled back.

"All they needed were bits and pieces of dinosaur DNA to make real dinosaurs," Roger corrected her. He'd spent most of his free time for over a month doing research on the animals, as they had captured his imagination. In that, he supposed, he wasn't much different than most other men and boys. "Ninety-eight percent the same as you and me and every other animal, remember? It's only the bits and pieces that make us different."

Tina was shaking her head. "Reptile and amphibian DNA…for all we know they used canine DNA as well."

"Is that your specialty? Genetics?"

"No, but I know enough about biology to—" She stopped, and frowned. "I have enough *respect* for biology," she corrected herself, "to know that what they did, what they created, for an *amusement park*," she spat those two words as if the very taste of them disgusted her, "was wrong."

She shook her head violently. "That's what's wrong with *el mundo*. People who do what they can, instead of what they should. Lobsters aren't supposed to be four feet long. Strawberries aren't supposed to be the size of your fist. *No es normal.* As soon as scientists figured out they could bring extinct animals back to life, they started doing it. The dodo, the quagga, the sabertooth tiger, aurochs, mastodons, the giant beaver, glyptodons, the giant sloth. Just about everything that went extinct in the Pleistocene. Dinosaurs—and they are not dinosaurs, they are a patchwork quilt of different animals made to look a certain way, and I doubt they behave in any way similar to what *el verdad*, the true, real dinosaurs did—dinosaurs are just the worst example of this, not the first. Science for entertainment's sake."

Mike frowned. "What's wrong with entertainment? Isn't zoo attendance at its highest in its history because of the 'extinct' exhibits?"

Tina shook her head quickly. "Nothing's wrong with entertainment, it is scientists doing things they shouldn't, for all the wrong reasons. The fast and loose rush to recreate extinct animals for entertainment…well, the laws haven't kept up with the science. Private ownership of these manufactured animals has resulted in them being released into the world, accidentally or on purpose, into a world that they do not belong to."

"So now you're against private ownership?" Roger asked her.

She huffed. "Never mind." He wasn't listening to her, he simply wanted to argue. Just like her father.

"So you should be happy that they're here to shoot some of them," Corey said, nodding at the Rudds. "Donating some dollars to the local economy, as well."

"I didn't make the animals or build the park," Roger said to her. He added pointedly, "And I didn't tear it down, either, letting all those animals loose. That's on your countrymen."

Seeing as there were no sympathetic ears on the helicopter, Tina frowned, crossed her arms, and looked out the window. "*Turistas*," she muttered unpleasantly.

Mike wasn't happy at all that they'd ganged up on her, but had a feeling that if he tried to cheer her up it would only go badly. Instead, he looked at Seamus.

"What did that soldier say to you in the hangar?" Mike asked him. The contractor, who'd been staring out the window at the brown hills far below, looked at him. "It sounded like 'mascara.'" He wondered if it was a swear word.

Seamus chucked. "*Escara*," he told the young man. "Short for *escarabaja*, which means beetle. That's what they call us, since we wear the armor." He tapped knuckles on his chest plate. Seamus actually preferred the traditional fabric battle fatigues, the type the Mexican Army troops wore, to the new armored uniform, but a 50/50 cotton/poly blend didn't stop bullets.

"*Escara* is a word that means something all on its own," Tina said to him, her eyes defiant. She'd turned away from the window and was staring at the two of them. "It means scab." And with that she went back to staring out the window.

Seamus looked at Mike and jabbed a thumb at Tina. "I like her. She's feisty." And he winked.

Tina heard him in her headset, and stared daggers in his direction. "You can forget about that ever happening, *mercenario*." Corey snorted.

"Personally, I've always preferred gladiator to mercenary, although I think most gladiators were slaves," Todd said. Both sliding doors were closed now that they'd gained speed and altitude, and he was sitting facing Roger, next to Tina. He glanced around the cabin. "But gladiator sounds cooler."

Seamus leaned back in his seat, looking thoughtful. "With this war?" he asked slowly. "And the butchers we're fighting, drug dealers who murder children and behead women? I think bestiarii would be more accurate."

"What?"

"With two i's at the end, not a y," Seamus said. "Bestiarii. They were the gladiators who fought wild animals." He went back to silently staring out the window and didn't catch the surprised looks sent his way.

* * * * *

Chapter Five

"Sierra Bravo Six, this is China Control, over," Hansen heard over the radio. The pilot checked his watch, then his illuminated 3D HUD map, part of the electronic upgrade package installed on the old bird a few years before. They'd been in the air over twenty minutes, and were about a third of the way to Victoria Base.

"China Control, go for Sierra Bravo Six."

"Sierra Bravo Six, we have reports of SAMs in the area around Linares. I need you to immediately divert to heading two-four-zero degrees. That should keep you clear of the danger zone. Stay on that heading, then at the waypoint turn and approach Victoria Base heading one-two-zero degrees. I am transmitting your new route now, over." Before he'd even finished speaking the heads-up map in the cockpit displayed the new route for them to take, including GPS waypoints and altitudes, burst transmitted from China Control.

"Roger that. I have received and copy the new route, China Control." Hansen banked the helicopter hard to the right.

Delian eyed the new route. "They've got us diverting way the hell out to the middle of nowhere, *and* scraping the undercarriage." The co-pilot keyed the radio make. "Uh, China Control, Sierra Bravo Six, if we've got SAM problems, why are the altitudes so low? Final leg shows us only five-zero-zero AGL, over."

"I don't know anything Sierra Bravo Six, I'm just a monkey pushing buttons over here. That is the route I was told to give to you. Maybe there's other traffic in the area. Be advised, Operation Green Spear kicked off this morning. That's that major offensive they've been planning for a while near Guadalajara."

Guadalajara was about 350 miles southwest of them, nowhere near their regular route, but both pilots knew they might be called down to help out as Raven was always light on aircraft. Delian frowned, not happy with the information he'd been given. Hansen glanced at his co-pilot, then keyed the mike. "Sierra Bravo Six, roger that. Thanks for the heads up."

"You got it. China Control out."

No one in the cabin had missed the hard banking turn. "What's up?" Seamus asked over the intercom.

"SAM activity around Linares," Delian told him and the rest of the passengers. "We're being diverted. Shouldn't add more than an hour to the trip. Also, Operation Green Spear started this morning. The two are probably related, I'm sure the G's are pissed."

"Sam activity?" Tina asked. She thought her English was nearly perfect, but those two words together didn't make any sense to her. And…."Gees?"

Todd undid his seat belt, then hooked the cable hanging from the ceiling to the strap on the collar of his uniform. The cabin filled with swirling warm air as he slid open the door. He grabbed the handles of the mini-gun and pulled it upright. "G is for guerrilla," he told her. "And SAM is for Surface-to-Air Missile," he said, all trace of humor gone from his voice.

"Can you shoot down a missile with that thing?" Tina asked him. She wasn't sure exactly what the big gleaming gun was capable of.

"No, but where there are missiles there are men. And this works very well on men."

When he heard "surface-to-air missiles," Mike felt a little chill inside and leaned forward so he could see his father past Corey. Roger could see he was worried.

"Should we be concerned?" Roger asked Seamus. He seemed to be the de facto leader of the contractors.

"I'm sure it's just a precaution," Seamus told him. "When the SAM itself, flying in your direction, is your warning that something's amiss, *that's* when you've got problems. And Guadalajara is the other side of the country, hundreds of kilometers from here."

Because he was curious, and also to distract himself from the thought of a missile heading toward them, Mike asked Seamus, "Have you ever seen a dinosaur?" He still wasn't quite able to believe that such a thing was real, even though he'd seen the news footage.

"Well laddie, they're not standing around waiting for tourists to come take their pictures. They're like any other animal out there. The plant eaters are hiding from the meat eaters, and the meat eaters don't want to get spotted until they're ready to pounce. If they hear a car or a helicopter, most of the time they'll disappear into the bush before we see them."

"So you haven't seen one?" He was crestfallen. Maybe PaleoSafari, Inc., was a scam after all.

Seamus smiled at the look on the boy's face. "I've been fighting in this bloody country for near a decade. Have I seen dinosaurs? Sure. Seals, diplos, massos, Syntax, two baby anks, even a triceratops. Probably half a dozen other species over the years, although I'll be honest with you—in person I've only seen less than half of those. The rest was camera footage off helis."

"The helicopters have cameras?"

"Gun cameras on a lot of the cannon and mini-guns."

"They're shooting dinosaurs with the mini-guns?"

"I'm sure some wankers have, but the footage I saw they were just running the cameras, not the guns. Boys of all ages get stiff willies when they see dinosaurs, and pilots here do a lot of flying, cover a lot of ground, have much more opportunity to spot the beasties. I just don't want you expecting to spot herds of them wandering the plains as we're flying around up here. Maybe in twenty or fifty years, if they're left alone to breed, but there's not quite that many yet. If you're here to hunt, chances are you're going to actually have to *hunt* them."

"Seals?" Roger said.

"Coelophysis." Pronouncing it 'seal-o-physis,' Seamus spelled it for him. "Pack hunters, about nine feet long with the tail, run on two legs. Nasty buggers if you let them surprise you. Pretty much what the movies would have you think velociraptors are. You do know about them, right?"

"Know what?"

"That the movies had them all bollocksed up. Scary killing machines my arse. Velociraptors were maybe two meters long, almost half of that tail, and when the lab boys grew a few they discovered they were covered in feathers. Looked like big turkeys bred with greyhounds. Hell on schnauzers and poodles, maybe the odd toddler, but not exactly the dry land version of sharks. Actually, a lot of the smaller dinosaurs were found to have feathers, or a weird fuzz that I'm told later evolved into feathers."

"Yeah, I've seen the pictures." Fuzzy dinosaurs were neither scary nor cool, but luckily they weren't all that way. "What about tyrannosaurs?" Mike asked him hopefully.

Seamus had to laugh. Boys. It was always about the T. rex. "Pangaea only ever had two, if I remember correctly, a male and a female. And the male I know was killed ten years ago near San Luis Potosi by some drunken FRAP boys, they posted video of it online. I'm sure the skull's mounted in one of their bloody hideouts. The female could have died out in the desert somewhere, with no one the wiser. It's a big country. So I wouldn't get my hopes up."

Their course deviation meant they had to climb over the Sierra Madre Oriental mountain range, crossing over the middle of the huge Monterrey National Park. Stretching north and south along the mountains for almost two hundred kilometers, the park encompassed half a dozen peaks at or above 5,000 feet in elevation. The pilots stared down at the ridges and canyons which, for mountains, were rather gentle. It was an old mountain range, and the gradual slopes were beautiful, most of them covered with spruce, pine, and oak trees. The southernmost tip of the National Park was only a hundred klicks—sixty miles—from the former Pangaea, and many people assumed some of the dinosaurs that had survived were in the National Park.

"Oh, hey, look," Delian said to Hansen, and pointed out the nose of the bird. "Have a look out the right side," the co-pilot said over the intercom.

Mike practically leapt in his seat, and pressed his nose against the window. He spotted the herd immediately, running, maybe because of the helicopter. He was trying to figure out what kind of dinosaurs they were, but his brain was having a hard time deciphering what his eyes were seeing. Then he realized the animals weren't dinosaurs, they were a group of wild horses, about eight of them. He grumbled and sat back in his seat. Seamus saw the look on the boy's face and hid a smile.

"You ever seen anything, flying in this area?" Hansen asked his co-pilot, peering down through his side window.

"I saw something big once, by a river. Some long-tailed herbivore, I don't know what it was. I couldn't drop lower to check it out. You?"

"A small herd of something. I don't know what they were, but there were about ten of them at the edge of a clearing. We went down to check them out, but they scattered, disappeared. They were the size of small horses, I think, only on two legs, and greenish brown."

"Creeps me the hell out, thought of things wandering around down there that'd be happy to eat me, and big enough to do it. It was the same thing when I was stationed in Africa with the lions and tigers."

Hansen glanced at Delian. "I'm guessing you don't swim in the ocean much. Sharks."

The older man shivered. "God no. Purpose-built killing machines always looking for their next meal, somewhere out of sight underneath me? Screw that. I've seen that horror movie." Danny Hansen smiled, teeth gleaming in the sunlight, and took another look out his window.

Ten minutes of flying and the helicopter was crossing the western edge of the mountain range, and past it was the vast plateau that took up so much of central Mexico. The low hills faded to flat brownness that seemed to stretch forever. The plateau stretched for 500 kilometers before running into the Sierra Madre Occidental mountain range near Mexico's west coast. When they hit the GPS waypoint and turned the bird left toward Victoria Base, the co-pilot looked out his window at the ground below.

"There is nothing down there," Delian observed. "You lived down there, you'd have to drive an hour just to get to the middle of nowhere." According to the HUD, the only town within twenty miles was a little speck called Santa Rita, parked alongside Route 57. Once they made the turn the bird was back on a southeasterly heading and aimed back toward the Sierra Madre Orientals.

"Whoever plotted this route should have his ass kicked," Delian remarked. "Waste of time and fuel."

"It's the scenic route," Hansen said with a smile. His eyes flicked to the gauges. Good thing they'd topped off at China Base, otherwise the tanks would have been uncomfortably empty by the time they touched down. He clicked on the intercom and spoke to the passengers. "We're about a hundred and ten klicks out from Victoria Base, so we should be down on the ground in about forty minutes, tops."

Delian eyed the mountains coming up. "You going to keep us at five hundred feet?" That was what their new flight plan called for. "There can't be any other air traffic, not out here. And there are no Gs in the area, only mud farmers and sheep herders."

"I do that, we'll be going up and down and up and down. It'll be like flying nap of the earth," Hansen said, staring out the windshield. Lower altitude made it harder for them to be spotted, and gave the missiles less time to lock on, but there were trade-offs for everything. Close to the ground meant much less response time if missiles did lock on. Also, flying nap-of-the-earth was very similar to riding a roller coaster. He glanced up through the top of the windshield, then back at the civilian passengers. You could never tell who was likely to be a puker. "I think we could do with a little more air under our skids."

* * *

Ciudad Victoria, or Victoria City, was the capital of the Mexican state of Tamaulipas. The city had a population of over a quarter million people, but it was far enough north that FRAP had never had much of a presence. The city maintained a large airport, General Pedro J. Mendez International, ten miles east of the city on Route 70, but for some reason, the Mexican Army didn't like it. They'd built their own airport and base twenty miles to the southwest of the city. It was beside a river, in a long valley between two fingers of the Sierra Madre Orientals, north of the intersection of Highways 101 and 126. There wasn't anything in the area other than a few farmers and their fields. After America joined in the war effort, "Victoria Base," as it was re-named, became a joint military operations center and was the main base controlling operations in northeast Mexico. Which sounded more impressive than it actually was—Victoria Base was mostly used as a refueling point for aircraft and vehicles heading further south. Northeast Mexico was the quietest region in the country, and apart from paying locals for intelligence on Raven activities, FRAP hardly had a presence.

Since they'd changed course, they'd flown over mountains and high plains, and were now heading back over mountains. They'd hardly seen sign of another human being, but that hadn't stopped the contractor Todd from keeping the sliding door open, his hands on the mini-gun. Roger was annoyed by the wind buffeting everyone in the cabin but didn't say anything. At least it wasn't hot.

"This really is beautiful country," he observed, looking down at the green and brown hills. The mountain range below them was closer in appearance and elevation to the Appalachians than to the Rockies, more rolling giant hills than jagged towering peaks. People paid a lot of money for sightseeing air tours in places not nearly as picturesque. He looked across the cabin. "Michael," he said into his microphone. His son looked his way. Roger pointed out the door. "I think that's the kind of terrain—" and then his microphone died.

There was a loud bang and the Blackhawk shuddered as if it had been kicked in the side by a giant. All the instrument panel lights in the cockpit went out, and the helicopter started to drop.

"Dead stick! Dead stick!" Hansen yelled. "Emergency re-start!"

"Mayday Mayday Mayday, this is Sierra Bravo Six, we've lost power and are going down," Delian calmly said as Tina screamed from the back. He and Hanson began frantically hitting buttons and flipping switches. "Radio's dead, I've got nothing." He had to yell it so Hansen could hear him over the wind.

Mike's eyes went wide. He felt his stomach come up into his throat as the helicopter dropped and began rotating. "Shite," Seamus cursed and smacked the button to drop the visor on his helmet.

"Keep transmitting," Hansen told his co-pilot. "Damn, I've got no electronics, can we do a manual re-start?" He stayed on the stick and the collective, trying to control the autorotation.

Delian had been hitting every button and toggle switch possible. "No, I don't think this is a short, it looks like everything's fried. Mayday Mayday Mayday, this is Sierra Bravo Six, we are going down." He told the younger pilot, "You know what to do. Keep it level, autorotate down, try to control the rate of descent. Time your glide. You see a place to land?"

The helicopter was spinning to the right as it fell, which traditionally was the reason the pilot was the right stick. Hansen looked out the window as he fought the controls. "We're in the mountains, nothing's flat. I've got trees everywhere. Hold on back there!" he yelled over his shoulder.

The helicopter began spinning faster and faster and Mike found himself being pulled sideways in his seat. The soldier on the door gun lost his footing and floated up in the air, then was halfway out the open door, one hand still on the mini-gun, restrained only by his tether as the G-forces made Mike's face feel hot. He vomited, and the bitter fluid was whipped away from his face. The world outside the open doorway past Todd was a spinning blue/green/brown blur. Tina was screaming wildly. The wind was whistling around the cabin.

"We've got smoke coming from the engine," Delian said, peering upward. "What the hell happened?"

"Brace for impact!" Seamus yelled at the cabin, and wedged his boots against the seat opposite.

"Coming up on the mark, keep it level," Delian said calmly. "Get ready for the burn!" he yelled over his shoulder at the passengers. He switched back to the radio, even though he thought it was a waste of time. "Mayday Mayday Mayday, this is Sierra Bravo Six—"

"If they work," Mike heard the pilot respond, then suddenly there was a roar, and he was pressed down in his seat, getting heavier and heavier. The helicopter was still spinning, and out the open doorway and windshield there was nothing but a blur of greens and browns. Mike got heavier and heavier, and Tina stopped screaming.

Then the roar stopped, and they began falling again, pulling up against their seatbelts. Tina opened her mouth to scream once more, but before she could draw a breath the helicopter hit with a huge crunch and the sound of tearing metal.

* * *

Someone coughed, and there was a groan. The smell of smoke and JP8 fuel filled the air. Mike opened his eyes to see Seamus straightening up in his seat. The contractor had lost his helmet, and there was a small cut along his jaw. The air between them was filled with floating particles.

"Well, that was exciting," Seamus said drily.

Mike blinked at the words and thought to look around the cabin for his father. There he was, still in his seat, holding the back of his head. "Dad?"

Roger looked over at him, squinting, and gave him a thumbs up. His head hurt too much to talk.

The helicopter was not quite level, in some sort of uneven grassy field. Seamus could smell something electrical burning. "Where's me shaggin' helmet?" he said, looking around. He was still in a bit of a daze. He'd been in helicopter crashes before, but nothing that harsh. His helmet was nowhere to be seen.

"Sound off. Who's not dead?" There was coughing behind him, in the cockpit. Tina in her seat next to him was dabbing a bloody nose.

"My ass hurts," Corey, sitting next to Mike, told Seamus. "How are you?"

Seamus grimaced. "Nothing that half a bottle of whiskey wouldn't fix for a night." He tried opening the sliding door next to him, but it was jammed. He braced his feet and pulled with both hands, but it wouldn't budge. "I guess we're going out that way," he said, pointing out the open sliding door on the left side of the bird. The floor slanted gently in that direction. "Todd? Where's Todd?" The doorgunner wasn't in sight.

"I'll check on him," Corey said, standing up with a grunt. He grabbed his slung rifle with a hand and hopped off the bird. Seamus turned in his seat and looked into the cockpit. "How are things up here?"

Hansen jerked his helmet at his co-pilot, who was slumped against his door and not moving. The door was crumpled, and the glass was spiderwebbed from the impact. It appeared the left side of the nose had hit the ground first. "Check on him."

Seamus climbed out of the helicopter behind Corey and, letting his rifle hang from its sling, fought with the co-pilot's door for thirty seconds, finally forcing it open with a curse. Delian had blood running down his face, and his head hung at an odd angle. The examination didn't take Seamus long. "He's dead," he announced, leaving the man in his seat. He looked across Delian's body at the pilot, who was moving slowly. "How about you?"

"I think my arm's broken," Hansen admitted, wincing. "Other than that I think I'm fine. Just pissed." He pulled his helmet off with his left hand and threw it at the controls of the dead helicopter. "Well, that sucked." He looked at Delian and shook his head. "Goddammit."

"Don't blame yourself mate, you got the rest of us down alive," Seamus said. He took a step back from the helicopter and looked at it. The fuselage was crumpled where it rested on the ground, and several of the rotors had snapped. A thin line of smoke trailed from the engine, the housing of which appeared damaged.

"Seamus," Corey said. He gestured. Seamus stepped to the edge of the helicopter, and Corey grabbed the cable which had connected their doorgunner to the ceiling of the helicopter. The cable was still there, but the hook at the end had snapped off.

"Jesus shite," Seamus said. "Anybody notice how high we were when we lost him?" All he got was head shakes and confused looks. "*Mierda.*" He turned and looked around. The helicopter had crashed into a small oval clearing running west to east. The clearing was uneven rocky ground covered in grass and low scrub brush with a gentle slope down to the north. A thin mixed evergreen forest surrounded the clearing, and the trees were tall enough to block Seamus' view in every direction but north—and there he could only see more trees running down a long slope and back up the next, maybe a mile away. He cupped his hands around his mouth. "Todd! Todd!" There was no response.

Roger climbed carefully out of the helicopter. Seamus grabbed his elbow and made sure he didn't fall. Roger hissed.

Seamus looked down and saw a huge welt on the man's left elbow. "Oh, sorry." He let go. "Any other injuries?"

Roger stopped only a few steps away and leaned against the side of the Blackhawk. "Banged my head, but it's not serious." He paused. "My back," he admitted. He could barely stand upright, but he waved a hand at Seamus. "Don't worry about me, check on them."

Tina had her nose pinched closed as she climbed out. "I banged my nose on something, but I think that's it," she said. She pulled her hand away, hoping that the bleeding had stopped, but felt a trickle come out and clamped back down.

"I'm fine," Mike said from inside the bird, not quite believing it. Maybe he'd be sore in a day or two, but now, with the adrenaline still coursing through his system, he was feeling no pain. He could taste puke in his mouth, but didn't remember throwing up.

"Good." Seamus pointed at the pilot. "Help him out," he told Mike. "Careful, his arm's broken."

Mike climbed out past the contractor and looked at his dad who was hunched over and making a face. "You okay?"

"Yeah, yeah, I just wrenched my back. Go help the pilot."

Seamus turned and saw Corey a few feet away, looking at him, and the two men stared at each other. "Could've been worse," Seamus said.

"Could've been better," Corey observed. "I don't suppose you've got a palm on you?"

"That would work out here? Not bloody likely, mate. It's in my locker at McAllen. And no encrypted satphone; the one I've normally got nearby is sitting back at Victoria. Anybody have a sat-linked palm?" he called out. He got nothing but shaking heads.

"You don't have your palm?" Mike asked his dad. Roger had told his assistant he'd be leaving it in the car, but Mike hadn't believed he'd actually do it. His dad lived on his palm.

"No, I left it in the Scout. The radio's completely out?" Roger asked.

"Appears that way," Seamus said. He looked from him out at the clearing, then took a few steps to peer around the helicopter. It had crashed thirty feet from the base of a nearly vertical bare rock cliff. The rock was near white—limestone?—and looked too crumbly to climb. The top of the cliff ended in a grass-topped ridge maybe fifty feet above the helicopter's rotors, and the ridge sloped down behind the bird. Near the tree line about a hundred meters to the west the lowering rock face had crumbled and looked easy to climb. He pointed at Corey. "Okay, you search the clearing, see if you can find Todd. Or anything else of interest. Head into the woods, but don't go too far, don't want to lose you too. Tina—you think you can help him? Two people can cover twice as much ground." From behind wings of black hair that had escaped her ponytail she nodded. "And don't forget to look up. He may be wedged in a tree. And see if you can find my bloody helmet. My swede's not good for much but it's the only one I've got. I'd prefer not to get domed crossing a hill."

Mike pulled out his own palm, which seemed to have survived the crash unscathed. No bars, no service, searching for a signal. So it wouldn't burn out the battery looking for a signal that wasn't there, he shut it off.

Corey and Tina walked off across the grass, angling in opposite directions. Seamus walked around the front of the Blackhawk as Mike was helping Hansen down from the cockpit. "Ow! Crap! Yeah, it's broken," the pilot said. He was cradling his right arm.

"How's the rest of you?"

"I banged my legs up pretty good, but that's just bruises. I can walk, I'll be fine."

Seamus nodded, and pulled a folding knife out. He opened it and held it out for Mike to see. "You think you can cut up one of the seats in back, maybe a seatbelt or two, and make a sling for his arm?" he asked the teenager. In the distance he heard Corey and the woman yelling Todd's name.

Mike had taken basic first aid a few years before, and still remembered about folding fabric into triangles to make slings. He nodded, and Seamus handed him the knife. Then Seamus looked at the pilot.

"What the frig happened?"

Danny Hansen shook his head. "Hell if I know. There was an explosion, not a big one, and everything died. Power, radio, everything. And Chris said the engine was on fire too."

"It looks torn up," Seamus observed. "But if the engine blew, that wouldn't, shouldn't blow the electronics. Right?"

"Right. So like I said, I don't know what happened."

"This bird's got an emergency beacon, correct?"

"Yeah," Hansen said, then paused. "But…."

"But….?"

Hansen lowered his voice. "We're out in the middle of nowhere, but I swear to God we were hit with a localized EMP. That's exactly what happens when they down a bird. And if that's what happened, then I don't know if the beacon is working."

An electromagnetic pulse? That would be bad news. "Aren't they EMP shielded?"

"On newer rotary wing aircraft, Kraits and Copperheads. Not on these old things."

"Can't you pull it out and check on it?"

Hansen shook his head. "They're designed to be crash proof, so I couldn't crack it open without the proper tools. So we've got no way to know if it's broadcasting."

"Shit."

"China transmitted our new flight plan to Victoria Base I'm sure, so once we're overdue they're going to start trying to raise us on the radio. When that doesn't work they'll send out someone to look for us. I don't think we're as much as half a mile off our route, and we're right out in the open, so they'll have no trouble spotting us. I'd give it two, three hours tops."

"How far are we from Victoria Base?"

Hansen thought back to the route. "Fifty kilometers, direct line over the mountains. Thirty miles. Maybe. Not far. We shouldn't have long to wait."

Seamus thought for a second. "If it was an EMP, we might be waiting less time than you think. Don't mention the EMP to the civilians. No call to worry them needlessly."

Mike came walking around the helicopter with several wide green strips of nylon seat material. "See if you can get the radio working," Seamus told the pilot. Seeing the man was about to argue, he said, "You never know til you try." Hansen frowned as Mike started wrapping up his broken arm. Seeing that the kid seemed to know what he was doing, Seamus tried opening the jammed sliding door of the bird from the outside, but the helicopter's frame had been bent enough from the impact that the door wouldn't budge. He climbed into the bird through the cockpit and retrieved the first aid kit. Roger Rudd was sitting awkwardly against a large rock about thirty feet from the tail of the bird.

"How bad is the elbow?" Seamus asked him, squatting down.

"I don't think anything's broken, I just banged the hell out of it," Roger told him, working the elbow a few times slowly. The knot on it had already swollen to the size of an egg. "My back hurts worse." Compared to his back, his head hardly hurt at all.

"Pulled muscle, or do you think you pinched a nerve or a disc?"

Roger shook his head. "I don't know. It's—it hurts bad now, but what scares me is how much worse I think it's going to feel after the adrenaline wears off."

"Adrenaline's a hell of a pain-killer," Seamus agreed. He dug around in the first aid kit and handed Roger two packets of ibuprofen. "Hold on." He got up and walked over to the Blackhawk, returning a few moments later with a bottle of water. "That should take the bite off."

"Pilot dead?" Roger asked him.

Seamus looked down at the older man. "Co-pilot. Pilot's got a broken arm. Considering he found the one clear flat space for miles around to put us down in, I'd say he did a brilliant job. I shudder to think what my gob would look like if we'd spun down into those trees, or that cliff-face."

Corey came trudging up through the long grass, Tina a few steps behind him. "No sign of Todd. Didn't see your helmet either. We checked about a hundred yards out from the clearing. It's pretty open under the trees. You want us to check farther in?"

Seamus shook his head. "If everything goes as it should, we'll have an SAR bird here in an hour or two. That crew can help us search for his body or maybe spot it from the air."

"You think he's dead?" Tina asked him. Her nose had stopped bleeding, but dried blood covered her chin and her neck. A little had soaked into the strap of her tank top under the light green button-down shirt she used to keep the sun off her skin.

"If he didn't land in the clearing, then he went out of the chopper when we were still at least a hundred feet up and spinning fast. So yes." Seamus pulled several moistened wipes out of the first aid kit and handed them to her. "For the blood on your face," he told her. "I don't have a mirror, so you're going to have to improvise. I opened up the back of the bird, there are bottles of water back there to help you clean up."

"Thanks." She walked off toward the Blackhawk, then stopped. "Sorry for all the screaming, when we were falling." She looked embarrassed.

"I thought that was me," Seamus told her. She looked at him, gave him a little smile, then headed for the helicopter.

"Well, it's a hell of a view."

Seamus looked around at the comment and saw Roger pointing to the west. There was a rounded mountain peak in the distance, rising above the tops of the pines at the edge of the clearing. "How far away do you think that is?" The sky was a light blue, with a few wispy clouds moving slowly.

"Miles," Corey said. "It's hard as hell to tell. Maybe if we knew how tall it was…"

"Well, I'm guessing we're up at least three thousand feet here," Seamus said. "Lot cooler, did you notice? So that's got to be ten thousand, easy. Not much more than that, though. There are trees all the way to the summit." The men stared at the peak in the distance. The fact that the tall pine trees thinly scattered around its slopes resembled green fuzz was the best guide they had to estimating distance.

Corey squinted. "I think some of those slopes have been logged," he said. "Not recently, but I grew up in logging country, and it looks like those trees were thinned out. So we're not quite in the middle of nowhere."

"Hmm." Seamus turned, and looked past the bird to the top of the ridge above. There was nothing but blue sky beyond it. He caught Corey's eye and jerked his head, and the younger contractor followed Seamus a few yards away.

"All right. You didn't find Todd. So what did you find? You never could play poker worth a shite." He spoke quietly.

Corey looked around casually, then turned back to Seamus. "How good are you with dino species?"

"You mean telling which is which? Probably a mite poorer than the average wide-eyed eight-year-old boy, but I know a few, why?"

"See that clump of yellow flowers, 'bout thirty feet behind me? Line that up with that pine tree with the zig-zagging trunk, go maybe sixty yards into the trees, there's a body. The girl didn't see it."

Seamus' eyes scanned the treeline. "Todd?"

"Nope, not Todd. Just wander that direction when you get a chance, since we're trying to be all casual and not scare the civvies."

Seamus grunted. "Before I do that, check your optic," Seamus told him softly, looking around the clearing nonchalantly.

"What's up?" Corey said. He pointed his rifle in a safe direction and shouldered it, then hit the button to power the hybrid optic atop the weapon. He stopped, then hit the button a few more times, and then lowered the rifle and began fiddling with the scope.

"Problem?" Seamus asked, deliberately talking quietly and not watching the man.

"It won't power up." The optic mounted on his M7 carbine was a variable magnification hybrid sight, battery powered, switchable between thermal and amplified visible light (night vision) or used as a day scope.

"You can still see through it, though, and have a reticle, right?"

"Yeah, but no thermal or night vision, and no digital magnification. Just crosshairs. What about yours?"

"No electronics in mine, just glass and aluminum." He took his eyes off the tree line, and gave Corey a look. "Pilot thinks we got hit with an EMP. I'm beginning to think he was right."

"And here I thought the helicopter crashing was the bad news. So what should we do?"

"Stay with the bird. Even if it was an EMP, this isn't a known FRAP area. Search and rescue from Victoria Base should be here long before the G's even know we went down. But...." He looked at the Blackhawk. "Maybe we better inventory what we have."

"On it."

As Corey headed toward the helicopter Seamus walked back toward Roger Rudd. From the awkward way the man sat it was obvious he was in a lot of pain. "Any idea at all how high we were when Todd parted ways with the bird?"

Roger shook his head. "Once we started dropping I didn't see anything other than my life flashing in front of my eyes."

"Always depressing, that," Seamus said. He cupped his hands over his mouth. "Todd! Todd!" he shouted, then listened. There was nothing but the sound of the wind in the trees and some distant birds. "I'm going to go poke about a bit," he told Roger. "Never leave a man behind and all that."

Seamus walked over to the small patch of yellow flowers and looked at the tree line. He spotted the tree Corey had indicated and headed in that direction, holding his rifle as casually as possible.

Inside the trees it was a little cooler, the smell of pine thicker. The dead needles formed a thick carpet underfoot which softened his footsteps.

He counted his steps, and after fifty turned and looked behind him. The clearing was just a brighter area between the tree trunks.

The ground in front of him was mostly clear, sloping gently downward, with a few thin saplings and patches of knee-high ferns between the tree trunks.

Holding his rifle less casually he moved cautiously forward. The faint but unmistakable smell of blood hit his nose before he saw the body. It was half hidden by a fold in the earth, and Seamus walked around the far side to see it better.

The animal had a small head and a few spikes on the end of its otherwise unremarkable tail. Most of its bulk was in its body near its hindquarters. Alive, it had been a mottled medium brown, but that color was fading fast, where it wasn't obscured by the blood.

Stegosaurus. Seamus easily recognized the double row of spade-shaped plates on its back running along either side of its spine. This was a younger animal, less than four meters long including the tail, which meant it weighed in the neighborhood of the average cow. Plant eater, likely munching on the ferns and young trees.

Whatever had brought it down had done so with claws. Sharp claws, and a lot of them. More than one predator would be his guess. Which wasn't surprising. Smaller predators tended to work in packs, which is why plant eaters tended to move in herds. This one had obviously wandered away from the herd, or been separated from them, and then been brought down. Then they started snacking on the beastie's tasty bits.

There were long claw marks in the animal's neck, and its belly had been ripped open, intestines spilling out. There was a fan of blood and viscera stretching downhill from the carcass. Bite marks through the deep meat of its back legs. Seamus didn't find any of that worrisome at all. Circle of life and all that.

No, what concerned him was the fact that he could still feel the heat coming off the animal. Smell the fresh blood. Whatever had killed this animal had done so within the last hour, and had undoubtedly still been chewing on it when the helicopter had come screaming in.

Hands lightly on his rifle, Seamus looked up from the stegosaur and studied the woods around him. He wondered if the animal or animals who'd had their meal interrupted were close enough to see or smell him. And he wondered if they were still hungry.

* * * * *

Chapter Six

Seeing as someone else had already broken open the case, Mike pulled a bottle of water out of the storage area in the back of the Blackhawk and was drinking it when Seamus and Corey walked up.

"It's not that hot up here, but the air's dry," Seamus told the young man. "Make sure you stay hydrated." He glanced over and saw Tina and the pilot sitting on the ground with Roger, talking. "Take a couple bottles over to them, and a few of these protein bars. The lemon ones taste the least like ass. Here, take this ibuprofen to Hansen. It's not much for a broken arm, but it's better than nothing."

When Mike returned from the errand the younger contractor was going through the items in the rear of the helicopter, and Seamus was standing in front of the mini-gun. "What are you doing?" he asked Seamus. The man was flipping latches on the big ammo box.

"Just seeing what they—oh, you greedy bastards," he said as he flipped the lid open. "Bloody beautiful." He grabbed hold of the belt of ammo inside and pulled a long length of it out with a clank.

"What?" Mike asked, stepping closer.

"This mini-gun fires the 7.62mm cartridge, the same as Leonidas here," Seamus said, patting his rifle hanging from its sling. "And they've got it loaded with black beauties. I was down to my last mag of them."

"The M7 is chambered in 5.56mm," Mike said slowly, trying to remember the specs. "So these are bigger." He eyed the finger-sized cartridges in the long metal belt of ammo. The tips of the bullets looked weird; stepped, with black tips. "What are black beauties?"

With some difficulty Seamus pulled one from the metal belt and held it up. "This cartridge was originally designed around a thirty caliber bullet weighing a hundred and fifty to two hundred grains. What you see here is a twenty-two caliber tungsten-tipped bullet weighing just sixty-two grains, held in a thirty-caliber ferropolymer sabot which discards as soon as it exits the barrel." The small bullet had a tip that was painted black.

"It looks tiny," Mike admitted. "Why is that better than a bigger, heavier bullet?"

"Since it weighs half as much, it spits out twice as fast, and tungsten is hard. With the new gunpowders they've developed, I'm getting well over four thousand feet per second even out of my short little rifle. These little lovelies will go right through any armor they might be wearing."

"I thought the terrorists almost never wore body armor."

"Almost isn't good enough. Plus, the extra velocity seems to double the hydrostatic shock. Ever hear of that?" Mike shook his head. "Even though we're skin and bone, the human body is really not much more than a big bag of water. If you take your finger and slowly stick it into a puddle, what happens? Not much, right? Maybe a few ripples, and your finger gets wet. But take that same hand and slap it as hard and as fast as you can against that puddle. Completely different result. And you're the puddle. Tiny bullet or no, when it passes through at four thousand feet per second, it tends to make organs react as if they'd been dropped in a blender. And it does bloody well against their vehicles too, even the armored ones. Here, be a good lad." Seamus pulled several large loaded magazines for his rifle out of the pouches across his chest and dropped them on the floor of the helicopter. Mike saw the cartridges in the magazines were loaded with standard bullets. "You empty those, while I pry some of these loose from the belt. We'll switch 'em out. Look." Seamus slid the top round out of the first mag, and showed Mike how to use it to pop the other rounds out of the magazine.

They worked side by side for a while, the only sounds the metallic clanking of cartridges. The hard metal edges of the magazines dug into his hands as Mike worked. Twenty rounds fit into each one, so it took a bit of work to empty them out and fill them up again. He asked Seamus, "Did you call your rifle Leonidas? Did you give it a name?" That seemed weird to him. And kinda cool.

"The first prototype of this rifle back before you were born was called Project Leonidas. He was—"

"King of Sparta, I know. Died at the Battle of Thermopylae."

Seamus' eyebrows went up. "Excellent. I see you've been paying attention in class. I never want to die, lad, and so far that plan's working perfectly, but for professional soldiers, Leonidas pretty much set the standard for pithy one-liners and going out in a blaze of glory. Makes me all weepy just thinking about him." And he wiped away an imaginary tear. Mike smiled.

* * *

Tina chewed on the energy bar and washed the bite down with some water as she sat cross-legged on the grass. Several feet to her right was a small agave rosette, resembling nothing so much as a large green rosebud with sharp petals.

She studied it for a moment and decided it most likely was an *agave chiapensis*. Most people thought agaves were cacti, but in fact they were simply succulents with thorns. Pretty scenery, the smell of pine in the air, a healthy snack, pleasant weather…except for the throbbing in her nose it could almost have been a picnic. Well, the throbbing in her nose and the crashed, smoking wreck of the helicopter visible behind Roger Rudd. She turned to the pilot sitting next to her.

"What happened? Why'd the helicopter crash? Why'd the power go out?" She'd been terrified as they'd been falling, but since the crash, she'd surprised herself at how calm she was. How *not* scared, even after being in a helicopter crash, which was a first for her. Maybe it was because the forest was so serene, or maybe—and she found this a hard pill to swallow—it was because she was protected by men with guns.

Hansen shook his head. "I don't know." He'd climbed up onto the bird and inspected the engine as well as he could under the circumstances. There was no explosive damage, so they hadn't been hit with a missile. Shrapnel had pierced the cowling in several places, but from the inside out, as if the engine had disintegrated. "The engine's damaged, but it almost looks like it tore itself apart. I'm not sure why the electronics went out."

"Well, thank you."

He looked at her and finished chewing his mouthful of nuts. "For what?"

"Saving my life. We crashed, and all I got was a bloody nose."

Hansen was in no mood to be thanked. The crash had killed two people. He kept replaying it in his head, wondering if he could have, *should have* done something different. He'd been lucky simply to spot the clearing, much less successfully glide the Blackhawk into it. The controls had fought him all the way, and he was pretty sure at least one of his rotor blades was damaged before they'd landed, as unresponsive as the bird had been. He'd tried to flare the Blackhawk at the end, tried to soften the impact, but it had been like flying a bathtub. He could hardly focus for all the flashbacks and second-guessing going through his head.

Roger saw the look on the pilot's face, and knew what he must be thinking about. As much to distract himself from the pain in his back as anything he asked the young woman, "Did you say you've been out in the field for six weeks working on your graduate thesis?"

Tina looked away from the pilot, wanting to console him but knowing there wasn't anything she could say that would help. "*Mas o menos*," she said. "A week or two at a time, then a few days at the nearest university, staying in the dorm if possible or a hotel room. I'd clean up and organize myself, resupply, get transport to where I needed to go, and head back out. About half the time I was with other students, and spent three days with a whole graduate class and a professor in a semi-permanent camp outside Tuxpan."

"I bet that was interesting. But dangerous, especially for a pretty young woman. I imagine your parents were none too happy about it." He glanced over at Michael, who was over at the helicopter helping O'Malley with something. Good kid, always willing to join in and help out.

"You have no idea," she said with a laugh. "My father….I ended up putting my palmpad in a box and mailing it back to him so he would stop calling me. Five, ten times a day, it was as if calling to check that I was still alive became his job. I told him I was going to do it, mail him the palm, but he didn't believe me. When I got back into a town two days ago and called him from a borrowed palm, he was so *loco* mad. Especially since he originally wanted me to travel with an escort, one of his…employees. So that's why I ended up on the helicopter."

"To keep him from having a heart attack?" Roger joked.

"It's an old story. He's big in business, powerful, and always needs to be in charge. *El Jefe*. But I am not my sisters, I don't want to be primped and pampered and lined up at parties to parade for my future rich lawyer husband. He never understood that." Her parents had their first peek at her independent spirit when trying to plan her *quinceanera*. Her older sisters had loved their huge *quinceaneras*, and spent weeks in stores and looking through magazines with their mother, trying to pick out just the right dress. Tina didn't like dresses, had never been girly, and told her father that instead of throwing her a huge party she didn't care about he should buy her an electron microscope. That had not gone over well. The party had been memorable, if only for how miserable everyone had been.

"Maybe if I'd been a boy, but…." She shook her head, and the movement made her realize just how many strands of her hair had escaped from her ponytail. She went to work on it as she talked. "*Papa* loves me and wants to do things for me, but I need to do them for myself. He doesn't understand that. So I didn't argue when he arranged for me to fly special, Raven rides all the way home. I've given him enough headaches for a while." She looked around. "And now *this.*"

"I never had a daughter, but I understand," Roger said. "Where's home?"

"Mexico City."

"Your English is impressive," he said. "You have almost no accent."

"Only the finest private schools would do for *papa*," she said with a shrug.

"You're a biology student? What's your specialty? What's your graduate thesis on?"

"On how non-traditional farming techniques, using pesticides and artificial fertilizers and machinery to do all the work, seem to result in increased erosion when compared to traditional, organic farming methods."

"That sounds more like agriculture or horticulture than biology."

"The non-traditional farming methods drive away or kill off local fauna to a much greater degree, and my thesis is that this is key to the increased erosion. Animals and plants have always co-existed, and without one, there is no balance."

"Hmm. Interesting," Roger said, by which he meant *Boring*. It also sounded as if she was mixing a bit of socialism in with her science. He remembered back to college, where nobody worried about a little thing the rest of the world seemed obsessed with, *results*. But keeping her talking, keeping her mind off the fact that they had crashed in the middle of nowhere and had no idea when they might get rescued, seemed like the right thing to do. Plus it helped distract him from the pain in his back. "It seems to me that that would be a hard thing to prove. If not impossible. I mean, how do you even quantify the effect of wildlife, or the lack thereof, on erosion? How would you separate that from all the other variable natural factors, such as weather?"

The question energized her. "That's a good question, and I came up with a theory…." she began.

* * *

"Are we doing all of that?" Mike asked, staring at the length of belted ammo. There had to be thousands of rounds. He finished loading the last twenty-round magazine Seamus had given him and handed it back.

"No, that's all of my mags. Shame to waste it though, that ammo is almost twenty quid a round." He peered up at the Blackhawk's broken rotors. "Of course, the helo's a bit spendier...."

"We've got enough water to last us a week if we're careful, and food for two weeks if we eat like pigs," Corey said, standing behind them. "Although it's almost all straight protein. Basic aircraft first aid kit. Weapons...we both have our rifles, you've got your pistol, and the pilot has a sidearm. I'm not sure how cold it will get here at night but there's plenty of wood to make a fire if we need to." He'd pulled the rifle cases out of the back of the bird and set them on the ground. He pointed at them with the toe of his boot. "Those yours, kid? What do you have?"

"Hunting rifles," Mike said. He bent down and opened the first case, showing them the rifle his father had chosen for him. A traditional bolt-action hunting rifle wearing a scope gleamed on the foam interior.

"What's that chambered in?" Corey asked, wondering if it was a military caliber.

".375 H&H," Mike told them without hesitation. It was a traditional hard-recoiling big-game caliber. A century before it had been the most popular caliber used to hunt big game in Africa. He'd sighted in the rifle himself.

"And the other?"

Mike popped the latches on the other, heavier gun case and let the lid fall open. "What the hell is that?" Corey said. The young contractor squatted down and peered closer at the box-magazine fed, military-style rifle inside.

"Um, it's a...." He turned his head and called out. "Dad, what's your rifle called again?"

Mike's shout interrupted Tina going on at length about the life cycle of voles and for that Roger was very grateful. "Sorry," he said, and struggled to his feet. He limped over to where everyone was standing over his rifle case. "What? My rifle? That's almost a collector's item, that one. An Alexander Arms Ulfberht, bought it in an estate sale."

"An elf what?" Corey said. "What caliber is it?" He bent down and picked up the big black rifle, grunting at the weight.

".338 Lapua Magnum. Semi-auto. Ten-round magazines. For anything smaller than a buffalo it's complete overkill, but—"

"—but your plan was to be hunting dinosaurs, and they get bloody big," Seamus finished for him. "Not a bad choice if you're going to be riding around in a vehicle with a guide, but I wouldn't want to hump it up and down these hills."

"No kidding, this thing's heavy as a PKM," Corey said.

"Stop your whining, nancy; you see the dimples in the barrel?" Seamus said. "That's the lightweight model. I thought it looked familiar; they issued a few of those to Special Forces for sniping when things got interesting in Libya. Not that it was ever boring over there. Good for men at a mile, or disabling a lorry." There was also a pistol in the case, a Glock. "What caliber is the Glock?"

"Ten millimeter," Roger said. "Last ditch backup, although I know it won't do anything against something really big."

"Shoot out its eye, or stick it in its mouth and empty the magazine, you're sure to get a beastie's attention, no matter its size," Seamus assured him.

"Stick it in its *mouth*?" Mike said in disbelief.

Seamus shrugged. "Well, if you happen to already be there...."

Corey snorted and shook his head. "What the hell is an 'ulfberht,' anyway?"

"It's a Viking sword," Roger told him. He'd had to look it up himself.

Roger looked over his shoulder at Tina, then at the contractors. "I know Aarne probably asks you to take it easy on the paying customers, but honestly, how much trouble are we in? This is a country in the middle of a brutal civil war, and here we are...."

"The cities are at war," Seamus said. "And the southern half of the country. There's nothing up here to fight over. And honestly...." He made a face and shook his head. "This war could be over in a year if the U.S. Congress got off their collective fat arses and just let us fight it."

"Fight it how?"

"With a real commitment of U.S. troops and equipment. This is a secret war, innit. Politicians have to lie about every dollar they send our way, which means hardly any top-of-the-line toys. No thumpers, no sentry turrets, hardly any UAVs worth a damn. We've been fighting a war for ten years with hand-me-downs and obsolete tech."

Mike knew from his video games that "thumpers" were autonomous robots about the size and shape of polar bears. They were heavily armed and armored. Sentry turrets were computer-controlled tripod mounted belt-fed machineguns that could be programmed to fire on anything moving, or warm-blooded, or both.

"As for troops," Seamus went on, "when it comes to bodies Raven is smaller than a midge's dick. Maybe five thousand bodies, and less than a quarter of those are actual trigger pullers. Officially we are only here as advisors to the indigenous forces, and yet we've fought *La Fuerza* to a standstill. Hell, they don't even have any aircraft. If we had an actual professional army on our side I wouldn't give the bloody FRAP more than a year at the outside."

"If we could ever find Timotéo and blow his shit up I think the war would be over right there," Corey opined.

Seamus shook his head. "You've got a lot of true believers in the ranks. Kill him and he becomes a martyr for the cause, and they fight all the harder."

"Who's Timotéo?" Roger asked.

"Timotéo Sandoval. Head of the *La Fuerza* cartel before the war and believed to be the leader of FRAP, even though officially it is run by a collective of generals," Seamus told him. "Brutal bastard, but smart. Hasn't been seen in public in almost two years, and we've never been able to find his headquarters. Pretty sure he moves it regularly. Killing him might not end the war, but it sure wouldn't hurt even if it does make him a martyr. Raven actually has a bounty on his head, although they can't legally call it that. Just that anybody who kills or captures him gets a 'performance bonus.'" He smiled. "And a big damn one at that."

"I'm going to go find a bathroom," Corey told Seamus, and twirled his finger, signaling that he was going to have another look around. Seamus nodded.

"And I'm going to sit back down," Roger said. He patted Mike on the shoulder and then limped away.

Mike watched the contractor head toward the tree line. "We don't have to worry about anything coming after us here, do we?" he asked Seamus. He looked past Corey at the shade under the trees.

Seamus grinned at the boy and said without hesitation, "What'd I tell you before? When we came screaming in and hit, anything within earshot went running arse over teakettle in the other direction, and is probably still going." Seamus looked up at the co-pilot's open door, and saw Delian still slumped over. That wouldn't do.

"Can you help me move him?" he asked Mike. "I don't think it's right to leave him in there, I'd like to put him out of sight behind the chopper."

Mike blinked and looked at his father. He had absolutely no desire to touch a dead body, but he didn't want to act like a scared girl in front of the tough soldier, much less his father. Besides, it wasn't as if anybody else could do it, his dad's back was hurt and the pilot's arm was broken. Well, Tina would probably help Seamus, if he asked her. She was tough. But there was no way he was going to let that happen. Be more of a wimp than the girl? He'd never be able to live with himself.

"Yeah," Mike said, swallowing.

He was relieved when Seamus only had him grab the man's legs, but still found it hard to look away from the man's bloody face as they carried his body over to the base of the cliff. He'd seen a lot more gruesome things in movies, but this was real. That made it completely different, somehow. More disturbing.

"C'mon," Seamus said to the staring teen. He jerked his head. "Help me go through the cockpit. I don't know if Corey looked in there."

Seamus stepped up into the pilot's open door. "Oh," he said. "Wouldn't do to forget this." He pulled the PDW out of its mount and handed it back to Mike. "Secure this for me," he told the young man, trusting that if he was going hunting he knew a little bit about gun safety.

Mike stared at the weapon in his hand, a sense of déjà vu washing over him. He knew what this was, he knew *exactly* what this was, a Blackbird. The rifle's curves felt very familiar in his hands, but the weight didn't. He was surprised at how heavy it was. His thumb found the safety, made sure it was on, then he reflexively extended the collapsible stock.

Seamus poked around, but other than the shoulder bag holding another four loaded magazines for the PDW there was nothing of value in the cockpit. He jumped down and turned, then stopped. He stared at Mike, at how the young man was holding the stubby rifle in his hands: crossbody, muzzle pointed in a safe direction, stock now extended and just out of the shoulder pocket, and his finger alongside the receiver, away from the trigger.

"You...you weren't in the military, were you?" Seamus asked him. "No, you're too young."

"No," Mike said, shaking his head. That was a weird question. "Why?"

"Because you look well ally, mate. *Ohhh*, let me guess. Action Box? I'm right, aren't I? What's your favorite game?"

"I still play 1944, but my absolute favorite is Man O'War. Man O'War 4."

That explained everything. Video games had had photo-realistic graphics for forty years, but the real breakthrough had been the interactive game systems, those that allowed and even required the players to move their bodies during play. Action Box was the current game system against which the rest were compared. Players stood in the "action box," a 6'x6' portable unit with 360-degree video and audio. Original models used white fabric walls on which images were projected, but current versions were open-framed and the images holo-projected. The box had lasers which could 'see' the player and transmit his or her position and posture to the game computer. For the first person shooter games, there were full-size replica shells of real guns into which players placed their controllers. For most games the players wore glasses which allowed the computer to see exactly where the player was looking, and the same was true of the sight on the fake gun.

Combat games had gotten so detailed that players who didn't display proper weapons handling, accidentally pointed their weapons at digital teammates, or didn't make effective use of cover while under fire were penalized. The games were so realistic, with 360-degree player interaction, that the military was using a derivation of the game system to train their recruits. Seamus knew Raven was using commercial Action Box game systems and Man O'War games to train up some of the Mexican Army troops in the field. Nothing built muscle memory better than repetition. Plus, the games were fun as hell.

"I watched how the characters in the game carried their weapons and moved and imitated them, as it kept me from accidentally sweeping them with my muzzle, which gets you penalized. And I didn't get killed as much," he told Seamus. "That's the only way you get any good at the game. You play?"

"Occasionally. When I'm not getting shot at for real," Seamus told him, then winked to take any bite out of the comment. He was actually very familiar with Man O'War 4, which took place in the Caliphate and featured numerous Special Forces missions. He missed that war. "What's your weapon of choice in the game?

The corner of Mike's mouth tilted, and he hefted the Blackbird. "This."

"Aye? So tell me about it."

Mike smiled, then stepped up to the challenge. "This is the M12, nicknamed the Blackbird, a magazine-fed semi-auto rifle designed as a Personal Defense Weapon. You said the prototype for your rifle was Project Leonidas? The original prototype of the Blackbird was called the Honey Badger."

Seamus cocked his head at that. "Seriously?"

Mike nodded. "It is chambered in .30 Blackbird, which is the latest name of a cartridge that has seen more last names than an actress in Hollywood." That line came straight from one of the grizzled sergeants in the game, voiced by veteran Hollywood actor Randy Max. "It was first the .300 Whisper, then the .300 Blackout. It features an integrally-suppressed twelve-and-a-half inch barrel and mounts a simple red dot reflex sight that is passively powered by fiber optics and always on. Thirty-round magazines. Two different kinds of ammo, super- and subsonic. The subsonic 200-grain ammo makes it as quiet as a cough, at least in the game, and there's hardly any recoil, but it won't go through body armor." That was one of the reasons Mike liked using the Blackbird in Man O'War 4—it forced him to do head shots on enemy soldiers a lot of the time, which made the game more challenging. "The military guns were originally designed for sentry elimination, then caught on for pilots of aircraft which went down behind enemy lines, to defend their position until rescued or to escape and evade to friendly territory. However, they are being used much more widely than the military planned, much like the M1 carbine in World War II." Mike's weapon of choice in the game 1944 was—surprise, surprise!—the M1 carbine.

"I guess you do know what the hell it is," Seamus said with a grin. Boys and their toys, was it ever not so? "You ever fire one in real life?"

Mike looked down. "Um, no sir."

"You thinking of going into the military?"

Mike shrugged. "I don't know what I want to do. College, I guess, but...." He shrugged again.

Seamus nodded. "Well, I know what I want to do," he told the young man. He pointed at the cliff rising over them. "I want to climb up to the top of that ridge and see what I can see."

Mike stared up at the nearly vertical crumbling rock face. "You can climb that?" he said dubiously. There were a lot of handholds, but it still looked amazingly dangerous.

"No, but I can walk over there," Seamus said, pointing to the west end of the clearing, "where it slopes down to our level, and walk back up to the top, hopefully without breaking a sweat."

"Oh," Mike said, chagrinned. "Can I come?" he blurted out.

Seamus smiled. The boy wasn't slow, and knew when to keep his mouth shut when there wasn't anything to say. "Sure."

"What should I do with this?" Mike asked, hefting the Blackbird.

Seamus looked at the young man, and didn't say anything for at least ten seconds. "Hold onto it," he said finally. "Take this, too." He slung the shoulder bag containing the four additional magazines for the Blackbird over Mike's neck.

They walked out from behind the Blackhawk and headed along the cliff wall. "Going up top, to have a look see," Seamus called out to Corey, who was walking through the grass toward the rest of the party. The other contractor nodded.

Roger turned and saw his son was going with the man, then did a doubletake at the black weapon in his son's hand. "O'Malley," he started to say.

"We're fine, thanks for asking," Seamus replied without looking at him. "We'll wave from the top."

Roger opened his mouth to argue, to call out, but then he shut it and watched his son follow the contractor. Michael was cradling the rifle like it was his baby and smiling as if it was his birthday. Not quite the vacation Roger'd planned, but at least it wasn't boring. He snorted, then winced. Damn. He hoped he wouldn't need surgery, something in his back seemed seriously askew. When the hell was the rescue chopper going to show up?

Roger reminded himself to ask Seamus what kind of death benefits Raven provided their contractors. Probably little, if any. If the dead men had families, maybe he could help them out financially if they needed it. Perhaps set up an educational trust for their children. Roger didn't feel responsible, or any sort of 'survivor guilt,' but he did feel somehow....involved. He hadn't known the dead men, but he'd been there when it happened. It had been twenty-five years since the first and only time he'd seen someone die, and that had been a car accident.

The clearing was wider than it had looked, and from the Blackhawk's tail, Seamus counted 163 steps before he passed the first tree. The grass died off quickly under the trees, smothered by a thick carpet of dead needles. Up near the cliff Seamus could see for close to a hundred meters through the trunks.

"It smells nice in here," Mike said, breathing deep. "What are you doing?"

"Looking for Todd," Seamus said. "The problem is he's wearing this damn armor with reactive camouflage. I might be staring at him right now and not see him." He was looking for odd shapes on the ground more than colors that didn't belong—more often than not it was a man's silhouette that gave him away. That, and movement. Todd wasn't likely to be moving. "Todd!" he yelled, not expecting any response. He didn't get one. "Todd!" Loud noises were also likely to keep any wild animals at a distance, a fact of which he was well aware.

"Don't the new armored uniforms have tracking chips in them?" Mike asked. "I thought I read that somewhere. You could find him that way."

"Two problems with that," Seamus explained to him, still staring beneath the trees. "First, I don't have any of the equipment I'd need to track down one of those chips. And deuce, even though those chips were supposed to be passive and not broadcasting their position, if *we* can send out a signal and ping them, so can our enemies. Encryption didn't matter, all they had to do was triangulate location. The first gen armored uniforms had locator chips, and bio-sign sensors which gave off more electrical signals, and we learned right bloody quick what a bad idea that was. No more chips in our uniforms or our weapons."

"Oh."

"Let's move along, maybe we'll see something from up top," Seamus said. To their left the ridge sunk toward them, and neared ground level about thirty meters inside the tree line.

"This looks as good as we're going to get," Seamus said. He and Mike clambered ten feet up a slope of loose rock peppered with tufts of grass and small cacti and found themselves atop a wide ridge. There were trees in front of them, but halfway to the summit the ridge rose out of the trees, covered by nothing but grass and small bushes.

Mike followed Seamus as they trudged up the gentle incline in silence, until something occurred to him. "What was that right before the crash?" he asked. "We were falling, then there was a roar and we almost stopped. Then we started falling again."

"Emergency thrusters," Seamus explained. "Single-use solid fuel rockets designed as a last ditch safety feature, mounted underneath the fuselage. Four of them, angled down and out. They're connected to an altimeter and designed to be immune to EMPs. In fact, that was why they were designed, to keep people alive in helis that have been zapped. They ignite at 200 meters AGL—above ground level— and are supposed to burn for 5 seconds, slowing you down from terminal velocity. I don't think these ones burned for the full five seconds, but then again they probably haven't been serviced for fifteen years. To be honest, I'm surprised they worked at all. Like as not to have flipped us ass over teakettle."

"Were we hit with an EMP?" Mike asked him.

Seamus realized he might have just stepped on his juicy bits with the boy. "Um, no. I don't know. I don't think so. But when the electronics went out the effect was the same. These birds were retrofitted about twenty years ago, when it appeared the world was going to war with China. Resistance to EMPs was all the rage." He nodded at Mike. "That's why the sight on that Blackbird is fiber optic. Even though it works just fine, it's a bit of antiquated technology, but it's immune to EMPs. No circuit board."

Mike found himself panting more than what he was expecting. He'd been on the swim team for the last three years, and played basketball with his friends, and thought he was in pretty decent shape. "How high are we? I'm really breathing hard," he said to the contractor as they passed the last of the trees and continued up the grassy uneven slope.

Seamus had noticed the same thing. "I thought we were around three thousand feet, but from the way I'm breathing out of my hoop I'm guessing we're closer to five," he told the young man.

The highest point of the ridge was a gentle slope covered in short grass and scrub brush, warm in the bright sunlight. Mike spotted a few small wildflowers peeking out here and there. "Pretty."

Seamus stepped close to the edge and looked down. He was directly above the helicopter. He waved down at the group, and Corey spotted him and waved back. Seamus stepped back and looked around. "Hell of a view."

Mike pulled out his palm, turned it on, and checked to see if he had any bars standing atop the ridge. Nothing. He took a few photos of the helicopter and the clearing. Seamus noticed what he was doing. "Your palm works?" he asked in surprise.

"Yeah. It's not satlink enabled, though, so no service. I have to shut it off or it will run the battery down looking for a signal.

"It wasn't damaged in the crash?"

"No. Look at this case it's in, Dad bought it for me, it's ridiculous. Laced titanium or something, supposed to keep anybody from hacking your data, but it looks like it would stop a bullet. Probably cost more than the palm."

"That's probably it, then."

Gentle slopes covered in evergreen trees stretched away on all sides, and they could see for miles in most directions. The ridge they were standing on appeared to be the tallest point between them and the high peak to their southwest. From the higher vantage point, Seamus was able to see the rounded mountain was farther away than he thought, maybe five miles. If he'd had a proper map he would have known the mountain was San Onofre, with an elevation of over 3500 meters, or 11,000 feet. To the north of the crash site, the ground rose up and down in gentle green/brown hills that seemed to lose height farther north. To the east, toward the center of the Sierra Madre Orientals, were more mountainous foothills. The closer ones weren't any taller, but a few miles away they gained elevation.

To the south there was a big shallow bowl, at least a mile wide, stretching off into the distance for miles. The valley was bordered to the east and west by wavy ridgelines. Their slopes were covered by trees but the summits were bare grass and open fields.

"I think we came in from that direction," Seamus said, pointing northwest. "How good are your eyes? You see anything? I doubt you'll be able to see Todd, but broken tree branches, anything like that, where he augered in?"

Mike wasn't paying attention to him, he was looking south, along the western edge of the valley. Along the top of the ridge there, way out...he squinted, and then used a hand to shield his eyes. "Hey, look at that," he said happily. "That was quick."

"What? What are you looking at?" Seamus turned around, and Mike pointed.

"Couple of cars heading our way," Mike told him. "I think there's a road on top of the ridge."

"Where, I don't see anything."

Mike stepped up next to him and pointed. "Look for the dust, I think they're on a dirt road. Still way out there, a mile or two, but they're heading in our direction." He was excited. The crash hadn't been part of the vacation plan, and he felt really bad about the guys who had died, but he didn't know them. It was hard to feel too sad about people dying whom you didn't know. He was just glad that he wasn't hurt, and his dad only had a sore back.

Once they got to Victoria Base, his dad could get some painkillers, and they could head out hunting. Even if his dad's back hurt too much to do anything, the whole experience had already been the coolest thing ever. A real adventure. Secret military installation, helicopter ride, walking around with a real Blackbird in his hands. And now he could tell Brad and Jerdy that he'd been in a helicopter crash. A freaking helicopter crash! Not that his friends'd believe him. Thinking of that, he pulled out his palmpad again and stepped near the edge of the cliff. He took several more shots of the horizon and the downed helicopter, so he had proof. His dad saw him and waved. Smiling, Mike waved back, then thought to check the display again, just in case. He had no more signal at the top of the ridge than he'd had down at the crash site.

The boy's eyes were better than his, and even squinting, Seamus could barely see the moving smudge. He flipped the lever on his riflescope, switching it to 4X magnification, and raised his rifle to his shoulder. It took him a few seconds, looking through the optic, to find the moving vehicles.

"Jesus shite!" he cursed.

Mike turned around. "What? You get stung by a bee?"

"A bee? What? No! That's not a rescue party, mate, it's the fooking FRAP!"

* * * * *

Chapter Seven

Tina climbed to her feet and worked her neck. It wasn't sore, not really, but she had a suspicion that it would be tomorrow. What was it the Americans called it when you were in a car accident? Oh, yes, *whiplash*.

The young contractor, whose first name she'd learned was John, was standing a few feet away, staring across the clearing.

"How old are you?" she asked him. She started walking slowly, to stretch her legs.

Corey looked around. "Me? Twenty-five."

She nodded. She was twenty-four herself and thought he had to be about the same age. He took a few steps to catch up to her. "How did you end up working for Raven?" Tina was genuinely curious. She just couldn't envision how a person ended up working as a mercenary, or contractor, or whatever they wanted to call themselves.

"I joined the military right out of high school. I liked it and was good at it. This is more of the same, only for a lot more money."

Tina made a face; she couldn't help herself. *A lot more* Mexican *money*, she thought. *From Mexican oil.* She knew where it was coming from. Hybridge saw their opportunity and had taken it; the American corporation was at best supposed to be an equal partner with Pemex, Mexico's state-run oil company, but from everything she'd read and seen they'd just about taken over drilling and refining crude oil in her country. It wasn't lost on her that the parent corporation of Hybridge also owned Raven—Americans were taking the profits from Mexican oil and fighting their civil war with it, as if Mexico was incapable of taking care of itself. Nobody but politicians and company stockholders seemed happy with the situation.

"What?" Corey asked. He'd seen her expression; she hadn't hidden it quickly enough.

She opened her mouth to respond but then stopped and cocked her head. There was a small pile of gray rocks at one end of the clearing, and on the other side of it was a plant about two feet tall. It had a thick brown trunk with a rough patterned surface and a crown of green fronds. Small cone-like flowers were just emerging from the walls of the stem. "This can't be here," Tina said.

"What?" Corey wasn't sure what she was talking about.

"This is a bennettite. In fact, it's *Monanthesia*, I'm sure of it." At one point she'd seriously thought about becoming a paleobotanist, and the plants of that era were distinctive.

"What, that little ugly tree?"

She shot him a dark look, then went back to staring at the plant. "Yes, this little ugly tree. *Madre Dios*. Except *Monanthesia* became extinct in the cretaceous period. That was one hundred and fifty million years ago."

Corey shrugged. "So they were wrong about it being extinct," he said. Then something occurred to him. "Or they brought it back, like they did the dinosaurs. Dinosaurs have to have something to munch on, right? Maybe they filled their park with plants they knew the dinosaurs—the plant eaters—would want to eat." The trunk of the little tree resembled a pine cone or a pineapple, with overlapping brown scales.

Tina blinked in surprise. That made sense to her, although she'd never heard mention of engineered flora in Pangaea. But the audacity of it—what were they thinking? They weren't. That was the problem, as she'd said earlier. The mercenary scientists who'd created the park and the creatures in it were only thinking about what they could do, not what they *should* do. Of course they recreated plants from the dinosaur era; why not let that genie out of the bottle too, but…. "Why is it here?" she asked.

Corey didn't understand the question. "'Cause it's sunny?" he said. There were ferns all over the clearing and underneath the trees, this to him was just another fern, albeit much, much uglier.

"No." She shook her head violently. "How far are we from *La Reserva de la Biosfera el Cielo?*"

"What?"

She sighed. "From Pangaea, how far are we from the dinosaur park?"

Corey thought. If they were fifty klicks northwest of Victoria Base… "Ninety kilometers or so."

"Could they have spread this far, this fast?" she asked herself. If so, what did that say about the Mexican landscape? Were the spores and seeds being spread by the wind or by animals? What other unnatural plants were spreading from the park around the countryside, polluting the environment?

The yelling made them both look up.

* * *

"We've got FRAP incoming, two vehicles, maybe three minutes out!" Seamus yelled, hands cupped around his mouth. He gestured southwest, then moved his arm down to point at the forest to their west. "They're probably going to come in from that direction. Hansen, you take Rudd and the woman into the trees that way." He pointed east. "Keep going til you're out of sight of the clearing and find something to get behind that'll stop bullets."

"They coming here?" Corey shouted back.

"Close enough." Seamus glanced over. The smoke from the Blackhawk was just a thin trail, but it was visible above the ridge. Maybe they'd seen it, or seen the helicopter go down, although that seemed unlikely. FRAP didn't do random patrols this far north, so close to Victoria Base. They might have a few informants but no infrastructure. Maybe the Guadalajara offensive down south had spurred them into some rash decision making? Something must be happening.

"Michael!" Roger yelled, struggling to his feet.

Mike stared at his dad, then his eyes ran down the slope to his left. If he hurried, he could be back with his father in no more than two minutes. Seamus looked at the teenager standing beside him, a panicked look on his face, and touched his arm. "Hold on there boy," he said softly. "He'll be safer up here," Seamus called to Roger.

Roger stared up at his son standing on top of the cliff, then looked around the clearing. He wanted to argue, wanted his son by his side, but atop the cliff, out of sight, might be the safest place for him.

"You stay down!" he yelled to his son, pointing. "You stay out of sight! And do whatever he tells you to!"

"I will," Mike yelled.

"Come on, let's go," the pilot said. He awkwardly pulled his pistol from its chest-mounted holster with his left hand and started walking toward the eastern tree line. He turned and looked at Roger and Tina. "We've got to move."

"Where do you want me?" Corey called to Seamus. He eyed the helicopter. It was the only thing in the clearing big enough to hide behind which would stop bullets, which meant it was the first place they'd look, if they were actually coming. Corey suspected they were just a random patrol, but you had to plan for possibilities, not probabilities.

Seamus pointed to the north, across from the cliff and the helicopter, where the trees were closest. "Find some defilade over there. Wait until they're all the way into the clearing and out of their vehicles, and light 'em up. I'll wait up here out of sight until you go loud. Hopefully we can catch them in a crossfire." As incompetent as most of the draftee Mexican Army was, the rank-and-file FRAP guerrillas were even worse. Most of them had no formal training and were piss-poor shots, if they were sober and their weapons worked. The only thing they were good at was brutality.

"You don't want to just fade into the woods?" Corey asked.

"And go where? We've got wounded, and for all we know, they've got dogs or thermal optics. We know they've got vehicles, and the trees are spread thin enough they can drive through them. They'd only need a minute to ride us down. We go on the run, we've lost any advantage we might have. And once they see the bird they're not going to leave without a search." He pointed over the cliff at the Blackhawk. "This bird is our anchor. This is where the Raven SAR team is going to come." He glanced over his shoulder. The two vehicles were already out of sight. It appeared that the road disappeared into the forest directly west of their location.

"Shit," Corey said, and with a last look around began jogging across the clearing. He lowered the ballistic visor on his helmet.

"Are we going to have a gunfight?" Mike asked, eyes wide.

"A gunfight? I hope not." Mike nodded, feeling a little relieved, until Seamus continued. "If we have a gunfight then something went wrong. If they show up, my plan is to simply slot the bastards before they know what's what."

* * *

"Come on, come on," Hansen urged Roger, as the middle-aged man paused by the crumpled helicopter.

"Hold on," Roger said. With a grunt of pain he bent down and grabbed his Glock from the open rifle case and stuck the unloaded pistol into his pocket. He saw his backpack with the ammo in the back of the helicopter and went for it.

"What are you doing?" Tina nearly screamed, panic inching up her spine. It was taking all of her willpower not to start running toward the trees. Not to start crying.

Roger found the box of ammo for the Glock. "All right, let's go," he said, starting after Hansen, who was halfway to the tree line and waiting for him. Roger looked longingly down at the Ulfberht, but he knew there was no way he could go running through the woods with the big rifle, not with his back. Simply walking hurt. But two pistols were better than one. He looked up at the top of the ridge high above, and saw his son's face peering down.

"You be safe!" Roger yelled at him, walking backward slowly, fighting the urge to throw up from the worry. As tree branches blocked his view of his son he shouted, "Get out of sight!"

* * *

Seamus saw Hansen move into the trees with his two charges, and Corey begin looking for a spot across the clearing from the rock face. Seamus stepped back from the edge and looked around the top of the ridge. No cover up top, but the rock face would stop anything short of rockets they might throw his way from down below. Of course, he'd have to stick his head over the edge to see them, much less shoot at them, and his bullet-resistant helmet was nowhere to be found.... Well, every plan had its soft spots.

Staring at the forest to the west, Seamus saw something rise out of the trees about a quarter of a mile away. At first he thought it was a hawk—he'd already seen one of those—but then he realized what it was "Down!" he growled at Mike, then tackled the boy and laid on top of him, trying to cover as much of his body as possible.

"What?" Mike said in a panic, squirming.

"Shut up and don't move," Seamus whispered in his ear.

Face in the long grass, a rock digging into his cheekbone, Mike could only see out of one eye. He didn't see anything but grass, the smell of dirt in his nose, and couldn't hear anything other than a few bird calls and the hum of insects. Then, after thirty seconds or so, there was a faint whirring sound overhead.

Seamus again wished he had his helmet, but this time for its reactive camouflage. He knew his armor would be mottled shades of brown and green, mimicking the ground around him, but there was nothing disguising the shape or color of his head. Forcing himself not to look, he heard it take a wide curving path, swooping over his right shoulder without hesitation. Then he heard the whirring change tone. It was hovering.

Daring to look up, Seamus didn't see the drone at first. "Don't move," he whispered to the boy, then crawled forward on his belly to the edge of the cliff. There, in the center of the clearing, hovering ten feet below the top of the ridge, was the drone. The surveillance drone had four rotors, each a foot in diameter, and was about four feet across. It was painted bluish-gray, for aerial camouflage, and if Seamus hadn't seen it against the dark green of the pines it might have been on them before he even spotted it. It was sure to have a camera, but was too small to be armed. Most drones didn't have any audio capability, but you could never be too sure.

So much for it being a random patrol.

The drone hovered for another thirty seconds above the Blackhawk, then did a slow circle of the clearing, staying about thirty feet off the ground. There was no need for it to be that low, and Seamus suspected the operator was trying to draw fire. Either that, or the camera on the drone was low resolution. There was no sign of Corey; wherever he was, he'd gone to ground, and *he* had his helmet.

After skimming the perimeter of the tree line, the drone returned to the helicopter, and Seamus watched it angle off to the side. The operator had spotted Delian's body. The drone hovered above the body for nearly a minute, performing a slow pirouette, then returned to the center of the clearing and hovered in place forty feet above the ground, just below the level of the ridge. Seamus wormed backward.

"Drone," he whispered into Mike's ear. "Probably can't hear us, but I'm being safe. You stay here, and don't panic when the shooting starts." Mike nodded, face still in the dirt. He was thinking that he probably would have still been in the open down in the clearing when the drone arrived if he'd decided to join his father. Seamus inched forward again, until one eye cleared the grass at the edge and he could see down into the clearing.

A minute later the low growl of engines could be heard. Gradually they grew closer, somewhere in the trees, and there was the crunching of underbrush. Without warning the nose of a tan pickup appeared between the tree trunks on the west side of the clearing, and the vehicle stopped with a lurch.

Engine idling, the lead vehicle stayed just inside the trees. Seamus saw the drone dip down and do another slow circle of the clearing. Whoever was operating it was either inside one of the vehicles or in communication with them. Seeing nothing, it moved to the center of the clearing and hovered again. Seamus looked back at Mike and made a pushing gesture with his palm, telling him to move off the left. He didn't want the boy anywhere near him when the shooting started. Mike crawled sideways, one hand white-knuckled around the Blackbird.

The vehicles slowly moved out of the trees at a crawl, a beat-up four door pickup spray-painted tan followed closely by a newer Vaquero, a lightly armored personnel carrier. The roof turret of the Vaquero was occupied by a stubble-faced FRAP soldier in a camouflage shirt behind an ancient belt-fed PKM machinegun. He slid the big gun back and forth, searching for threats, but nothing appeared. The other occupants of the vehicles were invisible behind the glass.

The pickup stopped thirty feet from the tail of the Blackhawk, the Vaquero right behind it. Most of the doors of both vehicles opened, and men climbed out, talking. They wore various camouflage patterns, parts and pieces of uniforms from various countries and eras. In their hands they carried the typical FRAP hodge-podge of weapons. Seamus heard "*¿A donde se fueron?*" and other comments from the men as they spread out and headed toward the helicopter, rifles up. He quickly counted seven men on foot, plus the one in the gun turret. He couldn't see if there was anyone left in the vehicles.

* * *

Peering through the grass across the clearing, Corey watched the men get out of the vehicles and walk toward the helicopter. At least half a dozen of them, more than he would have preferred, but none of them were wearing armor.

Most FRAP assholes couldn't shoot worth a damn. Corey estimated he was about forty yards from the vehicles, his back nearly to the tree line, and well hidden thanks to the reactive camouflage of his armor. He also had a small rise six feet in front of him. Hopefully all that would be enough. Heart pounding in his chest, he squeezed his arms together, rising up onto his elbows. He pulled the buttstock back into his shoulder, ignored the walking men for the moment, and trained his rifle on the one man who could be a serious threat to him, the roof gunner. The crosshairs of his scope were not nearly as steady as he would have liked as he took up the slack of the trigger.

At the shot, the man fell back down inside the Vaquero. Instinctively the soldiers scattered, yelling and shooting in all directions, suppressive fire as they ran for cover. The report had echoed off the rocky cliff face, and none of them knew exactly from which direction it had come. Corey fired at two of them running past the helicopter and saw one fall, then the rest of the men guessed his general direction. Shouting and cursing, they fired in his direction on full auto while retreating behind the vehicles. Corey heard the rounds snapping above his head, and blindly fired short bursts to keep them focused on his position.

Seamus popped up on one knee on top of the ridge and shouldered his rifle. At least four of the buggers were hunkered down in a row, hiding behind their vehicles, almost directly below him. It was a buffet line. He started pulling the trigger as fast as he could, walking his crosshairs up the line of crouching men.

Three soldiers died before they realized where the shots were coming from, but then Seamus threw himself backward as the survivors' answering full-auto bursts tore up the edge of the cliff and whipped past his face. He scooted to the right, shouldered his rifle, and then popped up to fire a few shots. Return fire caused him to duck low.

Corey heard the shouting and wild return fire as Seamus shot down at them. He took the opportunity to move backward and took a knee behind a tree trunk. Popping out, he peppered the remaining soldiers with harassing fire. There was movement far to the left of the vehicles, and he saw one of the FRAP men hiding underneath the nose of the Blackhawk. Corey fired at him without result, then steadied himself against the trunk of the tree and hit the soldier, killing him. He looked back toward the main group in time to see the pickup truck start moving. Passenger door flapping, the driver turned left and floored it. The pickup aimed straight toward Corey's position and a man appeared over the roof, standing in the bed of the pickup.

Bouncing wildly across the uneven ground, the pickup kept gaining speed, the man in back firing at him one-handed on full auto. Corey fired in bursts at the driver, shattering the windshield, but the truck kept coming. Making a quick decision, he moved his hand forward to the second trigger and fired a grenade from the launcher on his rifle. The grenade went through the truck's windshield and exploded, blowing out all the windows and peeling half the roof back. The man in the bed disappeared, but inertia kept the truck speeding straight at him. The truck left the clearing at thirty miles an hour and Corey dove backward, yelling.

Mike heard the crump of the grenade, and then the crash. Unable to stop himself, he lifted his head off the grass enough to see the pickup at the far side of the clearing. The roof had been split open and smoke was billowing from it where it was wrapped around a tree. If that's where Corey had been there was no sign of the contractor. He looked over at Seamus, who was busy reloading, then back down at the clearing. He heard shouting in Spanish.

Seamus glanced over at the smoking pickup on the far side of the clearing as he finished changing magazines. He scooted to the side another few feet, and popped up to fire. There was at least one more man down there, using the rear of the Vaquero for cover. He couldn't get an angle on the man. Where was Corey? "Come on you arsehole!" he shouted, trying to bait the guerrilla into sticking his head out. He hammered black beauties into the rear body panels of the gun truck, trying to hit the man. The guerrilla popped up on the far side of the vehicle and fired a long burst from his AK-47 at Seamus, then ducked back down.

Mike found himself on one knee, peering over the edge. Seamus had worked himself to the right during the firefight, and now he didn't have an angle on the last remaining soldier, who was hunkered down behind the armored SUV. Mike could see him, or at least see half of him as he crouched by the rear bumper, reloading his rifle. Seamus hammered the truck around the man, blowing holes in the bullet-resistant glass, the noise deafening, but it seemed there were too many layers of armor for his 'black beauties' to get all the way through. The man got a fresh magazine into his AK, and Mike raised the Blackbird, reflexively flicking off the safety. The amber dot of the weapon's reflex sight appeared in front of him, quivering on the FRAP soldier's head. The soldier swung his rifle around, firing a burst—Mike blinked—and then the man was on his back on the grass, thrashing around.

"Finally," Seamus yelled, partially deaf from all the shooting. His ears were ringing. He could see the man's kicking feet past the rear tire of the Vaquero. They slowed, then stopped. Seamus swung his rifle around, sweeping the clearing. He heard a few groans, but nobody shot at him.

"Corey. Corey! You queen, you'd better not be dead!" Seamus was riding the adrenaline high, and couldn't stop smiling. He loved his job.

Corey wiped the sweat from his face and eyed the front of the pickup wrapped around the tree. If the tree hadn't been there he would have been run over for sure; as it was he got hit by flying headlight glass, and a piece of bumper had whanged off his helmet. "Yeah! I'm still here," he shouted back, a little shaken. He stood up, shouldered his rifle, and peered out into the clearing, using the pickup for cover. He didn't see anything moving.

"Well, that was fooking exciting, wasn't it?" Seamus said to Mike with a grin. Then he saw the rifle in the boy's hands, saw that Mike was up on one knee, and thought back to the last gunman, nearly out of sight behind the Vaquero.

"You see anything?" Seamus called. He couldn't see Corey, but figured the man was somewhere in the shade under the trees beyond the destroyed pickup. "I can hear some moaning, but I can't tell where it's coming from." His ears were ringing something awful from the shooting.

Corey scanned the clearing from side to side from behind the pickup. "Nothing moving that I can see. I've got cover here, why don't you come down?"

"I don't see anybody," Mike told Seamus, still looking over the edge. Anybody *alive*, is what he meant. He saw plenty of bodies. He found himself staring at them. His heart was hammering in his chest so hard he thought his ears were going to pop off. He couldn't decide if he was going to faint or throw up.

"Moving," Seamus called, and backed away from the edge. "Come on," he said to Mike. He jogged down the slope until he was nearly at the level of the clearing but still out of sight. Mike followed him on autopilot. "Stay here until I tell you it's clear," he told the boy. Then he scrambled down the slope of loose rocks and approached the Vaquero, rifle up.

It took him about a minute to check the bodies around the vehicles. One man quivered and died as he watched, all the rest were already dead. "There's at least one guy in the Vaquero, one in front of the Blackhawk, and another under it," Corey called to him.

"Anybody get into the trees?" Seamus asked, walking toward the Blackhawk. The man inside the gun truck was missing half his head. The one under the bird he soon saw was dead.

"No." Corey moved forward and peered inside the smoking cab of the pickup. The scene was ugly. He found the body of the man who'd been shooting at him from the bed of the pickup. He was about twenty feet from where the truck had accordioned into the tree. The man's shirt was soaked in blood from where he'd been peppered with shrapnel wounds from the grenade, but he was still breathing. "I've got one alive," he told Seamus. The soldier appeared semi-conscious.

"Mike!" Seamus called out. The young man appeared at the far end of the ridge. "Go get the group," he told him, pointing into the woods. "Yell out as you go so they don't shoot you." Mike nodded and began running toward the far tree line.

Seamus walked over to the FRAP soldier and squatted down, just in time to see him let go of his last shuddering breath and die. "Well hell," he said from his squat. "So much for getting any answers out of him." He glanced over at the truck wrapped around the tree. "Good job on the valet parking. Go check the rest of the bodies for intelligence," he told Corey. Seamus stood up and strode back toward the Vaquero. He'd seen the control console for the drone in the front seat, and wondered what else might be inside.

Mike stopped about thirty feet inside the trees. He couldn't see anyone, but the ground under the trees on this side of the clearing was more uneven with a few large bare rocks jutting up through the carpet of pine needles. "Dad!" he yelled. "Dad! It's okay to come out." He waited, and was about to go further into the woods when he saw movement at least a hundred yards in, past the large base of a fallen tree.

"You okay?" Roger called to his son. Listening to the shooting— and not being able to do anything but listen—had been the hardest thing he'd ever done in his life.

"Yeah, yeah, we're all okay," Mike said. "Everybody's fine."

"Okay, we'll be there in a minute," Hansen called out as they began trudging through the trees. The pilot was relieved—thank God the contractors had done their job right, because he wasn't a good shot with a pistol to begin with, even when he could use his right hand. The shooting hadn't lasted much more than a minute, so apparently only a few guerrillas had shown up.

"Are you okay?" Roger asked Tina. She looked a little pale.

"I do not like feeling helpless," she said. Cowering behind the fallen trees, listening to the gunfight, had been terrifying, in part she knew because she had no control over the outcome. She shook her head. Helicopter crash, gunfight in the forest…it was all so unreal.

A minute later everyone was back in the clearing. Tina couldn't stop staring at the bodies.

"Ladies and gentlemen, we've got five minutes and then we are out of here," Seamus told them. The Vaquero was still running and the gauge showed half a tank of gas. He pointed at it.

"What? I thought we were staying here, with the helicopter," Roger said. "This is where the search team is going to look."

"We can't afford to sit around and wait for them," Seamus said. "We are leaving. This wasn't random; they were looking for us. Either they saw us go down, or they heard the Mayday on the radio."

"Are you sure?" Tina asked.

In response, Seamus pointed at the drone still hovering above them. Nobody in Hansen's group had even noticed it up there, and they all did a double take. "That is not standard issue, and this is not a FRAP area. They are way out of their comfort zone, coming up here. And if that's the case, there might be more vehicles on the way. Corey," he said to the younger man. "Do you know how to land that thing? I'd like to be able to take it with us, just in case."

"Yeah, if we've got the controller."

"It's in the Vaquero. While you're in there, clean it up a little, would you?" He was thinking about the body still inside which was missing half its head and had bled all over the rear compartment. "Okay," Seamus said, clapping his hands to get everyone's attention once again. "Five minutes, then we're leaving." He pointed at Tina. "You have a backpack in the back of the Blackhawk?"

"Yes?"

"Take everything out of it that won't keep you alive. That means any clothes not warmer than what you're wearing now, cosmetics, books, spare underwear, I don't care. Toss it. Then fill it back up with water bottles, protein bars, whatever will fit. This is no longer a vacation that's been sidetracked; consider us down behind enemy lines. Go."

He pointed at Roger. "Same goes for you, but I want you to grab that Ulfberht and whatever ammo you brought for it. Put it in the back of the gun truck and don't use it unless I say so. Leave the bolt action hunting rifle here. You can bill Aarne for it later."

"I know how to shoot. I'm not a bad shot," Roger said with a frown.

"And I believe you mate, but that rifle fires a big fecking bullet. How bout we save them for when we have a big fecking thing to shoot?"

Corey was in the front of the Vaquero, examining the drone controller. Seamus asked him, "You find any intelligence on the bodies?"

"I grabbed two palmpads, they're in the back there. If they're not password protected maybe there's something on them." He'd also taken a decent amount of cash off the bodies—you never knew when you might have to buy your way out of a bad situation. "They were mostly carrying AKs and Fire Snakes, knives and a couple rusty pistols. Mixed uniforms, no unit markings. What about you?"

"Nothing."

Even though the AK was a design that had been around for over a hundred years, it was so reliable and easy (and cheap) to manufacture that it was still being produced in nearly a dozen countries, and Seamus saw that three of the FRAP rifles were new AK-47s manufactured in Kurdistan. He tossed two of them into the back of the Vaquero along with a dozen spare magazines. The "Fire Snake" was the issued rifle of the Mexican military, officially the FX-05 *Xiuhcoatl* which meant "fire snake" but literally translated into "turquoise serpent" in tribal Nahuatl. The guerrillas had undoubtedly taken them off Mexican soldiers they'd killed. "Mike!" he called, sticking his head around the corner of the truck. The boy was by the helicopter, helping his father and the girl pack, and turned around at the sound of his voice.

"Yeah?"

"Grab about a six-foot section of that mini-gun belt and bring it over here. I've got some mags I'd like to get bombed up if we get a chance."

Hansen came walking up. "SOP is we're supposed to destroy an aircraft if we can't recover it," the pilot told them.

Seamus looked at Corey in the front seat. "How many more grenades do you have for your launcher?"

"Three."

"Then I'm not wasting one on the bird," Seamus told Hansen. "Check it out, make sure we're not leaving any intelligence in it. Pull the pins on the feeder/delinker on that minigun and have someone help you toss it into the woods—I don't want to leave a working weapon and we can't take it with us. And check your co-pilot's body, make sure he doesn't have anything on him. Maybe grab any personal effects he might have."

"Should we....should we be leaving him here? I mean, if we're taking a vehicle?"

Seamus stopped moving, and shook his head. "Feck me, you're right. Wouldn't want anyone to leave me in the middle of nowhere if I got zapped, not right to do that to him. Corey, drive this thing over there, have the boy help you load the body into the back."

Corey looked back at him. "And Todd?"

Seamus looked over his shoulder into the trees, then back at the young contractor. "Hopefully we'll be able to come back to look for him, but that's out of our control now. If he's still alive, he's on his own."

Tina could barely lift her backpack by the time she'd finished stuffing it with water bottles, but they drove the big armored SUV up close to her. She didn't see the co-pilot's body in the back until she was about to drop her backpack onto it.

"Just push the rifles out of the way. It's going to be a little cramped," Hansen told her. He helped as much as he could with one hand.

"Why is he back here?"

"Don't know when we might be able to get back. Wouldn't be right to leave him here."

She nodded. The man was right, but the thought of riding around with a body in the back creeped her out a little bit.

"All right! We're taking too long. Everybody grab their monkeys and parrots and mount up; we need to get moving. Corey, you're up top." Seamus looked from Hansen and his broken right arm to Roger and his son. He reached into the back of the Vaquero and retrieved an AK. He shoved it into Roger's hands. "You've got shotgun," he told the man. "Okay, everybody get their arses into the Vaquero. And don't mind the body."

Seamus slammed the driver's door as Roger settled into the seat next to him with a grunt. Roger had dug the holster for the Glock out of his pack and now wore it on his hip. The AK felt alien in his hands.

"Muzzle up, in a vehicle," Seamus told him. "That way if the bloody thing goes off you've only got a hole in the roof, not the drive train." Seamus reached over and touched a lever with his finger. "That's the safety, flip it toward the trigger when you're ready to go." He threw the big vehicle into Drive and began turning in a circle to head out the way the enemy had arrived.

"The only thing that worries me," he said softly to Roger, who was freely perspiring, "is that where we need to go, we'll be driving down the same road those FRAP bastards came up looking for us."

* * * * *

Chapter Eight

There were ferns and small saplings underneath the tall pines, but the trees themselves were spread thin enough that driving between their trunks presented little problem. The land slanted downward before them at a gentle angle and was level enough that the big vehicle barely rocked as the tall knobby tires ate up ground. Seamus was able to spot the trail made by the FRAP vehicles and trace it back through the forest, but he kept the Vaquero at little better than walking speed.

"We're probably all alone out here, but keep your eyes open," Seamus told his passengers.

"Is this thing armored?" Roger asked him nervously.

"Yes. Doors and windows should stop most small arms fire."

"One of the windows back there was blown partway out though," Roger observed.

"I did that. Special ammo; we shouldn't have to worry about any of that incoming."

"Seamus, I forgot, I found a radio in the front seat," Corey told him. He waved the unit, which was a small handheld model. "It's digital, but I don't think it's encrypted." He clipped it onto his armor near his collarbone.

"Satellite?"

"No. I'm guessing in these mountains the range is pretty short too, not much more than a couple of miles."

"You think there's other guys close by?" Mike asked.

"Maybe the other radio's in the truck Corey blew up," Seamus said.

"There was something electronic in the front seat, but that grenade shredded it," Corey admitted. "Handheld. Might have been a radio."

"You hear any traffic?" Seamus asked him.

"No, but I'll let you know if I do."

After about two minutes Seamus saw a thin spot in the trees up ahead. They rolled into a small clearing, and at the far side they saw the small rise of a road running north/south. "Anyone remember seeing this road on a map?" Seamus asked. "Hansen?" He pulled up onto the road and turned south. "Just wondering how far it goes, and how we get from here to Victoria Base." He knew Victoria Base was southeast of them, across the mountains, but there were no direct roads. Once up on the grade he sped up to fifty kilometers an hour, about as fast as felt safe on the rutted gravel-strewn road.

"Not this road, not specifically," the pilot answered. "I doubt this one's even on our maps. There is a paved highway that runs roughly east/west somewhere south of us, which leads to Victoria Base. I'm guessing its thirty kilometers out or more, though. Highway one-oh something." The Blackhawk's GPS and illuminated holo-maps had spoiled him

The dirt road rose through the trees until they were on top of the ridge where Mike had first spotted the incoming vehicles. The road followed the ridgeline, winding back and forth like a snake.

"Isn't there a back road, a trail, which leads to Victoria from the north?" Corey asked. "Maybe we're on that."

"There are two-tracks and trails all over these mountains. The chances that we're on the exact right one that will lead us exactly where we want to go…I'll take your money, if you're in a betting mood," Seamus told him. "Our best bet is to head south until we hit pavement, then turn left. Unless anyone's got a better idea?"

"Won't we be heading right for any other FRAP troops that might be looking for us?" Roger asked him. "You gave us the impression that this was not a random patrol."

"The Orientals are an old mountain range, not nearly as rugged as your Rockies. Tabbing over them would almost be fun, if we were all uninjured and fitter than a butcher's dog." He gave Roger a pointed look. "That, however, is not the case. And even though it looks *muy macho,* this Vaquero can't handle any real mountain climbing, if I even knew a route. So, until we find a turn-off, this road is our best bet. Even if they are looking for us. But I doubt that; I can't imagine they'd send more than two truckloads of troops this far north."

"You think they crashed our helicopter?"

"I'm not ruling it out, mate. Which begs the question, why?" He looked at Roger. "How much are you worth?"

"What?"

"The K and R business is booming in this country. Has been since the days of the cartels, before the war. Kidnap and Ransom," he said to Roger's questioning face. "Find a businessman, preferably foreign, snag him, and ransom him out. So, how much are you worth?" Behind the front seat, Tina bit her lip and her eyes darted to Roger.

"My salary's not that much," Roger said.

"Yes, but how much are you *worth?* And are you anybody important?"

Roger frowned. "Founder and CEO of the Pearl Sapphire luxury hotel chain." He thought for a moment. "With my shares in the company, stock where it is, right now I'm worth maybe three hundred million?"

Seamus nearly drove off the road. "Dollars? Shit, mate, I'd known that I might've kidnapped you myself."

Mike was surprised. He knew they had money, they'd always had money, but not *that* much. His dad never talked about being rich or acted it. He'd just always been a busy businessman. That's all Mike knew about what he did. Suits every day, long days at the office, business calls at night, and trips all the time.

"Yes, but…how would *they* know?"

Seamus shrugged. "Well, if old Aarne sold us out, I'm going to have a serious talk with him when we get back. Drugs may be their meat and potatoes, but K&R still pays FRAP's electric, ladies and gentlemen. My guess is they heard about our high roller here, somehow, and decided he was worth the trip north. Ten million or so would keep them in rice and beans and AKs for a bit."

"You don't think it could be for some other reason?" Tina asked him. She was trying to pay attention to the conversation in the front seat, if for no other reason than it kept her looking away from the co-pilot's body on the floor near the back door. Small eddies swirled around the rear of the Vaquero from the fractured back window.

"I'm open to competing theories," Seamus said. He glanced over his shoulder. "Mike, you want to start pulling some of those black beauties out of that belt? You've got a couple of my mags that need refilling." He smiled at the boy before turning back to the road. "You handled yourself well back there." He looked at Roger. "You should be proud of him. Kept his head on straight."

"I didn't do anything," Mike said, putting the magazines on the floor between his feet. Mostly he'd laid on the grass and been terrified.

"Well, you popped that one FRAP bastard I couldn't get an angle on right nicely," Seamus said.

"What?" Roger said in surprise.

Mike blinked, and his hands froze. "What? I didn't shoot him. Did I?"

"Well if you didn't, God reached his finger down to smite him." Seamus shrugged. "I couldn't hit him, and Corey was napping under that pickup. Count the rounds in your magazine, if you want to know. If you didn't shoot, there should be twenty-nine in the mag, one in the chamber, for a total of thirty. You got nothin' to be ashamed of, lad."

"What are you talking about?" Roger said, outraged at the soldier. He turned to his son. "Did you shoot someone?"

"I…"

The Blackbird was lying across Mike's thighs, and he looked at it hesitantly. Suddenly it looked completely different to him. It was no longer a video game toy made real, it was something more. After a second's pause, he depressed the magazine release and let the rifle's magazine slide into his hand. He stared at the loaded rounds in the top of it, wanting to know…and yet scared. Terrified. He'd had the rifle up, the sight's red dot on the FRAP soldier's head. He remembered flicking off the safety, but he honestly didn't remember pulling the trigger. The soldier had raised his rifle to fire at Seamus—and then fallen backward, shot. Mike looked at Corey. "You didn't shoot him?"

"Which one?" Corey said. He'd been a little busy dodging trucks and bullets to keep close track of how many men he'd shot in the firefight.

"Last man down. He was at the rear of the Vaquero," Seamus said from the front seat.

Corey frowned, then shook his head. "I don't think so." He saw the expression on Mike's face, and pulled the Blackbird magazine out of his hand. With a thumb he pushed down on the loaded rounds in the magazine—the stack moved not quite an inch before bottoming out. Then he raised his eyes and looked at Mike. "There's twenty-eight rounds left in there," he told the kid. He tossed him the magazine.

Mike caught it, his face frozen. "Are you sure? You didn't count them."

"You go right ahead," Corey told him, then pointed to Mike's hands. "But fill his mags up first." Corey got off the seat and stood up inside the gunner's hatch, manning the roof gun. Mike stared at the magazine in his hand, then looked up to see his father staring at him.

Roger didn't know what he felt—sad, horrified, maybe even another emotion, way deep down inside. One that he didn't want to examine for fear that it was, in fact, pride. "It'll be okay," he told his son.

Mike pressed his lips together, looked down at the Blackbird magazine, then shoved it back into rifle. He grabbed the mini-gun belt and began roughly stripping the rounds out one at a time. Had he killed someone? Maybe he had. He honestly couldn't remember. Shouldn't he remember something like that, taking a man's life? Shouldn't he feel different? He didn't know what to think. He didn't know what he was feeling, other than numb at the realization that he might have killed someone. A bad guy with a gun, sure, but still....

Roger turned to Seamus, anger making his neck red. The color rose up from his collar to his cheeks, finally reaching his forehead, where a vein pulsed. "I can't believe you made him shoot someone!"

"I didn't make him do anything," Seamus said flatly.

"He had to kill a man!"

"Yes. He *had* to. No shame in that. The shame would be in not doing it, when the time came." He looked over his shoulder at Mike. "Hopefully that's the last time any of us has to pull a trigger before we get back to base, but be aware, none of the other rifles we have are chambered in Blackbird, and we're not likely to find any more til we get back with friendlies. With your spare mags, you've got a hundred and fifty rounds, total. Well, minus one."

* * *

Eduardo Manuel Echevarria—Eddie to his wife and friends, "*Gordito*" to the media and the public, and Señor Echevarria to everyone else—glanced up from his tablet every few seconds out of habit, but very little of what he saw out the tinted windows of the SUV registered.

Everywhere was crowded. The small narrow streets in the slums where he was born so many years ago were crowded with faces. Poor, hungry, angry, scared, hopeless faces, for the most part. The highways were crowded with vehicles jockeying for position, ignoring the painted lane markers. The small open-air *tianguis* where Rosita had shopped since she'd been a young girl living with her family, a short distance from the vehicle, was crowded with wooden stalls.

The stalls were all bare brown wood, had been forever. Every one of them looked ready to collapse, leaning into each other, falling in slow motion, but that didn't stop the foot traffic, the business, the constant conversations. It never had. Even when the war visited Mexico City, the *tinaguis* in *Barrio de Tepito,* perhaps the worst neighborhood in the city, kept doing business. And, in fact, the guerrillas avoided Tepito—nothing of value for them there, nothing but poor people with nothing to lose.

Echevarria glanced over at his wife, who was biting into a peach, then out the window at the last of the broken stalls falling behind them as the vehicle accelerated. "You pay too much," he chided her softly. He knew it was a sentimental gesture. In spite of what most people assumed of her, she had a kind heart.

She smiled behind the fruit. "I don't pay enough," she told him. They'd had the same conversation, or variations of it, for twenty-seven years. At least once a month, she demanded to go to the neighborhood where she grew up, buy a few things, talk to people. Buy a few more things, at inflated prices. Hire some of the dirty children to carry her purchases to the car, and pay them far too much for a few minutes of their time. And even though he hated that she did it, because of the risks, he loved her for doing it and never thought to tell her no. Not that he was in any way convinced she would obey him.....

The residents of Tepito had a kind of pride belonging to perhaps the most dangerous neighborhood in Mexico City, and they loved his wife who, at every opportunity, proudly announced that she was from *Barrio de Tepito.* This was the first time he'd accompanied her to the market in years, though. He almost never was out of the office during the day. But today was different. He'd made time in his schedule. Time for family.

He grumbled and used a thumb to flip rapidly through the tablet. He preferred hands-on electronics to the glasses or helmets which stuck your head in a virtual world. Not that he didn't use them, but he liked being able to look at the world around him whenever possible. "I'm going to be in meetings all day tomorrow," he said with a sigh.

"I thought you set aside some time…"

"Today," he reminded her. "Today." He checked his watch. "The flight should land in ninety minutes."

"You are too busy," she scolded him for what felt like the ten-thousandth time. He looked at her and made a face, and she reached out and patted his hand.

"Life is what we make of it, but it is not always what we want." It was perhaps his most famous quote. Just because he'd found it true in his personal life didn't mean he was happy about it.

"But we are fine," she said with a smile, setting her hand on his.

He squeezed her fingers. "*Sí*, we are fine," he agreed. Then he glanced down. "Except for your sticky fingers."

She laughed, and her eyes sparkled as they had that first day they'd met, so long ago. She moved the peach away from her mouth and pursed her lips. "Kiss me, and I'll get you even stickier," she challenged him. He began to lean toward her when his palm rang.

She rolled her eyes theatrically. "*Ay, Dios,*" she said.

With a smile he pulled his WorldView eyeglasses out of his suit pocket and put them on. A tap on the temple, and he could see and hear whoever was on the other end of the call. As Eddie began talking business she stared out the window at the passing city. Even though there hadn't been any serious attacks in the city in years, it was not the same. She could feel it, see it on the faces of her countrymen. They were scared. The war had been dragging on for close to a generation, and it was grinding the whole country down. Mexico City itself had seen combat, but for the past five years the only thing the *terroristas* had been able to pull off inside the city were random bombings which killed as many innocents as they did soldiers and police. *La Fuerza* was not nearly as popular in the city as they were in the south.

The inside of the SUV smelled of leather and the overripe fruit she had happily paid too much for. She set the peach pit down on the center console and pulled out a bottle of water. After taking a swig from it, she leaned forward and hit the button which slid down the blastproof glass shield between the front seat and the rear of the vehicle. José, in the passenger seat, turned and looked back at her.

"José, Manuel? Would either of you like a bottle of water?"

"*Gracias, Señora*, but I have a cola," José told her. He had a square head and thick black hair cut to stubble, and never looked comfortable in the suits. He then looked at Manuel behind the wheel and smirked.

"What?" Rosita asked. She was missing something. She could only see the back of Manuel's head as he shook it. His neck was thick with muscle.

"I've already had too much water, Señora," he admitted. "What do the Americans say? 'My teeth are floating?'"

"I see a beautiful mountain stream, hear the water trickling between the stones, glistening in the sun...." José said to him, trying hard not to laugh. He lifted a can of Coca Cola into view and took a loud slurping sip.

"José, you're terrible," she scolded him. "How long before we arrive?"

"Depends on the roadblocks," Manuel said to her, keeping his eyes forward. She saw his head bob, and looked past him to see a police roadblock up ahead. There were only a few cars in line in front of it.

Their belt radios crackled, and Manuel slowed the vehicle down. Their tail car, an identical black SUV, roared around them and rolled straight up to the police barricade, ignoring the vehicles already in a queue before the roadblock. By the time Manuel coasted their SUV to the roadblock, the police were already waving the two big vehicles through. Two minutes later, they were pulling up in front of the big office building downtown.

Beni and Al climbed out of the lead SUV and were joined a second later by José and Manuel. The men spread out along the sidewalk and looked in all directions. At first glance, they looked to be businessmen, standing there in their dark suits, but Al and Manuel were discreetly carrying compact submachine guns. Most of the pedestrians passing by on the sidewalk never even noticed, but those that did gave the men a wide berth.

The sidewalk here was twenty feet wide. There were six steps up, then another twenty feet of variegated marble flagstones to the front doors. Two uniformed officers from building security stepped out the front doors, nodded to the bodyguards, and looked around. Their bright blue uniforms were spotless, and their white patent leather belts and holsters could have been props for a costume, but the holsters held real pistols.

When no threat was apparent, Beni moved to her door and opened it. He was the head of their security detail. "*Señora*," he said, nodding to her. His instinct was to hold out a hand to help her out of the vehicle, but knew she didn't like it. Instead, he opened the door and stepped back, his eyes constantly moving. Except for the expensive suit, he was unremarkable in appearance—lean build, just over six feet tall, with dark brown hair over brown eyes. In the sunlight Rosita saw age lines starting to form around his eyes—she'd never noticed those before. From a distance he still looked younger than he was.

Rosita stepped from the SUV and waited for Eddie.

"*Sí, claro*," she heard from inside the vehicle, then the beep as he ended the call. With a sigh, he made his way out the open vehicle door and stood next to her.

"I should retire," he said, straightening his suit coat. It was something he said once a month.

"You would go *loco* within a week," she said once more, and it was the truth.

All of their bodyguards twitched at the shriek, and Rosita spun to see a very short and fat woman rushing toward her on the sidewalk, arms out. Beni moved to put himself between his charges and the woman, but Rosita put a hand on his shoulder as she saw the look on the woman's face.

"Ay, Maria, Maria, is it you? It is! I love you!" the woman gushed. Her hands were up and shaking with excitement. "You are my favorite!"

In her short heels, Rosita had eight inches on the woman, although they probably weighed the same. She smiled widely and dipped her head slightly. "*Gracias*. You are too kind."

The woman stopped and stared up at Rosita with wide eyes. "You are even more beautiful in person. That Roberto was a fool for leaving you."

"He had a brain tumor," Rosita reminded her gently. "He did not know what he was doing."

The woman waved a hand angrily. "Then he should have died. The writers should have killed him off. Instead he follows around that blonde *puta* Gabriella like a dog on a leash."

Echevarria stood on the sidewalk a few feet away and couldn't help but smile as his wife dealt with the fan. The woman seemed to be of a machine-made type: thick, intense, working class; and display-ing a consistent tendency to confuse events on the soap opera with reality.

He'd met Rosita when he'd made a large advertising buy on *La Vida Loca* and visited the set. Years before, it had started as a short-run telenovela, but it had been so successful it had become serialized into what the Americans called a "soap opera." Rosita played Maria Conchita Lopez on the show, a smart and savvy law school student, the only honest person in a family filled with liars and thieves and killers.

The story Rosita and Eddie told for years to reporters who'd asked was true; it really had been love at first sight. She'd been ten years his junior, and taller than him in bare feet, and he'd never been handsome, so of course everyone thought she was only interested in his money. But his critics didn't know the man that her beloved Ed-die was, how much love and humor and happiness his trademark scowl concealed. They'd been engaged within six months and mar-ried a year after that. Rosita had continued her role as Maria for an-other three years, until she'd given birth to a daughter and given up acting for motherhood. The writers had pregnant Maria—by then a young idealistic attorney working for the Prosecutor's office—die in a fiery car crash, murdered by a family friend who turned out to be a bank robber.

Rosita had thought her acting days long behind her, even though her character on *La Vida Loca* consistently appeared on lists of all-time favorite soap opera characters. One evening two months after her youngest had gone off to college, she'd run into her old producer at a charity fundraiser. *La Vida Loca* was not only still on the air but seeing a resurgence in popularity. The producer sensed an opportunity—they could bring Maria back! It didn't hurt that in many ways she was at least as beautiful as she had been twenty years before when she'd left the show, and even more famous considering who her husband had become. Storyline was easy: her character had in fact faked her own death and been put into witness protection. Fan reaction at the announcement of her return had been truly and gloriously *loco*. She had returned as the gruff but glamorous prosecutor with a heart of gold causing no end of grief to the troublemakers in her own family.

Rosita didn't need the money—far from it—but with all her children married or moved out her big house had been too quiet. Still, she had only agreed to a small role on the show, as she didn't want or need a full-time job. Her part only required several days of work a week, about three months a year.

As the fan giggled with his wife over some arcane aspect of an absurd plot point, Eddie leaned in close to Beni's ear. "Whenever you can pry her away and get her upstairs, check on the flight. It should have taken off by now."

Beni nodded, not taking his eyes off Señora Echevarria. Eddie then headed into the building, accompanied by the rest of his body-guards.

After several more minutes Rosita was able to disengage herself from the woman, and Beni followed her up the stairs and into the lobby. The two uniformed guards closed the blast-resistant doors behind them and escorted the two around the wave scanners in the lobby. Rosita treated them with a smile and a nod.

"Do you think I'm a fool for going back into acting?" she asked Beni in the elevator. She looked at his reflection in the elevator's mirrored walls. Beni had been with them longer than anybody else. Eddie had met him not long after Rosita had given birth to her youngest daughter. She still wasn't sure how the two had met, as they seemed a most unlikely pair, but Beni never shied from the truth, no matter how ugly it was. She could always count on him to be honest with her.

He had an angular face and never spoke much. Beni shrugged at the question. "I see that it makes you happy. And you playing Maria makes so many others happy." He shrugged again. "And they pay you very well for it. How is that foolish?" She smiled and patted him on the arm.

Eddie was on the old-fashioned desk phone, and Rosita was pouring herself a lemonade from the bar in his office fifteen minutes later when Beni entered. She glanced at him and was immediately troubled by the look on his face. It was even more expressionless than usual, this in a man who had made a career out of never show-ing emotion when he was working.

"What is it?" she asked him.

Eddie finished his call and looked up at his head of security. "Beni?"

"I have been on the palm with General Santos and Raven Command since we arrived." Beni stopped and took a breath and swallowed. "The helicopter that she was on cannot be contacted. It never made it to Victoria Base. Efforts to reach it by radio have been unsuccessful. It is not on their radar."

"Are you—are you saying it crashed?" Rosita asked, horrified.

Eddie held up a hand to calm his wife, then looked to Beni. "Did they radio for help? Is there any emergency beacon?"

"Not that any of the stations are picking up. No one reported receiving a distress call. It is entirely possible they had mechanical issues and had to set down somewhere. There is a lot of open land out there, a lot of mountains in the area that could be interfering with the signals. It was a Raven helicopter, and General Santos assured me Raven is looking into it. They have already launched several aircraft to search the area, see if they can pick up any beacon signal. He told me that you should not worry, there has been no report of a crash. The mountains could block the signal from an emergency transponder. Santos said he will contact me directly if any of the tracking stations pick up radar contact or reestablish radio communications with the helicopter."

"And Raven?"

"They confirmed that the helicopter she was to get on arrived at China Base, but they seem to be having some problem getting any information beyond that."

Rosita was pale and shaking. "My Rita?" she asked in disbelief.

She looked at her husband. His scowl had deepened, and he had gotten very still. That was the surest sign she knew that he was upset. "You reminded them who she is?" he said quietly.

Beni nodded. "I made it very clear to them exactly the magnitude of the situation, but they were already well aware."

Rosita cursed and dug in her purse. Echevarria turned and looked out the window behind him. His 65th floor window in *Torre Cielo* afforded him one of the best views of downtown Mexico City there was to be had, but at that moment he wasn't seeing the city at all. All he was seeing was the face of his youngest daughter, his beautiful, headstrong, brilliant daughter. Who was now missing; the helicopter she was riding in disappeared.

As Rosita stood there, palm to her ear, there suddenly was a ringing sound in the room. Echevarria pulled open one of the drawers of his desk and scowled at it. "She mailed us her palm, remember?" he told his wife. He slammed the drawer shut. Rosita fought back sobs. She threw her palm onto the couch and hugged herself.

Echevarria turned back to look at Beni, a man whom he'd known for almost twenty years, who he knew like a brother, and whom he trusted with his life.

"Find the helicopter. Find her. Take whoever you need, take whatever you need, do whatever you need to do."

Beni nodded once, then turned and left.

* * * * *

Chapter Nine

"This road's in good shape for being in the middle of nowhere, but it doesn't look like it sees a lot of traffic," Seamus observed. The crash site was maybe five kilometers behind them, and the dusty road arrowed almost due south. It ran along the top of a ridge line, or near to it. To the right was an uneven forested slope running slightly uphill to a crest maybe a quarter of a mile out. No telling what might be past the jagged crest in that direction.

On the left was a long valley paralleling the road. The slopes were covered with trees, mostly pines, but the floor of the shallow valley was thick meadow grass, mostly green, but with hints of brown and gold, and the occasional wildflower. Past the valley, the slopes rose up in undulating waves that kept on going—the foothills of the Sierra Madre Orientals. "How far are we from Victoria Base?" Roger asked. "Fifty miles?"

"Straight line, about thirty miles," Seamus told him. He pointed to his ten o'clock, southeast, then put both hands back on the wheel. The Vaquero liked to wander across the bumpy road, even at a sedate 60 kph. And at that speed they were still putting up a big tail of dust behind them, easy to see. They were sorely exposed on the elevated road, but there was nothing to be gained by mentioning that to his civilian passengers, who were already a bit panicked. "But it's in that direction, over the mountains. No direct route. I'm not even sure if there's an indirect route. Most of the trails around these mountains are a lot older than the base. There wasn't much of anything there before the base, so I don't know how many if any of the roads and trails through the mountains—"

He was interrupted by Corey yelling and pounding on the roof above their heads. Seamus stomped on the brake. "What?" he yelled.

"Vehicle ahead!" the contractor yelled again.

"Bloody hell," Seamus cursed. He couldn't see anything yet, but Corey had a better vantage point up top. "Friendlies?"

"I can't tell. It's just over a rise, maybe a mile out. Mostly I'm seeing dust. There any binoculars down there?" Their trailing dust cloud enveloped them, and Corey coughed and spat.

Seamus cursed and opened his door. He stood with one foot on his seat and one on the door handle to get some elevation and brought Leonidas up. He switched the scope to 4X but couldn't see anything because of the dust cloud drifting down the road. Seconds dragged by, and finally the dust thinned. By that time the far vehicle—or at least the dust cloud—was visible to Roger sitting in the front passenger seat. He squinted but couldn't make any details.

"What is it? Raven? Army?" Roger said hopefully.

Seamus cursed again and lowered his rifle. He looked through his open door at Roger. "How much did you say you were worth? Three hundred million? *Pinches culeros Fuerzan.*" He jumped back in his seat and had the vehicle moving before his door was all the way closed.

"FRAP?" Corey yelled from above.

"You got it mate!" Seamus yelled back. "A pickup and what looks to be a bloody fooking troop truck. Maybe they haven't seen us yet."

"Nothing's coming over the radio."

Seamus made a decision. "Hold on!" And with that he wrenched the wheel to the left.

The Vaquero got airborne for a few feet as it left the edge of the road and started down the long grassy slope to the valley. The grass-covered ground was softer under the wheels, though less even, but that didn't stop Seamus from accelerating. Roger had forgotten to put his seatbelt on and was bounced against the door and ceiling before he let go of the AK between his legs and belted in.

"Jesus! You're going to bust an axle, slow down!" Roger yelled at him. He looked over his shoulder and saw his son had his feet braced against the opposite row of seats and had his palms pressed against the roof. The girl, Tina, had lost her balance and fallen on top of the co-pilot's body in the back. She looked sick as she scrambled back onto her seat.

"You hear what I told you, mate? I said they had a troop transport." The Vaquero bounced crazily as Seamus sped across the width of the valley, heading for a low spot between two hills opposite them. His knuckles were white on the steering wheel to keep from being thrown about the cab of the truck. "That means troops."

"Where are you going?"

"We're exposed as a priest without pants in this pretty little meadow. I'm hoping that leads us somewhere," Seamus said, nodding ahead of them. To their right, the valley stretched wide and open and green, running north to south. Low hills bordered it to the east, but directly in front of them there was a low rocky saddle with only a few trees. "No trail, but we should be able to get over it no problem. We get out of sight, and they didn't spot us on the road, everything's posh."

Seamus powered the Vaquero up the short slope, tires spitting gravel and pine needles. He weaved it between the few trees. Engine roaring, the vehicle nearly left the ground as it crested the slope, and he had to wrestle for control of the wheels as they slid on the long grass on the far side. He hooked a right. A hundred feet farther, Seamus stomped the brake, and the vehicle slid to a stop.

In front of them was a narrow vale with steep treed slopes to either side, curving out of sight to the southwest. Seamus jumped out of the gun truck, rifle in hand, but waved at everyone else to stay inside. He jogged back up the slope to one of the trees he'd driven around and looked in the direction they'd come. In two seconds he'd seen all he needed to.

"You're a bleeding idiot," he cursed at himself. From where he was standing all the way back across the wide meadow and up to the road was a double set of dark tire tracks through the grass, so obvious an imbecile could spot them. And there, on the road right above where the tracks started, maybe half a mile away, just stopping, were a pickup and a large cargo truck, its open bed filled with men. As he watched several of the men jumped down and gathered by the pickup. At least one of them pointed in his direction, although they couldn't see him.

He growled and spat and ran back toward the Vaquero. Corey's head and shoulders were sticking out of the hatch where he stood behind the roof-mounted PKM machine gun. He flipped the visor up on his helmet. "I know that look."

"Tracks in the grass are like arse-afire airport landing lights," Seamus told him. He stared at the narrow valley before them. At least it was heading in the right direction. "Let's see where this one takes us," he said, jumping back behind the wheel.

Mike helped Tina buckle her seatbelt before Seamus got the armored vehicle moving once again. She was a little freaked out after having fallen onto the dead body. There was some of the dead man's blood on her sleeve, but Mike didn't want to point it out to her.

"It'll be okay," Mike told her as they started bouncing around in their seats again. He looked forward out the windshield and saw they were heading down a narrow gorge, the slopes tree-covered all the way down to the grassy floor. Something scraped the undercarriage loudly as Seamus bounced through a shallow stream. Mike'd been trying to reassure her, but the girl stared at him as if he hadn't spoken at all.

* * *

El Tejón stood at the edge of the road and stared at the tire tracks. They cut almost a perfectly straight double line across the valley, the grass dark and matted where the wheels of the vehicle had rolled over it. The fresh tracks ran right up to a low spot between two hills, then vanished. He looked up at the sun, then back at the valley. They were heading nearly straight east, he reckoned.

He stood an inch over six feet, with glossy black hair that was too long. He'd been too busy in the last few weeks to get it cut. His high cheekbones were cliff edges, and combined with the hair, made him look like a character actor. He wore a long-sleeve button-down khaki shirt over brown canvas work pants, eschewing all the bits and pieces of camouflage that his men simply adored. Peeking above the collar of the shirt on the left side of his neck was the tip of a shiny scar. On the right side of his neck, the edge of an old tattoo was visible, the tail of a snarling lion which covered the right side of his chest, the result of a bad mix of tequila and youth—he'd been a brazen young man who'd just survived yet another firefight with the Army putas. Over one shoulder was slung a battered Sig Sauer MPX submachine gun and on his hip was an American Army .45 pistol even older than the submachine gun. He prized them, because he'd taken both guns off the first American he'd killed, a military policeman.

"Maybe it is a farmer," one of the men standing behind him said. He was short and hairy and looked none too bright, but at least he kept his rifle pointed in a safe direction.

"In an armored Vaquero?" Domingo, his lieutenant, replied derisively. "*Idiota.*" He stepped closer to his *Comandante*, who still stared across the valley. They'd caught sight of the Vaquero just before it disappeared behind the hills.

"Any answer on the radio?" he asked Domingo without turning around. It was a beautiful, warm, sunny day. A perfect day to be working, if you were a farmer. But there were no fields within kilometers. And who would want to be a farmer?

"No. But that could be the other squad."

"Or it just as likely could be the Army; they use Vaqueros. Where do you think we get ours? If it is Miguel and his men, where is the other truck? And why don't they answer their radio?" He would have preferred all four vehicles arrive at the crash site together, in case there was trouble, but they'd gotten separated on the road, and Miguel had rushed ahead, as his sergeant always did. Out of sight, out of radio range, out of his head with the thought of claiming their prize. Maybe his impetuousness had finally been his undoing. "No, we need to know before I go chasing tire tracks, no matter who might be at the other end." He turned and looked at Domingo, then the small flatbed truck. Many of the men who'd been riding in it had taken the opportunity to jump down and walk around or relieve themselves. Maybe half the men had combat experience, but the rest were untested. All the new faces were volunteers, but he still wished his regular platoon of combat-hardened men had been available. They'd been down south, preparing for a rumored Army offensive that had materialized just that morning. "Take this truckload of *troncos* with you to the crash site, and inform me by radio."

"*Comandante?*" One of the younger guerillas raised his hand sheepishly, then pointed. "I see some smoke, very far away."

The boy looked barely out of high school, and of dull farmer stock, but there was no arguing that young eyes could be sharper. *El Tejón* found the battered pair of binoculars in the Toyota pickup and focused them on the ridge several kilometers to the north. After about thirty seconds of searching he finally spotted the narrow column of thin smoke. That was right in the area where the helicopter should have come down. He lowered the binoculars and nodded at Domingo. "Leave me two men."

"*Sí, Comandante.* Back in the truck you *maricones!* Run!"

"Domingo!" He pointed at the teenager who'd spotted the smoke. "Let him be your eyes." The boy opened his mouth in surprise. The great *Comandante* wanted *him* to help?

Domingo nodded, then yelled at the gawking boy, "You heard *El Comandante!* Get in the cab. See if you can keep me out of trouble. What is your name?"

"Francisco."

The big truck accelerated with a loud growl of its diesel engine and a black cloud. *El Tejón* watched it for a second, then turned his attention back to the tire tracks, staring at where they disappeared into the distance. The two men with him spread out and watched for trouble, rifles at the ready.

He had not been born *El Tejón*, of course. No mother should so burden a son by naming him "The Badger." His birth name was Daniel, his family name a close kept secret known only to a few, to prevent the Army from enacting retribution. At twenty-eight, he was the youngest *Comandante*—Major—in *La Fraternidad Progresista para un Mexico Nuevo*. He had earned his nickname when fifteen, fighting the Mexican Army in a small but brutal engagement in Puebla. The guerillas had been cut off and they'd been forced into a bloody retreat, with house-to-house combat. At one point, young Daniel had been fighting a soldier not much his senior. He was out of ammo and had lost his knife, but he managed to knock the rifle out of the soldier's hands. As a last resort, he had ripped the soldier's throat out with his teeth. The act was witnessed, and his legend began. As with so many legends, some of it was true.

After several minutes, he checked his watch, then used the binoculars to scan the far side of the valley. "What is on the far side of those hills? Do either of you know?" He looked over his shoulder at the two FRAP soldiers Domingo had left with him. They were both veteran guerilla fighters he had fought with in the past, and like most men who had survived more than a skirmish or two, only went by nicknames, to prevent the Army *cabrones* from jailing and torturing their family members. Tuco had enormously thick black eyebrows, and Chi-Chi never stopped with the tales of his feminine conquests. Both men shook their heads.

"*Señor*, I have never traveled this far north to fight," Tuco admitted. He did not look happy about it.

"We have a map, but you have seen it, it is nearly worthless," Chi-Chi remarked. He nodded to the southeast. "More hills and low mountains between here and Victoria. Very few roads, and not many trails. What exactly is on the other side of *those* hills…" He shrugged.

El Tejón was himself feeling nervous being that far north, not that he would show it. They were so far outside of FRAP territory that the area wasn't even considered contested—it belonged *mano total* to the American *escaras* and their lapdogs the Mexican military. Not that there was much to fight for. The towns and villages in the area were few and far apart; there were few farms, and no factories or mines.

On their trip north, the first night they'd hidden the vehicles in an abandoned warehouse identified for them by sympathizers. The second night, they'd overnighted in a large barn belonging to a believer in the cause. Outwardly, both nights he'd been relaxed, but he was ever aware of possible betrayal and set guards just in case. Travelling south with their prize would be infinitely more dangerous.

The radio crackled. Domingo's voice was faint and scratchy, but understandable. "*Comandante*, Miguel and his men, they are all dead. The other truck is here, destroyed. So is the helicopter, empty. Whoever was in it must be in the Vaquero."

He frowned. Miguel was headstrong, but he was no fool, and had had half a dozen men with him. And they were all dead? That was extremely troubling. "Get back here as fast as you can, then." If Miguel had been so easy to ambush, perhaps…. He got back on the radio. "And Domingo, switch to the alternate frequency." Then he stared at the mountains. His prey would not have gotten far. The two men with him eyed the distant hills nervously.

* * *

The Vaquero bounced along the winding floor as fast as Seamus dared push it. A flock of birds took flight from the long grass ahead of them.

"Where's this go?" Roger asked the contractor, staring out at the valley. "Do you know where we're going? Have you been here before?" He was trying to get some sense of the situation, find some sort of control over what was happening. Knowledge was power.

"Mate, I'm making it up as I bloody go," Seamus told him through gritted teeth. He glanced at Roger and smiled. "But I do have rather a lot of experience at that, if it makes you feel any better." He knew there was no way this quiet little valley would run all the way down to Victoria Base, but Seamus hoped that it might stretch for a ways and perhaps lead him to a trail he could take up into the mountains. Any road in any direction was preferable to being boxed in by the FRAP, or engaging in direct combat with them when two-thirds of your force was tourists or injured.

The narrow valley doglegged to the left, and Seamus followed it. As soon as they were past a tumble of dead trees, they got the bad news; the valley ended a quarter mile ahead of them.

"Now where do we go?" Roger asked as Seamus cursed. Seamus stuck his head over the steering wheel and then against the window of his door. He looked up at the steep slopes to either side of them, looking for roads, trails, or clearcuts for power lines, but he saw nothing.

Corey ducked down inside the rear of the Vaquero. He held onto the edge of the roof hatch with one hand to keep from being knocked over in the bouncing vehicle. "I've got radio traffic. Somebody calling for Miguel. Miguel's not answering. Don't even know if it's those guys behind us on the road. Now what? We make a stand?"

"With a bunch of civilians and wounded?" Seamus shook his head at Corey.

"I've got one good arm," Hansen said from the back.

Tina didn't know what the soldier was talking about, and peered between the seats out the windshield. They were rapidly coming up on what seemed to be a wall of trees. "Are we trapped?" she asked.

"Surrendering isn't an option?" Roger wasn't a coward, but he liked exploring his options, especially since what was supposed to have been a nice hunting trip with his son had turned into some sort of war movie.

Seamus glanced at him. "If they are interested in ransom, then you'll probably be fine. At most you'll lose a finger; they like cutting those off and sending them back to prove they really have you. And maybe they won't kill your son, if you beg real nice. Me, Corey, our lovely pilot back there? They'll kill us all straightaway. Hopefully. If not, they'll torture us before they kill us. And you?" he said, turning in the seat to look at Tina. He knew she could hear him. "You they'll rape for, well, for the rest of your life, however long that is. Personally, I prefer Plan B."

He stomped on the brakes, and the Vaquero skid-bounced to a stop. Roger looked out the windshield to see they were surrounded on three sides by steep slopes. Up close the trees—which were mostly pines—weren't as dense as they appeared from a distance. The slope made the branches appear as a thick dark green wall, but at ground level he saw most of the trees were at least ten feet apart. Even so, the slopes were far too steep to drive up.

"Unass the vehicle!" Seamus called out. "Everybody grab what they can carry. If you've got extra clothes tie them around you." He opened his door and jumped down.

"Where are we going, O'Malley?" Roger demanded. He didn't want to move from the seat, his back hurt too much.

Seamus pointed up the slope in front of them. "Up there."

Roger stared at the incline. It had to be a thirty degree angle, and while there was little underbrush under the trees, the ground was covered in dead pine needles which would slip everywhere. His breath was already a little short, just sitting in the seat, because of the elevation. And the pain.

"This is an armored car!" he barked at Seamus, spreading his hands inside the cab. "And you want us to abandon it? We should have stayed on the road."

Seamus looked at him. "Maybe we should have, but that's not an option now. Let's pray the buggers chasing us really are hoping to kidnap you."

"What? Why would you say that?"

"Because it means they'll do whatever they can to not shoot at us, because they might hit you. Maybe we can work that to our favor."

"How do you even know they're FRAP? The men you killed back at the helicopter weren't wearing uniforms, and their vehicles, this vehicle, aren't marked."

"If you've got truckloads of guys with guns and they're not Mexican Army or Raven, they're FRAP. Or soldiers with one of the drug cartels. Bad guys one way or the other," Corey told Roger. The old guy looked like he was used to being in charge and wasn't taking the change well. "The only place you see that stupid shield and hammer FRAP logo is on their press releases."

"Stop talking and move!" Seamus shouted. "We've got about two minutes. We need to be up that hill and out of sight before they show up."

"You got a plan?" Corey asked him.

"Don't I always? You think you can pull the PKM off that mount, drag it up the hill?"

Corey looked at the belt-fed machine gun on the roof. PKMs were built for reliability and durability, neither of which was consistent with light weight. "Sure. Sounds awesome. Was hoping you'd ask," he said, deadpan, then began tugging at the mount, trying to disconnect the gun.

Roger climbed out of the cab and walked around to the rear, listing to the side and limping badly from the pain in his back. "Should I grab that?" he asked Seamus, nodding at the rifle case which contained his big .338 Magnum hunting rifle. He still held the AK Seamus had given him in one hand.

Seamus looked from the big rifle case to the AK in the older man's hand. He shook his head. "No, too big and heavy. You can't even stand upright. Just grab some mags for that AK from the back here and hightail it up the hill."

"We're just going to leave it here for the FRAP to take?"

Seamus stopped moving and stared at the man. "You might be a great bloke to have on my side in the boardroom, but right now all of your boardroom experience is worth exactly four-fifths of five-eighths of fuck-all. We're not in your office; we're in mine. And we don't have time for you to question every fooking thing I say to you. Just do it. There are people coming here to kill us, or worse. Stop worrying about your precious goddamn gun. I'm more upset about having to leave the body of our co-pilot, who gave his life to save yours."

Roger, chagrinned, clamped his mouth shut and grabbed some magazines off the floor of the armored truck, moving out of the way for the girl.

Tina jumped down from the rear of the Vaquero and dragged her backpack toward her. Filled with the water bottles and protein bars Seamus had told her to grab, it was heavy, maybe fifty pounds. She set it at the rear of the Vaquero and was squatting to fit her arms through the straps when Seamus stopped her.

"I'll take that, Rita," he told her. "You get up the hill. Go," he told her firmly when it appeared she wanted to argue. "You've got two good hands, help those who need helping up that hill, fast as you can."

"It's Tina," she said reflexively, but moved to help Roger.

"Mr. O'Malley, did you know these were here?"

Seamus looked into the Vaquero to see the boy had pulled a seat up to reveal a storage compartment. He put a foot up on the back bumper so he could see what was inside.

"You're bloody beautiful son, come over here so's I can give you a kiss," Seamus said with a smile. "No I did not. I'll grab those, get up the hill after your father." He then quickly held up a hand, staring at the Ulfberht. "Think you can make it up the hill with that beast on your shoulder?" he asked the boy. "And as many mags and ammo for it as you can fit in your pockets?"

"Yeah, I think so." Mike turned and looked out the Vaquero's windows at the hill, then back at Seamus. "How far up the hill?"

"Just keep going til I tell you to stop. Or the shooting starts, in which case find something to hide behind. Corey! You fondle that pig any longer you're going to have to propose."

"I think I've got it," Corey said. "You want to come around the side so I can hand it down?"

Seamus moved around and took custody of the PKM. Corey hopped out the back of the vehicle and took the heavy gun out of Seamus' hands. "We headed anywhere in particular?" he asked, staring up at the pine-covered slope in front of them. "Not that I don't enjoy walks in the country. The air's so fresh and clean."

"Isn't it though? For the moment, up is good enough," Seamus told him. "I'll be right behind you." He jumped into the back of the Vaquero, heading straight for the storage bin Mike had found.

With every step a sharp shooting pain stabbed Roger in the middle of his back, and he was gasping before he'd gone a dozen steps. Sweat popped out on his forehead, and he rested an arm against a tree trunk as he tried to find a position where his back hurt less. Hansen, the pilot, was ahead of him and trudging up the slope.

Hansen was trying not to lose his footing on the pine needles, because he only had one good hand and his pistol was in it. Finally he decided that was dumb and holstered the gun. Where the slope got steeper he put his hand on the ground. He was panting and sweating, but he kept going. He wore the sling and had the hand of his broken arm tucked into his web gear on his chest, but if he moved too quickly, a sharp pain would shoot through the dull throbbing ache.

Roger saw him disappearing into the trees up ahead. The man had a broken arm and was still outpacing him. Gritting his teeth, Roger pushed off from the tree and started up the slope again. Before long, he was on all fours, his lungs burning as he fought the pain and the altitude. He saw he was dragging the AK through the needles and dead branches, but barely had the strength to lift it. The Irishman had been right, there was no way he could have dragged the Ulfberht up the hill.

"Here, let me help." Roger looked and there was the girl at his elbow. She put his free hand over her shoulder and together they pushed forward and up.

"You okay, dad? You want me to help?"

Roger looked up and his son was there, looking concerned. He had the black military rifle in one hand, and the big Ulfberht over his shoulder. There was a bag hanging over one of his shoulders, heavy with magazines for the giant rifle. All the military hardware hanging off his son disconcerted Roger a bit. He would have loved to hand the AK over, but Mike was sweaty and panting from trudging up the slope already weighed down with one of Roger's rifles. He couldn't give him the AK too. His pride was already wounded quite enough, thank you, by having to be helped up the slope by a woman less than half his age. He shook his head. "No, I'm okay, we're okay," he gasped. "How much farther?"

"I don't know," Mike told him, panting. It was a lot harder getting up the slope with the big rifle over his shoulder than he thought it would be. It had to be the elevation, because he knew he was in shape, yet he was panting like a smoker. A fat smoker. "You've barely gone fifty feet. Just keep going. Follow the pilot."

"One step at a time," Tina panted in Roger's ear. He was heavy on her shoulders, and the thin air was burning her lungs. The only thing that made her push as hard as she was going was the thought of the FRAP terrorists coming up behind her. She would have kept glancing behind her if Roger's arm hadn't been in the way. She'd been worried about those young soldiers in the hangar at China Base, but only distantly—she doubted they would have actually tried anything. FRAP guerillas, on the other hand…she'd never seen any except on the news, but she'd heard a lot of terrifying stories. Rapes and beheadings of women were common. Most of the time they occurred in that order.

The young contractor powered past them with the big machine gun in his arms, his legs working like pistons. Roger was dismayed at how slow he and the girl were moving in comparison. Only Mike saw how hard Corey was working to get up the hill that fast, his eyeballs looked about to pop. Mike kept pace with his dad and Tina, not wanting to leave his father's side.

It felt as if someone had stabbed him in the middle of the back and was twisting the knife every time Roger took a step. He heart was racing from the pain, and he was gasping from that and the altitude. Sweat was running down his face freely. Every step was a struggle, every step was pain, and he focused on the slope and putting down one foot in front of the other.

He looked at the girl and saw her face was dark red with the effort of helping him up the hill. "Sorry," panted harshly at her, after trying three times to get enough air in his lungs to speak. She nodded but didn't waste air responding.

"Move, up the hill, fast as you can," they heard from behind them.

Seamus felt like he was moving through syrup between the elevation and the girl's backpack. Jesus Mary, had she stuffed an entire elk into the rucksack? He was on all fours more often than not moving up the hill to keep from tipping ass over teakettle with all that weight on his shoulders. He took the opportunity to pause and eyeball the scene. Even with the 'rita helping him, Rudd was struggling. Seamus looked past them and saw the boy, Michael, nervously keeping pace nearby. Corey and the pilot were maybe twenty meters up the slope.

"How much farther?" Mike asked Seamus, more for his father's benefit than anything.

"Keep going," Seamus said, trying not to sound too winded, without any luck. He glanced back down the slope, then past the Vaquero into the valley. No sign of company, yet. He stayed behind the older Rudd and his helper, covering the rear. The girl looked good from any angle, but he had to admit that the view he got walking behind her as she struggled up the slope with Rudd was spectacular.

"I...I don't...." Roger gasped, stumbling and falling to a knee.

"Sure you do," Seamus said cheerfully, there at his other elbow in an instant. He helped the man up, giving a nod to Tina, then stood in place and stared out at the valley as the pair continued their struggle upward.

How long had it been? Close to five minutes. Where were their pursuers? Maybe they were worried about walking into an ambush. Seamus knew he would be, with tire tracks that obvious in the grass. He also realized that the people following them didn't know quite who they were, or how many of them there might be. Probably. Maybe they hadn't even seen that the vehicle which had turned off the road had been their own Vaquero.

"You getting anything on the radio?" he asked Corey, who shook his head.

"It's a piece of junk, I think it's older than I am. Some garbled conversation a few minutes ago, but I couldn't make any of it out other than '*domingo*.'"

"Sunday?' Wrong day of the week. Keep listening."

About a hundred meters up from the valley floor the slope grew steeper, and their progress slowed. "Where the hell are they?" Mike asked Seamus from a dozen paces upslope, looking past him out at the valley. Most of the valley floor was blocked from view by the branches of the trees around and below them, but the woods were quiet except for the sound of a few birds and the occasional angry chitters of what were probably squirrels. Pursuing vehicles should have been easy for them to hear.

Seamus looked over his shoulder, then at his watch. It had been eight minutes since they'd stopped the Vaquero. They were at least two hundred meters up the slope, maybe a hundred meters above the valley floor. Not even halfway to the summit of what amounted to a low ridge. Glacially slow going, but every step was visible agony for the senior Rudd.

About forty meters past Mike, Corey and the pilot had paused by a large fallen tree. Seamus cupped his hands around his mouth. "Hold there," he called to Corey, just loud enough for the man to hear. Corey gave him a thumbs up.

"I need to...stop...and rest for...a minute," Roger gasped, falling onto his side. His face was so red, nearly purple, with a vein throbbing in his forehead, Seamus was worried the man was having a heart attack.

Tina looked up at Seamus, who nodded. They needed to push on, but not if it meant killing Rudd with the climb. He stepped up to them and turned around. "Take a minute. Get some water out of the pack."

"I...don't need...water...I need...air," Roger gasped from where he lay on his back.

Seamus stood and looked around through the gaps in the trees. Climbing up and down mountains aside, it was much prettier country than he was used to fighting in. Smelled a lot nicer too. He would take pine-scented woods over alleys filled with burning garbage any day.

Maybe half the valley floor directly below them was out of sight behind trees. He scanned what he could see and the surrounding slopes for movement, but he didn't spot anything. Behind him, Tina drank half a bottle of water, then knelt down and offered it to Roger. His face was blotchy red, and his breath was still harsh in his throat, but he nodded and took the plastic bottle gratefully.

Mike came down the slope toward Seamus, trying hard not to slide on the loose needles underfoot. "Where are they?" he asked. "Do you think they were just locals or something?" He wondered if maybe they should go back down to the Vaquero and drive out, since the other vehicles obviously weren't coming. And his dad couldn't take much more hill climbing.

Seamus opened his mouth to answer, then cocked his head. He looked out and down at the valley, but nothing was visible.

"Was that...?" Mike said.

Seamus grabbed him and shoved him at his father. "Grab him, get up there as fast as possible," he said, his voice low. He pointed upslope at Corey and Hansen. "Get behind cover,"

Tina looked up. "What?" A second later she heard the sound of a vehicle echo faintly off the hills. The look she gave Seamus was one of wide-eyed terror.

* * * * *

Chapter Ten

Despite his father's weak protests, Mike hung the Blackbird on its sling over his shoulder and pulled Roger up. With him on one arm and Tina on the other, they dragged Roger up the slope as fast as they could, hearts thudding in their chests. At first, their harsh breathing drowned out the distant sound of the engine, but it grew steadily louder.

Seamus trudged up behind them, turning every few steps to look back. He caught a glimpse of a vehicle between the trees as it moved slowly across the valley floor, but didn't see enough to identify it. It might have been the pickup he'd spotted on the road earlier. The low growl of a diesel engine echoed off the hills.

Corey heard an engine—no, there were two vehicles, one with a deeper pitch than the other—and waved at the staggering trio below him to hurry. "Come on! Get up behind me," he urged, trying to keep his voice down. The valley was so quiet he wasn't sure how far the noise would carry.

When they were a dozen steps below the big fallen tree where he was set up Corey jumped down the slope and grabbed Tina's arm. "Head for that, get down behind there," he told her, pointing at a large jumble of rocks about twenty meters away. Gasping, Tina nodded. Thankfully the rocks were at nearly the same elevation, and even though walking sideways across the slope was tricky, it was a lot easier than going up. She pulled Roger along and Mike let go of his arm, wanting to stay with the young soldier

"This is the best cover anywhere near," Corey told Seamus as he clambered the remaining distance up the slope.

Seamus eyed the thick tree trunk lying sideways across the slope and nodded. It would probably stop rifle rounds, at least for a while. Corey had laid the PKM across it. Hansen was sitting behind the fallen tree. Seamus shrugged off the heavy backpack with relief and set it next to Hansen.

"Stay low, stay quiet," he told the two men. "Don't fire until I do." He eyed Hansen's broken arm. "Corey, give him your carbine, he can fire it one-handed off the log. Single shots," he told the pilot. "And only shoot if you see something to shoot at. We might need every round."

Hansen was older than O'Malley and outranked him, but he didn't bristle at being ordered around. He simply nodded. He was a pilot, and a damned good one, but he had absolutely zero ground combat experience. The sergeant seemed to have that in spades, in addition to a naturally commanding personality. Hansen grabbed the M7 and checked to make sure there was a round in the carbine's chamber. Firing it left-handed would be awkward, and he wasn't the best shot to begin with, but he'd be damned if he let himself be captured. He'd seen what they did to prisoners, with beheading usually the most pleasant option.

Seamus nodded at Corey. "You work the PKM. How many rounds do you have for that thing?"

"Almost a full belt."

"Well if we get to shooting, don't spare them. We have to retreat from this position it'll be very dodgy, and it shouldn't be for a lack of shooting back." He looked at Mike, who was standing nearby, looking a little lost. "Lad," he said as gently as he could. "There might not be any shooting. There might be a lot. The only way we get off this hill alive is if you help out, like you did back at the cliff. You go about twenty steps that way," he pointed to their right flank, "and find a big tree to hide behind. A tree's not perfect cover, but it's about all we've got up here. This mountain is a bloody bitch to climb, but if we did it, so can they. And we can't have them getting up above us. They can't flank us, do you understand? If they do that, we're dead."

Mike swallowed and nodded.

"You see anybody getting close, you shoot them," Seamus told him. "Otherwise, don't shoot until you hear this beast barking," he jabbed a thumb at the PKM, "and then only shoot if you've got a target."

"How many guys are there?" Mike asked.

"A dozen, maybe fifteen," Seamus said. He grabbed the Ulfberht off the lad's shoulder and dumped it behind the fallen tree. "Don't fret. Between the slope and the fact that they don't know how many of us there are, we actually outnumber them. Now move."

Corey eyed the three fragmentation grenades hanging off the front of Seamus' armor. "Where'd you get those?" he asked.

"Saint Nick," Seamus said. "Made it off the naughty list for once, didn't I? And he left presents for everyone." He pointed downslope in the general direction of the Vaquero, then jogged sideways across the slope to where Tina and Roger were crouched behind a jumble of rocks. Behind him Corey frowned.

"Where's Michael going?" Roger asked Seamus. He'd seen his son trotting off in the opposite direction.

"To get behind cover, same as you. Don't worry about him, he'll be fine. Anything happens, you keep your heads down. I know you've got that," he pointed at the AK lying across Roger's thighs, "but you're in no shape to use it. Unless you see them on top of us, or circling around the side to flank. But I don't think that will be an issue. Unless they've got dogs."

"Dogs?" Roger huffed. "What are we doing?" He demanded. The pain on top of the ridiculous situation he found himself in was making him angry. "We don't know who these guys are, or if our rescue beacon even went off. Now we're halfway up a mountain? Going where? What's the plan?"

Seamus looked him in the eye. "The plan is to stay alive, mate. Now get down, and keep your gob shut."

* * *

They crawled along the valley floor, following the tracks in the grass. As soon as they rounded the bend and saw the Vaquero, he had them halt. From inside the Toyota pickup, *El Tejón* studied the Vaquero with the binoculars. It appeared empty, with several of the doors open. There might have been something on the floor in back, but the shadows were too dark for him to make out any detail.

He scanned the slopes around and above the armored vehicle but didn't see any movement. The men in the bed of the truck beside them shifted restlessly, fondling their rifles.

"They left the Vaquero to climb the hills?" Domingo said from the driver's seat. He frowned.

"What would you have done?" he asked his lieutenant.

After thinking about it, Domingo shrugged. "All their options are equally bad."

"Go slow," he told Domingo. He rolled the window down and spoke to the driver of the big truck. "Spread out so we are not one target. Keep pace with us, and if you see anything, stop and yell out."

"*Sí, Jefe.*"

The vehicles crawled across the grass. *El Tejón* wasn't too worried about an ambush, he knew he had the numbers and the guns, but he hadn't survived twenty years of combat by rushing blindly into the unknown. Although he did have to wonder who had been in the Vaquero. Other than those of his men, there were no bodies at the helicopter—had the entire crew and all their passengers survived the crash? He'd been assured the crash would be rough but easily survivable, but you never knew. Although Domingo did say there was a little blood and vomit inside the Blackhawk. Miguel and his men seemed to have been outfought, whether by ambush or otherwise. Worst case scenario, if everyone on the bird was not just alive but armed and healthy...say four or five *escaras*, and at least one passenger, his target. Against he and his sixteen men. He'd gone into danger against far worse odds, but never when trying to secure a prisoner. And failure, with this mission, would not be tolerated. Nothing like that had been said, of course, but the importance of this mission to the cause had been impressed upon him at every meeting during the planning stage. He'd been brought in very early, which spoke to how much they valued him. He'd even met with Timotéo once.

He shook his head at his own doubts, his weakness. It was an important mission, and they had entrusted it to him. Because they knew he would not fail them; he never had. And he would not this time.

The vehicles drew ever closer to the abandoned Vaquero, and finally *El Tejón* had them slow to a snail's pace. "Do you see anything?" he asked Domingo.

"No. I don't think they would have had time to get over the top yet, even if they plan to run all the way to Victoria Base. So they are in the trees, somewhere. Maybe watching us."

"Of course they're watching us. Let them watch." He eyed the armored vehicle, then the slopes surrounding them on three sides, then the men standing in the flat bed of the truck. If their prey had been interested in ambushing them, they would never get a better target than a truckful of men. But no shots broke the stillness of the valley air. He climbed out of the Toyota.

"Spread out," he told his men, gesturing. "Keep your eyes open. See if you can find where they went. Their tracks should not be too hard to find." Would it be a chase up and down the mountains? His hope for an easy grab at the crash site had been foolish, he saw that now—*when did things ever go easy?*—but a little exercise would not kill his men. And he had no doubt he could push them harder than the *escaras* would be willing to travel. It was only a matter of time, now.

The men jumped down and spread out in a skirmish line on the grass, rifles up. They advanced slowly, heads turning this way and that, but there was nothing to be seen. *El Tejón* followed behind them, eyeing the open rear door of the Vaquero. There was something back there, maybe some gear they left rather than carry it up the slopes.

The line of men approached the Vaquero. "*Comandante!* There is a body back here," one of the men excitedly called to him. That got the attention of a few other soldiers, and they clustered around the vehicle

"*Escara*," someone spat.

"What is that?" They were staring at the big case on the floor in the back. One of the men pulled it out and flipped open the lid.

"Empty."

"There is a drone back here." The man held it up. *El Tejón* was glad to see it—maybe he could use it to scout the slopes and spy his prey.

"What else did they leave?" Eager to find more spoils a man climbed up into the back of the gun truck and began searching the body of the American. Some peered in the windows, cupping hands around their eyes to better see.

"*Idiotas!*" Domingo yelled at them. "Like a cat with something shiny. We are not here for you to fill your pockets. Find where they went."

One guerilla opened the driver's door of the Vaquero to look inside. He heard a clicking sound and something heavy hit his foot. He looked to see what it was. There was an object in the grass and he stared at it for a second. Then his eyes flew wide. "*Grenada!*" he screamed, and had time to take one step before it exploded.

* * *

The muffled *Crump!* of the grenade going off was quieter than he'd thought it would be. Then there was shouting, and full auto weapons fire. None of it came anywhere near them; it seemed to be directed into the trees immediately around the Vaquero, far down the slope. Seamus peeked around the tree he was behind and looked downhill, but couldn't see anything. A single voice rose above the shooting, and the firing tapered off. An officer or sergeant, Seamus presumed. There was more shouting, much of it angry, and at least one person crying out in pain.

"The hell was that?" Roger hissed at him from fifty feet away. Seamus looked over to see Roger had gotten partway to his feet to look over the rocks at him. His face was twisted up in pain.

Seamus violently gestured for him to get down, and put a finger across his lips. But then he tapped one of the grenades hanging off his armor, so the man would understand what had happened. Roger frowned, then ducked back behind the rocks.

Seamus looked at where Roger and the girl were in relation to the PKM and Mike. He decided that their right flank was covered better than the left, and moved away from the rock pile. About a hundred feet away there was a thick tree that had his name written all over it, and he moved quickly and quietly in that direction.

* * *

Mike jumped at the explosion and gunfire and ducked back behind his tree, sweaty and scared. As soon as he figured out everything seemed to be happening far below him he peeked out. The uneven ground falling away before him was empty. He could hear distant shouts and curses of men. A lot of men. With nothing to do, his imagination began to run wild, and fear worse than he'd ever felt before froze him solid.

He stared down at the Blackbird in his hands in disbelief. What the hell was he doing? He wasn't a soldier. It was a crazy dream that was turning into a nightmare, but he couldn't wake up. He could hear men screaming in pain and smell smoke. This wasn't fun anymore. It wasn't an adventure; it was terrifying.

* * *

"*¡Comandante! ¿Esta bien?*" Domingo rushed over to him.

El Tejón sat up in the grass, his ears ringing so loudly he barely heard his lieutenant. Domingo had blood running down his face.

"Yes, I am fine. See to the men." He waved him off and looked at the scene in front of him.

The Vaquero had blocked most of the grenade's blast, but the armored vehicle was the reason so many of his men had been clustered in a tight circle. The blast had lifted it a few inches into the air. The vehicle now listed in the grass, tires shredded, with smoke pouring steadily from under the hood. He saw at least two bodies on the grass, not moving, and many men were wounded. Several of the wounded were clutching at their legs, and he realized that they'd been hit by shrapnel flying beneath the Vaquero as they huddled around it like dumb cows. He shook his head and cursed their stupidity. He was stunned, but he'd been far enough away to avoid any damage from the blast—or so he thought. It was only when he tried to stand up that he realized he had been injured.

Balancing on one foot he pulled up a pantleg to see that he was missing a chunk from his right calf. Painful, but not serious or life threatening. Limping slightly, he walked over to watch Domingo and one of the other soldiers providing first aid to several of the wounded. Most of the other men were doing nothing but standing around in shock. That would not do.

"You! You! And you!" *El Tejón* barked, pointing at the three men in turn. "Spread out. Watch the trees and our rear, make sure we do not have any unwanted visitors while we tend to the injured. The rest of you—whoever is not wounded, I want you at the base of the slopes. Find where they began climbing! Their tracks should be obvious."

"*Si, Jefe.*"

Domingo fought valiantly to save the life of the most severely injured man, but he'd been hit throughout the body by a dozen pieces of shrapnel. He bled out in minutes. There were two other men with serious injuries—they'd live, but were out of the chase. A handful of others had minor wounds but could still fight. Their wounds were tended to while the other guerrillas stared up at the slopes around them, gripping their rifles.

"You are injured?" Domingo asked him worriedly, wiping his bloody hands on the grass. He could see the blood on his *Comandante's* pant leg.

"My pride." A shake of his head. "It is nothing." He surveyed what was left of his men. Three dead here, and two too injured to continue. Tuco was dead, and Chi-Chi was one of the two too injured to continue; both had been veterans he could hardly spare. He'd left Guerrero with four vehicles and twenty-five men. He'd lost half his vehicles and, counting wounded, over half of his men. The drone controller was shredded and useless. What men he had left were scared. And he hadn't yet laid eyes on the people he was pursuing. This could not continue.

He walked back to the pickup, and he bent over to grab a bottle of water off the floorboard, but he felt a buzz in his pocket. *El Tejón* pulled the satellite phone out and checked the display. Encrypted incoming call. He punched in the four-digit decryption code and put the phone up to his ear as he walked toward the rear of the pickup, away from his men.

"*¿Si?*"

"We have been expecting an update." The satellite connection made the man's voice flat but *El Tejón* had no trouble recognizing the voice of his immediate superior, General Aponte.

"Yes sir. I was waiting to call until I had something to tell you."

"Oh? Video feed from the drone indicated the strike was on target, and should have downed the helicopter. Have you reached the crash site?"

El Tejón took a deep breath. This was not going to be enjoyable. "I sent my two fastest vehicles ahead to search for the downed aircraft. They found the helicopter, but apparently were ambushed. The target is now on foot in the area. We are in pursuit."

"Ambushed?" The General's tone was icy. "How many men did you lose?"

He took another deep breath. "I have lost nine men so far. The crash was apparently not severe, and the *escaras*—"

"Of course the crash wasn't severe; we wanted the target alive!" the General shouted in his ear. "You've lost nine men? How many escaras have your men killed?"

"Several," *El Tejón* lied. "In spite of being ambushed. My men were so ferocious even in defeat the *escaras* ran like dogs. But we are close now, and they are on foot in the hills. They cannot escape."

"Have you even seen them yet? Do you even know if the target is still alive?" The General sounded apoplectic.

"The crash only killed one *escara*. After the ambush they saw us coming and panicked. They abandoned their vehicle and took to the hills. But I am sure the target is with them, and we are in close pursuit."

"*Comandante*, you were given this assignment because you seemed to be capable of handling it. But talking to you, I am not reassured."

"Sir, we will accomplish our mission. Nothing short of death will stop us."

The General seemed almost to growl. "That is what I am afraid of. Do not disappoint us. And keep us updated on any developments."

"Yes, Sir," he responded, but he was talking to a dead line.

He closed his eyes and put the phone away, feeling the sweat on his forehead. First, he gathered his thoughts, then he gathered his men at the base of the nearest slope. The tracks of their prey in the pine needles were fresh and obvious. "If this was supposed to be an easy mission, I would have asked for idiots, but I asked Colonel Taveras for his best men, and he gave me you," *El Tejón* said to the faces all around him. "The *escaras* kill us while hiding in the sky, while cowering behind their armor. Most of them fight like cowards, but," he said, sweeping his arm at the hills around them, "today they have no aircraft, no armor, no radio. They are a trespasser in our country, on foot, and today they will get the kind of fight they deserve, against the kind of men they most fear. You." He looked at them pointedly, then up at the hills.

"They are probably up there waiting for us. Not many of them, less than we have here, and they will be scared. You know how important this mission is. Failure will not be tolerated. Even if they put up a fight, it will not matter, because you know what is at stake. You will not fail me, you will not fail the cause." He looked at them and saw the pride on their faces.

He lowered his voice. "The two injured will stay here and wait for our return, guarding the vehicles. That leaves eleven of us, and we will split into three groups. Three men will go straight up, following the tracks. Four will go to either side, to flank the *escaras*. And surprise them, if they are waiting. Maybe they are still running *como* rabbits, but we will find out. I will be with the group on the right, in the fight with you." He unshouldered his MPX submachine gun and extended its stock. "Now move, quietly. You have all been shown pictures of our target." He paused. "Kill everyone else."

* * *

Far to the south General Miguel Aponte stared at the satellite phone in his hand. He had an expression as if he'd eaten something that was now seriously disagreeing with him. The speaker had been on for the call and he looked around the room.

"We sent four vehicles and how many men?" General Ruben Flores asked from the far side of the billiard table. Flores was tall and slender with thick black hair, almost the exact physical opposite of Aponte, who was short, squat, and bald. He sipped whiskey from a glass tumbler, then set it back on the bar.

"Enough so that if some got captured or killed during the trip north there would still be enough to get the job done, yet not so many as to immediately attract attention," Aponte told him. They'd argued for weeks about the plan. Ultimately, they'd all signed off on it. And now, at the first hint of trouble, they wanted to start assigning blame. Flores, especially and as usual. "That they made it that far north without incident I find surprising." He studied the hardcopy map of the area spread out on the billiard table.

"So do I, listening to that *cabrón*. So cocky last week, and now when it is time, when we need him most, all he has for us is excuses." Flores looked over the liquor choices as the whiskey was about gone. The bar in the hacienda's game room did not have much of a selection. The room was well appointed, with an expensive billiard table, dart board on the wall, bar, leather chairs, and a flat screen so big it took up most of one wall. The stucco walls were painted a friendly peach color that did not fit the mood of the occupants. Idly he wondered who the last occupants of the villa had been. *La Fuerza* had liberated it some time in the past, but had only been using it for about a year, mostly a staging area for men and supplies. Command staff had been on site for less than a month.

"This is too great an opportunity for *La Fuerza*, we must not fail!" General Martin Ramos shouted. He had been leaning against the wall and shoved himself off of it, jabbing a finger at Aponte. "You picked this man!" His deep voice echoed around the stucco walls, and the man guarding the doorway glanced into the room briefly.

Aponte seethed inside but didn't let it show. Ramos was always criticizing others' decisions rather than making any of his own. It was safer. "*El Comandante* is a skilled field commander, that was how he was chosen for this mission in the first place," Aponte reminded his fellow Generals. "I have faith that he will do his best."

"Yes, but will that be good enough?" a voice asked from behind them. The three generals turned. Timotéo Sandoval rose from the leather chair and walked to the billiard table, where he placed a hand on the map. Sandoval looked nearly ten years younger than his true age of sixty, which added to his mystique. He had only a touch of gray in his close-cropped beard and the trim body of a much younger man. The famous pearl-handled knife at his belt glinted off the sub-dued lighting in the room. "Show me, where did the helicopter go down?"

"Right in this area," Aponte told him, pressing a finger to the paper.

Sandoval studied the map, frowning. "Closer than I would like to Victoria Base, but there doesn't seem to be anything in the area but mountains." He backed up half a step and took in the whole map, eyed how far north Aponte's finger was compared to their usual operating areas. "If this Comandante fails, how far away are our next closest forces? I know we don't have any men stationed that far north, much less equipment or vehicles."

Ramos cleared his throat, and a greasy smile slid over his face. "That is not entirely accurate."

* * *

Manuel wrestled the armored SUV through the light traffic on the *Circuito Exterior Mexiquense*. To the right were the endless streets, filled by the millions of people living in and around Mexico City. At one point, the population of the greater Mexico City area had been pushing 25 million, but the war had caused many people to flee the country. To the left of the highway was the airport, stretching long and flat. There were several rows of chain link fences topped with razor wire separating the highway from the airport property, as well as concrete barriers.

"What do you think happened?" he asked. When he got no response he looked at Beni in the front passenger seat. The quiet man was staring out the window. "Do you think it was a crash? Maybe she never got on the helicopter."

Beni turned to look at him, then went back to staring out the window.

"If it was an Army helicopter, I'd be worried, but it was Raven, right? Their helicopters are better, and their pilots are much better. Even if they had problems it probably just set down somewhere out of radio range." Manuel looked at Beni again, but got no response. But that was Beni, always keeping everything inside. Manuel, he talked through everything, especially when he was nervous. He glanced out at the huge open space of the airport behind the fences.

Finished two years late and eighteen percent over budget, the new Mexican International Airport—officially *Aeropuerto Internacional de la Ciudad de Mexico*—was the biggest and had been expected to be the busiest airport in Latin America. Built in the *Zona Federal del Lago de Texcoco*—the Lake Texcoco lakebed—the construction project ended up taking seven years. Situated northeast of the city, the X-shaped main terminal was six million square feet and featured an airy lightweight roof with spans in excess of 100 meters. Initially, the airport sported three runways, two 4.5 km in length and one 4 km in length, with room for an additional three runways. In aviation terms it was referred to as a "hot and high" airport—due to the high elevation and high temperatures the air was thinner, so airplanes taking off required longer runways.

Unfortunately, the airport was finished in the early days of the war, and within three years, it had been attacked twice by FRAP. The airport was still the busiest in Mexico, but because of the war, it had fallen to fourth busiest in Latin America behind Sao Paolo-Guarulhos and Rio de Janeiro in Brazil and El Dorado in Colombia.

The Mexican Army didn't have enough troops to fight the war, much less protect high value targets, so it contracted site security out to various companies. Because it was a Tier 1 target, Raven provided physical security for the airport, at a hefty fee.

Manuel downshifted and barely touched the brakes as he took the exit used mostly by airport employees heading in to work. The swerving SUV was honked at fiercely by several slow-moving vehicles. He took the turn toward the private hangars and pulled up to the security checkpoint with a tiny chirp of rubber.

The Raven employees working security at the airport were not the same breed fighting the war, but they were a step above normal security guards. The two men who stepped out of the guard shack were Mexican nationals and wore dark blue well-maintained airport security uniforms, complete with sidearms.

Manuel rolled down the window and from the passenger seat Beni leaned over. "Señor Echevarria," he said curtly.

The guard stiffened and looked to his partner, who had just verified the license plate on the vehicle. His partner nodded, and without another word, the first guard stepped back inside the small building and hit the button to open the gate. Manuel drove along the backs of the private hangars, directly toward the small military section of the airport.

The runway at China Base was too short for Señor Echevarria's Gulfstream G850, even though it was the fastest non-military aircraft in the country. But he had gotten on the phone, called in some favors, and as soon as they cleared the more heavily armed guards at the second gate separating the military section from the rest of the airport, Beni pointed at the V-35 Peregrine sitting on the concrete pad in front of them.

"That is the ugliest helicopter I've ever seen," Manuel said, staring at it. "It would make fat girls feel pretty. And thin." The big craft had two short wings, each tipped with a rotor. As it sat on the pad the wings were vertical, the rotors aimed at the sky. Manuel had seen airplanes like this before; when it took off the wings would rotate forward and act as giant propellers. It was halfway between a helicopter and a plane, and looked as awkward as a newborn horse. It had a camouflage paint job, splotches of greens, browns, and tan.

"Stop here and let me out," Beni told him. As soon as the SUV stopped, Beni jumped out. "Park and grab your gear," he told Manuel as he grabbed his bag from the back seat. "I will find the pilot." He jogged off.

"You the VIP?" Ted Billings looked the lean Mex up and down. A hard type to be sure, but dressed in an expensive suit. The pilot didn't know what to make of him. "Buddy, I don't know who the hell you are, but you must have some pull if you can get Lucille to do taxi duty when there's an offensive going on." The frontline heavily-armed tiltrotor craft could transport 30 soldiers and their gear in addition to the four-man crew; instead they were burning fuel for only two guys. Billings wasn't so young and gung ho that he was itching to be where the bullets were flying, but he didn't like his time being wasted either. Still, orders were orders, and these had come from someone so far up the food chain, they were only two steps removed from God.

"Lucille?"

Billings slapped the side of the fuselage with a gloved hand. "That's her name. She and I have been through a lot together." He eyed the man in the suit, who looked maybe thirty-five. "Where are we going?"

"China Base."

Billings pulled out his map and checked it quickly, frowning. "Okay, 700 kilometers, not quite 450 miles, we can make it there easy with the fuel we've got in the bird since we're flying nearly empty.

Better radio ahead and make sure they've got some juice there to fill us back up." He eyed the second Mex as he jogged up carrying a bag of his own. Both their bags looked heavy. The second man was a bit younger and stocky with muscle. Also in an expensive suit. Not his regular clientele at all. Were they spooks? Mexican government didn't run a lot of white collar intelligence operatives, but they didn't quite look like civilians, either. "Just the two of you, right?'

"*Sí*. When can we leave?"

"Soon as my crew gets back from hitting the head and playing grabass with the *señoritas* in there. Go ahead and store your gear in back, and pick a seat. Flight time's going to be just under two hours."

* * * * *

Chapter Eleven

Corey was hunkered down behind the fallen tree, PKM against his shoulder. He could just see Seamus far off to the left, peeking out from behind his tree, and the kid was off to the right, but closer. Beside him, the pilot was breathing heavily, nervous. Corey himself felt a few pangs of fear, but that was natural. He was scared, but he wasn't worried. On high ground with a belt-fed, with his armor and helmet and a big tree for additional cover in front of him? He'd been in far worse situations. And Seamus O'Malley had his left flank. The man had been working for Raven in Mexico since Raven had been in Mexico, longer than just about anyone, and the stories about him, if even half of them were true, shit, if even *one* of them was true….

The human eye spots movement much more easily than it does colors. Camouflage doesn't do you much good if you're moving, even the reactive camouflage of his armored uniform. Seamus stayed behind the big tree he'd picked and edged his head out enough to peer down the slope with one eye. Nothing.

Between the uneven ground and the tree trunks and the occasional bush he could see downslope maybe thirty meters. The entire valley was quiet, with the occasional chirp of a bird or the scratch of a squirrel. The air was dry, strong with the scent of pine needles. The ground underneath his boots was soft with a layer of decomposing needles several inches thick. It made traversing the slope treacherous, but the brown needles muffled footsteps as effectively as pillow down. The last he'd heard from the guerrillas was some faint talking several minutes before, then nothing. He assumed that meant they were on their way.

* * *

The slope would have been difficult to climb even if he hadn't had a chunk torn from his leg. *El Tejón* could feel the wound throbbing under the field dressing, but he did his best to ignore it. He wasn't used to the elevation either. With his feet slipping in the dead pine needles it was unnatural to look at anything but where he was going to step next, but he forced himself to scan the slope above him and to either side, looking for any movement, anything that stuck out. The slower pace meant at least he wasn't gasping for air.

He was as far to the right of the men following the tracks up the slope as he could be and still keep them in view. The difficult terrain aside, they were moving deliberately so as to not walk into an ambush. Not that there was a lot of cover for their prey to hide behind; under the tall trees there was little but the occasional scraggly bush and jumble of fallen branches.

El Tejón stepped behind a tree and looked behind him. He couldn't tell how far they were above the valley floor, but the vehicles were blocked from view by the trees. The three men with him were spread out along the slope, moving carefully but not using the trees for cover as much as he would have liked. They seemed convinced that the people they were pursuing were still on the run and likely over the ridgeline, and he couldn't say they were wrong. But still....

"Move from tree to tree," he said very quietly to the men, and demonstrated a zig-zag pattern up the slope with his hand.

"*Sí, Comandante,*" the man closest to him said, panting in the thin air. He stepped behind the trunk of a red pine and slung his rifle over his shoulder. From his belt he produced a canteen and took a long pull from it. The soldier sighed in pleasure at the cool water coursing down his throat, then his head burst apart like a dropped melon. Everyone around him instinctively dropped to the ground as the sound of the rifle shot echoed around the valley.

Lying on the ground *El Tejón* stared in shock at the lifeless body of his man sliding down the hill, most of his head gone. The bullet had passed right through the tree the man had been using as cover, a tree with a trunk two feet thick—how was that possible? Somewhere above them a machine gun opened up, and men started screaming.

* * *

By the time Leonidas came down out of recoil, the men around the soldier he'd targeted had dropped to the ground and were scrambling for cover. Seamus fired at them as Corey opened up with the PKM. He'd been pretty sure the black beauty would zip right through the tree trunk, and he'd seen the bloody spray from the hit that proved he'd been right.

There was yelling, and the guerrillas opened up on full-auto. Seamus tucked himself behind the tree but none of the incoming fire hit close to him, it seemed to be concentrated on Corey. The young contractor was firing controlled bursts at the men downslope, chewing up the trees they'd taken cover behind. Hansen was next to him, firing single shots at any movement.

Seamus took a deep breath, then leaned out from his tree, rifle up. He caught one of the FRAP bastards out in the open thirty meters downslope and put a bullet through his chest. As the man fell, a look of surprise on his face, he squeezed the trigger of the AK in his hands. With one long burst he emptied the magazine of the rifle. The bullets whipped by Seamus and clattered upslope, some spanging off rocks. Seamus heard a very feminine scream, but didn't let himself get distracted. He fired at glimpses of movement, put bullets through every tree trunk that was a likely hiding spot, even as Corey continued to pour full auto fire at the guerrillas. There was a lot of shouting downslope of him, mostly curses.

Seamus emptied his magazine and grabbed a second. As he was reloading one of the guerrillas must have spotted him. Bullets kicked up dirt all around, and he felt a few thud into the tree he was hiding behind. The incoming sounded like it was from a submachine gun, which meant it didn't have nearly enough power to penetrate the tree trunk. Enemy return fire increased, but nothing else hit nearby. When he popped out from the tree, Leonidas up, the guerrillas were calling out a retreat and running down the hill, firing blindly behind them as they went. Seamus fired at them, but they were jumping down the steep slope and sliding on loose needles, falling and rolling; they were out of sight so fast he didn't think he hit anyone else.

Seamus waited for a minute, which was long enough for his hearing to begin to return to normal. There was no more return fire, only distant shouts. It sounded as if the guerrillas had retreated all the way down the slope to the valley floor. He jogged across the slope to the rockpile and peered over it.

"Everyone still alive?"

Roger was grim-faced, Tina was pale and looked terrified, but they both nodded at him.

"Cracking," Seamus told them. He pointed upslope. "Ladies and gents, time to gather your potpourri and gift bags and exit to the rear."

Roger frowned. "Why? They're not going to try that again." Roger was pleasantly surprised at how quickly the guerrillas had fled once the shooting had started.

"No, they're going to try something different. They're not going to bugger off. And we don't want to be here when next they show up." He held out his hand to the older man and Roger reluctantly took it. Seamus saw the man wince as he pulled him up.

"I know your back hurts. But we've got no choice. Rita, if you could keep helping him, maybe we can stay far enough ahead of these bastards to make it to Victoria Base without losing anyone else."

"It's Tina," she said reflexively.

Seamus scanned the slope above them. The ground seemed to get a little more friendly fifty meters up. "Get going, we'll catch up," he told them.

"But—" Roger began.

Seamus cut him off. "You're the slowest moving nesh here. Get your arse moving up that hill." Then he headed for Corey.

"That was over almost before it began," Corey said, nearly sounding disappointed. There were a few wisps of smoke trailing from the barrel of the PKM. Hansen had only fired a few rounds from Corey's carbine, and shooting left-handed he had no idea if he'd hit any of the dodging shapes he'd seen downhill. Corey had been doing most of the shooting, showering the pilot with hot brass cases.

"Aye. We could hold off a hundred trained men on this slope. But them running off so quick...I don't know if that means they're dodgy cowards or smart and recognized they were in a meat grinder. Let's not stick around to find out. Bin the pig, grab the Ulfberht and start heading up."

Corey stared at the PKM. He'd barely burned through half the 100-round belt. "Not that I love the thought of dragging it up and down more hills, but why the hell do you want me to leave the PKM and take the dinosaur rifle?"

"I think this just turned into a footrace, and we're going to need to move as fast as possible. The pig will just slow us down. That," he pointed at Roger's big hunting rifle, "that might be his dinosaur-hunting rifle of choice, but that's not what it *is*. That is one of the finest heavy sniper rifles ever made, capable of killing a man a mile away. We might need to do just that. Plus, you know," he said with a shrug, "dinosaurs. The smell of blood's in the air. Head on up after Rudd and the girl and keep them moving as fast as possible. I'll see about his son."

Seamus found Mike right where he expected to find him, about a hundred feet past Corey's position, standing behind a thick tree trunk. The boy looked stunned.

"Son! Time to go. You unhurt? Good. Let's go catch up to your father. That was a bit exciting, wasn't it? Lots of shooting on our part, lots of arse over tit on theirs. Anybody pop up this way?" Seamus looked downslope but didn't immediately see anything.

"Um, I—I think I saw three. Three or four." Mike was blinking erratically.

Seamus cocked his head. "And?" He stared at the boy pointedly, then looked around again. There, about twenty-five meters away, there was something on the ground....a body? And another about ten meters to the side.

Mike looked at Seamus, then down at his feet. "They...they didn't see me. They were looking over at the other shooting, coming up as fast as they could. And then...when I fired...they didn't hear it. Because of the suppressor." He looked at the Blackbird in his hands, then up at the soldier. "They never—I mean when I was shooting they didn't even...they just kept running up the slope. Right at me. Didn't—didn't know I was..."

"Son, how many did you shoot?" Seamus asked gently.

"All of them." The boy seemed about to cry, and swallowed loudly.

Seamus blinked twice, then told the teenager firmly, "Good. Better us than them. I knew I was right to trust you over here on your own." He put his hand on Mike's shoulder and gently moved him. "Now go find your father and help him get up the hill. I'll go check on these knobs who bothered you. Go," he told Mike, when the boy hesitated. "There's more where these bastards came from, and they're not going to leave us alone even if we ask nicely. We don't want to be here when they get back." Seamus watched him walk away, still apparently in some minor state of shock.

Mike stopped after going about thirty feet and turned around. "Don't tell my dad about this, okay?" His dad had been so upset about him shooting one guy, maybe, and here he'd shot at least three for sure. He was freaking out.

Seamus stared at him for a second, then nodded. "Mum's the word," he agreed. "Now go. But reload, if you didn't already." He watched to make sure the boy kept moving. Then Seamus turned and started down the hill, wanting to examine at least a few of the bodies. Maybe they'd be carrying some information that could tell him specifically who they were, or if he was right about why they were after his group.

* * *

"C'mon, up you go, let's keep moving," Seamus told Roger, grabbing his elbow to help him over a rocky patch. He'd taken over for the girl, who looked exhausted, although they were nearly to the top of the ridgeline. They found themselves walking through patches of sunlight. The slope was getting gentler, and the trees were thinning out a bit. "We get up to the top it'll be easy as biscuits," Seamus assured him. Roger was sweating heavily, fighting against the pain with every step.

Corey was up ahead of them, scouting. He came pushing back through the bristly bushes as Seamus and Roger finally reached the top of the ridge. The trees were thin enough that Seamus had a clear view all around for miles, at least where there weren't higher peaks to block his sightline. There were no roads or buildings to be seen, just trees and scattered clearings. To the east, the hogback ridges appeared to get progressively higher, and they all seemed to be running roughly north/south. He was pretty sure they were in the Mexican state of Nuevo Léon. Whether they were technically in the Sierra Madre Oriental mountains or still in the foothills or even on the edge of the Mexico plateau didn't much matter. Roger Rudd was having a hard time, but the elevations around them would barely be considered foothills in the Rockies. The real mountains were to the east.

Seamus pointed south and spoke just loud enough for everyone to hear him. "Let's follow the top of this as far as it will take us. The less up-and-down we have to do the better." Far to the south the ground seemed to get flatter, but maybe that was simply an optical illusion.

Once they'd reached the nearly even ground everyone seemed to want to rest, but Seamus would have none of that. "Rest while you're walking. I'll take point," he told Corey. "You follow up behind, and keep the stragglers moving." He wanted to start running, or at least jogging, for he knew the guerrillas would be right after them, but simply walking was a struggle for the would-be dinosaur hunter, and Hansen's broken arm didn't make him any faster.

They walked in silence, the group spread out in an uneven line. Roger couldn't quite do a normal pace, but the uneven ground on top of the ridge was much easier to traverse than the steep slope. The pain still hit him short and sharp with every step, but he pushed himself against it. It was a pinched disc, or a torn muscle; nothing compared to what he'd suffer if the guerrillas caught up to them. He looked around and saw Mike was half a dozen steps behind him, looking glum. Roger wanted to sit down and talk with him, let him know that it was okay what he'd done back at the crash site, that he still loved him, but he and Mike didn't exactly have a history of heart-to-heart talks. And their current situation didn't exactly lend itself to conversation. At least he'd made it through the brief gun-fight on the hill without a scratch.

"You okay?" Roger asked his son quietly, panting a bit in the thin air.

Mike looked up and saw his father starting back at him. Mike swallowed and nodded and looked away, trying to push away the flashback images filling his head.

"I'm proud of you," Roger told him. "Don't worry, we'll get through this."

* * *

"Did you think this would be easy?" *El Tejón* spat at his men. Those with prior combat experience looked angry, which was good. The virgins who'd just been blooded on the mountain looked terrified, which was to be expected. "If it was easy, anyone could do it." He laughed, trying hard not to make it sound forced. He looked around, and did a quick head count of men. Six, he'd lost another six men. *Madre de dios.* He was down to less than a third of the force he'd started with, and had yet to catch more than a glimpse of a shadow of his prey, or hear anything other than the girlish scream somewhere above him as he was ducking behind a tree. His men had been firing wildly, mostly as they retreated, and he doubted they'd hit anything.

He looked at the slope they'd just run down, then the ones to either side. He pointed off to the right. "We go up here. Quick as cats, quiet as mice. At the top we will turn left and pick up their trail, which should not be hard to spot. They will be heading south by east most likely, toward Victoria Base." Their commander treated them all to a flat stare. "You are brave men, young and strong with the will to fight these imperialist Americans and their traitorous lackeys. I have shown you the picture of who we are after. Do any of you doubt that we can catch them in these hills? Not just catch them, but catch them quickly?"

They shook their heads at him. "Of course not!" he crowed. "And we will avenge our fallen comrades, do not doubt that. Collect your gear. Domingo, lead them up the hill."

El Comandante turned to the men sitting in the pickup truck. Chi-Chi had suffered a dozen shrapnel wounds to his legs from the grenade. None of them had punctured any major blood vessels, but he was too torn up to continue on foot. The soldier with him was barely out of his teens, and his left arm had been torn down to the bone by the grenade blast. Domingo had wrapped the wound up tightly, and luckily that was enough to slow the bleeding to a trickle. If he'd had to apply a tourniquet that would not have boded well for the arm.

"You two," *El Tejón* told the injured men. "I do not know how long we might be gone, but you are here to guard these trucks for when we return. They will get us home safely." He looked around the narrow valley, at the slopes above them. "We are out of the way here, nearly out of sight, so you should not be bothered by the Army or *escaras*, but stay alert." He glanced at the back of the troop carrier. They'd placed the bodies of the grenade victims there. He wished he had a tarp or blanket with which to cover them, but nothing of the sort was available. The flies were gathering above the bodies, and soon they would begin to smell. Such was war; an ugly business, but necessary. He hoped they'd have an opportunity to recover the bodies on the slope, and at the crash site, but knew that was a practical impossibility. If—when, when they returned with their captive, they would need to head south, and quickly.

"*Si, Comandante.*"

El Tejón slapped Chi-Chi on the shoulder then jogged after the rest of his men.

* * *

Seamus leading the way, they followed the top of the ridge for half a mile, wending through sparse bushes and long grass for the most part. The ridge sloped gently downward, so they were able to make much better time than they had climbing the steep slope. Still, the fast walking pace felt no better than crawling to Corey and Seamus who knew the guerrillas wouldn't be far behind. Corey had to keep pressing Roger to maintain a good pace.

The ridge angled west and kept dropping, and finally Seamus had them leave it and turn east. The ground was level and they walked through tall dry grass and rosewood bushes, prickly pear cacti and small succulents, scaring off birds and a few chipmunks. They pushed through a small copse of ponderosa pines, trudging between their thin reddish trunks, and started up the slope of the adjoining hill. "Oh great," Roger gasped, looking upward, "another hill." Even walking downhill hurt, and there were shooting pains lancing through his entire back, but he took a deep breath and started up the incline. The first half of the gentle slope in front of him was open meadow, mostly brown grass with scattered low cacti and scrub brush.

The group walked past blooming cholla cacti with their pink flowers and blue and yellow wildflowers in the grass, blind to the beauty all around them. The shadows of small wispy clouds scudded across the hills, and the call of a predator bird echoed far off. The grade was much less steep than the first hill, and they kept a good pace, even Roger.

At the treeline Seamus stopped and looked behind them. The group's path through the grass was clearly visible from a distance, all the way to the belt of pines. He turned back around and watched the girl and Rudd Senior trudging up the slope in the shadow of the trees—mostly pines, with a few firs and broadleaved diehards mixed in. The tracks under the trees were easy to follow, but could only be seen from a few feet away.

Seamus snagged Corey as the younger man was heading by. "You have any wire on you? Cord, spare shoelaces, anything?"

"There's a small spool of paracord in the pack on your back," Corey told him. "Stuffed it there myself. What do you have in mind?" He stared back at the way they'd come, expecting at any minute to see their pursuers. He scanned the slopes looking for movement, colors, listening for the sounds of men. So far, nothing, but at the speed they were travelling, it was only a matter of time.

"Giving us some breathing room," Seamus said. He eyed the obvious scuffmarks of shoes through the dead needles and struggling grass inside the treeline, and studied a pair of younger oaks on either side of the tracks.

At the top of the slope, Mike and the pilot, Hansen, broke through a line of bushes to find themselves once again in the warmth of the sun. They blinked in the light and looked around, only to discover they were standing on an old dirt path of some sort.

"This will be a lot easier to walk on."

Hansen looked at the teenager. "I doubt we'll be sticking on the path."

"Why not? It's headed in the right direction." He pointed to the south over the winding dirt trail.

"I don't know. Seems like that's what they'd expect us to do. I'm not looking to get caught."

The rest of the group arrived almost all at once, everyone gasping in the thin air. They stared at the unexpected path before them and blinked in the bright light.

"Are we taking it?" Roger asked. The hardpacked dirt looked so much easier to walk on. And the path was nearly level, running along the crest of a ridge.....

Seamus looked up the trail in one direction, then the other. He moved away from the group so he could study the ground. At first he thought it might be a wild game trail, but it was too wide. It had to be manmade. He didn't see any tracks in the dirt, though, no footprints or tire treads, so it had not been used recently. An old hiking trail? He lifted up one boot and looked at the ground beneath, then stomped and raised his boot again. "Yes," he told them, pointing to the south. He kept his voice low; he knew how far sounds could travel in the hills. "We can make better time, and it'll be harder to track us. This ground is so firm you can hardly tell where it's been trod on. We needed some luck; maybe this is it. Everybody take a bottle of water out of this pack and drink it as we move, this mountain air is dry. But don't throw away the bottles, no need to leave the wankers breadcrumbs."

The weight on his shoulders lightened noticeably as the group dug out half a dozen bottles from the pack. Corey handed one to Seamus and an energy bar.

"Walk while you drink," Seamus told them. They were just standing there sucking down water. He looked at Roger and said pointedly, "As fast as you can."

He walked next to the sweating man as Roger emptied his water bottle in a few quick gulps. "So where should I put this?" he asked Seamus, gesturing with the empty bottle. They were at the tail end of the group, with Mike and Corey on point maybe twenty yards ahead. The pilot and the girl were having a quiet conversation as they walked.

"Top of my ruck still open? Stuff it in there." He paused long enough and bent down slightly so Rudd could stuff the empty water bottle inside the pack, then he was off again. Roger struggled to keep up with him. His elbow that he'd banged in the crash was swollen and sore, and he couldn't fully straighten his left arm, but that was a mere distraction compared to the pain in his back. He made sure to keep the AK-47 in his hands pointed away from everyone else in the group. The rifle had been heavy when he'd picked it up, and it seemed twice as heavy now with his elbow throbbing worse than an infected tooth, but he'd be damned if he'd complain. He knew it was his slow pace endangering the group…and not just that. It was *him* endangering the group. He was the reason they were being pursued by the guerrillas, the terrorists. He was experiencing not a small amount of guilt over that.

"You want an energy bar?" Seamus asked him, holding one out.

"Thanks." Roger struggled a bit, figuring out how to unwrap it without dropping the rifle, but Seamus never stopped moving. Roger kept up with him, eventually tearing open the wrapper with his teeth. The bar was gone in three bites, and after he finished, Roger found he was hungrier than before he'd eaten.

The view from the hiking trail, if that's what it was, was rather scenic. The route it took ran along the crest of a line of rocky hills, heading generally south. There was a little up and down, but the hardpacked dirt made it a much easier trek. The sun was starting to drop off their right shoulders, and even though it was warm on their faces the air around them was cool. It would probably be a chilly night.

"Damned if it isn't a beautiful day out here," Seamus remarked, enjoying the light breeze on his face. He watched a hawk riding a thermal in the distance, and the smell of juniper was in the air. The hills around them had light tree cover, a conifer forest with the occasional oak and the rare clump maple, speckled green and brown. He saw no sign of man's presence other than the trail they were on. He turned around and walked backwards, keeping an eye on their rear. The trees were thicker behind them, completely blocking the view of the trail to anyone approaching from the direction they'd come. "How's the back?" he asked Rudd.

"It hurts," Roger replied tersely. He sighed and said, "Being fat doesn't help either. I was expecting to be driven around in some sort of luxury ATV tricked out for hunting, and instead I'm carrying an AK-47, being chased through the mountains by terrorists." He shook his head and snorted at the absurdity of the situation, then looked around at the surrounding hillsides as they walked.

"What's the frown about?" Seamus asked him.

"Nothing. Well, we're walking through forests and fields. But I haven't seen anything bigger than a squirrel. Paying as much as I did to PSI, I was expecting, I don't know—"

"Herds of dinosaurs traipsing about, begging to be shot?"

"I suppose. There's still a tiny bit of my brain still wondering if it's all a big scam. I know the creatures are real—I've seen video of them in zoos—but the idea of them wandering around out here in the wild but the Mexican government, our government, keeping it a secret...." He tried to shrug, which was a mistake.

"I've got more ibuprofen, but not much," Seamus told him, seeing the flinch and wince.

Roger shook his head. "Back's not too bad, walking on this. We stop for any length of time I think it'll really stiffen up, though. Save it for then."

"Don't plan on doing that any time soon. We have to assume they're racing to catch up. Even on this trail we're moving slow." *And as visible as panties on a church floor*, he thought. At least to anyone south of them. The bright sunlight made the walk nice and comfortable, but they were plainly visible to anyone who might be atop any of the adjoining hills.

"So what do we do? If they're going to catch us anyway?"

"Nothing's for sure, mate; don't fall into that pit of despair yet. One thing I do know for sure is that I was sugarcoating it before. What'll happen, when they catch us? They'll keep you alive, because you're money to them. But your boy, Michael? The only person who'd pay ransom for your son is you, and you're here. He's not valuable to them at all. They catch us, you they might tickle with their knives a bit, just for fun, but the rest of us are dead." He glanced up ahead and said softly, "Well, not the girl, but you don't want to even think about what they'll do to her. So I'd keep putting one foot in front of the other."

Roger scowled, then increased his pace enough that Seamus couldn't keep up with him walking backwards. The contractor smiled thinly to himself and nodded.

* * *

"You look like you know what you're doing with that thing," Corey told the kid as they followed the path. Mike made sure to always keep the rifle pointed away from everyone else as he walked, safety on, and kept his finger off the trigger.

The blood seemed to drain out of his face and pool in his stomach, where it churned, but Mike nodded and grunted out thanks. He glanced down at the Blackbird in his hands, then out at the surrounding hills.

"Is it okay to talk?" he whispered.

"Long as you're quiet." Corey nodded ahead of them. The slopes fell away in all directions. The path wound down a long thinly wooded slope and up another, clearly visible ahead for half a mile. "Trees are getting thin around here. Anybody out there will see us before they hear us, so keep your eyes open." The reactive camouflage and armor plates of his uniform were great in a firefight or an ambush, but it wasn't designed for comfort when it came to forced marches. Or maybe it was the damn dinosaur rifle on his shoulder; the thing was getting heavier with each step. He shifted it to his other shoulder and licked his lips in the dry air. They were starting to crack, and it was only going to get worse. He knew he was in front with the heavy rifle to set the pace for the kid's fat father in back, but he still moved at a brisk pace. This wasn't a nature walk, no matter how pretty the view. Between the rifle and the elevation, though, he doubted he was doing better than three, maybe three and a half miles per hour.

"Aren't they behind us?" Mike looked over his shoulder, but all he saw was the rest of the group strung out along the trail. Mike had the bag containing the magazines for the Ulfberht over one shoulder to spare Corey some weight. Over his other was the sling bag containing the Blackbird magazines, one of which was now more than half empty, but he didn't want to think about that.

"You plan for an enemy's capabilities, not his probabilities," Corey told him, breathing heavily.

Mike looked at the man who wasn't much older than he was. "How long have you been a soldier?"

Corey glanced at him, then back out at the nearby hills. "Seems like forever. But I've only been with Raven a few years. Before that I did four years in the Marines. Joined right out of high school." Corey didn't mind talking. It kept his mind off the weight on his shoulder, the chafing all over his body from the rubbing plates, the burning in his lungs....

"No college?"

Corey shook his head. "Never had any interest. I got good enough grades, but...." He would have shrugged if he hadn't had a heavy rifle on his shoulder. "Had two brothers, one older and one younger, and I was always fighting with them. All the time. And dad was pretty damn strict too. So going into the military didn't seem like it would be much of a change for me, except I'd be getting paid to get yelled at. Boot camp wouldn't be too bad, army life would be easy. And I'd get to shoot people and blow things up. At least, that's what I thought."

"Not so easy?"

"It was in some ways, in others it was a lot tougher. But I liked it and was good at the job. I had a combat MOS, and saw some action. No shortage of brushfire wars around the world even if you ignore the Caliphate. I found out that I could handle myself pretty well. So when my enlistment was up I joined Raven."

"But why? Why didn't you stay in the Marines?"

Corey looked at him and saw the expression on the kid's face. "What, and keep fighting for my country, instead of a corporation? Trust me, I am fighting for America, only the name at the top of the check's different."

"So then why'd you get out?"

"Seriously? You have any idea how much they pay? I'm making five times as much with Raven as I was in the service. I do this for another five years and I can retire. At age thirty."

"If you don't get killed," Mike couldn't help but blurt out.

"You can get killed crossing the street. Plane could crash into your house and kill you while you're sitting on the toilet. You could choke to death on a ham sandwich. At least out here if I die, it'll probably be because somebody was trying to kill me and was better at the job than I am. I'll take those odds. For the money, I will definitely take those odds."

* * *

"How bad is your arm?" Tina asked the pilot as they walked together. Her breath was short, and one of her lips had already split in the thin dry air.

"I get a sharp pain if I come down too hard on my heel, but mostly it just aches. I can move it a little bit, so it's only a hairline fracture or something like that. Luckily. Lot luckier than Delian."

Tina wasn't sure who Delian was, probably the co-pilot who died. She didn't know what to say about that. The pilot's face darkened. "Do you have any family?" she asked him, thinking changing the subject might be a good idea. Hansen was older than her, with a little gray in his hair, but she always found she had a hard time judging the age of black men. They didn't show the wrinkles nearly as much. When she asked about his family Hansen's face lit up.

"A daughter," he told her. "Emily." His hand moved to the front of his uniform, where there was something small and pink hanging from the second button. She hadn't noticed it before.

"What's that?"

Hansen glanced down, unaware he'd been rubbing it. He laughed. "It used to be a little plastic pony. She loves ponies and gave it to me as a good luck charm. But toys don't do well in combat zones." He pulled his hand away and she saw that it was now just a pink pony head dangling from his button. She smiled.

"She just turned five last month. I'm actually doing this for her, so she can afford to get into whatever college she wants. She's smart, like her mother, so if she wants to become a doctor or lawyer or biologist," he nodded at Tina, "working, flying for Raven for a few years will earn me the money to make that happen. Your father do the same for you?"

"Papi's never had any trouble making money in business. The cost of *universidad* was no problem, the problem was I was too much like a boy for him. He wanted to see me in dresses, like my sisters. Or maybe it's that he still thinks of me as that little girl, that five year old," she nodded at Hansen, a smile on her face, "with bows in her hair, playing with plastic ponies."

"Fathers never want to see their little girls grow up," Hansen admitted.

"Or discover boys," Tina added, her mouth twisted into a wry smile.

"Oh God no."

They both laughed, then abruptly stopped at a sound in the distance. The entire group slowed down and looked around as the booming sound echoed around the hills. They couldn't tell which direction it had come from. At the rear Seamus waved for them all to keep going.

"What was that?" Roger asked him.

"If you're being chased by a superior force, and you can't go faster," he nodded at Roger, "you do whatever you can to slow them down. Such as booby-trapping your trail with a grenade, so they're forced to slow down and keep an eye out for tripwires. It was a bodge job, but hopefully it was enough."

"Do you really think we can stay in front of them all the way to Victoria Base?"

Seamus shook his head. "No, but all we need to do is keep them from catching up by nightfall. After dark they won't be able to track us."

"Are you sure?"

Seamus half-turned as he walked and pointed at the trail behind them. "You can see our tracks in the dirt, but only if you're close. And that's in direct sunlight. At night, even with a full moon? Bollocks. I couldn't do it, so I know these sheep-shagging idiots can't.

Unless they've got torches and use them, in which case you don't need to worry about anything."

"Why?"

"Because that means they're bloody imbeciles."

"But even if they do stop because they can't see, they'll pick up our trail in the morning."

"Right. Which is why as soon as it's dark we'll get the hell off this trail. They'll probably keep going in hopes that we stopped to rest and they can ambush us while we nap. Hopefully they'll go right past the point we stepped off the trail and waste a lot of time backtracking in the morning when they realize their mistake. Right now all we have to worry about is making it until sunset. Speaking of which, I should set another tripwired grenade, keep those villains honest." His face split into a wide grin.

Roger looked at him and shook his head. "You are way too damn happy about all of this. Helicopter crash, gun fights, getting chased through the mountains by FRAP...you love it, don't you?"

Seamus looked at him and smiled even wider. "Of course I do. Why else would I be in this bloody business?"

* * * * *

Chapter Twelve

Billings' voice popped into their headsets. "We're about a minute out. China Base is at our eleven o'clock."

Beni and Manuel popped their seatbelts and stood up. They stared out the small porthole-type windows, but it took them quite some time to spot it—because they were looking for their idea of a military base. "China Base?" Manuel said derisively. "China Parking Lot."

"It's mostly a refueling stop for non-fixed wing aircraft heading to and from the States," the pilot told them, not disagreeing.

Beni glanced forward into the cockpit, then at the two crewmen in their helmets sitting with their backs against the forward bulkhead in jump seats. One of them was reading a soft-cover book, the other playing a game on his palmpad. Their knees occasionally bumped the big Gatlings.

On either side of the aircraft stood an electric Gatling gun on a swinging mount. Beni had never seen one in person before and was surprised at how big they were. Their ammo boxes were the size of suitcases. The side doors could be slid open, and the guns brought into action by the crewmen in a few seconds.

Pilot, co-pilot, a crew chief and a crewman. Beni looked at the cargo bay of the aircraft. It had to be twelve feet wide and close to forty long, and it was empty. Empty but for him and Manny. He grabbed hold of a hanging strap as the vehicle slowed and flared in approach.

"You have any idea how long we're going to be here?" Billings asked him.

"No."

"Fair enough." Billings looked at Chris Evers, his copilot, and hit the switch so only she could hear him. "Taxis charge by time and distance, right? Should I tell them we only accept American dollars?" She smiled but didn't respond.

It was extremely interesting to Beni. As they approached the aircraft slowed greatly, and then the nacelles containing the rotors began to tilt up. Soon they were almost vertical, a helicopter-type blade on either side, forward motion all but ceased, and the aircraft settled directly toward the pavement. As soon as the aircraft was on the ground, the crewmen unbuckled. One of them slid the door open for the men, then jumped down to chock the wheels.

Beni put his sunglasses on and stared out into bright sunlight and swirling dust. The air was dry and smelled faintly of brackish water. He stepped down from the Peregrine and crouched slightly as he walked toward the closest building, a hangar with an open door.

The interior of the hangar was a black rectangle devoid of features until he grew close. Then he saw the Mexican Army soldiers slouching in chairs or on crates. As he entered the shade one of the young men stood up and sauntered toward him.

"Where is the office, or wherever they have the radio room?" Beni asked, glancing around at the bored soldiers.

The soldier who'd gotten up stopped in front of Beni and smirked. "Who are you that you want to know?" he asked with a bored sigh. He flicked a smile over his shoulder at his compatriots.

They got V-35s in from time to time, but they were rarely visited by men in suits, and all of them were white. *Este traje* was no gringo, and he had a hard look about him, but the country was filled with hard men. Time to have a little fun, as *el sargento* was otherwise occupied.

Beni ran his dark eyes around the room before he calmly answered, "The man who in three seconds will separate your head from your shoulders and ask the boy behind you the same question while trying to keep your blood off my shoes." He stared unblinkingly at the sullen and probably stupid teenager in uniform as he heard Manny come up behind him. The young soldier licked his lips and stared at the expressionless man in the sunglasses before him, and the equally hard and much more muscular suit behind him. It only took him half a second to decide that messing with well-dressed strangers who had been given a private ride on a Peregrine was perhaps not the best idea he'd had.

"In the next building, *Señor*," he told Beni.

Beni found a pale puffy man in Raven coveralls eating a donut in the smaller air-conditioned building. The man frowned at them. "You the VIPs?" he asked. "I'm Wilson, Communications Officer on duty." He hadn't been expecting to see natives, even ones in fancy business suits. Maybe they were politicians? Seemed a bit young for that, though.

"Yes."

Wilson waited for more, and when it wasn't forthcoming asked, "Who exactly are you gentlemen with?"

"A concerned citizen," Beni told him, then got to the point. "A helicopter left here this morning, headed toward Victoria Base. It never arrived. What can you tell me about it?" He stared at the pudgy unimpressive man.

"Not a damn thing, I've only been on since noon," Wilson told them. "Nothing in or out since I came on. Let me grab a coffee, and I'll see what I can find out for you."

Beni and Manuel stood by impatiently as the man made himself a cup of cream and sugar to which he added trace amounts of coffee, then followed him into the China Base control room, such as it was. It was as unimpressive as the man, a small room with a few old computer monitors and keyboards. Beni had been waiting for news since he had left Mexico City, but no one had any for him. Even though it didn't show on his face, he was uneasy.

Wilson tapped a few keys, then a holo screen lit up in front of him. Waving his hands through the display in midair, it seemed to Beni the man knew exactly what he was looking for. And when he couldn't find it he was just as easy to read.

"That's weird." He panned back through the flight logs and data records and radio transcripts. "You're sure it left out of here? Records show no arrivals or departures today at all. But that can't be right, I heard the damn helicopter come in when I was in my bunk. Blackhawk. I can recognize them in my sleep."

"Whoever was working here this morning confirmed with Victoria Base that the helicopter arrived and then departed on schedule. That was," Beni checked his watch, "almost seven hours ago."

Wilson was shaking his head as he flipped through the holo folders in front of his face. "Yeah, no, I believe you. Like I said, I heard the dang thing come in when I was in my rack. But I can't find any record of it here. No radar record, no radio recordings, nothing in the log." He was totally confused. "Well what the hell? Did he compile it and store it in a new location? We running new procedures I don't know about?"

"Who was working here this morning?"

"Charlie Travers," Wilson said distractedly. "He's on days, we're running twelve-hour shifts with no days off until we can get a third man here. It's been killing me. Okay, the hell with it, let me try this." He stopped flipping through the virtual folders, killed the heads-up display, and went to work on the keyboard, fingers tapping quickly. A monitor in front of him flickered to life, and soon all sorts of windows and folders were open on-screen. Beni turned and looked at Manny, who shook his head. Manny did not look happy. The expression on Beni's face, as usual, was unreadable.

"Where is Charlie?" Beni asked the man.

"Probably in his bunk," Wilson said distractedly. "Or watching a movie in the bunkhouse. Not much else to do here."

"Where would that be?" Manuel said.

"Building behind this one."

Manuel left without a word. He was back five minutes later. "The bunk house is empty," he said. "The soldiers said that Travers took one of the trucks and headed out this afternoon, a few hours ago."

"Must have been right after I went on duty," Wilson said distantly, peering at the screen and shaking his head. "Shit, the backups aren't even running, how the hell did that happen?"

"Does he often leave the base?" Beni asked him.

"What? No. There's not much more to do in China than here. Well, bad food and worse whores," the man admitted. "And not necessarily in that order."

"Have you found anything?" Manuel asked him.

"No, not yet, I'm still searching."

Manuel turned the man's swivel chair so he had to look away from the screen and let go of the keyboard. "Can you come with me to the bunk room and show me which bunk is his?"

"Why?"

"Please," he said politely.

Beni watched the two of them go, then turned and studied the computer screen. It was covered with open windows, each one filled with lines of fine text. The two men were back shortly.

"I don't get it," Wilson was saying as they came through the door. "Why would he take off? He knows we're not due to get any relief until next week, earliest."

"¿Que?" Beni asked.

"His things are gone," Manny informed him.

"Not all of them," Wilson argued, defending his co-worker out of reflex. He sat back down in front of the terminal.

"Everything he might want to have with him if he wasn't coming back. Most of which he would not need if he was heading out for *enchiladas o putas.*"

After another ten minutes the communications officer was no closer to finding any of the records they needed. "I think the system's been wiped," he said. "If it was, he did a great job, because there's no evidence of a wipe, and it's only the last twelve hours or so that's missing. But it's not there. Anywhere."

Beni pulled out his palm and placed a call.

"¿Si, Beni?"

Beni spoke in Spanish. "The radio man who was on duty when the helicopter departed for Victoria Base has left and taken his things with him. As if he is never coming back," he told his boss. "The files here have been wiped, so we have no record of their route or GPS waypoints, no recordings of their radio chatter, no evidence that they were ever here."

There was silence on the other end of the phone for several seconds. "But they were there, yes? She was there?"

Beni pulled the phone away from his face. "Do we know for sure she was here?"

Manny nodded. "The soldiers remember her very well. Apparently you are not the first person today to threaten to cut them."

Beni smiled and put the phone back to his ear. "Yes, she was here." The smile disappeared. "But we seem to have no way to determine where she went. There are all sorts of aircraft flying in and out of Victoria Base from every direction, and General Santos told me that none of them has spotted any wreckage."

"That's what I was told. No distress calls either." Señor Echevarria breathed heavily into his ear for a few seconds, then told him, "Stay there. I will make a phone call."

"Who are you guys? What the hell is going on? Who was on that chopper?" Wilson asked, visibly nervous. He hadn't done anything wrong, but knew that wouldn't stop him from getting the blame, if they needed a scapegoat.

Beni ignored him. "We wait," he told Manny.

The bigger man scowled, then glanced out the doorway. "Coffee?" he asked Beni.

"Water."

Beni was sipping from a water bottle five minutes later when his palm rang. "Yes?" he said in English, gambling on the most likely language this conversation would require.

"This is Colonel Richard Kresge with Raven Command, Victoria Base. Who am I speaking to?"

"Beni Trujillo, the personal representative of Señor Eduardo Echevarria in this matter."

"Well Mister Trujillo, it seems we've got a Blackhawk that's gone missing. I'm aware of the situation, and am told that we received no Mayday and can't seem to find it through the usual means. No response on the radio. Their transponder is off, broken, or out of range. Their emergency beacon has not been activated, or is not working. Mexican military aircraft have searched the corridor between China and Victoria for several hours without success according to General Santos, who is the person who alerted me to this greasefire. No other aircraft has spotted a crash site or unexplained fires or smoke, and no civilians have reported seeing an aircraft go down. And now I hear that there is no record that it was ever at your location? Is that correct?"

"Yes."

"Well, we'll see. Let me speak to the communications officer there."

Beni hit the Speaker button and set the palm down in front of Wilson, who was visibly sweating. "Who's on the call?"

"This is Colonel Richard Kresge, Raven Command, Victoria Base. My computer here tells me that the Communications Officer on duty there should be Specialist John Wilson, ID 3YU87563. Is that you?"

Wilson recognized both the colonel's name and voice. "Yes sir." He was sweating even harder now.

"Well, it sounds like we are missing some records of a helicopter, Specialist, in addition to the helicopter itself. This is not good. In fact, this is the exact opposite of good. Expect a videoconference request in three, two….." There was a loud beep, and a flashing red icon appeared on one of the screens. Wilson typed in his authorization code, and the big monitor lit up with the image of a lean middle-aged man in a pressed Raven uniform. He was on his feet, leaning slightly forward, a man sitting in front of him at a keyboard out of frame but for one shoulder. They were in some sort of command module, with electronic suites visible behind and all around them. The colonel's eyes flicked around his display, cataloguing the men in front of him, which told Beni the man could see them standing behind Wilson. The colonel did not acknowledge them but instead arrowed right in on Wilson. "Mister Wilson, how about you walk me through this hairball."

"A Blackhawk landed and took off here this morning, Sir, but I can find no record of it in the system. I know it was here, I heard it, but the Specialist on duty before me…I don't know if he deleted the information from the system or what, but I've got no flight plan, zero radar or transponder data, no radio transmission recordings or the automatically transcribed text, nothing. Even his duty log is missing from the system." Wilson threw up his hands in frustration.

"I see. Why don't you walk me through what you have done to search for and recover this information," the colonel instructed him. He leaned back and crossed his arms.

Wilson gave his superior a step-by-step rundown of what he had done—and attempted to do—to pull up the data. It took several minutes. When he was done, the colonel was silent for several seconds before speaking. "Considering I didn't understand half of what you just said to me, Specialist, I think I've established to my own satisfaction that you do know your ass from a hole in the ground when it comes to your job, and that I am going to be of absolutely no help to you."

Beni and Manuel traded a look as Wilson sagged in his chair. "Oh."

"I do, however," the colonel continued, "have a whizbang communications tech here who assures me that if the information still exists in your system, he can direct you to it." The colonel pointed to the man sitting next to him and took a step back. The seated man scooted over—his chair must have had wheels—and he gave a nod to Wilson. The colonel's whizbang tech was skinny as a rail and looked like a teenager.

"You did what you were supposed to, tried every procedure in the manual to recover lost data, but there are a few tricks I can show you that aren't in the manual," the tech told Wilson. The two men then proceeded to have a rapid and highly technical discussion that had Wilson tapping keys and flipping through information on his displays at a frenetic pace.

"And let me guess, that folder's empty too?" the tech on-screen said ten minutes later, looking a little frustrated.

Wilson shook his head. "No, it's not empty, it's not there at all. The entire directory has been deleted." He peered at a screen to the side filled with text. "And the subroutines to enable it are—crap, they're gone."

The other tech nodded, and an admiring smile came across his face. "Damn, he did everything but splash gasoline around and light a match." He looked over his shoulder at Colonel Kresge. "Sir, their entire mainframe and software system has been gutted. I'm surprised the lights are still on over there. We have so many redundant systems that to remove all of the records he had to take a digital axe to the computers."

"So that's it?" Kresge asked him. "There's no way to retrieve the information?"

"Oh, I didn't say that," the tech said with some measure of pride in his voice. He turned sideways in his chair so he could address the colonel directly. "Raven loves duplicated effort for no good reason most of the time, but in this case it's going to serve us well. All the relay stations around the country, which boost our radar signals and radio communications, don't just relay that information but record it." He looked above the monitor at a map of the stations. "That Blackhawk should have passed within range at least two of those relays even if it went down within half an hour of leaving China Base. It will take me some time to track down which relays actually recorded passage of the bird, especially if it deviated from its flight plan, but I know I'll get something. I can access all their data remotely. Once I find the right stations, they'll give me speed, altitude, direction of travel, maybe even recorded audio traffic."

The colonel nodded. "Well, get on it son, we may have people bleeding or dead somewhere waiting on us to save them."

The tech gulped. "Yes sir."

Kresge looked at the video display. "We'll get back with you as soon as we have something," he told the men waiting at China Base and cut the feed.

Beni stared at the black screen, then looked at his watch. Wilson spun around in his chair and looked at his two visitors. "You guys want chairs? It might take a while; I don't know."

"What is a while?" Beni asked him.

Wilson shook his head. "Your guess is as good as mine. I'm going to get more coffee."

* * *

Twenty-six minutes later (by Beni's watch) Wilson's display pinged, and the same flashing icon appeared. When he signed in to the videoconference, there was the colonel and his tech, only the tech was looking a little more animated.

"Did you find something?" Beni asked.

"Yes. But first let me tell you that I checked our system, and Travers has not used his ID card to gain access to any equipment or secure area controlled by Raven since he left China Base. All your vehicles have GPS trackers on them, and only one of them isn't on base. I'm guessing that's the truck Travers took earlier today, and I've located it. It is eleven kilometers northwest of your position and hasn't moved in hours. Guessing it's parked. From the map it is right in the middle of a small town. General Bravo? Is that a person or the name of the town?

"That's a town right up the road, straight up 40. Bigger than China, but not by much," Wilson said.

"Okay, well, put that on your to-do list. But first let me play you something," the tech told them.

Sound came out of the speakers above their heads. *"China Control, this is Sierra Bravo Six. Clear to take off for Victoria Base?"* The recording was good quality.

"Sierra Bravo Six, affirmative, you are clear to take off."

"That's Charlie!" Wilson said. He looked around the room, feeling vindicated.

"Hold on, that's not all of it," the tech on-screen told them. "This next traffic comes twenty-two minutes later." He hit a button and sat back.

"Sierra Bravo Six, this is China Control, over."

"*China Control, go for Sierra Bravo Six.*"

"*Sierra Bravo Six, we have reports of SAMs in the area around Linares. I need you to immediately divert to heading two-four-zero degrees. That should keep you clear of the danger zone. Stay on that heading, then at the waypoint turn and approach Victoria Base heading one-two-zero degrees. I am transmitting your new route now, over.*"

"*Roger that. I have received and copy the new route, China Control.*"

A new voice came out of the speakers. From the background noise it was coming from the helicopter, probably the co-pilot. "*Uh, China Control, Sierra Bravo Six, if we've got SAM problems, why are the altitudes so low? Final leg shows us only five-zero-zero AGL, over.*"

"*I don't know anything Sierra Bravo Six, I'm just a monkey pushing buttons over here. That is the route I was told to give to you. Maybe there's other traffic in the area. Be advised, Operation Green Spear kicked off this morning. That's that major offensive they've been planning for a while near Guadalajara.*"

"*Sierra Bravo Six, roger that. Thanks for the heads up.*"

"*You got it. China Control out.*"

Kresge leaned forward. "No reports of SAMs around Linares that I can find. No record that anyone in command here or anywhere gave him that route and instructed he divert Sierra Bravo Six." He glanced at something off to the side. "The new route he gave them had the Blackhawk swinging far west, over the mountains, coming in to Victoria from the northwest. Not much of anything out there. Sparsely populated at best. We don't have regular routes there, and neither does the Mex Air Force, such as it is. We've got GPS data from three relay stations that show they followed the new route, but then they went out of range. We don't have any relay stations in the Orientals."

Beni leaned toward the screen. "Have you had any reports of trouble in that area today?"

"I've got someone looking into that," Kresge told him. "But like I told you, the area is sparsely populated even for this region. My computer is telling me the largest town in the area is Doctor Arroyo, which I've never even heard of. I have no idea if it even still exists; this country is filled with ghost towns."

"Do you have satellites available?" Manuel asked.

The colonel smiled thinly. "Under normal circumstances I might tell you that there was no way one missing chopper containing a few civilians would rate re-tasking a satellite, but I'm not so sure that's true given who called me in on this." He looked at Manuel, then Beni. "I've spoken with General Santos on this, and I believe your boss in fact got the President of Mexico involved." It sounded as if he didn't know whether to be amused or offended by that. "But in this case I can tell you straight that no satellites are available, because they've all be re-tasked to support the Guadalajara offensive, where we have men under fire. Daughter of an important man or not, she has only been missing for a few hours, and that's not enough to re-task Keyholes. Maybe in a few days." He shrugged and tapped his tech on the shoulder. "We are sending you all the data we have, including the projected flight path and last known radar contact, but that location is much closer to us than you. We have already launched UAVs and I am scrambling two helicopters on a search and rescue mission; we are leaving here in two minutes."

"You are going?" Beni asked.

The colonel nodded. "I don't like being told my business by rich men who know the right ears to whisper into. But that's not what this is any more. I've got a bird missing, a flight officer diverting aircraft with bullshit and then doing a disappearing act, and a sincerely bad feeling that this is going to get much worse before it gets better. So I am now personally involved." He nodded at Beni. "I have your number. I will call you as soon as I learn something, but it could be hours, or days, if they didn't come down somewhere near their new route. You can check out the truck he took, maybe he's at a bar nearby tying one on, but I doubt it. I don't know what else there is for you to do there."

Beni stared at the colonel. "Do you have Señor Charlie Travers' personnel file there?" he asked.

The colonel frowned. "Yes. Why?"

"It appears he and I have much to discuss," Beni said flatly, his face expressionless. "Perhaps there is something in his file which will help me locate him. A photo would be helpful. And the exact location of the truck in General Bravo."

Kresge stared back at Beni for a few long seconds. The expensive suits didn't fool him, Echevarria's two men were not clueless boardroom types or even thugs but obvious hard professionals. They looked more than capable handling themselves and asking tough questions of rough people. He nodded at his tech. "Send it."

Within a few seconds Wilson had the digital file in his inbox and opened it so Beni could look at it. Beni stared at the photo of Travers for a few seconds, then looked at the rest of the contents. "Twenty pages? Send this to my palm," he told the tech and gave him the number. "And can you send his photo twice, once as a separate file?"

"Yeah, I can do that," Wilson told him, relieved that he'd somehow avoided any blame in this whole giant mess.

It took about a minute, and then Beni's personal device vibrated. He checked the screen and saw he had the file and the photo as a separate attachment. Nodding, he then looked at the pudgy communications tech. "We need a vehicle," he told the man.

* * *

The light was fading as they drove into General Bravo in a borrowed Raven pickup. Technically it was unmarked, but it was painted flat Army green, and they got a lot of looks as they drove along Route 40, Autopista Monterrey-Reynosa. Everyone knew who the truck belonged to.

Beni was driving, and Manuel had an old folding map open on his lap. "Slow down, we're almost there. Two more blocks."

The GPS put the missing Raven truck right on Route 40 at the corner of Calle Lerdo de Tejada. Route 40 was concrete, cracked and faded in the bright sun. The side streets were all uneven asphalt. They rolled by listing cinderblock walls and low buildings made of plain concrete, sometimes gray but often painted bright colors.

"I see it," Beni said. The green truck was parked in a small lot on the right on the next block. It appeared empty.

Beni pulled to the curb a hundred meters from the other truck, and they walked the rest of the way. He assumed Travers was long gone, and had abandoned the truck here, but on the very small chance he hadn't they didn't want to spook him by parking another Raven truck right next to his.

Manny drew his pistol but kept it down along his leg as he approached the truck, on the off-chance Travers was inside, sleeping. "Empty," he said, standing next to the truck while trying to appear uninterested in it, just in case Travers was nearby, watching. Beni turned and looked around. Route 40 here had businesses on either side of the street. Travers had parked in the lot of a small furniture store that was out of business. There was a bar on the next block with a winking sign, and a hardware store across the street, but every other store or shop seemed to be out of business. The war had not been good for business anywhere in Mexico, even in small towns removed from the fighting.

"The keys are in it," Manny said in surprise, staring into the truck.

Beni looked through the window. "He probably hoped it would be stolen." Any other vehicle probably would have been, but a truck obviously belonging to Raven, a company made of combat-hardened *mercenarios*? A battered truck wasn't worth that much trouble.

"The bar first? Maybe he's in there, drunk."

Beni looked at the winking light. "Yes, together, and then when he's not there and no one there has seen him, we can split up." He frowned. "We will not find anything here."

"You never know," Manny said optimistically, taking the keys out of the ignition and pocketing them.

They were back to Travers' truck in twenty minutes. Nobody at the bar or any of the other nearby open businesses remembered seeing any gringo that day, and did not recognize Travers from the picture on Beni's palmpad. None of the businesses had exterior security cameras, at least that were functional. Beni searched the truck Travers had abandoned without finding anything.

"So now what?" Manny asked as Beni sat behind the wheel. Manny was standing beside the open car door and shivered a little in the cool breeze. The temperature had noticeably dropped and the wind cut right through his thin suitcoat. The sun had set while they'd been asking questions in General Bravo.

"It has been hours, hours, and hours, but maybe…." Beni said. He thumbed through the contacts on his pad and placed a call.

"*¿Si?*"

"I am sending you a picture of a man," Beni said without introduction.

"Are you sure you are not presuming too much?"

Beni smiled thinly. The man on the other end of the call did not like him much, for many good reasons. But the man was an Inspector with the *División de Inteligencia, Policia Federal,* and knew who Beni worked for. "Senor Echevarria would consider it a personal favor if you could get this photo out to all of your men stationed at the border." He pulled the palm away from this head and used his thumbs to quickly send off the photo.

"Who is he? Business competitor? *La Fuerza?*" The man on the other end of the line chuckled.

"An American, a Raven employee."

"*¿Una escarabaja?* Is he armed?"

"Not a soldier type, an office worker. I don't know if he's armed."

"And why is he important? Ah, I have the photo. Not very dangerous looking. A criminal?"

"He may have been involved in an attempted kidnapping. Near Monterrey." Beni had not been given permission to pass on knowledge of Tina's situation, so he was deliberately sparse with details. Even though he thought the inspector was probably trustworthy, there were many men in the *Policia Federal* who would be exceedingly interested to learn that the daughter of the great Gordito was missing. But there was no one who might be of more help, *agentes del División de Inteligencia* were stationed at every border crossing in the country, north and south.

"How nicely vague of you."

"I think he is in America already, but if not I need to talk to him. *Es muy importante.*"

The man on the other end of the line grunted. "Well, it would be nice to inconvenience the *escaras* for once. I will have my men watch for him. If he tries to cross, we will grab him. Should I contact you at this number?"

"Yes. And do not delay; time is critical."

"Isn't it always?"

"Drive the other truck back, I'll follow you," Beni told Manny as he disconnected the call. "Then we can search Travers' bunk area more thoroughly. Maybe there is something useful there. Check the garbage too."

Manny looked at him. "Do you believe she is dead? Helicopters crash all the time. *La Señora Rosita*, I think she would handle it better. Take strength from her other daughters. *Pero El Señor*, I fear it would break his heart."

Beni shook his head. "I will not believe she is dead until I see the body. And maybe not even then."

* * * * *

Chapter Thirteen

As soon as the sun faded in the west, the sky filled with an explosion of stars. Within a few minutes the moon slipped above a ridge, but it was a waxing sliver and barely shed any light on the ground. When Seamus could no longer see his boots on the trail he hissed and snapped his fingers to stop Corey, still in the lead.

"You been doing a pace count?" he asked Corey, his voice low.

"I've got close to three miles on the trail, maybe a mile and a half before that once we topped that first hill, although with all the up and down it's hard to judge."

Seamus nodded, then when he realized Corey couldn't see him said, "That's about what I figured. Time to leave the yellow brick road," he announced. The rest of the group had gathered close, their faces invisible. The air had cooled, and the hills were beginning to echo with the sounds of nocturnal animals. The heights around them were no better than dark clouds in the starlight. Night vision equipment would have been useful, but both the scope on Corey's carbine and the optics in his helmet had been destroyed by the EMP. They could only hope the guerrillas didn't have any night vision or thermal optics.

"We're going to leave the trail up ahead," Seamus told them quietly. "I'll lead the way. It will be slower going. Stay close, but more importantly stay quiet. No talking now. None. Not even whispering. We don't know how far they are behind us, and I don't want them to hear us floundering around in the bushes. Let's go."

He resumed walking down the trail, but much more slowly than before. Even in the few moments they'd been stopped, the night had grown darker, and any rocks or uneven spots on the trail were impossible to see. The trail meandered down a long slope, and he could sense rather than see that perhaps half a mile in the distance the trees and brush thinned out a bit. To either side of them the bushes were tall and thick, looming walls in the dark. Up ahead would be a much more convenient and logical place to leave the trail, which is why Seamus stepped off the packed dirt path and pushed his way between two bushes, stepping carefully. Clump oaks or maples, probably, but they were little more than gray clutching shapes in the dark; treeland ghosts.

His boots crunched over dead leaves and twigs as he shoved through the foliage, doing his best not to get a branch in the eye. His pace was slow, deliberate; one step at a time, not trying to eat up distance but rather make as little noise as possible. The group kept close behind him in single file. Inside the trees it was even darker, and they drew together, close enough to touch.

He'd rigged another grenade booby-trap maybe a mile back on the trail. They'd never heard it explode, which wasn't necessarily a bad thing. If the G's had spotted his well-concealed trip wire that meant they were moving slowly. They could be following the trail, very carefully, or paralleling it through the brush on either side— either way, the guerrillas hadn't caught up to his group before dark, which was all he could have hoped for.

Seamus led them through thick underbrush, across meadows whose openness they could sense but not see, and through crowds of fragrant pines standing stiff and still. The sky was full of stars, but the light they threw to the ground did nothing to illuminate their way.

They hiked up and down slopes, breath harsh, no talking except for the occasional muffled curse as someone got jabbed by a branch or brushed against an unseen cactus.

Seamus hadn't navigated by the stars in...ever, but it was oh so easy when the sky above you was lit up like glittering diamonds on black velvet. So far from anywhere civilized, even the white wisps of the Milky Way were plainly visible. He would have liked to lie on his back and watch the heavens turn above him, dream of younger days, but that wasn't the job. Polaris, the North Star, was right where it was supposed to be, and Seamus kept the group heading southeast as well as the terrain allowed. He had a sense they'd been heading south more than southeast, simply because it was easier to follow the ridges than traverse them, but that wasn't much of a problem. He knew there was a main highway which ran straight west from Victoria Base. Shagging it cross-country if they drifted far enough to the west to miss Victoria Base completely they'd hit the highway. All they'd have to do then is stop a vehicle and catch a ride in to the base. That was a long way in the future, though, at least another full day at the speed they were travelling, even if there weren't any surprise delays.

After several hours, the steady up and down became a long uneven slope downward. He wasn't too happy about that, because he knew what it probably meant. Twenty minutes later he found his suspicions were correct—they'd come up against a steep mountainside. He couldn't tell how tall it was, could only see far above him where the slope ended, and that only because that was where the stars began. The rest of the group clustered around him at the base of the slope. It was so dark he could only identify them by their voices. And they all sounded exhausted.

"We stopping?" Roger whispered hoarsely. His back was killing him, and he'd been running on fumes for an hour. Walking blindly in the dark, even slowly, would have been exhausting even if there weren't guerrillas chasing them. His nerves were shot, as were his legs, his back, his arms…. He stared blindly forward, sensing rather than seeing the hill in front of them. "Is that a wall or a cliff or something?"

"Or something. Grab some bottles out of my pack everyone, water your gullets. Then let's get to it. We'll stop for the night once we're up top." They'd done maybe three kilometers in the dark, although his pace count was a little messed up. He'd have to check with Corey when they stopped.

Hands groped blindly toward him, and touched his face. He turned so they could access the pack, and soon he heard the creaking of plastic bottles and the sighs as they down the cool water. The load on his shoulders lessened somewhat but the pack still felt twice as heavy as it had when he'd first shouldered it at the Vaquero. He wasn't spent, but he'd be glad to be quit of this steeplechase. Someone found his arm and slid a bottle of water to his hand. The mountain air was so dry his lips were cracked, and his tongue felt thick in his mouth. He cracked the cap and sucked at the water gratefully. With his eyes fully adjusted to the dark he could just barely see the slope in front of them was rocky and tangled with underbrush.

"Everyone make it this far? Sound off," Seamus said softly.

"I'm here," Mike announced. His feet had turned to lead, and his arms ached from carrying the Blackbird, but he wasn't complaining. The arduousness of the day had helped keep his mind off what had happened back on the hillside.

"*Sí, estoy aquí,*" Tina said. She was so tired it took her a few seconds to realize she'd spoken in Spanish. "I'm here," she repeated needlessly.

"You haven't lost me yet," Hansen announced. His broken arm was killing him, and his feet ached from all the walking (pilots didn't walk, they flew, dammit), but he was still alive. He had a little girl to get home to and was looking forward a few strafing runs on FRAP emplacements as a little payback for all this bullshit mountain hiking. His hand found the pony head and fiddled with it.

"Yeah, I'm here. But I can't even see to climb," Roger complained.

"If they come after us tonight, would you rather have your back to a wall with nowhere to go, or would you rather be up there?" Corey asked him, a soft voice floating bodiless in the dark. Working out regularly was one thing, but humping up and down mountains for hours had shown him that he wasn't in nearly as good shape as he'd thought he was. He was tired and not a little bit pissed off. "High ground worked pretty well for us before. I'm not exactly looking forward to dragging myself up there either, carrying your heavy damn dinosaur rifle, but you don't have to like it, you just have to do it. Especially since they're going to all this trouble for you and your fat wallet."

Roger opened his mouth in the dark, then closed it. There was nothing for him to say after that.

"I'll help you Dad," Mike said from somewhere nearby.

The climb would have been challenging during the day, if they'd all been healthy and knew the route. On a near moonless night, with a third of the group injured, the ascent was nightmarish.

They fought their way up through steep brush-choked fissures littered with loose rock an inch at a time. Before they'd gone thirty feet, Seamus had relented and pulled the girl's machete from its sheath on the pack—it was the only way they were going to get up the mountain, and that fact to Seamus outweighed the inherent dangers of swinging what amounted to a short sword in the dark.

After a hundred feet, the heavily overgrown V-shaped crack opened up into what might have been a steep dry watercourse. The walls were mostly rock, pale in the starlight. The channel split and

Seamus took the left fork, only to have it dead-end ten minutes later at a completely impassible vertical rock wall. They backtracked and found the right fork passable but filled with long-thorned cacti and unsettled boulders. They scrambled upward, often on all fours, several of the group barely avoiding broken ankles as the boulders shifted.

Their harsh panting echoed off the limestone. None of them had the energy or breath to talk, even if they weren't afraid that any pursuers might hear them. Several times the group froze as some small creature scurried away from them in a panic; the dislodged pebbles seemed as loud as gunshots.

Roger was in agony. It felt as if he was being stabbed in the back with small knives, and the pain was shooting down his buttocks and the backs of his legs as well. For most of the climb, he was on all fours, dragging the AK across boulders and using it as a walking stick. Mike tried to help him but the path was so steep, or narrow, or the footing so treacherous, that most of the time he had to make his own way. Sweat was running off his face and dripping from his nose and stinging cuts on his hands he didn't remember receiving. Every step took conscious effort, and he soon lost track of time.

The rocky channel narrowed to hardly wider than his shoulders, then he sensed rather than saw a wall in front of him. He looked up from the ground and there was a rock face inches from his nose. Roger blinked, wondering where Seamus and the one or two others in front of him had disappeared to, then saw the rock wall was only a few feet high. A pale hand appeared in front of his face, and he grabbed it gratefully.

Compared to the dark crevice, the top of the ridge seemed brightly lit, the sky above him filled with stars and the thin crescent moon. He recognized Seamus' outline in front of him. "Christ, is this it? Please tell me we're at the top," Roger gasped as soon as he had the breath. He set the AK on the ground and put his hands on his knees. If they weren't at the top….

"This is it mate," Seamus assured him. "But don't fall over just yet, head over there where there's a little more cover." He pointed to a clump of bushes fifty feet away. "And don't get any ideas, no fire."

The top of the ridge was nearly level but less than a hundred feet wide. It was spotted with bushes but not many mature trees. Roger stumbled toward the thicket. He discovered a small clearing enclosed by bushes, young oaks, and a handful of cedars. He almost stepped on the girl, who was sitting on the ground, head hanging low, half asleep already. "Sorry," he mumbled. He moved a few feet to the side and eased himself to the ground with a succession of groans and gasps. The earth was covered with a fine layer of dead leaves and needles, but was blessedly free of rocks. He was asleep before he could finish the thought that his back was going to be even worse in the morning after sleeping on the cold, hard ground.

Corey was the last one up the slope. "I'd feel a sense of accomplishment if I didn't know we were going to have to do the same thing all day tomorrow," he told Seamus as he got a hand up the last few feet, panting harshly. "Damn, I'm out of shape."

"You and me both," Seamus agreed. The two contractors stood and looked around as well as they could in the dark. They were atop a ridge running roughly north/south. The view to the west, the way they'd come, was pure blackness with only a few folds of the land evident. They saw no lights, heard nothing from anyone that might be following them. To the east, the land seemed to drop away into a deep valley lost in shadow. The valley floor could be fifty feet down or five hundred; they'd have to wait until morning to check it out. There was a steady soft breeze from the west that was cool on their faces. Seamus shivered as the sweat on his neck dried.

"No way to get up here without making a shitload of noise just like we did, at least not at night," Corey said. "Here, let me get another bottle of water. I'll take first watch."

"What is it, nearly midnight? Wake me at three and I'll take it to dawn."

Corey twisted the lid off the bottle and sucked half of it down. "Roger that."

* * *

"No, I'm telling you, she had the face of a...what dog is that? The one whose face is all smashed in, as though it was running fast and hit a wall blind?" Chi-Chi turned to the young man beside him.

Francisco shook his head, then it came to him. "Pug?" He'd given up trying to find a position inside the cab of the truck which was comfortable; now he was simply trying to ignore the pain in his mangled left arm. He couldn't tell if the bleeding had finally stopped because the bandage was so heavy with blood. Ambushed by a grenade before he'd ever gotten a chance to fire a shot. He'd felt helpless listening to the firefight on the slope, but then when so fewer men had come back down than gone up....

"*Si, si,*" Chi-Chi said, laughing. He scratched his thin beard. "Pug. Barely sixteen years old and the face of a pug, complete with moustache. From some small town way down south near the border, probably had dirt floors in her house. She drank three *cervezas* so fast I thought it was a race, and assumed that meant she could hold her liquor." His face split in a huge smile. "No! Never had a drink before! Took the opportunity of *La Fuerza* coming into town to sneak away from *Mami* and *Papi* and live a little. Flirt with danger."

"So a drunk ugly girl?"

"That's just it!" Chi-Chi nearly shouted, waving his hands. "She was ugly as a pug, as an ugly pug, but after *tres cervezas* she was ready for anything. I took her into the back room, and when her clothes came off, I tell you I couldn't believe it. Below the neck she was a sculpted goddess, perfection…especially her *chichis*."

Francisco shook his head. "Chi-Chi, have you ever met a girl whose *chichis* weren't perfection?" Every story he told was about some conquest, *una chica bonita con chichis grande y magnífico*. He had the nickname for a reason; that was for sure.

One corner of Chi-Chi's mouth curled up in a smile. "*Sí, muchos,* but why would I talk about them?"

Francisco smiled, then winced. "Can you start the engine and run the heater? I'm cold."

Chi-Chi looked at the younger man with concern. Francisco was pale, and shivering. There was hardly any white left in the bandage on his arm. The bleeding seemed to have stopped, but the boy had lost a lot of blood. He'd been trying to distract the young soldier from the pain in his arm with his stories, but it hadn't quite worked.

"Sure, sure." Chi-Chi looked out the windshield of the truck, but couldn't see anything. The sun had set hours before and they'd heard nothing and seen less. Chi-Chi had faith in *El Tejón*. He knew the man was a great leader and fierce in battle, but the *escaras* could be treacherous. This war had been the death of many great leaders. He turned the key on the truck halfway and first checked the fuel gauge. Half a tank, plenty to run the engine for a while. Stuck in the small narrow valley, a fire probably would have been okay, but he didn't want to get off the truck's bench seat, much less walk around looking for branches to burn. Even though they didn't look nearly as gruesome as Francisco's arm, Chi-Chi's legs had been chewed up badly by the grenade shrapnel. The truck started immediately, another good sign.

While waiting for the heater to warm up, Chi-Chi pulled out some jerky. "You want some?' Francisco shook his head. "Well, have some water, you need to replace your fluids." Chi-Chi screwed the cap off a bottle of water and handed it to his companion.

"How long do you think they'll be gone?' Francisco asked after taking a sip.

"No way to know," Chi-Chi said with a shrug. "Could be back in two minutes, could be tomorrow."

"Tomorrow?" His arm was killing him. "What if they don't come back?" Francisco looked out the windshield into the darkness and tried not to think about all of his fallen compatriots.

"Don't think like that," Chi-Chi warned him. "*El Tejón* is a great leader. He will catch up to the *escaras,* exact vengeance, and collect our prize. Things in war do not always go as you plan. Most often they are harder and take longer. Did you think you would be sitting here with me now instead of out there on the hunt? No. But we will both live to fight another day, unlike *nos hermanos muertos.*" He nodded in the direction of the other truck whose bed was filled with the bodies of their fellow soldiers who had not been so lucky. "Ah, see? Better than a campfire," Chi-Chi said with a smile, holding a hand over a heater vent. The air was starting to get warm. He turned up the fan, then cracked a window.

"*¿Cigarillo?*" he asked, pulling out a small thin cigar which looked much like the jerky he'd been eating. Francisco shook his head.

Chi-Chi lit the small cigar with a battered lighter and inhaled deeply. He blew the smoke out the cracked window with a sigh. "I ever tell you about the blonde in Reynosa?" he asked Francisco, then cocked his head and looked out the side window.

"What?"

"You hear something?" When Francisco shook his head, Chi-Chi looked back out the windows, squinting, but could see nothing. He'd heard something, though. Suspicious, he grabbed the switch on the truck and turned on the headlights. The grass in front of them lit up all the way to the edge of the slope and the trees. After so long in the dark, the weak headlights seemed bright as searchlamps.

"Did you see that?" When the lights had come on, Chi-Chi thought he'd seen something—a flicker of movement at the treeline—but now there was nothing. He stared at the spot, then looked all around the truck. The reflection off the glass kept him from seeing much of anything.

"No, what? I don't see anything. Do you think it's them coming back?"

Frowning, Chi-Chi grabbed his battered Fire Snake and opened the door. He hadn't realized how much the heater had warmed the inside of the truck until he felt the chill air on his skin. He sucked in air as he put weight on his feet and all the cuts on his legs flared with new pain. Hopefully they wouldn't start bleeding again. "They'd yell for us," he told Francisco. "Just stay there, it's probably nothing."

Rifle in hand, he stepped away from the open door and peered past the headlights, then up the slope. He could hear a few distant birds, and the wind sighing through the trees, but no human sounds. Bright as they were, the headlights were feeble compared to the great darkness all around them, and the black slopes reaching high above them seemed to be leaning in over the trucks. Chi-Chi stood and listened for thirty seconds but heard nothing but sounds of nature.

With a painful limp, he walked around the back of the pickup, muttering, blinking his eyes in a vain attempt to regain some of his night vision. The grassy valley floor behind the trucks was a vast dark emptiness.

Chi-Chi caught a whiff of something ugly and walked around to the other side of the pickup. The flatbed truck was parked a dozen feet away, and in the glow of the headlights he could see the bodies in back. Probably starting to bloat and smell in death. Such a shame, really, so many men having to die for the cause. He shook his head in disgust at how long the war had dragged on, then jerked his head back to stare at the pile of bodies. What was…was that an animal? Eating the bodies? The shape was odd, he couldn't quite identify it as it tore into the corpses, but that didn't matter. One more indignity….

He jerked the rifle up and was about to yell to scare off the animal when he was hit from behind. Chi-Chi grunted and went down hard, the pain in his injured legs sharp. He grabbed for his rifle and rolled onto his back, not knowing what had knocked him down. Facing away from the headlights all he could see at first was black, but then several of the shadows moved. The sinuous shapes were on him before he could fire a shot.

Francisco jerked as a sharp scream erupted seemingly right outside his door. "Chi-Chi!" He looked around, but didn't see anything. "Chi-Chi?" Are you playing a joke?" Somehow he didn't think so.

Something thumped against the side of the truck, rocking it. Francisco pulled away from his door, any thought of opening it forgotten. In fact—he looked across the cab at Chi-Chi's door, hanging open into the night. There was movement in the corner of his eye, and he jerked his head to stare out over the hood. Something had been out there, right at the edge of the headlight illumination near the trees, but was gone now. "Chi-Chi!"

He heard an unsettling sound that he couldn't quite describe. Francisco's eyes were drawn to the blackness outside the open driver's door. Shivering in fear, he stretched across the seat to close the door with his injured arm. His arm was cold and numb, and he glanced down at the heavy blood-soaked bandage around his bicep.

When he looked up there were orange eyes glittering at him outside the door, low to the ground.

Francisco lunged for his AK on the dashboard as the creature leapt into the cab of the truck with surprising speed. The truck shook back and forth violently, and the screams continued for quite some time.

* * * * *

Chapter Fourteen

"Three of a kind." Chris Evers laid her cards down on the table for the rest of the aircraft's crew to see.

"Seriously?" Sweeney, the crew chief, shook his head. It looked as though he'd bitten into something sour. "I thought you were bluffing."

"Don't you know by now she never bluffs?" Hatch, the other crewman, asked. "Why do you think I folded as soon as she started betting?"

"Only thing I pay attention to is when she gets the shakes."

"Not much chance of that this trip." Evers said, trading a look with Billings. Everyone else on the crew thought the co-pilot was psychic, and to be honest, she didn't know what it was. All she knew was that she always got the shakes right before they were going to get incoming fire. Every time. The first time it had happened she'd been in the middle of nowhere, taking an old Osprey in for mainte-nance. Her hands started to quiver, and thirty seconds later their aircraft was getting incoming from a squad of guerrillas caught out in the open where they weren't supposed to be. The worse the shakes, the more incoming they got. She couldn't explain it and had stopped trying to. If it was God, she appreciated him giving her and the crew a heads up when the shit was about to hit the fan.

The co-pilot collected her winnings, which in this case was a pile of toothpicks they were using as symbolic money. Toothpicks were a lot easier to transport and in no danger of being stolen when out in the danger zones, and no great loss if the box got misplaced. Whenever they got back to base the losing crewmen (or woman) paid up in actual cash.

Ted Billings smiled and tossed in his now worthless cards. They were huddled around a small table in the communication building's break room. Still at China Base. How many hours had it been now? He checked his watch. Near midnight, and he'd started the day early. "How long are we staying here?" he asked, looking over his shoulder.

Beni was standing in the doorway, looking at nothing, as he had been for hours. "Until we have somewhere to go, we go nowhere," he said firmly. His face looked tired, but his suit still looked fresh off the rack.

Billings sighed. What a waste. Lucille sitting out there on the helipad, cold and dark. The bird wanted to fly. She wanted to hunt. Not that he was in any hurry to rush down to join the Guadalajara offensive—there were plenty of aircraft involved—but it seemed a huge waste to have a Peregrine up here doing less than nothing. Still, he had his orders. Billings held up his hands in surrender. "Whatever you say, but I'm going to need a nap if we're up much longer."

"There are bunks in the next building," Manuel told him, sipping another cup of mediocre coffee. He was eyeing the chica, the co-pilot, as he had been ever since she'd pulled off her helmet and revealed that thick mane of strawberry blonde hair. Until she'd taken her helmet off he hadn't realized how pretty she was, or seen how curvy she was under the flight suit. He liked her nails, too, trimmed short but with a coat of light pink polish. He happened to be between girlfriends at the moment….

"Are you old, old man, or are you just afraid I'm going to take all your money?" Evers taunted.

Billings smiled. "Maybe a little of both." He wasn't the oldest pilot working for Raven, but he'd logged the most flight time on combat missions. That total, he observed, wasn't likely to go up on this chauffeur assignment.

"Hey, he's only five years older than me, are you calling me old too?" Sweeney asked the co-pilot.

"You must be. If you think that 'stache looks good your eyes are definitely going. Glaucoma maybe." The rest of the crew laughed as Sweeney stroked the bushy moustache which trailed down the sides of his mouth to his chin.

"The ex-wife wanted me to shave it. Not that she ever used a razor for me. That's why she's the ex," he said with a smile.

"Good priorities there," Evers said with a shake of her head.

Hatch snorted. "No more stories of the ex-wife, please."

"At least I've got stories. The rest of you are boring. Ted's old, that's his excuse," he said, winking at the pilot. "Flies around with the left turn signal on, talks about the weather making his joints ache. You are dictionary definition boring," he said to Hatch. "Wife, kids, dog, picket fence back home, boring blah yawn. You were my only hope," he said, pointing at Evers. "Finally, someone on the crew who likes girls as much as I do, but can we get any romantic details about your dating life? No. No stories at all. Won't share any juicy pictures. Which is just cruel. So it's up to me. I remember, there was this one girl back in Kansas City—"

"No dating stories!" the rest of the crew said in unison, then looked at each other and laughed.

* * *

Beni didn't know he'd fallen asleep until his vibrating palm woke him. He jerked upright in the uncomfortable plastic chair and dug the device out of his suit pocket even as he checked the time. Almost 5 a.m. He didn't recognize the incoming number.

"¿Si?"

"I have never seen a man more nervous who appeared less capable of doing harm," Beni heard in his ear. Even half asleep he recognized the purring voice of Inspector Ramon Torres, *División de Inteligencia, Policia Federal.*

Beni sat up straighter. "You have him?" he asked Torres. Manny was sleeping nearby, lying sideways across three of the lumpy plastic chairs. Beni didn't know how the man could do that without paralyzing himself.

"He tried to cross at Juarez with a crowd of migrants, apparently dressed *como un campesino.*" There was an unpleasant laugh in his ear. "He almost made it."

"Juarez?" Beni cleared his throat and tried to picture Mexico in his head. Juarez was more than halfway to California, maybe eight hundred kilometers away. Why had he tried to cross the border so far from China Base, and so many hours later? "Are you sure it is him?" He stood up from the chair, feeling his back pop in several places. He brushed at the wrinkles in his suit.

"My men found his Raven ID when he was arrested. And a handgun. And five thousand dollars in cash. They sent me his picture, and it is your man, unless he paid someone who looks exactly like him to cross using his ID. He claims he had a few days off, has done nothing wrong, and wants to know why we're holding him, something I would like to know as well. Luckily I will be there in ninety minutes and can ask him myself."

That froze Beni, and he realized he could hear the sound of a straining vehicle engine behind Torres. He didn't want the inspector interrogating the man at all, but especially not without him. And Torres knew it, which was probably why he was racing to Travers' location. In fact, Beni wouldn't be surprised if Torres had held onto the information until he could be sure he would beat Beni to the prisoner. "Do not do anything until I get there," Beni warned the man, striding quickly from the communication center's break room.

"Oh, you are coming?" the inspector asked innocently. Beni could almost hear the smile on the man's face. He knew that he'd have to fill Torres in on the details of the incident if he expected him to cooperate, and the inspector knew it too. He was in the *División de Inteligencia*, and secrets were his business. Travers was also in his custody, and Beni knew Torres would never let him talk to the man alone. Still, he had some leverage.

"I know I don't have to remind you who I work for, and by extension, who you are working for. This man has information that I need, that is vital to solving a serious problem."

"He is in the custody of the *Policia Federal*, which makes him our responsibility. We decide who will talk to him. Or not. As for you...I'm not sure if my superiors would be happy if I let someone with a criminal record talk to a detainee."

Beni bit his tongue and counted to three silently before answering. "*Si, claro*, he is your prisoner, and you are free to do with him as you wish." He was trying not to pant as he jogged from one building to the next. "But if anything you do or say to him jeopardizes my investigation I can assure you there would be more than just your career on the line. This is far bigger than just the two of us." He paused for that to sink in. "Perhaps we could question him together?" Torres wanted in on it, even though he didn't know what "it" was.

"Wait for you? How long will you be? You did tell me time was critical." His tone was light, almost mocking.

"Hold on." Beni threw open the door of the sleeping quarters and flicked on the light. The crew was asleep on bunks in their flight gear, having grown tired of waiting. Beni strode to where the pilot was curled up on his side and kicked the bunk. Billings groaned, then cracked an eye.

"Juarez," Beni told him, holding the palm to his chest to block the sound. "How long?"

"Juarez?" Billings repeated. He sat up and rubbed his face for a few seconds. "Ciudad Juarez? Have to check the charts but...three hours, maybe less? There's an airbase south of the city where we can land. Ummm, what's it called?"

"Raven designation is Norton Station," Evers groaned from her bunk, eyes still closed. "Jesus, it feels like I just fell asleep."

"Three hours," Beni said into his palm. "The Raven airport south of the city, they call it Norton Station. You can pick me up there."

"You're flying in on a Raven plane? *¿Con escaras?* This gets more interesting by the minute. Three hours, then."

* * *

Eddie Echevarria was awake and staring out the window of his office when his desk phone rang. The city stretched out below him nearly to the horizon, a bright wash of color, as if God had kicked glowing coals across the country-side. From this far up, the city looked peaceful and quiet. In fact, the city was waking up for another bright, noisy day.

He answered his phone on the first ring, but still his wife stirred where she lay on the leather sofa, covered by a blanket he hadn't known he had in the office. "*¿Si, Beni?*"

"No word on her or the helicopter yet, but the Raven colonel himself is in the search. The helicopter was diverted from its regular flight path by the Raven aircraft controller at China Base. He told them it was because of missile activity, but that was a lie. Almost immediately afterward, he left the bas, and abandoned his vehicle in a nearby town, but not before destroying, or trying to destroy, any record of the aircraft."

Echevarria frowned and thought it through. "Diverted where?"

"Over the mountains, to the west. Many fewer people, but the Ravens tell me there is nothing else out there of interest."

"So not *to* something, but away from something? Prying eyes?"

Rosita sat up on the couch, the blanket falling from her shoulders. She had not changed her dress from earlier in the day, only taken off her high heel shoes. She squinted at her husband, and he pulled the phone away from his head and put it on speaker.

"He sent them to the middle of nowhere with a lie and then went on the run," Beni said, his voice echoing around the office, which was filled with polished hardwood surfaces.

"So he took money to do this," Rosita said, approaching the desk. It wasn't a question. Her bare feet made no sound on the wood floor. "Why else leave the *escaras*, if not for money. And they pay very well, so to abandon his career, it had to be for a lot of money. Enough for him to retire somewhere, hide. But from who…what is that noise?"

"My aircraft getting ready to lift off. Sir, I have a contact with the *División de Inteligencia, Policia Federal*. I asked him to have his people look for this man, the aircraft controller, and he was just located trying to cross the border at Juarez. They have him in custody. I am heading there as soon as I get off the phone with you to talk to him."

"What do they know?"

"*¿El División de Inteligencia, Policia Federal?* Only that the man is a Raven employee wanted for questioning about a potential kidnapping in the Monterrey area. That is all. But my contact, Inspector Ramon Torres, will want more, *need* more, before he lets me see the man."

"Do we have any other information? Any other leads?"

"Until the Raven colonel finds the helicopter, no."

"Then tell him whatever you need to, to gain access to this man. We need to know what he knows, find out why he did it."

"Torres. Is he a bureaucrat or a hard man?" Rosita asked, staring fiercely down at the phone. "Will he do what needs to be done? Or allow it to be done?'

"*Sí, Señora*. He is not a bureaucrat."

"Then do it," she said sharply. "Do whatever needs to be done. This is my daughter, Beni. My youngest daughter. If anything has happened to her, this man…." Her face began to quiver, but she bit down on the anguish, blinked away the tears.

"All that is in my power, Señora," Beni said calmly then ended the call.

Eddie stared at the silent phone for a few seconds then at his wife leaning over the big desk, fighting her emotions. He stood up and walked to the refrigerator and grabbed a raspberry-flavored water, her favorite. He uncapped the bottle. "Beni will do all he can," he assured her, handing her the water.

Rosita drank from the bottle then shook her head. "And what is that? What can he do?" she asked. "I mean, I have known him for fifteen years, maybe twenty, and he is a strong man, but I do not know him. I see him in his suit every day with his stone face, but I do not know who he is. He was young when he came to work for us, and I was so busy with the girls. How did you find him? Where does he come from? He is far too young to be a retired police officer, but he is not the type anyway."

Eddie smiled. "No, not police. I...saw something in him. Offered him a job. Sent him to the bodyguard training, the security schools."

"He must have been barely out of high school when you hired him. What did you see in him? Why did you do it?"

Eddie turned to stare out the windows at the city. The lights reflecting off the pollution gave the sky the false look of dawn. "Because he saved me. So I saved him."

* * *

"It's cold as hell up here."

Seamus glanced toward Corey but couldn't see him in the dark, not in his camouflage uniform. He heard Corey's boots crunching softly on the dry grass as he approached. A peek over his shoulder showed him the sky above the mountain range to the east starting to lighten, but it would still be a while before dawn.

"Could've used my helmet last night, that's for sure," Seamus agreed, keeping his voice low. He was sitting cross-legged on the cold ground, staring west. His ears were cold, the lower half of his body was numb, and if it had been any lighter he was pretty sure he'd have been able to see his breath. The land below was still in shadow with no sign or sound of any pursuers.

"So you're saying I'm a dick for complaining, since I have a helmet?" Corey asked, the smile evident in his voice. He took a knee beside Seamus and stared off into the distance. "Anything?"

"Not a bloody thing. And I can't decide if that has me worried or not. Don't really care for running for my life, but it would have been nice to hear them stumbling by down below, never the wiser."

"Any aircraft? Raven should be searching for us by now."

"Something, probably a helicopter, far to the west several hours ago, but that's it. I can hope that they're looking left, right, and centre for us, but it's a big country, and there's a war on. Even with our big spender I don't know how much of a priority we might be. They still asleep?"

Corey grunted. "Wrapped up tight in one big shivering ball. Nobody was dressed to spend the night in the mountains, sleeping on the ground. Hopefully this will be over before anybody gets pneumonia." They stayed quiet for a while before he said, "You know, I've been meaning to say something for a while. I'm no expert, but for an Irishman you don't sound very Irish."

Seamus smiled. "I've spent too much time in Her Majesty's bloody fookin' army, haven't I? I sound like a right Englishman now, or at least that's what I'm told at the pubs whenever I make it back. Actually, my mates tell me I have an American accent."

"American accent?" Corey asked in disbelief. "You sound like goddamn James Bond."

"James Bond was actually Scottish," Seamus felt obliged to point out.

"Whatever. Leave it to the English to muck up their own language, as you would say."

"What are you on about?"

"You either mispronounce everything or call it by the wrong name. A boot goes on your foot, it's not part of a car. Neither is a bonnet. They're cookies, not biscuits. Potato chips, not crisps. 'Anticlockwise' is not a real word. Valet—it's a French word, so there should be no question of how to pronounce it—the same way the French do. Yet you Brits say va-*lett*. And it's ass, not arse."

"A gormless Yank schooling a para on grammar? Lookit the goolies on you, and with a face like a bulldog licking piss off a nettle."

"I don't even know what that means. Are you flirting with me?"

The two men laughed together quietly in the darkness.

Sometime during the night when he was so cold his teeth were chattering and his hands were numb, and he thought for sure he was slowly freezing to death, Mike lost all his inhibitions and wrapped his arms around Tina. It was self-preservation, not ardor. She was shivering just as violently as he was, even though they'd put on every piece of clothing they had or could find in the pack. Grabbing her had been a reflex; he'd done it without thinking, but she hadn't resisted. Pressed hard against her back the cold didn't disappear, but gradually they helped warm each other to some small degree. It was still miserable lying there on the ground, just not unbearable. He thought perhaps being wrapped around an exceedingly attractive woman might keep him from falling back to sleep, but he was too tired.

The next thing Mike knew he was blinking awake in the gray light of fresh dawn. At first he didn't know where he was, then suddenly the images of the men charging up the hill at him filled his mind. The flashbacks were in slow motion, but then it had seemed to happen in slow motion. The men had never seen him, and in fact weren't even looking in his direction, they were looking off to the side where all the shooting was occurring.

Mike raised the Blackbird thinking he wouldn't have to shoot, that it was all some sort of mistake, but there was no mistaking the murderous intent in their eyes or the rifles in their hands. Even so, he didn't want to shoot, didn't want to kill anyone else. When they were so close to him he couldn't take the fear anymore he shot the first one, the man farthest up the hill, pulling the trigger until he fell face first into the pine needles. None of the other guerrillas heard the Blackbird going off or didn't recognize the metallic sound of a suppressed carbine as gunfire. Maybe they thought the first man down had simply tripped. They didn't realize they were under fire, didn't see Mike hiding behind his tree, and kept coming. He shot the next one, and the next....

"*¿Esta bien?*" he heard in a worried tone. He realized he was squeezing Tina so hard he was hurting her.

"Sorry," he said quickly, embarrassed and guilty for reasons he couldn't explain. He relaxed his arms and started to pull away from her.

"Not yet," she said quietly, touching his forearm. She gave a small shiver and pushed back against him. "The cold is like death." She shook her head slightly, brushing her hair against his ear. "I do not know how people can do it, living in snow."

"With thick coats and hot chocolate."

Tina frowned. "But it would melt, no?"

"Melt?" It took his sleepy and half-frozen brain a few seconds to catch up. "No, hot chocolate is not chocolate that has been heated up, it is…warm chocolate milk. You wrap your hands around the cup to warm them up, and blow the steam from the top of it until it is cool enough to drink."

"*Como* chocolate flavored coffee? That sounds good. I have never been so cold. I am stiff as a piece of wood."

Mike guessed the temperature had possibly dipped into the forties during the night, and he'd been in plenty of colder weather. But never without a coat, all night, sleeping on the ground. His hands were stiff and aching and nearly numb, and he couldn't feel the side of his body pressed against the thin layer of leaves and pine needles. A slightly thicker long sleeve shirt over a t-shirt was not suitable attire for sleeping outdoors in such weather, but that's what he had. They'd all been dressed for the weather at sea level; at the crash site, 5000 feet of elevation, the temperature had been twenty degrees cooler. He wouldn't have been surprised if they'd climbed another thousand feet or even more while fleeing the guerrillas. Without moving his head to keep from disturbing the girl he looked around and saw his father about a dozen feet away. His father had a light jacket, so he wasn't so thinly dressed, but still he and the pilot had hugged up to combine body heat sometime in the night.

The girl smelled of sweat, and dirt, and faintly of body odor, but she still smelled of girl, and more importantly felt like one—what little he could feel with his cold-deadened arms. As...inappropriate? as it was, Mike was enjoying the forced intimacy. He hadn't had a girlfriend for almost a year, and those twenty minutes on the couch in Brad Sozogni's basement kissing Emily Miller didn't count for much. His friends, high school...it all seemed a universe away. He couldn't see Tina's face, only one ear peeking out through her hair, but he was glad she no longer seemed angry with him and his father.

"I know you don't really like the idea of us hunting dinosaurs," Mike said, trying to keep his teeth from chattering. He was talking quietly to keep from waking his father and the pilot. "But I guess you won't have to worry about that."

"It's not that I don't..." Tina said, then gave a little shake of her head. "It does not matter. *Si*, we have been a little too busy for that."

"No, I didn't mean that. Well, yes, we've been busy, but I mean it's too cold. Too cold up here for dinosaurs, they'd die or go dormant or whatever, since they're cold-blooded."

"No, actually, they're not," she corrected him. "Well, not completely."

"What? I thought they were like snakes or lizards, and those are cold-blooded. Aren't they?"

"Well—again, you know how I feel about the dinosaurs, that they are not really dinosaurs, but your father is right, they were made with dinosaur DNA. And we have learned a lot of things since fossils became flesh and blood. Biologically, physiologically, many dinosaurs are more closely related to birds than lizards. The scientific consensus is that birds are a group of theropod dinosaurs that evolved during the Mesozoic Era. Large meat-eating dinosaurs had a complex system of air sacs similar to those found in modern birds that helped pump air through their lungs."

"So they're warm-blooded?"

She shook her head next to his. "There is not just either/or," she told him. "Thermoregulation in animals *es muy* complex. There are warm-blooded animals, *si*, and cold-blooded animals, but there are a number of species that are somewhere…what is the phrase? *El medio*, in the middle. Endotherms are warm-blooded, like people. But there are actually…is it three? Yes, three types of warm-bloodedness, homeothermy, heterothermy, and poikilothermy. Warm-blooded animals that hibernate for long periods are heterotherms, and their metabolic rates can vary wildly. But just because a bear can sleep for a month and slow its heart does not make it a cold-blooded lizard."

"Okay."

As she lectured him the textbook knowledge floated back up into her conscious mind. She'd read a lot about dinosaurs, and the living creatures going by that name, while she'd flirted with the idea of becoming a paleobotanist. "Ectotherms are the true cold-blooded animals you are thinking of, such as lizards and turtles and snakes. But there are also stenotherms, a cold-blooded animal that can only survive within a very narrow temperature range. The surprising type is the eurytherm, a cold-blooded animal that can function in a wide range of temperatures. They are technically cold-blooded, but can operate almost as a warm-blooded creature. From everything I've read on these 'dinosaurs,' some of them seem to be eurytherms. It is actually quite interesting, and their study has opened up many new avenues of scientific discussion on related topics."

"So they're cold-blooded, but being cold doesn't slow them down?"

She nodded her head. "*Si.* But there is a lot of evidence the smaller dinosaurs were actually warm blooded, as are their bird descendants. They've found fossils high up on mountains where it would have been too cold for ectotherms to survive. And the extremely large dinosaurs, there is a theory for them…." She searched her memory. "Gianto…no, gigantothermy. They were cold blooded, but because they were so large their very size and mass helped them regulate their heat and behave as if they were warm-blooded, or close to it. Studies of bone histology and body type has a lot of scientists convinced that it actually depended on the species of dinosaur as to whether it was warm or cold blooded. That has been the case with these created dinosaurs, but their DNA is so polluted, no true scientist wants to make any conclusions about the real dinosaurs based on these creatures' metabolisms."

"Well, being warm blooded didn't really seem to help us last night."

"It kept us alive," she told him. "Uncomfortable, but alive."

Mike nodded his head in agreement, but arms wrapped around and body pressed against a pretty girl…he wasn't so uncomfortable any more. "What about it being so dry? I thought dinosaurs lived in swamps or jungles."

"Some did, but paleontologists have discovered fossils all over the world, in what at the time was every kind of climate you can imagine. Even along the south coast of Australia, which with continental drift at the time was much nearer the South Pole, and temperatures wouldn't have been much different than what we have here right now. The Triassic period, immediately before the Jurassic, was warm but arid with extensive deserts, even sand dunes. Those deserts lasted through the Jurassic period. They had conifer forests similar to the ones we've been walking through too."

Mike didn't know whether to be anxious or happy at the thought that they still might see some dinosaurs.

* * *

The sun was up, somewhere behind the mountains to the east, but the land before them was still in shadow, gray. Seamus was surprised how much of the countryside he could see looking west, the direction they'd come. Past the steep slope at his feet the land was rolling hills, carpeted with trees and thick scrub.

"It doesn't look nearly as tough a climb when you can see it," Corey said, peering over the edge at the slope they'd crawled up the night before. He sat back on his heels beside Seamus and looked around. "Are we the highest point?"

"This ridge is higher than anything to the west of us except for that peak we could see from the crash site. To the east you go further into the Orientals, and those mountains are taller." The closest ridge to the east, behind which the sun was rising, looked several kilometers away and was significantly higher than their current spot. "I'm hoping we can head more south than east today; I'm bloody tired of climbing." To the east there seemed to be a valley between them and the high ridge, but it was still dark and filled with mist or fog.

Seamus suddenly squinted off into the distance. Leonidas was lying across his lap, and he lifted the rifle and put his eye to the scope.

"What is it?"

"Movement," Seamus said softly, then lowered the rifle. "Just a deer." He looked at the younger man. "What say we go wake up the sleepyheads, see if anybody's been rude enough to freeze to death in the night."

* * * * *

Chapter Fifteen

"Oh my God, I can't even move."

Seamus looked at Roger on his side on the ground, trying to sit up. He looked a bit like a turtle on its back trying to roll over. "Take your time, stretch, do whatever you need to do. I'll grab you some ibuprofen out of the pack. You want someone to help pull you to your feet?"

"No!" Roger said sharply, holding up a hand. "Not unless you want me to scream. I've got this, just—give me some time." His entire back was one big screaming knot.

"You've got ten minutes, and then I am pulling you to your feet. We can't afford to wait any more than that, and we can't have any screaming." He looked around. "Anybody needs to use a toilet, find a friendly bush somewhere close. And stay away from the edge of the slope we climbed last night, I want us to stay quiet and out of sight."

Mike was jumping up and down nearby, trying to warm up a little. When Seamus had come stomping into the clearing Tina jumped to her feet and headed off to pee or something, and all the heat they'd been generating together vanished. Mike was left feeling abandoned. "Do we have any food?" he asked Seamus.

"There are still a few energy bars in the pack." It was sitting on the ground open and he gestured at it. "Some full water bottles as well, under the empty ones. Everybody grab one of each but bury your trash, no need to advertise we were here. I want to keep a few empty water bottles in the pack in case we find somewhere to fill them up again." He nodded at Mike. "We're about as high up here as we're likely to get. Wouldn't hurt to pull your palm out and power it up, see if you've got a signal."

"Right."

"How far did we travel yesterday?" Hansen asked. He sniffed and rubbed his running nose, pretty sure the brutal night had given him a cold.

"With all the climbing it's a bit hard to keep straight, but at least a quarter of the way to Victoria. Maybe as much as a third." Disappointed groans greeted his pronunciation.

"That's it?"

"We walked for hours."

"We didn't really get moving until the afternoon," Seamus told them. "We avoid steep climbs and any firefights, we can easily halve the remaining distance today."

"How are we going to avoid climbing?" Roger asked bitterly. He was doing his damndest to stretch his back and only getting about an inch of movement, accompanied by stabbing pain. At least the pain made him forget about the cold.

"We've got a tall range to the east of us, a few klicks away, but I don't see any reason why we'd need to climb it. We can follow this ridge south as far as it goes, do as few elevation changes as possible. Last night I wanted the high ground in case we had to make a stand. But I haven't seen any sign of pursuers."

"What about search craft? Are they even looking for us?"

"Nothing close enough to signal. I saw a helicopter last night far off to the west, maybe near our crash site."

"Still think leaving the crash site was a good idea?" Roger asked. Mike lifted his palm up and turned, but the device still couldn't get a signal.

"Considering they sent another two vehicles full of men after us on that slope yesterday, yes," Seamus told him bluntly. "That crash site was not defensible mate, not if they were careful and didn't come in blundering like the first caravan of idiots. They'll find the crash site, widen the search, find either a vehicle or bodies or some evidence of our second dust-up yesterday, and then Bob's your uncle, we're golden. They'll figure out what's going on and where we're likely to be heading."

"How long is that going to take?" Mike asked.

"Actually, I'm surprised it's taken this long," Hansen said. The pilot sniffed and shifted his broken arm which was aching painfully after being cold all night. "We should see helicopters doing search and rescue in this area any time."

"But until we do," Seamus said, "we need to keep moving." The gray dawn was quickly turning to the thin bright light of morning. He looked at Roger, who still wasn't even into an upright seated position. "Mate, you need some help stretching? Or maybe getting up? Moving might help loosen you up a titch. Because sitting here hoping they don't show, that they just gave up, is not a sound tactic."

Roger took a deep breath, blew it out, and held out a hand to the contractor. "Yes. But slow. I was serious about screaming."

* * *

"D o those hurt?" Mike asked.

Tina was examining her hands as they walked. Her hands and arms and legs were covered in thin cuts and scratches from the hike the night before. Some of them were lined with dried blood, and stung. Her shorts had been wonderful when the weather was oven hot, but in the cold and dark, walking through bushes and past cacti? Not so much.

"It is not so bad."

He offered his bottle of water. "You want to wash them off?" Her hands and knees and elbows were dirty as well. So were his, but he wasn't a pretty girl.

"Yes, but I think we should keep the water to drink, just in case."

"Yeah, you're probably right." They were following the ridge to the south, working their way through thin brush and tall grass on a nearly even slope. It was an easy walk, at least for the moment. Mike looked over his shoulder. "Dad, you doing okay? Is the walking making your back any better?"

"It's not making it any worse," Roger said through clenched teeth. The pain was making his eyes water, and he couldn't walk without hunching forward and listing a bit to one side, but he was moving. "Don't worry about me." He peered up at his son. "How are you doing?"

"Fine," Mike said quickly. He could tell his father wasn't talking about his body but rather his mind, after shooting someone the day before. If his father knew the whole story… "Cold all night, but, uh, you know." He walked a little faster, and Roger fell behind, no chance of keeping up with his back in the shape it was.

The top of the ridge began narrowing, and before they'd traveled south for five minutes, the sides fell away. The ridge became too narrow and treacherous to walk on, all jagged rock, so they had to choose a slope.

"Right or left side, west or east?" Corey asked Seamus.

"Not west, I want to keep this thing between us and anybody that might be following." Seamus looked to the east. The far ridge was several kilometers away, and in-between was a wide valley, still in shadow and filled with morning mist. Although they couldn't see the floor, the valley seemed to stretch quite a distance to the south. "Let's stay on the east slope."

The slope proved to be rocky and steep, and they found themselves gradually descending. Ten difficult minutes later Mike felt wetness on his face and looked around, only to realize they were moving down through the layer of fog covering the valley floor. The fog was thick and still, pearl white and thick as a cloud. "This is neat," he said quietly. The fog muffled the sound of his voice and made it seem as if he was whispering. "Like flying through clouds in an airplane."

The moisture made everything slick, and they had to take their time clambering over the glistening rocks. Whether it was the thick fog or not, sounds echoed oddly around them, and the entire group grew quiet.

"No running off," Seamus called out from the back of the line. The fog was so dense he could only see about fifty feet in front of him. Hansen was in the lead, a fuzzy gray silhouette, and he waved with his good arm to acknowledge he'd heard.

Before they'd descended another fifty feet they were clear of the fog, which hung thick above their heads like gray cotton candy. It made the morning as dark as a stormy afternoon, and even without the fog they couldn't see farther than a quarter mile to the east. The valley floor was just below, and when they reached it Seamus called a halt and looked around.

"That was cool," Mike said, staring upward at the fog layer.

"That must happen here a lot, trapped moisture, look how green the valley is," Hansen observed. The valley floor was long field grass and jumbled rocks, but instead of the mostly brown grass they'd been seeing this was dark green and glossy.

"Air currents must cause a bit of a microclimate between the two ranges," Tina observed. "More precipitation, yes, more humidity, but also it's warmer, do you feel? Only a few degrees, but that can make quite a big difference. I'm surprised we've already reached the valley floor, it looked deeper from up above." She guessed they'd only descended about two hundred feet. She peered to the east. The uneven ground was hard to see in the dim light.

"It's a little wide open for my taste, but at least the fog will cover us," Corey said.

"Until it burns off," Seamus said. "Okay, let's keep moving. Watch you don't trip on the rocks."

After several minutes, Corey, who was now in the lead, came across a narrow but well-used game trail heading south. The dirt path was a little easier walking and seemed to be heading in the right direction, so he began following it. Five minutes later he stopped so quickly Tina almost bumped into him.

"What is it?" she asked reflexively, then looked past him. The valley floor stretched off to their left toward the other ridge, but in front of them it abruptly ended. In a cliff. "I thought the valley might be deeper than this," she observed, taking a few steps to peer over the edge. She could see more green several hundred feet below. "This is maybe a plateau or upthrust geological artifact at the end of the true valley bottom." The cliff falling away before them seemed to be a near-vertical rock wall.

"How do we make it down?" Seamus asked, stepping forward.

"Animals found a way down," Hansen observed, pointing at the game trail. The trail hugged the right side of the valley and hooked around a chair-sized boulder out of sight.

"Unless the trail was made by lemmings," Roger said quietly.

Seamus heard him and laughed. He walked forward and looked past the chalk-colored boulder. "Yes, there's a way down here. Looks a bit steep, and slick, so everyone be careful."

"Up top I assumed the trail was made by deer, but this freaking thing has to be the work of mountain goats," Corey swore ten minutes later. They were maybe a third of the way down what was nearly a vertical rock wall, very carefully picking their way along a path that was either narrow or steep or slick or some combination of all three. He wasn't scared of heights, but the fact that one wrong step could send him plummeting to certain death had his heart rate way up.

"*Es loco*," Tina agreed, directly in front of him. She was shaking her head and couldn't stop looking over the side of the trail to the valley floor far below.

"Don't look, you'll only make it worse," Corey told her. She turned and he could see from her eyes how close to panic she was. "Just look at the cliff next to you, and hold onto it with a hand every time you take a step."

"But I don't want to slip!"

"Then look at the trail. And relax."

"Relax!" she said indignantly.

"You are a smart woman, probably smarter than me. So tell me, if the ground was only a foot below the trail, would you be so worried about falling?"

"No," she admitted.

"The trail is as wide as a ladder for the most part, and only slippery in spots. You have very expensive boots with textured soles designed specifically for this kind of work. So keep putting one foot in front of the other and let your boots do their work. Keep your brain out of it."

Corey'd had to take the big sniper rifle off his shoulder thirty feet down the trail, as it kept bumping the cliff face or making him feel off balance. He already had his carbine hanging off his chest from its sling. The last thing he wanted was the big rifle's weight pulling him backward toward the edge. After mulling it over for a few seconds he ended up using the Ulfberht as an improvised walking stick, placing its buttstock on the trail ahead of his feet, feeling his way along. It wasn't fast, but he could still move faster than Roger with his injured back.

"There's a flat spot up ahead, we'll stop and take a rest there," Seamus called back some time later. He was holding onto the rock face to his left with one hand and Leonidas with the other as he moved along a stretch of the trail that resembled a stone staircase, except it was barely a foot wide and the stones were covered with slick moss. The game trail was seemingly the only way up or down the cliff on foot and zigzagged back and forth across the cliff face.

"At least it's finally warm," Mike said.

Behind his son, Roger lifted his head in surprise. Mike was right, as they'd climbed down from the ridge where they'd overnighted, the temperature had risen ten, maybe fifteen degrees, and the air was noticeably more humid. Roger was sweating, but that was more a result of the effort he was making fighting the pain in his back than anything temperature related.

The flat spot was barely larger than a dining room table, but compared to the narrow trail it seemed big as a concert hall. There was enough room for all of them to sit down, but just barely. "And look what we have here," Seamus said happily, eyeing a trickle of water running down the cliff face. It ran across the flat expanse of stone in a rivulet an inch wide.

Seamus unshouldered his backpack and handed out the remaining bottles of water. "Drink up," he told everyone. "Best place to store water is inside your body. Then I can refill them."

"Is that water safe to drink?" Roger asked. Mike had to help him sink down into a seated position. Sitting still hurt him, but slightly less than standing, and at last he was finally able to put the AK down. It seemed to have tripled in weight since the day before.

"Probably. But we don't have anything to treat it with anyway. Maybe we can boil some later if we find something we can use as a bowl. If not, well, we should have walked out of here well before any of us comes down with dysentery or giardia." Seamus finished his water bottle, the last full one in the pack, and held it under the trickle of water. There were a lot of trickles running down the rocky cliff face, but he could only reach one of them from the ledge.

"Lovely," Hansen said with a thin smile. He was sitting closest to the edge and looked around as he sucked down the contents of his water bottle. There were dozens of tiny streams of water running down the imposing cliff face, and they made a gentle hiss as they bounced down the rock. While the thick layer of fog was high above them, the air around them was hazy with mist. The mist gave all the greenery below a grayish cast. Then his head twitched and he looked to the south, toward the valley out of sight below them. "Hey...." He cocked his head.

"What?" Corey was standing next to him.

"Is that...." Hansen peered into the fog overhead, but the sky was nothing but a gray blanket so thick it was hard to pinpoint the direction of the sun. But as he listened the faint sound grew slightly louder. "Yep."

"Is that a helicopter?" Mike asked. He had excellent hearing. The sound was faint, and muffled. Maybe from the fog?

"Blackhawk," Hansen said, as soon as he was sure. "Way out there. A mile at least."

"Yeah?" Seamus said. He still couldn't hear it. Too many gunfights. "Probably searching for us." He stared upward at the thick fog layer. There was no way any search crew could spot them at the moment unless they were using thermal optics, and even then he wasn't sure how well they worked through thick fog.

"Does anybody have a flare gun? Or tracer ammo?" Roger asked. He could hear it now.

Seamus shook his head. "Sorry mate." He stuck another empty plastic bottle under the thin stream of water.

"Maybe we should have stayed on the ridge where we slept," Tina said.

Seamus shrugged. "Maybe. But they still might not have spotted us. Or that ridge might be full of guerrillas now, poking over our tracks. Best to stay on heading to Victoria, and keep the villains to our rear."

It took almost a minute to refill each bottle, but at least the water was clear. He screwed the cap on the next one as tight as it would go, stuffed it in the bottom of the pack next to an oddly-shaped hard-case. He cracked open the silvery-gray container to reveal a camera, then closed it back up. He began filling the next bottle. It was a maddeningly slow process.

"Is that your camera in the pack?" he asked the girl. It had originally been her pack.

"Yes, why? Did it get damaged?" The case it was in was supposed to be nearly indestructible.

"If I'd known it was in there I would have dumped it out at the Vaquero," Seamus told her. "Have your father buy you another one. Do you know how heavy this bloody pack was when we started out?" He wanted to be mad at her, but he knew he had only himself to blame for not fully exploring the pack's contents before he slung it over his shoulder and started hiking up and down mountains.

"Don't throw it away," she said in a panic. She'd had the Nikon with her for all of her graduate studies and used it to document her findings.

"Most of the energy bars and half the water bottles are gone now. Even filling the ones we have back up the pack will barely be half full." He sighed. "Much as I'd like to toss it over the edge..." He sighed. "Hell, I've carried it this far."

"Thank you," she told him sincerely.

"Look at that, that's pretty," Mike said, staring upward.

The rest of the group followed his gaze and saw a bright yellow butterfly lazily fluttering down the face of the cliff. The mist gave the light an odd focus, and at first the butterfly seemed right above their heads. But it kept coming closer, and closer, until finally it bobbed and fluttered right above their heads.

"Holy crap," Hansen said, staring at it.

Seamus pulled back against the rock face of the cliff, his eyes wide, the half-full water bottle in his hand forgotten. The butterfly danced an arm's length above his head, yellow with gold and red highlights on its wings. It was beautiful, but what had grabbed their attention was its size—its wingspan was easily over a foot. Seamus could feel the gentle puffs of air on his cheeks from its wings, which were tissue thin and nearly translucent. The butterfly bobbed lazily above him, then drifted out into the open air away from the wall and the group. Then there was a loud buzz and a wet crunching smack and the butterfly was gone.

"What the hell was that?" Hansen said, scooting back from the edge. He looked around nervously.

"I think it was a dragonfly," Roger said in disbelief. It had hit the butterfly like a hawk going after a sparrow.

"A dragonfly? The thing was a foot long, maybe a foot and a half!" Corey peered down over the cliff but couldn't see anything.

"And me without a helmet," Seamus said, checking the misty air around them for any more giant flying insects.

"I'd settle for a shotgun," Hansen said. "Do those things have stingers or claws?"

"Giant dragonflies? They had those back during prehistoric times, right?" Mike asked Tina. "You think they brought those back to life for Pangaea too?"

"Not just the dragonfly, that butterfly as well. The dragonfly has to eat something." She climbed to her feet, a disgusted look on her face. The benettite, the dragonfly, the monstrous butterfly...they hadn't even seen a sauropod yet, and still it was obvious Pangaea was polluting the countryside in many more ways than she had ever suspected. She thought hard, trying to dig up some of the information she'd ingested when she'd had that brief flirtation with paleobotany. Meganeura? Was that the name of the genus of the giant dragonfly? No, that wasn't right. She frowned. They weren't actually dragonflies but rather griffinflies, the largest insects ever discovered, but totally extinct. Insects pollinate plants, so any study of the plant life of the period had included the insects. If she remembered correctly they had wingspans as long as her arm. And as scary as having something that big whirring by your head was, they only ate smaller insects. "You are in no danger from them. But I don't understand it."

"What?"

"The prehistoric era was filled with much larger insects than we have today. Scientists have concluded that was because the atmosphere at the time was much richer in oxygen, over thirty percent compared to the current twenty percent."

"So?"

"So I am not sure how they managed to work around that with these new—" she looked at Mike "—Frankenstein's Monster dragonflies. While there might have been a sealed hyperoxic exhibit at Pangaea for them to fly around in, if anything, the atmospheric oxygen content in these mountains is lower."

"Maybe they breathe nitrogen," Hansen opined.

She made a sour face. "At this point nothing would surprise me."

All of their heads snapped around toward the valley floor out of sight through the mist below them as a loud bellow rolled up the cliff face from the valley below.

"What the hell was that?" Roger asked. "Was that a cow?"

The low bellow was answered by a much louder trumpeting that echoed hollowly in the mist.

"*That's* no freaking cow," Hansen said.

"That sounded like an elephant," Mike said.

Seamus eyed the game trail where it left the landing and continued downward. Twenty feet farther on it cut back on itself and disappeared below them. "I'd wager we're going to find out."

"Is it too late to head back up the cliff?"

* * *

Beni felt his palmpad buzzing in his pocket as he sat in the Peregrine. He pulled it out and didn't recognize the number. He spent several seconds trying to figure out how to take a call while wearing a headset in a noisy aircraft, then answered the call and wedged the flat Sirion datapalm between his ear and the headset.

"*¿Sí?* This is Beni."

"Mister Trujillo, this is Colonel Kresge, Raven Command. I have found our missing helicopter."

"You have? Is she there? Is she all right?" Beni smacked Manny dozing beside him and the man sat up, looking around. When he saw Beni was talking to someone he leaned his head in close.

"Let me tell you what I have, then you can ask your questions. I have the helicopter. It went down along their redirected flight path, along the western border of the Orientals." Kresge stood on top of the cliff overlooking the crash site. He'd gone up with one of his men mostly for a better signal, but also to check something out. And he'd found the empty brass cases he'd been expecting. A quick examination of some of the dead guerrillas had seemed to indicate they had been shot from an elevated position while in a crossfire. They'd been professionally ambushed.

"It crashed?" Beni couldn't stop himself from asking questions, but the colonel ignored him. After finding the crash site and circling it for a few minutes and seeing no movement and receiving no incoming fire Kresge's helicopter had set down in the middle of the gravel road about a quarter mile away, the closest spot clear enough and flat enough to safely land a bird. He and his men had proceeded on foot, as had the troopers in a second Blackhawk. Both the aircraft were now circling the area providing overwatch with their mini-guns and cannon.

"The crash looks pretty bad, but I've seen worse. This was not mechanical failure, the helicopter was brought down. By a Shrike, which is, well, it's a kind of kamikaze drone that fries the electronics with an EMP just before burying itself in the nearest heat source, in this case the engine. Titanium. My man found pieces of it still in the engine cowling. They're actually French, but I've seen them in our inventory. I'd heard that FRAP might have a few but never seen them actually use one. Guess they saved it for something special. The crash didn't damage the Blackhawk too badly so it couldn't have been too extreme, and there's more vomit than blood in the chopper. When we arrived we found no Blackhawk crewmembers or passengers, but we have found half a dozen dead FRAP guerrillas and evidence of a firefight. Questions?"

Beni found he was gripping the seat hard enough to turn his knuckles white. "Let me be sure I understand you. She was not there. No helicopter crewmembers were there. But you have dead *La Fuerza?*" Manny's eyebrows went up and his expression went dark. "Has she been kidnapped?"

Kresge heard the question as he stared down at the crash site, then looked out at the surrounding hillsides. Finally, he glanced up at the circling helis. Then he looked down at the fired shell case in his hand. The headstamp was LCOF, and the only ammo anyone was using in this war made at the Lake City Ordnance Foundry were the black-tipped sabot rounds feeding Raven helicopter mini-guns. The cases were in the wrong spot for them to have ejected from the mini-gun as the helicopter went down, which meant someone had stripped them from the belt and loaded them into their personal weapon. And he'd put money on the fact that no FRAP flunkie was smart or motivated enough to do that.

"I can't say this with one hundred percent certainty, but the evidence here strongly indicates that my men did their job and kept everyone safe. I've got one vigorously destroyed FRAP vehicle here, and tire tracks leaving the area. If the FRAP had been the victors I'd have dead friendlies here, the guerrillas aren't good enough to have won without a serious fight, which means wounded and dead on both sides. And they tend to execute wounded. It looks like they were ambushed. I'd guess the survivors took off in whatever second vehicle the guerillas showed up in. Something big, probably a truck, from the tread pattern."

"So where are they?"

"Tracks head west through the trees to a road, and from there it appears they turned south. Heading toward Victoria Base, presumably, which isn't too far away all things considered, but we didn't spot any vehicles in that direction before we found the crash site. I've got UAVs searching, and two helicopters here with me, but following the tracks from the air will be difficult at best. We'll be taking off momentarily and moving the search south and east. Now that we know their jumping off point it will help the search parameters immensely."

"Are they being chased? Why did they leave the crash site?"

"Unknown at this time."

Beni frowned. "But you are sure, the helicopter was brought down deliberately?"

"One hundred percent. And I'm not too happy about it. FRAP shouldn't be sticking their noses this far north. But that also means that they won't have as many men available as they would further south."

Beni nodded. "I am in a…" He snapped his fingers until the name came to him. "Peregrine. Raven Peregrine. I can have it sent your way if you need additional aircraft." The sun was up behind them, sending long shadows across the ground below.

Kresge blinked. "You're riding in a Peregrine?" That was a nicer aircraft than either of the two helicopters he had available to him. He was surprised at first, and still a bit put out at the resources dedicated to the search for a civilian, no matter how powerful her father was, but then the light bulb went off. She was important because the FRAP thought she was important. In going after her maybe they would misstep or overreach and provide Raven an opportunity to do some real damage to their ranks, or get some valuable intelligence. The missing girl wasn't an annoyance, he saw that now. No, she was an opportunity. "No, we've got all we should need here. And now that we've verified a FRAP force in the area, I'll have no problem getting whatever resources I need reassigned to this area for the search. It's just a matter of time, now."

"Thank you. I will inform Señor Echevarria, and please let me know if you find anything else." Beni thought it best not to inform the colonel that he was on his way to interrogate one of his men, even if the man had obviously sold information to the guerrillas.

"I will call you with any further developments," Kresge told him, then disconnected the call. They he punched in the number for his XO at Raven Command. He wanted every bird they had in the air, searching for FRAP activity, and every trigger puller on the base on five-minute alert in case they found it. The only problem was most of his birds were down south helping with the Guadalajara offensive. Along with most of his men.

"Tony! That tech screwed us on records, completely destroyed the manifest, but contact China Base, contact Central Command, contact whoever. I want to know how many of our men were on that chopper when it took off. I want names, ranks, their entire service records on my palm as soon as possible. And I want to know who else was on that chopper, or if it was just our VIP." He peeked over the cliff again at the dead guerrillas directly below him. Most of them seemed to have been stripped of weapons. And a few had been gnawed by animals. Since he couldn't say for sure what kind of animals, he'd neglected to pass on that bit of information to Echevarria's man.

* * *

"So her helicopter has been shot down and she is on the run?" Manuel said, scowling.

"With Raven soldiers," Beni said. He punched in Señor Echevarria's number to give him the news.

"Why do you look happy? She is being chased by *La Fuerza!*"

"I am happy because now I know she is not dead. She is alive, and fighting. You did not know her growing up, Manny." Beni smiled. "If there is one thing that girl is good at, it's fighting."

* * * * *

Chapter Sixteen

David Tejada maneuvered his new Toyota Furia hatchback around the concrete barricades designed to slow down terrorists, then pulled up to the entrance of the underground parking garage. He swiped his card and punched in his access code, then waited while the door rattled up.

He didn't get his own parking spot, he wasn't nearly senior enough for that, but arriving early as he usually did meant he didn't have a long walk to the elevator. His bag held his lunch—soda, apple, and gourmet sandwich that he made himself every day—as well as his issued EstrellaCorp tablet. The company tablet was a joke, as far as he was concerned, and he always brought his own with him to the office even though use of personal electronics on company time was frowned upon.

David waved his card at the scanner outside the elevator, and when the doors opened he bent down for the retinal scanner inside. While there were hundreds of other businesses in *Torre Cielo*, the only way to get access to floors 40 and above, the headquarters of *Corporación Estrella*, EstrellaCorp to the rest of the world, were these secure elevators. He punched the button for 42.

His supervisor saw him getting off the elevator and intercepted Tejada even before he could reach his cubicle. "Good, you're here early. I was about to call you."

"*¿Que pasa Reynaldo?*"

"You need to head up to Señor Echevarria's office right away."

"I'm—I what?"

"You need to go right now."

"What did I—I didn't do anything," he said in confusion. "*Señor Echevarria? ¿El Señor Echevarria?*"

"Yes. His office up on 65."

"I know where it is; I've just never been up that high. It's dangerous to your health."

"Just get up there."

"What time does he come in?"

Reynaldo shook his head. "He never went home last night."

"What's going on?"

"I don't know, but it's something big. He called down here himself, asking for a tech."

"And you picked me? Why?"

"Go," Reynaldo said in exasperation.

Heart hammering in his chest, David got back on the elevator and hit the red button for 65. The control panel beeped and he had to bend over for the retinal scanner again. He must have been approved, because the elevator began moving almost immediately.

At 65, the doors opened onto a small lobby with a tiny but prohibitively expensive teak desk. There was a surprisingly pretty girl behind it and, standing next to her, one of the uniformed guards, all muscle and scowl and holstered pistol.

He cleared his throat. "David Tejada. I was sent up here and told to see Señor Echevarria?"

She clicked her screen and nodded. "Yes, he's waiting for you. Door at the end of the hall." She nodded to her left.

Clutching his bag to his chest he walked nervously down the hall. It ended at a giant door covered with candy apple red wood. He lifted a hand hesitantly, then knocked. The door was opened a second later by the man himself.

"Tejada? Good, come in."

Señor Eduardo Echevarria was not the man that he was expecting. Hair askew, it appeared as if he'd slept in his suit. He even smelled stale. As Tejada entered the room, a woman stood up from where she was lying on the couch, and he recognized her instantly as Señor Echevarria's actress wife. But she looked horrible, face all blotchy from crying, and her dress appeared slept in as well. He nodded at her. "Señora."

Echevarria went back around his huge desk and sat down heavily. "Your supervisor tells me that you are the smartest man I have working in my IT department," Echevarria said without introduction.

David blinked. He was surprised Reynaldo had said that. It was true, he was just surprised Reynaldo had admitted it to anyone. "He is too kind."

"Is it true?"

"Well, I would never say such a thing myself, Señor. Your IT department is full of—"

"This is no time for bullshit, son. Are you the best I have?"

David paused. Echevarria's wife was standing off to one side, studying him. "I think so."

"Then I have a job for you. But let me first explain. If you pass on the information I am about to give you, let's just say that being unable to ever find a job in your field again would be the least of the problems which would befall you. Am I clear?"

David swallowed. "*Si Señor.*"

"Good. My daughter Margarita was on a Raven helicopter which crashed. Shot down by *La Fuerza*. She is being pursued by *La Fuerza* through the Sierra Madre Oriental mountains northeast of here. She is with Raven commandos, but no one has been able to communicate with them. An EMP destroyed their electronics, we think. Do you know what an EMP is?"

"*Sí Señor.*" David was blinking rapidly, trying to digest the information being thrown at him. He knew who Margarita Echevarria was; she was a cult figure among the employees. Youngest daughter of the great Gordito, fighting him at every turn, that photo of her in a bikini in the tabloids when she was seventeen. *Ay, que foto…*it was a rare EstrellaCorp male employee under the age of sixty who hadn't spent some serious time staring at it. The tabloid had called her the reincarnation of Sophia Loren, and David had had to look up who that was—but the resemblance was uncanny… although Gordito's teenage daughter had been noticeably bustier than the old Italian movie star. Then, at 18, she'd refused public marriage proposals from both an Austrian prince and a Saudi Arabian sheik. Neither man had ever met her; they just knew who her father was, and had seen *la foto infame*. She'd had no interest in the family business, or business at all, and instead had gone to school for something completely different—medicine, if he remembered correctly. And she was on a helicopter that had been shot down? *¿La Fuerza?* EMP? *Madre de Dios.*

"She does not have her palmpad with her," Señora Echevarria told him, finally speaking. "I do not know if she has another device, but she has not called and has not emailed us, so maybe she does not have any working electronics."

"And Raven seems to be doing all it can to find her," her husband continued. "But I would feel better if we could get into her email account, see if she has sent any messages."

"Or tried to," his wife added.

"Or last logged on, if that is possible. She has an Estrella email account, I can show you her address."

It was Rosita's idea, really, she was going insane with worry. Eduardo was pretty sure it was a waste of time, but doing something was always better than doing nothing. Beni's updates were few and far between, and while he was making progress, he still hadn't found his daughter.

"You want me to hack into her account? Even though you own the company, *señor*, and she is your daughter, I am not sure if that is legal."

"I am unconcerned with the legality of it," Echevarria said flatly. "I am only concerned as to whether or not you can do it."

David pursed his lips, trying to decide whether or not he wanted to dive head first into this. "If she has an email account with us checking her access to it is easy," David told them, deciding quickly. He had never been shy about taking risks. "Being that it *is* our system, we have numerous shortcuts installed to make such a thing as this easier. Many of them are government mandated, as you know."

Echevarria nodded. "I have asked the *Federales* and Raven to scan the area for any radio or data signals but apparently they don't have any of the technology they'd need for that in the area. It is rather remote and far to the north of where they normally fight *La Fuerza*. Is there a way you can get into her account, see if she has been sending emails or anything?"

David nodded. "Most likely. What about her other email accounts, addresses, profiles? Do you have a list of them?"

"She only has the one," the missing girl's mother said. "The Estrella address."

David thought about how to say it diplomatically. Hmm. "Señor. Señora. She is a strong-willed young woman who is famous for having fought and argued with you her whole life," he said slowly. "Do you think that the only email address she has is the one with the company you own? Please. She may even have another phone number or palm registered to her that she has not shared with you. I will find out all there is to find out. Although there may be nothing."

Eduardo nodded. "We know."

"How long?" Rosita asked him.

"Give me a couple of hours. Should I call, or...?"

"Come up here in person when you have something to tell us. We're not going anywhere."

* * *

Norton Station was little more than a huge expanse of cement surrounded on three sides by pre-fabricated rectangular buildings, all identical, and all throwing off glints of orange in the morning light. The only interesting thing to look at was the open hangar. There were two hangars, and the big door of one had been slid open. Inside, Inspector Ramon Torres could see sleepy mechanics eyeballing some huge helicopter as they sipped their coffees and tried to wake up.

The smell of rubber and kerosene and hot asphalt tickled his nose even though the morning air was cool and humid; it was as if the Raven base itself couldn't wait for the sun to start baking the ground and everything on it.

There were six helipads in the center of the base, such as it was, covering an area at least as big as two *fútbol* fields. They were all empty, so he knew the party he was waiting on had yet to arrive.

He rolled up to the guard house in his battered sedan, the morning sun peeking over the ground to the west. There was a radio partially hidden below the dash. The vehicle belonged to the *División de Inteligencia's* motor pool, and rattled so much he wasn't convinced it would remain in one piece on his high-speed journey north in the middle of the night, but it had.

To his great chagrin the guards would not allow him on the base, and he had to wait in the parking lot outside the double row of fences topped with razor wire. The guards knew who he was—they'd been told he would be arriving to pick up an incoming passenger—but that did not apparently grant him access to Raven property. As if this was their country, and he was *un turista*. So he sat in his dusty car, smoked, and fumed. His black suit was wrinkled from having been worn all day and then all night while driving. He wore his trademark narrow black tie. It hadn't been in style for so long it would probably be in style again soon.

Not quite two hours after he arrived, he heard the unmistakable sound of an aircraft approaching. A helicopter, and a large one, from the sound. When it appeared above the buildings on the far side of the helipads he frowned. It was big, but not a helicopter. No, it was *un feo híbrido* of helicopter and plane that looked too awkward to fly. Bristling with guns, it set down lightly on one of the center helipads and immediately its engines began winding down. Two men jumped down from the aircraft and jogged his way.

They stopped briefly at the gate to talk to the rifle-toting Raven guards, then walked to his car. Torres eyed their dusty and wrinkled suits, then flicked his gaze back to the impressive Raven aircraft. It appeared neither old nor battle worn, which made it stand out.

The car windows were down, and Beni leaned his elbows on the passenger side door. He peered in at the inspector. *El Federale* looked much the same as he had the first time they'd run into each other all those years ago—a narrow hatchet face, almost vulpine, jet black hair, with a permanent squint in one eye from a scar that ran along his left temple. "You still have him?" Beni asked.

Torres nodded, the smoke from the cigarette in the corner of his mouth snaking around his head. He glanced at Beni, then his companion, who was a little younger and much thicker. "*Sí*. This *escara*. Who is he?"

Beni glanced at Manuel, then back at the inspector. "Raven communications officer. He diverted a Raven helicopter off its flight plan and out into the country where it should not have been, where it was shot down. The passengers and crew of the helicopter are now on foot in the mountains, being chased by *La Fuerza* in an area far north of where those *cabrónes* should be." He paused and licked his lips. "Margarita Echevarria, Señor Echevarria's youngest daughter, was on that helicopter."

The Inspector digested that information silently for several seconds, then nodded. "I understand Señor Echevarria's concern, then. We should speak to this radio man. Get in. It is a fifteen minute drive to our station in Juarez."

The building housing the district headquarters of the *Policia Federal* in Juarez was a long low cinderblock building that decades past had been painted tan. After being brutalized by the sun and smog and windblown debris, it was now nearly the same color as the bare earth surrounding it. It had few windows and almost no character. Torres parked his dusty, creaking sedan in the lot and led the two men in the front door. Two policemen in full tactical gear stood outside the entrance holding battered CZ 805 assault rifles, looking bored. The *Policía Federal* had not stood idly by during the war, and the "Federales" had quite frequently participated in joint missions with the Mexican Army and Raven. Several of their headquarters in the south had been attacked by guerillas. In a civil war, the line between army and police was blurred and often broken.

Torres badged the uniformed corporal running the scanners in the entryway and asked to see the chief inspector in charge of the district. The officer eyed Torres and the two suited men with him silently, then waved over a younger officer working the counter. Torres, Beni, and Manuel weaved through a big, dusty, cluttered room. A few small windows provided a little brightness, but most of the illumination came from rows of fluorescent bulbs which gave off a sickly gray light. The interior walls had recently been painted an odd shade, halfway between light brown and light green. About half the desks were staffed by *Federales* typing on keyboards or peering at antique computer screens. It appeared as if most of the day shift hadn't arrived for work yet.

The chief inspector's office was in a back corner of the main room, with glass walls so he could look out on all his officers. His name was on the door. He was a big man with graying hair and a bushy moustache and sat behind a large wooden desk.

"Chief Inspector Rosas, I am Inspector Ramon Torres, *División de Inteligencia*. We spoke on the palm last night."

"No, we spoke on the palm this morning, as I am most confident it was well after midnight when you somehow obtained my personal number and woke me next to my wife, who was less than pleased. And she was again not pleased when my palm rang again half an hour later. That time it was not you but rather *El Comisionado General Sabado del Policia Federal.* The commissioner general told me to extend you every courtesy when it came to dealing with the American we were detaining. An hour after that my palm rang again, and my very angry wife answered it only to discover she was speaking to *El Secretaría de Gobernación."* The chief inspector looked bemused as he related that, rather than angry. "Now, while I know the *Policia Federal* is under the authority of the Secretariat of the Interior, I never thought I would actually speak to the Secretary himself." Beni and Manuel looked at each other. Apparently Señor Echevarria had been busy making calls.

"After being woken up so many times at my age, it is no surprise that I was unable to go back to sleep, and so I have been here for hours, catching up on reports, drinking horrid coffee, and waiting for you to arrive." He hoisted a large coffee mug off his desk and took a loud sip.

"I have been told that I am not to interfere with your operation, only provide whatever support you require and allow you to proceed at your discretion. That, *señores,* means I have all the information I need. I do not want to know who he is or why we picked him up. And whatever is going on here, I hope you can take it somewhere else very soon. *¿Comprendes?"* The three men nodded as one.

The chief inspector hit a button on his desk console and a few seconds later a male voice responded. *"¿Si?"*

"My office, Paolo."

Twenty seconds later a senior uniformed sergeant was standing in Rosas' doorway. "Sergeant, take these gentlemen to see our guest in Interrogation Room Four and make sure no one interferes with them."

The sergeant eyed the three hard men in suits and one eyebrow went up, but he controlled his curiosity and instead just said, "*Sí, Jefe*."

The sergeant led them toward the back of the building, down a hallway. He stopped in front of a door marked with a black 4. "The man is in there," he told them. He nodded at the unmarked door nearby. "That is the observation room. I will be at the end of the hall if you need me."

"*Gracias*," Manuel told him, then Beni opened the door and they entered the small room.

Charles Travers, communications specialist with Raven Corporation, was a singularly unimpressive man. He was pale and pudgy, with mouse brown hair. He was slouching in a chair and looked up when the door opened. He saw the expensive suits and looked relieved.

"Are you from the embassy? I keep telling these assholes they've got the wrong guy. I haven't done anything. Jesus Christ, I hate this shithole country."

"No Señor Travers, we are not from the embassy," Torres told him, speaking with an unnecessarily heavy accent while fighting a smile. He shut the door as the Raven man's face dropped.

The three of them looked at the man handcuffed to the table, then at each other. He'd been grabbed trying to cross the border at Juarez into El Paso, and they'd been told he was dressed "as a peasant." In fact Travers, over a checkered shirt and khaki trousers, was wearing a garish serape that he must have bought in one of the few tourist stalls left in the city. One that catered to drunk or legally blind *gringos* from the rainbow colors in the pseudo-traditional garment. He resembled more a hapless tourist than a peasant. Had that been his attempt at a disguise?

Travers looked from face to face, not liking what he saw. "Well, what the hell is going on here? I work for Raven; we've got an agreement with you people." He'd been trying to bluster his way out of custody since the minute he'd been arrested, with little conviction and zero success. "And I've done nothing illegal." Even he didn't sound like he believed it.

Beni glanced at the mirror on the wall facing Travers, then up at the corner where there was a tiny camera. "You should check the observation room, make sure none of this is being recorded," Beni told the inspector in Spanish.

Torres glanced at the two-way glass and nodded. He left the room and was back in thirty seconds. "All off."

Manuel glanced at him. "Still, you are an *Inspector con el Federales.* Even if the men high up have been making calls on our behalf, perhaps you should not be in the room for this next part."

"Because we *will* be getting answers," Beni said, not taking his eyes off Travers.

Torres stared at Echevarria's two men, then glanced at the *escara*, who from his blank expression as they discussed his immediate future had never learned to speak the language of the country in which he was stationed. *Idiota.* It was a smart suggestion, but still he bristled at it. "Have you done much interrogating?"

"No. I am sure you have more experience and are much better at it," Beni told the inspector. "But you are still an officer, with rules, regulations, laws to follow, even if you might bend them from time to time. We have been given free rein to do what must be done, but tomorrow, or next week, even next year, those men far above us may decide we went too far. If that occurs, nothing will happen to me. Señor Echevarria is an angel on my shoulder. But you, you will be a juicy target." Beni looked down, shook his head, then looked back up at Torres. "Believe it or not I am actually trying to protect you." He then nodded at Travers, who was sweating. "This one will not be so tough if he is convinced of the seriousness of his situation."

"Who are you guys?" Travers asked them, getting visibly uneasy. He didn't like the looks they were giving him, and didn't like that they were speaking Spanish in front of him.

Torres glanced at him and the corner of his mouth twitched in a small smile. "Perhaps," Torres admitted to Beni. "But I will be on the other side of this—" he knocked on the two-way glass "—watching." Torres left the room, and Beni and Manuel stared at the American.

Charlie Travers was sweating big rings under his arms. "Who do you work for? Are you with the Mexican government? I'm an American, I should be allowed to speak to someone in the embassy," Travers demanded without much force.

"We are with no government agency," Manuel told him. He pulled the serape over Travers' head and threw it aside. Beni took off his suit jacket, folded it, and set it on the floor in the corner farthest from the prisoner.

"Then who are you?" They ignored the question.

"How much did they pay you?" Beni asked him, loosening his tie.

"What? What are you talking about?"

"To divert the helicopter," Beni said. He had his tie off and folded it several times, then laid it on his suit coat.

"I'm…what are you…I don't have to answer any of your questions. I want a lawyer." Travers glared at them.

Beni nodded as he began unbuttoning his white shirt. It was dirty and wrinkled, but it was an expensive shirt. "I assume it was a lot of money, enough to get you to run from your job. I thought Raven paid very well, but apparently not well enough." He tugged his shirt tails out and pulled the shirt off. He was bare-chested underneath and Travers stared at him as Beni folded the shirt.

Beni was lean and muscled, but what Travers was staring at were the crude gang tattoos all over his arms and chest. They were faded with age but unmistakable. And then there were the scars, the obvious results of violence. His scarred and marked body stood in stark contrast to the expensive suit which had covered it. Travers looked from him to Manuel and back. "Who are you guys?' He tugged at his handcuffs nervously, but they were secured to the table by a sturdy steel ring. "Why'd you take your shirt off?"

"I don't want to get any blood on it." Beni dug a hand into the pocket of his trousers and pulled out a small pocket knife. He unfolded the blade and tested it with a fingernail. It was razor sharp.

Travers eyed the knife uneasily. It was tiny, not scary at all, but still…. "You guys are crazy. No, you're full of shit. You're bluffing. I'm an American, and I want a damn lawyer, now. And somebody from the embassy. This is bullshit."

"When someone commits suicide by slashing their wrists," Beni told the sweating man, pantomiming the act on his own wrist with the small knife, "quite often the first cut isn't deep enough. They get scared. Perhaps they don't realize the reality of the situation until the blade first sinks into their flesh." Without warning he pinned Travers' left hand to the table, palm up, and ran the little knife blade across his wrist. The blade was so sharp Travers hardly felt any pain but still he yelled. Then he stared as the red line appeared and blood began to seep from the shallow cut.

"Are you crazy? Help! Help!" He yanked at his cuffs and yelled toward the door. "They're trying to kill me in here! Help me!" Beni waited calmly until the man was done yelling. Not one *Federale* even opened the door to check on him. If Torres was watching on the other side of the mirror he gave no sign.

"I think they are called hesitation wounds," Beni told Travers, who had his good hand clamped around his injured wrist to slow down the minimal bleeding. "Quite often with successful suicides you will see many cuts across the wrists. Getting successively deeper as they get braver, or get used to the pain." He held up his small knife. "How much did they pay you?"

Travers was breathing so hard he was nearly hyperventilating, and his eyes bounced back and forth between Beni and the closed door. His shouts for help had produced no response. In a police station. What the hell? The big guy stood near the door, arms crossed, dark face expressionless. "You're nuts," Travers told Beni.

Beni nodded at Manny. "I will have him pry your other hand away and will cut you a little bit at a time, sawing away at your tendons and muscle until I get down to bone. And do the same to your other wrist. Then we will stand here and watch you die in a puddle of your own blood, having committed suicide using this small knife the *Federales* missed when they searched you." He held up the pocketknife next to his face. "Or you can answer my questions." He appeared to not care which option Travers chose.

* * *

The second Blackhawk had been on station for several minutes when Kresge's bird arrived, and still through the binoculars he could see that the noise of the aircraft wasn't enough to scare off the carnivores chewing on the bodies. They were moving around on two legs, whipping their long tails from side to side, and looked as big to him as dogs.

"That's pretty damn bold, isn't it?"

"They'll take off as soon as we touch down," the pilot assured him.

Syntarsus was suspected to be a pack hunter from the original fossil records, long before geneticists recreated them in a lab and determined them in fact to be a subspecies of the common coelophysis. Because their fossils were so abundant—30 skeletons were found in one location in Zimbabwe alone, which led to the pack hunter theory—scientists had a lot of their genetic material to work with. As a result, they were one of the earliest species brought back to life in the GenVen laboratories, even though their appearance was less than impressive.

Mottled brown in color, syntarsus was a theropod related to the much larger coelophysis. Six feet long with the tail (although the females were slightly larger) they had graceful builds. They were bipedal carnivores, with long back legs and small forelegs, and lived in hot and semi-arid locales during the early Jurassic period. Their hands had three claws and their long jaws were filled with short sharp curved teeth. Their role as an ancestor to birds was evident simply from their body shape and quick movements even before the first young animals grew crests of purple-black feathers on the backs of their heads.

Animal behaviorialists studying the first living samples observed they could run surprisingly fast, sometimes in excess of twenty miles per hour, and did in fact often hunt in packs. The creature had a larger than average brain, and scientists attributed its advanced hunting behaviors to that. Alone or in pairs, the Syntax, as GenVen's Marketing and PR division trademarked them, preferred to prey on smaller animals, but when working in a pack, they could successfully bring down game much larger than themselves. In the zoos and theme parks they were just another live exhibit, and not very interesting to observe unless they were fighting or eating. In the wild, in sufficient numbers, they had proven themselves to be fearless and successful hunters even of men. Raven helicopter pilots were the first to discover that the Syntax, like many of the theropod carnivores, did not show up well through thermal sights. They seemed to be able to drop their body temperature significantly when at rest.

Kresge watched the animals track his helicopter as it descended toward the valley floor about a hundred meters from the vehicles. They waited until the helicopter touched down, then seemed to call to each other before vanishing up the heavily treed slopes.

"That's just creepy," the co-pilot said over the intercom. "It's bad enough they look like killer bird lizards, and work in packs that big, but did you see the way they stared at us? Those damn things are smart. At least dog smart."

"Yeah." Kresge had noticed that too. The animals didn't seem to be nearly as afraid of the noisy helicopters as they should be. "They're probably not happy about leaving all that meat behind, so everybody keep an eye out. I don't think we'll have a problem, but there had to be twenty of those damn things. Those things'll kill you if you let them."

"Roger that, sir."

"How the hell did it take us this long to spot this?" he asked the pilot, staring at the scene before them. "We've got three vehicles here out in the open. Looks like a goddamn church social."

The man shrugged and nodded out the window. "It's a narrow valley, deep, with steep slopes on three sides. You almost have to be on top of it to see all the way down to the valley floor. I probably flew over this area five times without seeing the trucks."

Kresge and his people waited until the second Blackhawk landed before they started toward the vehicles. They could tell it was going to be ugly long before they got close enough to see the details.

"Damn, that's nasty," one of the carbine-toting contractors muttered, staring at the shredded bodies.

"I'm guessing the dinos didn't kill all these guys, and not just because they wouldn't have neatly stacked them in the back of a truck to snack on later," Kresge said to his men. Large areas of grass were smeared with blood, and clouds of flies hovered above the blood and the bodies, many of which were no longer whole. "So find out what did. Or who. What happened here? That Vaquero looks shredded, but the trucks seem to be in good shape. I'm guessing we had another dustup here, and recently because the bodies don't look more than a day old, and they don't hardly smell yet. Check the bodies first, and if any of them aren't FRAP I want to know. And keep your heads on swivels, we've got high ground all around us." The helicopter crew stayed with their birds, scanning the surround slopes with the miniguns. You could never be too careful.

They found the body of the airman in the back of the Vaquero, which had been shredded by some sort of explosion. The man only had a few predator bite marks on him, and it was difficult to determine what had killed him. The rest of the bodies were FRAP, and their causes of death was much plainer to see.

Kresge eyed the slopes around him. "Sergeant!" he called out to the man in charge of the tactical security team with him which was deployed in a perimeter. The man jogged up to him. Kresge pointed at the slopes. "I don't think anybody went back out through the valley, which means they went up these slopes. Victoria Base is what, that direction?" He pointed at the slope in front of them. "Take half your men, see if you can find us a trail, so at least we have an idea in which direction to look."

"Copy that, sir." The sergeant whistled, and in a minute, he and his men were out of sight, huffing loudly as they moved up the steep slopes.

"I'm guessing the Vaquero was boobytrapped, maybe with a grenade," his tech lieutenant told Kresge a few minutes later. "I found a pulled pin on the floor. Both the trucks are in working order, although the battery on the pickup is dead. Headlights were left on."

Kresge walked over to it and peered in through an open window. "What the hell happened in it?" he asked, staring at the interior. Blood had sprayed everywhere like special effects in a cheap horror movie. Except this blood was real, and the copper smell of it filled the air. Kresge waved the flies away from his face. There appeared to be chunks of raw meat and gnawed bones on the seat of the truck.

"My guess is a late night snack. FRAP's chasing our people and lost a few in a firefight. The main force continues the chase up the ridgeline, and I bet they left a few guys here to guard the trucks. The smell of the bodies must have been enough to attract the dinos, which looked like Syntax to me, and at night, in big enough numbers, they could have taken out a few sleeping Gs easy."

The sergeant and his men returned forty minutes later. They were sweaty and panting from the altitude and steep slopes. "There was another firefight about halfway up this ridge right here," the sergeant said, pointing. "Got another five FRAP dead for sure. No friendly casualties that we could find. Our crew continued up the slope and then headed south afterward. Their tracks were easy to see under the trees, because of all the needles, but up top it's grass."

"Can you tell how many of them there were, or if the guerrillas are still chasing them?"

The sergeant shook his head. "More than a couple and less than twenty, that's all I can say. As for the FRAP, my men found several individual foot trails heading up top from the surrounding slopes which I would bet were made by pursuing guerrillas."

"Thank you." He pointed around them. "Make sure all the bodies…or parts…are checked for intel. I want to know which battalion these bastards are from." Kresge pulled out his satpalm and contacted his second in command at Victoria Base. "Miller. We found a second location several miles from the downed heli. Evidence of another firefight between the FRAP and our people, with one friendly KIA. Ping our bird's GPS and rotate the UAVs to this position. It looks like our people are on foot and headed southeast in your direction, and I want them found. I've got three vehicles here including a Vaquero and a troop truck. Between the crash site and this location we've got over fifteen FRAP dead, and evidence of even more chasing after our crew. They brought in a troop truck, Tony, a fucking troop truck. In my neighborhood. If I had any doubts whether they knew who they were after, how valuable she would be to their damn cause, they're gone now. We need to get these guys."

"You say we've got one dead on scene?"

"Yeah. Delian." He gave his XO information off the man's dog-tags. "From his shoulder patches he was aircrew, probably the pilot or co-pilot. Find out for me. I'm still waiting for a goddamn list of who was on this aircraft."

"I'm working on it, got a partial one right now, just waiting on a few people to get back to me. If they make it out of this in one piece, you should put this damn crew in for battlefield commendations. Right now they're fifteen to one. It sounds like they're giving a good accounting of themselves."

"Get me that crew and passenger manifest. When we leave here both birds have to come back to Victoria to refuel, so I want those UAVs up. These people have been on the ground long enough."

"Roger that. I'll call you as soon as I have anything."

Kresge disconnected the call, then dialed Echevarria's point man. The call was answered after three rings. "Yes, hello?"

"Señor Trujillo, Colonel Kresge, Raven. Calling to give you an update."

"'Update' I am guessing means you haven't found her yet." Beni was sitting at one of the unoccupied desks in the main room of the police station. Judging from the amount of dust on the desk it had been vacant for some time. His shirt and tie were back on, although his suit jacket was hung over the back of the chair.

"You would be correct. I am several miles southeast of the helicopter crash site. The FRAP were pursuing our crew and presumably your young lady. Sometime yesterday, looks like, they got into another firefight. I have one crewmember dead, and multiple FRAP KIA."

Beni's face grew dark. "What is 'multiple'?"

Kresge sighed. "Between the crash site and this location I have about fifteen guerrillas dead on scene."

"Fifteen?" Beni asked incredulously. "How many did they send?"

"Unknown at this time." He deliberately didn't mention the troop truck, as there was no way to know how many men it might have carried. Although, between the truck destroyed at the crash site and the three at this location, the FRAP had dedicated a lot of manpower to this operation. "But however many they have left it appears they are pursuing the crew on foot through the mountains. It's been less than a day, and with this terrain, they can't have gotten too far. I have UAVs up and will have helicopters back on station doing search and rescue very quickly."

Manuel walked up with a bottle of water in each hand, and set one down on the desk in front of Beni. Manuel raised his eyebrows at the palm in Beni's hand, and Beni shook his head. Manuel scowled. Beni asked the colonel, "Can you track them?"

"We've got UAVs up now, and helicopters again soon enough. We can even search at night, using thermal. We'll find them."

"No, not that. Dogs. Do you have dogs that can track their scent? Follow them through the hills?"

"Oh. Uh, no, actually. We have bomb-sniffing dogs, but none trained for that."

Beni shook his head. "They mean to kidnap her. They know who she is. She is too valuable to their cause to let escape."

"Yes sir. We are operating under that assumption."

"It is no assumption. Your missing radio man from China station, Señor Travers? He was picked up by the *Federales* in Juarez, trying to cross the border. I just spoke to him."

"Juarez?" Trujillo had gotten there fast. "And you—what did he have to say?"

"That he was paid a million U.S. dollars to divert the helicopter to this route. He was contacted about three days ago. They knew she was going to get on a helicopter there, just not which one, or even which exact day. So they needed a man inside to divert it and then alert them when it was on the way."

"A million dollars? Shit, they do want her. And our communications officer, he just volunteered this information?"

"He was made to see the seriousness of the situation. Once he understood his options, he was very cooperative."

"Yeah, I'm sure I don't want to know." Kresge frowned. "How did they know he would be receptive to the bribe? Even a big one like that, most of my men would tell the FRAP to pound sand. Did they kidnap a family member of his or something?"

"They knew to call Travers because he has been on their payroll for a while, giving them minor intelligence on aircraft patterns and personnel movements, information on your chain of command. Apparently FRAP is paying a number of Raven employees around the country for such information."

"Well shit. What about his FRAP contact? Do we have that person?"

"All he ever had was a phone number, and a name, 'Fernando.' *El Policia Federal* checked the number but it is shut off and not registered in any name. I doubt that phone or palm or whatever it was is working anymore."

"Is he still alive? Because I will very much want to talk to Mr. Travers when this is over."

"*Sí*, he is alive, and unharmed. Mostly."

"I like the sound of that. Okay, I will call you as soon as I have anything further to relate. I will send a Raven detail to take custody of Mr. Travers, unless he's being held on additional Mexican charges?"

"No. They only picked him up because of me. I will tell them to expect your men."

"Roger that. And nice work. Hopefully I'll be talking to you soon."

"That is my hope as well."

Beni set his palm down on the desk and shook his head at his partner. "Manny, *La Fuerza* attacked the helicopter crew again and lost more men. Fifteen in all. And still they pursue."

"*Quince? Quince guerrillas?*" He cursed in disbelief. "How many did they send?"

Beni shook his head.

Manuel checked over his shoulder. Torres was nowhere to be seen. After the interrogation of Travers, he'd said he had calls to make, and had nearly turned purple when Beni told him firmly not to tell anyone that Eduardo Echevarria's daughter was being chased by *La Fuerza*.

"You are not a person who should even think to tell me what to do," Torres had spat. "You have powerful friends now, but we both know who you are. What you are." Beni had walked away from the man, his face a mask.

"Why does the inspector dislike you so much?" Manuel asked. "You never told me."

The corner of Beni's mouth twitched. "Ah, Manny, when I was young I was not so friendly and charming, and that is when we first met. And the inspector has not forgotten the man I was."

Beni never talked about his past, his life before coming to work for Señor Echevarria. Manuel didn't bother pressing him with further questions about it, because Beni never answered them. "So what do we do now?"

Beni didn't have an answer for him.

* * *

Kresge disconnected the call with Echevarria's man and waved at his sergeant on the far side of the trucks who was photographing the scene. He pointed. "Disable these vehicles. No need to make it easy for them." He raised his voice. "We need to get back on the hunt, people, and before we can even do that we've got to fuel up these birds. Grab whatever intel you've found. And weapons; we're not leaving any here for stragglers to pick up."

His satpalm rang, and he answered the call walking back to his Blackhawk. "Kresge."

"Sir, it's Tony. I think I've finally got a complete manifest of crew and passengers on that bird."

"Let me have it."

"Our KIA Christopher Delian was the most senior crew on the bird so he was probably pilot. The other stick was Daniel Hansen. He's got a solid service record, and both he and Delian are prior Air Force. Our girl was definitely on the bird, we confirmed that through indigenous troops at China Base. There were also two other civilians on board as well."

"Really? Who? Why?"

"Hunters. Roger and Michael Rudd. Might not have found out about them but our professional hunter here came walking in wondering where the hell his clients were."

"Dinosaur hunters? Great. What, brothers?"

"Father and son."

Kresge didn't like the sound of that. He took his seat in the Blackhawk. "How old is the son?" He envisioned a grade-schooler in a crashing helicopter, on the run from terrorists...dear God.

"Hein didn't know, but I called Aarne Anders. Boy just graduated high school, so at least he's not a little kid. Having a hell of a vacation I'd guess. As for the rest of the men, let's see.... Derrick Todd with the 5th TST." Miller had the electronic service record open in front of him and studied the man's face. "Doesn't look familiar."

"I think I recognize the name. Who else?"

"John Corey. Been with us two years, currently assigned to the 3rd TST." He scrolled through the e-documents. "Prior service, Marines. I recognize him, but I'm not sure from where. He's got a solid record. And one more." He opened the last file. "Seamus O'Malley. Sergeant."

"OMalley was on that bird?" Kresge blurted. He shook his head. "I guess I shouldn't be surprised. He hasn't gotten into trouble in almost a year." His men returned to the Blackhawk and took their seats, and the pilot began spinning up the rotors.

"You know him?"

"In your career, have you ever known those soldiers who, no matter where they were, trouble always seems to find them? That's Seamus O'Malley to a T. Look at his service record."

Miller skimmed the pages. "Hell, he's been with us a while. He fought in...." His eyes scanned down the list of operations and incidents. "Jesus, have we had a gunfight in this country he wasn't in the middle of?"

"I doubt it. He's lucky as hell, but I can't tell if it's good luck or bad. And only something like this would keep him away from the asshole rodeo we've got going on down in Guadalajara."

"So he's a shit magnet. But is he any good?"

The engines were getting louder and louder. Kresge reached for a headset as he yelled into the palm, "If he wasn't, he would have been dead years ago."

* * * * *

Chapter Seventeen

There was a Raven compound directly over the border in El Paso, apparently, and a group of four armed men in Raven uniforms arrived to pick up Travers in short order. Travers didn't know whether to be relieved or terrified that his own men were taking him into custody.

After they were gone the two men looked at each other.

"So we go back to Señor Echevarria?" Manuel asked.

"I do not know what else we can do, here or anywhere, Manny," Beni told him. "Colonel Kresge has said he does not need the aid of the Peregrine, but maybe when we get back to it he will have changed his mind."

Manny smiled. "And how are we going to get back to it? You and our chauffeur seem to have had words."

Beni cursed. "Perhaps one of Rosas' men can drive us." He pulled out his palm and placed a call to Señor Echevarria. He didn't have much to relate, only that the Raven communications officer had been picked up. He had received no additional updates from Colonel Kresge. Instead he was hoping Señor Echevarria had some good news for him for a change. Such was not the case. There was no news.

"Your contact *con El División de Inteligencia, Inspector Torres,* is he still there?" Echevarria asked him.

"I believe so."

"I would like to speak to him about this matter. In person. To-day."

Beni looked up at the ceiling. "*Si Señor.* I will see if he can make himself available. Provided our aircraft is still where we left it we should be back in Mexico City in...." he tried to guess the travel time, based on the two flights he'd already taken in the Peregrine. "Six hours?"

"*Bueno.*"

* * *

The farther down the trail they went the slicker the footing became. The cute trickles of water at the top of the cliff seemed to spread and multiply until it was as if they were scooting along the top of a treacherous wall in a misting rain. They clung to the cliff like monkeys and slid their feet sideways with small steps. It wasn't until they were finally near the bottom that they realized how warm and humid it had become. And that wasn't all.

"It smells like a jungle," Mike remarked.

Seamus was in the lead, and he took a break from white-knuckling the wall in front of him to look over his shoulder. "It looks like a jungle." He was surprised to see plants at nearly foot level. The dark stone forming the cliff face was covered with damp moss, and where it wasn't, it was slick with water. The narrow path they were on was no drier. Seamus hadn't looked up from his hands and feet for a while and saw the path sank into a thick mass of ferns and bushes barely twenty feet ahead. "Almost there." They hadn't lost anybody yet, but now they seemed close enough to the ground that if anyone did fall they'd likely barely be hurt by landing in the thick dark green underbrush.

The last six feet of the path seemed to have crumbled. Rather than risk it Seamus jumped down to the valley floor, which was covered with fine grass. He sank calf deep in a bog, and belatedly saw that the tufts of grass were islands poking out of standing water. "Bloody—watch your step when you jump down, it's a little swampy at the bottom. You're going to get your feet wet." Something jumped away when he landed, either a frog or small lizard, too quick and green for him to discern which. He peered upward past the members of the group inching along and saw how much water was dripping down the cliff face. He worked the cramps out of his fingers and shook water drops off Leonidas.

Mike jumped and then helped Tina down. She was shaking, but whether it was from exhaustion or terror at the harrowing descent he doubted even she knew. Seamus put his back to the cliff and scanned the valley floor in front of him.

The area immediately in front of the cliff face was overgrown, no doubt due to the ready water supply. There were ferns everywhere, knee to waist high, thick grass, horsetails, some man-high fronds with oval leaves and saw-tooth edges. Overgrown bushes, even small cypresses. He could only see a short distance as many of the bushes were at least as tall as he was.

Far above them, the fog cover had thinned to a bright haze, fuzzing the sun and dimming it enough that he could squint directly at it for a few seconds. The valley floor was much hotter and wetter than the surrounding slopes. How far had they descended? At least another five hundred feet. It seemed the crawl down the narrow switchbacking game trail had taken forever.

"What did you call this, a microclimate?" he asked Tina.

She nodded, busy retying her ponytail. She was surprised she still had her hair, with all the stress of the week. "The deep valley keeps it sheltered, and there doesn't seem to be any wind down here. All this water running down the cliff, and look—" she pointed "—there even seems to be a spring at the base of the cliff, bubbling up. It keeps the air full of moisture, which traps the sunlight and keeps it warmer."

Hansen splashed down next to Seamus. "Well, at least we won't have to worry about water for a while. We have any food left? I feel I ought to celebrate not falling to my death."

"And you did it all one-handed," Seamus agreed. He didn't want to set the pack in the bog water, so he turned around so the pilot could dig in it. "We should still have a decent supply of energy bars in there mate, but don't take more than one. We're not home yet." He watched Mike help his father down off the rockpile that marked the end of the game trail. Rudd's face was red and screwed up in pain as he sat back on the rocks, panting.

"It feels like we've been crawling down this trail all day," Corey said, jumping down next to Roger. "How long has it been?" He swung the big sniper rifle up over his shoulder to keep it out of the bog water.

Seamus checked his watch, an inertia model that hadn't been affected by the EMP. "Tad over ninety minutes, not including our break in the middle. Felt a lot longer," he had to admit. He stared up the cliff and couldn't see the top, which was wreathed in mist. It looked completely vertical, and intimidating as hell. His forearms ached from clinging to the rocks. "If nobody minds standing in some cool water let's take a few minutes here and everyone take a drink and have a bite to eat."

"Gunfighting, rock climbing, helicopter crash…." Roger said between pants. He felt ready to fall over or pass out, or both. He looked up at his son. "If he'd have known we were going to do all this I bet Anders would have charged us double." He fought through the pain to smile.

Mike shook his head. "Dad, jeez. You doing okay?"

"No, but I'm a lot better than dead. If my back didn't hurt this might almost be fun in a terrifying horrible nightmare kind of way. You want to grab me a water and an energy bar? I don't feel like moving just now."

"Sure."

Corey slogged over to Seamus and the two men turned to look out toward the valley, what they could see of it past the foliage. They were near the right wall of the valley, which was steep and covered in light green grass. It disappeared into haze in the distance, but then so did the rest of the valley. Farther south of them the valley seemed to open up.

"Looks like it runs straight south, although it might angle east way over there; it's hard to see," Corey observed. He squinted and put a hand over his eyes to shield them. The sun wasn't bright through the haze, but it did cast some glare.

Seamus felt hands digging in his backpack for water and energy bars. They froze as another loud bellow echoed across the valley, much louder. Whatever had made it sounded very close.

"What the hell is that?" Roger hissed. He clutched his AK in one hand, bottle of water in another. A fainter answering bellow reached their ears.

"Something that sounds big enough to not care what hears it," Seamus observed. He turned and caught Mike's eye. "You may get your wish to see some dinosaurs after all, junior." The soldier looked around the group. "Everybody stay calm. Some of the herbivores are just like cows, they'll stare at you with a stupid look on their face. It's only the carnivores you have to worry about, and for whatever reason all dinosaur carnivores, and I mean *all* of them, run on two legs. So they're easy to spot. If you see a dino on all fours, it's a plant eater. And if it sounds like that," he jerked his thumb over his shoulder, "chances are it's big enough it won't be scared of you. If it's not some farmer's damn lost water buffalo or something. So relax. If you think you see something else point it out to me, but for God's sake, don't start shooting."

He didn't think it would be a good time to point out just how hard dinosaurs were to kill, even the small ones, compared to similarly-sized contemporary animals. They had what he'd heard referred to as distributed nervous systems. The stegosaurus, for example, weighed over three tons yet had a brain the size of a plum. Much of the task of moving its body around was assigned to the rest of its nervous system, not its brain. Dinosaurs didn't feel pain the same way, and didn't have the same kill switches. Slow to feel the pain, slow to bleed, slow to die. Shoot a man through the heart, and if he could muscle past the pain he had thirty seconds (give or take) worth of oxygen in his red blood cells before he lost consciousness. Do the same to a dinosaur and you might be waiting five minutes before it took the hint. Sometimes even shooting them in the head, *through* the head, only slowed them down. What was that old phrase, "running around like a chicken with its head cut off?" It was as accurate when applied to dinos. He'd seen it happen, and the results weren't pretty.

Seamus didn't think there were too many small predators nearby as the air was filled with the loud sound of frogs and insects. After a ten-minute rest, during which they heard a few more bellows and some hooting that could have come from giant owls, the group pushed away from the cliff face. Seamus took the lead, his boots splashing through mud and water as he tried to keep an even distance from the steep slope on the right. The dark green plants dripped with moisture and wiped slimy fingers on him as he passed. Palms, deciduous bushes and clump trees, vines, swamp cypresses, even cycads crowded together in the warm damp air. As thick as the vegetation was, he was able to push through it without having to hack at it with a machete. Most of the plants seemed to give away before him, providing no more resistance than the big ferns covering the ground in an everpresent green blanket.

After less than a hundred meters the ground seemed to dry up, and as they moved away from the water, the undergrowth began to thin. Seamus broke out into a clearing ahead of the group and climbed a small rise. He looked left, across the valley, and froze. He was still standing there, blinking, when Hansen huffed up next to him. "What are you—oh, wow." The pilot stood there, mouth open, and gawked. The rest of the group joined them in ones and twos and stood staring at the valley laid out before them.

The bog beneath the cliff was fed by the water running down the cliff face and several underground springs. The water oozed slowly southward, all of the small watercourses gradually merging together, and the group had walked off at an angle to the stream that formed. Four feet wide at the mouth with a gentle current, the stream wound lazily southward along the valley floor.

A hundred feet distant, a small herd of protoceratops was crowded at the stream's edge drinking. The size of large pigs with armored frills on their oversize heads, the animals grunted and pushed at each other, trampling the bushes at the water's edge. As the humans watched one adult animal slid down the short bank and landed on its forelegs in the water. It snorted in surprise, but when it found the water less than a foot deep it lowered its head and drank.

Paleontologists had discovered so many fossil remains of the herbivores they had been dubbed the "sheep of the Cretaceous." The low browsers had heavy heads and beaks which they used to strip leaves and bark off plants. Their scaly skin was a rough mottled brown. There were maybe two dozen protoceratopsians, most of them full grown, with a few smaller juveniles being protected by their mothers.

The animals drank from the stream then wandered away, occasionally clamping their jaws on low foliage and ripping sideways. They chewed as they walked and seemed oblivious to the group of humans watching them.

"Plant eaters?"

Seamus looked around to see that it was Corey who had spoken. The young man was staring off into the distance. "You see them eating plants, don't you?"

"No, not them, *them*," Corey said, pointing. Beyond the stream the foliage thinned to small bushes and tall grass. Several hundred yards past the stream, maybe a quarter of a mile away from their small rise, was a small group of slender dinosaurs. There were maybe half a dozen of them near a copse of young conifers. The dinosaurs were light green with an irregular pattern, which was why Seamus hadn't spotted them. The animals had long necks and tails and as he watched one of them stood on its hind legs.

"You said two legs for predators, right?" Corey said.

"Those are massos," Seamus told him. He raised his rifle and studied the animals through his scope on magnification to be sure. "It's rearing up on two legs to get at the higher branches. It's eating leaves." The massospondylus specimens were ten to twelve feet long with their whip-like tails, and were narrow and darting with small heads. They were not lumbering grass eaters but rather slender and graceful, resembling gazelles. "Sometimes they run on two legs but I've only ever seen them eat greens. You've never seen them in person before?"

Corey was wide-eyed and shook his head. "A couple glimpses here and there, but nothing like this. It's amazing."

Seamus smiled and looked past Corey to Tina, who was staring at the protoceratops in fascination. "Frankenstein Monsters or no, you have to admit that is quite a sight," Seamus said, nodding ahead.

"*Sí*," was all she could say. She could smell the animals at the stream, and while they gave off the same barnyard animal smell as cows or pigs, somehow it was different. As was seeing the animals in the wild as opposed to penned up in a zoo. While her brain knew that genetically there was nothing natural about them, seeing the animals from so close, snorting and shoving at each other, drinking from the stream, she could not deny their reality. Anatomically, structurally, externally, visually, they were dinosaurs. Creatures millions of years extinct, made flesh.

"They look like lizard pigs with parrot heads," Roger said, squinting at the protoceratops. "Wonder if you could make bacon out of one of them, I'm starving."

"*Daaaad*," Mike said, but he couldn't keep the grin off his face. He was smiling so hard his face was hurting. Dinosaurs. Frickin' dinosaurs!

"You see those ones out there?" Roger asked his son, pointing at the massos in the distance. "They look more like what dinos are supposed to look like to me. These parrothead dino pigs seem like something you'd raise for meat."

"Well armored meat," Hansen said, staring at the bony shield which protected the animals' shoulders.

"Baconasauruses," Roger said. "Barbequeasaurus rex."

"Stop it, you're making me hungry," Hansen said with a smile, idly fondling the plastic pony head from his daughter.

"There's another herd of something small way out there," Seamus said, lowering the scope from his eye. The valley, which they'd first thought was long and narrow, was actually triangular in shape. They'd entered at the narrow tip. It stretched south from their position another mile but widened as it went. At its southern end it looked to be over a mile wide. There were steep slopes on all sides.

"Look at that," Seamus said to Corey, gesturing at the sky above them. It was still hazy, but half of the fog had burned off. "It'll take most of the day for the sun to burn off the fog, and it probably rolls back in every night. No wonder nobody's spotted these herds on satellite."

"No need to route satellites up here, all the fighting's been a lot further south."

"I'm guessing even that professional hunter at Victoria Base doesn't know about this little valley, because they don't care bugger all about us." He gestured at the protoceratops. Some of them had smelled the humans, and most of the rest had noticed them standing at a distance, but no alarm had been raised.

"How long do the babies take to grow to full size?" Mike asked Tina. The herd of protoceratops was gradually moving away from the stream. The mothers had shuffled their young to the center of the herd for protection.

She shrugged. "It depends on the animal. *Los pequeños*, the smaller ones grow to maturity faster. Those animals I'm guessing at least a year. Much larger ones at least a few years, perhaps as many as ten. The giant sauropods were so big it would have taken decades for them to get to full size."

Seamus looked farther south. The stream appeared to get wider and the vegetation grew thicker again. "We're going to have to cross it somewhere, and right there looks to be the easiest spot," he announced. "They've matted down all the shrubbery, at least on the far side. Then I think we can head southeast across this great bloody big plain and not have to worry about climbing for a while." He looked at Roger. "Sound good to you, mate?"

"Not as good as a soft mattress and a handful of Vicodin, but it'll have to do."

Seamus smiled. "Let's wait for the snufflers to clear out a bit; don't want to spook them or cause a stampede. They look too stupid to spook, but I wouldn't want to get hammered by one of those armored heads."

Roger lay on the warm ground and tried to stretch his back as the rest of the group continued to stare at the prehistoric scene before them, waiting for the grazing protoceratops to put some distance between them and the stream. After ten minutes or so they were about a hundred yards south of their watering spot.

"That should be good enough. You need a hand up?" Seamus asked Roger.

"I've got it," Mike told him, and held a hand out to his father. Mike helped him up, then picked the AK up off the grass and handed it to his dad as the rest of their group headed for the stream.

"Still think I need it?" Roger asked his son softly, staring at the rifle. "Seems like we lost them."

"I don't know." Mike never wanted to have to shoot at a person again, but not having a gun when guerrillas were chasing you seemed an even worse idea.

Roger looked at the rifle in his son's hands, and remembered the man he'd had to shoot back at the crash site. Whatever physical pain he was going through, he knew Michael's emotional pain had to be worse. "Shooting a man is a horrible thing to have to do, but when you get put into a position where you have to, there's no shame in it. I know we don't really talk much, but you didn't do anything wrong. And God forbid, I don't want you to think that I'm mad at you or anything. You did the right thing. I just wish you didn't have to do it, you know? That's all."

"Yeah, I know, Dad." Mike still hadn't told his father about the other men he'd shot on the piney slope and didn't want to. It hadn't even been a gunfight, he'd simply shot a bunch of guys who never even saw him. Bad guys, bad guys with guns, sure, but still. He flashed a fake smile at his dad. "C'mon, let's catch up."

Roger smiled sadly at his son's back. It was obvious he was upset, and Roger didn't blame him. But he didn't know what he could do to help him.

"Whew. They smelled better from over there," Hansen said, waving a hand in front of his face. The air above the stream was still carrying the scent of the protoceratops herd.

Corey saw the ground on the far side of the small stream was covered with fresh piles of scat, some of which were right near the water's edge. "Glad we drank the water upstream of that."

The stream was barely knee deep, and Seamus led the way across it. The herd of protoceratops was maybe forty meters away to the south. A few of them were staring at the humans and making odd grunting noises.

"Not sure if they like the looks of us or not," Seamus said. He gestured at his group, then pointed east. "Let's head this way for a bit until we get clear of this lot, then angle south a bit. Make for that far corner of the valley." With most of the fog burned off they were getting a better look at the steep-walled valley. "Mile, mile and a half of easy walking on level ground, in exactly the direction we want to go. Please, no skipping, but feel free to sing." He flashed a smile and took the lead, keeping his pace slow enough for Roger to keep up.

Once the humans moved away, the herd of protoceratops seemed to forget about them and went back to grazing, moving slowly southward. Mike glanced back a few times but his dad was right, they resembled prehistoric livestock more than anything else.

The wide valley floor was mostly covered by knee high grass, although there were clumps of bushes and clusters of trees here and there. Seamus angled a bit to the right, and he and everybody else gazed at the small group of massospondylus eating in the small thicket of cypresses ahead. From time to time one of them would stand on its hind legs and strip leaves and bark off a branch with its mouth, sometimes grabbing hold of the branch. The animals had a huge clawed first finger which they could curve over like a thumb.

The humans were walking in a line through the grass, and when they were a hundred meters or so away, the slender herbivores stopped eating and turned their attention on them. Seamus had led the group so that they would get no closer than fifty meters from the browsing animals. Unlike the protoceratops, the massospondylus seemed more skittish, and before the humans were within seventy-five meters several of the dinosaurs hooted. The animals loped away from the humans using an odd running jumping gait halfway between the bounding of a gazelle and the bouncing of a kangaroo. It made Tina laugh out loud.

"I thought you said only meat eaters ran on two legs," Hansen called to Seamus.

Seamus turned and walked backward. "No. Meat eaters only run on two legs, but not all dinosaurs who run on two legs are meat eaters." He caught Mike's eye. "More fun than the average school field trip, eh?"

Mike smiled and looked at the rapidly disappearing group of massos. He was glad he'd seen them, and seen them in the wild rather than in a zoo, but he didn't have any desire to take a shot at them. Maybe he never would have, even if the hunting trip had happened as planned; the vacation was about spending time with his dad more than anything else. Or maybe he would have been eager to take the shot. But, after surviving two firefights, and shooting at least four men who'd never even known he was there, killing an animal that was merely trying to survive in the wild didn't seem very sporting. He no longer had any desire to do it.

Seamus stopped and let the group walk by him. As Tina passed he winked and blew her a kiss. She rolled her eyes but couldn't help but smile. He fell in with Roger, who was sweating and wincing with every step.

"How's the back, mate?"

"You ever been stabbed? I imagine this is what getting stabbed feels like."

"Been hit with shrapnel, but that usually burns too, as it's the product of an explosion. Never been lucky enough to get stabbed. Few blokes have tried, though."

Roger shook his head. "How'd you get into this line of work?"

Seamus shrugged. "I was an aimless lad, smart mouth, always getting into fights, on the verge of getting kicked out of school, row after row with me mum and dad. Then the London riots happened, and they called everyone in. My father was a constable, what you'd call a police officer. He was manning a roadblock and someone tried to ram it. He got crushed, died on the spot. Random and stupid and pointless, but it helped me get my head on straight. Graduated school and went straight into the Paras, and I've been doing this ever since." He patted the pistol in his thigh holster. "This is my father's Walther P99, actually. Was carrying it on duty the night he was killed."

Roger tried to do the math in his head. If Seamus was in high school during the riots which had destroyed half of London, he had to be somewhere between thirty-five and forty years old. And he looked it, except for the gray at his temples. "Bit young for gray hair, aren't you?" he said with a smile.

Seamus pointed at his close-cropped head. "I earned every one of these little bastards, let me assure you. They could each tell a story."

Roger smiled. "How'd you end up with your father's pistol? He was police, but you're military, and I know the Brits banned private ownership of all firearms decades ago."

"The UK's been a police state since not too long after Orwell wrote 1984," Seamus admitted. "We've had a long love affair with overbearing governments ever since Charlemagne was stomping about. After all, we're subjects of the crown, not citizens. But the tighter the grip," he held up a clenched fist, "the more things slip through your grasp."

"I've got hotels all over, and try to keep a finger on the local politics, crime, anything that might affect its business. The crime rate around our hotel in London is one of the worst. Worse than Istanbul or Moscow. Worse than Detroit, if you can believe it."

They walked for ten minutes, everyone talking quietly. As relatively easy as the walking was, they were all sweating in the humid air as the sun burned off most of the mist above them. The thick grass concealed the fact that the ground was not nearly as level as it looked and sometimes rocky. They walked past thick patches of wildflowers, purple and yellow. Seamus turned and walked backward for a while. They'd made it halfway across the valley floor, and from there he was able to discern the valley was shaped more like a fat shallow L than a true triangle. The slope to the left had drawn close and even though they were a hundred meters or more away from its overgrown base it seemed to tower over them. The slopes on all sides were steep and covered with dark green vegetation, but he saw a lot of exposed rock. Roger would not enjoy the climb out at all.

Before they'd crossed the stream, he'd spotted a group of small animals far off in the valley through Leonidas' scope, at about the spot they'd reached. The animals had long since vanished. He had no idea if they were something prehistoric or just wild goats.

"Holy crap," Hansen said, and stopped. He was staring to the south. Everyone else looked, and from a dense patch of trees several hundred yards from them, a massive animal emerged.

Brown with wide stripes running down its sides, the animal pushed through the thicket with its wedge-shaped head, walking slowly on four thick legs. Its skull was broad with two pairs of sideways-pointing horns at the rear corners. It showed no teeth at the front of its mouth, just a beak which was stuffed with light green fronds. It chewed as it walked, seemingly oblivious to everything around it.

"Now that's a dinosaur," Corey said. "What the hell is it?"

After it cleared a patch of clump maples the giant animal angled slightly to its left, toward the stream, and they finally got a look at its tail—tipped with a massive bony club. The tail swung slowly side to side several feet above the ground as the animal walked.

"That's an ank. An ankylosaurus," Seamus breathed.

"Didn't you say you've seen one of those? Corey asked him.

"Not one that big. Look at the size of that beauty. It must be one of the original animals from Pangaea and survived in the wild all this time. It's massive."

The herbivore was eight feet tall at the hips and was thirty feet long. Its rear legs were slightly longer than the ones in front, all of them as thick as a man. The slightly flattened club at the end of its tail was three feet wide.

"Would this thing even kill something that size?" Corey asked Seamus, gesturing with the muzzle of the big Ulfberht on his shoulder.

"Not before it stomped you to pudding. That thing's got to be five, six tons, easy. And he knows how to scrap."

As the animal drew slowly closer they could see the scars on its hide. The ankylosaurus had large armored plates on its neck and shoulders, with smaller plates and spikes in rows down its sides. The plates were covered in horny hide, and the ones over its shoulders had deep scars. They were old and had healed up, but the ank sometime past had tangled with something big.

"It's from the late Cretaceous," Tina told everyone. "Alive at the same time as the Tyrannosaurs and the other large theropods, and the armor and tail club evolved as a defense against those giant carnivores."

"It's a tank," Hansen remarked. He cocked his head, thinking of his daughter and a trip they'd taken to the zoo. He reached up to touch the pony head. "Wonder if you could ride around on it, like they do elephants."

"It wouldn't even feel your weight," Corey mused.

"All those trees running along there behind it….I bet the stream took a turn and is following the valley floor. Following us," Tina said. It certainly couldn't run up the steep sides of the valley.

"You got your palm?" Roger asked his son. "Now would be a good time for some photos."

"Yeah, no kidding." Mike had forgotten he still had the device but found it in a cargo pocket of his pants. Even more surprising, the battery wasn't dead. The group stood and watched the animal as it came closer and closer, covering ground fast as a man walking. It passed thirty yards behind them, glancing in their direction once but otherwise paying them no mind. Its tail swished softly through the grass as it swung back and forth. They could hear its breath huffing in and out like the air from giant bellows.

The rest of the group started walking again but Mike stood where he was and watched the ankylosaurus. Maybe it was dumb as a cow—he didn't know—but it looked majestic; the slow-moving armored king of the valley. Or queen—he hadn't seen anything as the animal went by to determine one way or the other. He took more photos of its retreating backside but they didn't do it justice. He switched over to video and that was better—the slow sway of the animal's body and tail was like a metronome.

There was something else in the viewscreen of his palm, in the distance. Dark spots against the green. He squinted at them, then looked up over the device to see several animals had emerged from trees beyond the ankylosaurus. They stood upright. Mike was trying to figure out what they were when there was a sizzling snapping above his head, followed half a second later by shouts and the staccato sounds of gunshots.

* * * * *

Chapter Eighteen

E/ *Tejón* was having a bad day. Not the worst day of his life, that had probably been when one of his own *compadres* had accidentally shot him during a raid eight years past, but this was close. It had been Miguel who had decided to charge ahead to the crash site and gotten him and his men slaughtered, but as the commander of the mission, *El Tejón* took full responsibility for their failure. He himself had been leading the men when they set off the explosive hidden in the Vaquero and then were so skillfully ambushed on the slope. Two-thirds of his force wiped out before they'd even laid eyes on their target. But he preferred that straight-up fight to the ordeal which had followed.

Following the trail of what had to be half a dozen people through the hills was no trouble for anyone who was not blind. They found the trampled ground at the top of the slope and followed it as quickly as possible. One, two people walking through dry grass could have eluded them, hidden their sign, but half a dozen, most of them in boots? *Fácil.* His men walked fast, sometimes even jogging when the trail was obvious across a grassy field. *El Tejón* found himself at the rear of his men; not where he wanted to be, he preferred to lead, but his injured calf slowed him down.

Perhaps if he had been in the lead he would have seen the trip-wire, or sensed the trap, perhaps not. Domingo heard the metallic ping of the grenade lever flipping off and dove sideways but the man in front of him, the one who'd tripped the wire, caught the full force of the blast.

The rest of the men suffered scrapes and cuts, but other than a deep cut from shrapnel across Domingo's cheek they were miraculously unharmed by the booby-trap. He'd left the vehicles on foot with a mere six men, including Domingo. Now they were down yet another. *El Tejón* stared at the unlucky man's body, not even sure of his name.

Scrambling upslope not fifty feet past the tripwire they found the old trail.

"Did they take the path?" one of his veteran men, Martin Guitierrez, asked. He looked up and down it. It seemed too obvious.

Domingo left the group and went ahead thirty feet and studied the hardpacked earth of the trail to the south. Then to be sure he checked to the north as well. There was sign heading south, but not north. "They went this way." He looked at his leader. "Very hard to see the tracks."

"If we can't see the tracks on the trail, then we have to watch for signs of them leaving it," *El Tejón* told his men. He assigned half his group to study the grass and bushes on the left side of the trail, and the rest the right. "Move slower, and keep an eye out for tripwires."

The men headed out, their heads low and searching for sign. "They can't be far ahead. They could be right around the next bend," Domingo said quietly.

"I want to race after them as well, but we do not have enough men to risk setting off another trap."

"The sun is getting low, and then we won't be able to see any-thing."

El Tejón looked up at the sky and scowled. "As fast as you can, *mis hombres*," he told them.

As the sun sank in the sky he pushed his men faster and faster until they were barely scanning the sides of the trail, so it was pure luck that one of them spotted the second tripwire perhaps two kilometers down the trail from where they'd joined it. He hissed and stopped so suddenly he almost fell over, and the man behind him nearly collided.

"*¡Bomba!*" he said, a little too loudly. He held his hands out to either side so no one would walk past him.

Domingo patted the man on the back and knelt to examine the trip wire, which was cord. Thin wire would be better, harder to spot, but *los escaras* probably had to make do with what they had with them. He followed the cord to a large bush just off the trail and found a grenade tied there. "*Otra grenada*," he announced. Some of the men hissed, aware of how close they'd come to death yet again, still without having faced their enemies.

El Tejón would have bent down to examine the device himself but his calf ached horribly, and the shrapnel wound still seemed to be bleeding. His boot felt to be full of his own blood, but he had no time for weakness, his own or anyone else's.

Domingo made sure it had the pin, then clipped the tripwire and the cords holding the grenade to the stem of the bush. He hoisted it for the men to see. "Good luck," he told them, and stuffed the grenade in one of his empty magazine pouches. "*Vamonos.*"

But their good luck didn't last long. The men were hesitant to go too fast and miss another tripwire, and before long the sun dropped behind a ridge. It almost instantly became too dark to discern any sign on the trail even though the sky to the west was bright.

"It is suicide to go on, we must wait until the dawn," one of the men muttered when *El Tejón* told them to take a break.

"We will not be able to see if they've left the trail," Guitierrez told his *Comandante*.

El Tejón frowned in the dark. He knew the man were right, yet knew the people he was pursuing, if they were smart, were not stopping. They were using the dark to their advantage.

"*Comandante*," Domingo said to him. He held up a hand, and in it *El Tejón* could barely make out a length of the cord that had been used to make the last tripwire. "The dirt of the path is lighter than this cord, and I have good night vision. If I go slow enough I will be able to spot any tripwire. We may not be able to spot where they go off the path, if they do, but maybe we will. And if we are quiet, maybe we will hear them."

"*Sí*, it is a good idea. Do you men hear this?" he said to the soldiers sitting nearby. "Domingo will work the trail, spotting tripwires. He has the eyes of an owl. And we will be behind him, quiet as ghosts. We may not be able to see where the *gringos* left the trail, but do any of you doubt we will be able to hear a woman in the dark out here, crashing through the bushes? Complaining?" He forced a laugh. "And maybe they will be stupid enough to start a fire. Drink your water, then we are leaving." He didn't know if they believed him, and he didn't care. They had to move, had to do something. He could not bear sitting there until morning. Every minute, their quarry drew closer to Victoria Base. Waiting until morning meant the sure failure of the mission.

Quiet as ghosts they were not, but his men did make very little noise as they followed slowly behind Domingo, who was bent low to the ground. He kept to the middle of the path, where there was more bare earth. The light brown dirt seemed to catch some of the star-light above them and reflect it, so although he had to stay bent at the waist he could see more than well enough. Walking in that manner they made slow progress, but steady.

They inched along the trail like snails for kilometers, for hours. They heard nothing but creatures of the night, and never found another tripwire. Finally Domingo straightened up, holding his aching back. He stepped close to *El Tejón* so they could talk without their voices carrying.

"We have gone farther, much farther, than they could have gotten before dark I think. So if they were smart they should have already turned from the trail." He gestured ahead of them, his arm nearly invisible. Before them the trail ran up a long slope and turned to the west. "Before us the trail is even more exposed, and turns the wrong way for them. Unless they are *idiotas totales* they would have not come this far. If they had, we would have found another trip-wire."

"Unless the last was their only grenade. So where?"

"Did you see that gulley off to the left, about half a mile back? That is where I would have turned off. Easier walking, and it was headed in the right direction."

"They could have turned off anywhere." *El Tejón* scowled and looked around at the nearly black landscape around him. His eyes were fully adjusted, but only the vaguest details were apparent—clumps of bushes were dark amorphous shapes, trees were seen more by the stars they blotted out, and the trail was only a slightly less dark wide line under their feet, running off into the distance. "We could walk past them in the night and never know."

"We know where they are heading. They are somewhere in that direction." His lieutenant nodded to the southeast. "I would not be surprised if they had already stopped for the night. They probably have wounded. Plus the girl. If we somehow pass them, there is a lot of high ground from which to spy."

El Tejón nodded. Really, what choice did he have? They could sit on the trail in the dark and wait for dawn, which was still hours and hours away, or continue to search for *la puta rica*, whom he was hating more and more. Failure was not an option.

He urged his grumbling, exhausted men up and they trudged backward down the trail to the gravel strewn gulley. It did seem a likely spot to turn off, and headed almost directly southeast. With Domingo in the lead, they proceeded cautiously and quietly up what appeared to be a dry riverbed. It narrowed, and became choked with weeds and thorny bushes, and after an hour of struggle their path ended in a box canyon with walls too steep and crumbling to climb. With no sign of the Americans. Or sight. Or sound. Or smell.

The men swore when they reached the dead end but he didn't have time for their cursing. He led them back up the gulley and found the spot he remembered, where the slope to their east was gentle. Perhaps the Americans had been forced to backtrack as well.

The gentle slope seemed to be grassy, although it was hard to tell in the dark. There were clumps of bushes here and there, almost invisible in the night, and at first they could walk around them. Then the bushes grew thicker and more numerous, and when the men began having to push through them discovered they sported long thorns that quickly had them all bleeding from dozens of fine cuts.

The slope went nowhere, the summit a low hill that gave them a view of nothing but a sea of blackness all around. Navigating the descent of the far side was more treacherous as it was strewn with rocks. It ended in a wide ditch they followed for a bit until that, too, ended. They had a choice of going back or climbing one of the steep slopes surrounding them.

"You can rest at the top," Domingo told the exhausted men. He pushed them toward the east slope. As the men began stumbling up the slope he turned to his commander.

El Tejón was more than tired. He was feeling lightheaded and suspected it might have to do with blood loss from his leg wound. Even though he'd bound it and re-tied the bandage several times, it continued to bleed, because he continued to walk on it. His boot was filled with blood and his leg was both numb and tingling from above the knee down. He didn't know what that meant—he was no doctor—but assumed it wasn't good.

"*¿Esta bien?*" Domingo asked.

"I will be when we reach the top."

What was before them was more than a steep hillside, it seemed as if they struggled up a small mountain in the dark and cold, panting and cursing quietly. By the time they reached the summit, the sky in the east was beginning to lighten with the dawn. They found themselves on a ridge of some sort, breath visible in the air before them. To the east below them all was in shadow.

"A short rest." *El Tejón* panted. "Until the sun can show us the way."

"I will take first watch, *Jefe*," Guitierrez told him, putting a hand on his injured commander's shoulder.

"*Si, bueno,*" *El Tejón* said. He found a spot of grass to lie down on and was asleep by the time his shoulder touched the ground.

He awoke to see Domingo kicking Guitierrez, who was snoring on the grass. The man grunted and sat up. "*¿Que?*"

"You were supposed to wake me for my watch, *hijo de puta*," Domingo spat. "*Pinche maricón.*" He kicked the man once more for good measure, then saw his commander sitting up.

"How long?" *El Tejón* was shivering from sleeping on the cold ground, although the sun was warm on his face.

Domingo stared at the sun in the sky in front of them. From its position it was late morning. "Four hours?" The men were scattered around him like leaves on the grass, most of them still dead asleep. Domingo began kicking them awake, cursing.

El Tejón went to stand, only to learn that his right leg, the injured one, was completely numb below the knee. It was still there, but his pantleg was soaked in blood. The blood had soaked the canvas of his boot from the inside out. He didn't dare take the boot off, and he didn't want to unwrap the bandage as he had no more clean ones. He stood on his good leg and flexed his numb foot until the feeling began to return. By that time the rest of the men were awake.

While there were tall ridges in the distance, and far beyond them mountain ranges, a huge expanse of lowland before them was invisible, wreathed in a thinning blanket of fog which hung below their boots. He could see some green of the valley through the fog, but no details.

"Do we go down? Or stay up here?" The ridge they were on ran almost directly east.

If there'd been no fog he might have given a different answer, but the flatland below them was too large to ignore. He could see almost none of the valley floor through the white haze, which did not appear to be burning off quickly. *Los gringos* could be there below them, this valley was right on the way toward Victoria Base. "We go down." He wasn't looking forward to it, but the mission came first.

Domingo scowled at Guitierrez once more and cuffed his head, then shoved the man forward to take point. The descent was treacherous, down a slope covered with loose rock and thorny bushes, complicated by the fog layer which they pushed through a third of the way down. It made everything slick. One of the men fell and suffered a gash to his arm before they were down.

At the base of the ridge they found a stream crowded by plant life. The men had caught glimpses of it during their difficult descent and could think of nothing but drinking its cool clear water, as they had not brought nearly enough water with them. *El Tejón* allowed them ten minutes to relieve themselves and drink their fill of the stream, which seemed fresh, then they pushed across the shallow stream and into the thin belt of forest. From his vantage point on the slope it had looked as if the valley opened into grassland beyond the trees, but he hadn't been able to make out much detail with all the water vapor hanging in the air. Since they'd made their descent, the fog seemed to have thinned considerably.

The foliage was lush and green, and the air seemed much warmer in the valley than it had at the top of the ridge. The men pushed through the thick brush and emerged into the vast grassy plain which filled most of the valley.

One of the men gasped, and pointed. *"Madre de dios. ¡Es un monstruo!"* They all stared at the massive dinosaur several hundred meters distant, lumbering slowly in their general direction. It was as big as a truck.

Then Guitierrez swore and rapidly pointed past the beast. "There!" he shouted. "It is them!" And he raised his AK-47 to his shoulder and fired a long burst.

* * *

Tina screamed as the bullets whizzed by overhead and the group realized they were being fired upon.

"Guerrillas!" Mike yelled and turned and ran in the opposite direction in blind panic.

"Shit," Seamus said. He glanced over his shoulder, then waved at his people as they started to run. "Head for the slope!" He pointed over his right shoulder at the line of brush along the base of the closest slope a hundred meters away. "There's some cover there." He raised his rifle and fired at the guerrillas who had stopped shooting and were now running in their direction. He deduced in a second that they weren't shooting anymore because they didn't want to risk hitting Roger.

"Go go go!" He waved at Corey and Hansen, then fired another few quick shots at the FRAP to keep their heads down. He dumped the heavy pack into the grass and left it. The guerrillas were about three hundred meters away, much too far to hit any of his people except by luck. If he took a knee he could steady Leonidas enough to pick them off, but he felt too exposed in the middle of the valley floor—especially with no helmet—and he had people to protect. He began jogging backwards, trying to keep an eye on the FRAP without falling on his ass.

* * *

Guitierrez had barely finished firing before Domingo slapped his rifle down. "¡*Idiota!* You'll hit her."

"*Muchachos*, after them! They have nowhere to run," *El Tejón* urged his men, breaking into a jog. At the sight of the distant group all the pain in his leg had vanished. "But no shooting unless you have to, and you can pick your targets. We must be much closer." They fell in behind him and ran toward the retreating Americans as fast as they could. They soon drew away from him, outrunning their commander in eagerness to reach the *escaras* and their target.

The big lumbering beast ahead and to their left turned its head to stare at them, not sure of their intent. *El Tejón* hoped they'd pass by far enough away that it wouldn't be bothered by them, because it was the size of a garbage truck. He doubted his submachine gun would have any effect on it.

* * *

Mike was in the lead, sprinting for the short but thick tree cover at the base of the slope ahead. He had both hands on the Blackbird, pumping it back and forth, the magazine pouches for it and the Ulfberht slung over his shoulder banging against his hip. He wasn't panicking, not quite, the shooting had stopped, but he wanted to get away from the guerrillas. He didn't want to have to shoot any more people. He glanced over his shoulder and saw the rest of the group in a staggered line behind him, the guerrillas so far back they were barely more than dots. Mike had pulled away from his people, and even though it seemed unnatural he stopped when he saw how far back his dad was. Seamus was at his father's shoulder, urging him on, but still they were barely moving.

"They're not shooting because they don't want to hit you, but let's not make it easy for the bastards," Seamus said to Roger, jogging beside him. He glanced over his shoulder. The guerrillas were gaining on them, but were still at least several hundred meters away. Roger was gasping in pain but didn't stop moving. Still, it was all he could do to manage a slow jog.

Catching his breath, Mike turned and stared at the tree cover before them, maybe fifty yards away. They should be able to make it, but then what? More shooting? The trees were mostly young maples and cypresses with thin trunks that wouldn't stop any bullets. While the slope above them was rocky it didn't look as if there was anything at the base of the slope that would provide any cover. Although, what was...? He peered at a dark shadow under the trees, partially hidden by branches.

Hansen went running past Mike, holding his fractured arm and wincing with every step. "Stop!" Mike yelled at him. "Stop!" He turned around to see the rest of the group almost on top of him, running as fast as they could. "STOP!" he screamed, and grabbed at them.

Corey stumbled to a stop right in front of him, almost dumping the big rifle. "What?" he yelled angrily back in the kid's face, fighting for air, his face red.

Mike turned and pointed at the shadow under the distant trees. "That!"

Seeing that they had stopped their headlong run, and were perhaps alerted to its presence, the predator broke from the undergrowth and charged toward its prey.

The allosaurus had not yet reached full size but still was twenty-five feet long and weighed three thousand pounds. It was three shades of brown, well camouflaged for hunting. With its head low and tail high as it ran at its prey all they could see of it was its yard-long head, with short horns above its eyes. Below its staring eyes were jaws filled with dozens of curved serrated teeth like steak knives. It ran on two powerful hind legs, churning up dirt and grass as it accelerated to twenty miles an hour. Its arms were proportionately small but still larger than a man's, each with three strong fingers tipped with razor-sharp claws four inches long. A relic of the late Jurassic, the enormous carnivore could grow larger than a T. rex and was born to kill.

Corey's eyes went wide as the huge carnivore appeared out of nowhere and ran straight at them. "Holy shit!" He dropped the Ulfberht and grabbed at his carbine. "Seamus! SEAMUS!"

"What? Oh, for love of—everyone shoot, or we're meat!"

Mike began firing first but the muffled thumps of his sound-suppressed Blackbird were lost as Corey and Seamus began pouring fire into the creature which had already halved the distance between them. Hansen wrestled his pistol out and began firing at the thing one-handed, and even Roger, after staring at the nightmare for an unbelieving second, raised the AK which had been nearly forgotten in his hands and began firing. Even though she had never fired a gun and doubted she could hit anything with one, merely standing there as the huge animal bore down on them made Tina feel helpless.

Through his dancing optic Corey saw the hits on the animal's head and chest, furrows appearing as bullets glanced off its thick angled skull. At first the swarm of bullets didn't slow it, but then Seamus began hammering the beast in the face with his black beauties. Holes appeared in its snout, one of its larger teeth exploded, and blood sprayed from the back of its neck as the hypervelocity bullets tore through it.

Finally the animal slowed and shook its head, as if it was getting attacked by a swarm of bees. Corey found himself with an empty weapon in his hands, as did every other member of the group, as the animal slowed to a walk thirty feet from him.

"Reloading!" Seamus shouted.

"Get out of here!" Corey yelled at the animal as blood began to well from the dozens of bullet wounds it had suffered. He dug for a fresh magazine as the animal began walking around the group at a terrifyingly close distance. Then it roared. The ground seemed to shake with the noise, and Tina's involuntary scream was lost in it. They stared at the rows of shark-like teeth in its mouth. The giant predator was both beautiful and terrifying. They could smell the beast, a rank odor mixed with fresh blood. It smelled like death.

Seamus got his rifle reloaded first and slammed the bolt home. "Go pick on someone your own size you wanker!" he yelled, and fired twice into the allosaurus' face. He blew off part of the horn above the creature's left eye and that made it shake its head and take a step back. Corey finished reloading his carbine and fired several rounds into the side of the carnivore's skull. It shook its head at the pain, roared once more but not as loudly, and finally, grudgingly, loped away from them into the valley.

They stood and watched it move away, in shock at what had just happened. "How is it still moving?" Hansen said in wonder. While his pistol was near useless, the men with rifles had mercilessly pounded bullets into the beast's chest and head. Blood was running down its flanks.

"I think it's dead on its feet, mate, but it might take the better part of an hour before it figures that out." Seamus stared after the animal, heart hammering in his chest. He almost felt bad about having to shoot the thing; it was magnificent.

The allosaurus kept moving away from them at a slow trot, then after a few seconds it accelerated once again, having spotted more prey. The guerrillas scattered and started shouting and shooting wildly as the carnivore accelerated toward them.

Seamus laughed with joy at the sight. "Go go go!" He said to the group, pointing at the nearest slope. "On it and up it. I don't know how well that thing can climb something that steep, but hopefully not at all."

* * *

At first *El Tejón* thought the *escaras* were firing at his men, but then he saw the beast. Flying at them as if it had wings. And, he had to admit, he was conflicted— seeing the *escaras* eaten like meat by one of their own zoo monsters would have poetic justice. But he needed the girl alive.

His men had drawn away from him but stopped when they saw the huge beast charging the other group. *Los Americanos*, firing wildly, were finally able to drive the animal away, but then it started walking in his direction. Then running. His men began to panic.

"*¡Mierda!*"

"*¡Vamanos!*"

Several of his men pointed at the huge lumbering dinosaur forty meters away, paused in the center of the valley, and began running toward it.

"Run for that one, hide behind it." The size of a trailer, the animal was the only cover to be had on the open valley floor.

"Maybe the two will fight," someone said hopefully.

The second, much larger dinosaur had turned at the unfamiliar sound of gunfire. It was so big and so well armored that it was in no real danger from any carnivore, and the loud sounds seemed more like thunder than any noises a dangerous animal might make. Then it spotted the allosaurus running in and hunched its shoulders, preparing for a fight.

The guerrillas fired as they ran, but most of their rounds went wide of the running predator drawing close and slowed it not at all. Its face was the stuff of nightmares, all teeth and blood.

The ankylosaurus didn't know what to make of the small strange animals running toward it, making loud noises, but it recognized the danger in the carnivore closing quickly. It roared at the allosaurus and swung its tail back and forth aggressively.

Carnivores are generally much smarter than herbivores. It is a function of evolution—it doesn't take much intelligence to sneak up on a blade of grass. The ankylosaurus might not remember, but the allosaurus did—several years past they'd met. The allosaurus had tried its best to kill the big herbivore, and had given the animal the scars on its armor plates. Its claws and teeth had had no effect on the much larger creature, and then the ank had delivered a glancing blow from its tail to the allosaurus' leg, nearly fracturing it. It had been partially numb for a week.

The carnivore saw the ankylosaurus and had no wish to attack it, but the small weak-looking animals were running toward the big creature, confusing it and making it agitated. It was in pain, but the small slow-running animals seemed easy prey. And it was very hungry. Still, it slowed as it approached the ankylosaurus, trying to figure out how best to snag one or two of the prey animals circling the big beast without getting in range of its tail club. It remembered that tail very well.

* * *

"Up, up, I want to get above the treeline, so I can see," Seamus urged them, powering up the slope. They were all close behind him.

Fifty feet above the floor of the valley there was a ridge of crumbled stone. "Here!" Seamus shouted, pointing. He dove behind it then came up with Leonidas to his eye, scanning for threats.

Corey set the Ulfberht on a large flat rock. "Where's this sighted in at?" he shouted to Roger, who was struggling up the slope. "What distance?"

"A hundred yards?" Roger gasped, trying to remember.

Corey and Seamus looked out over the thin belt of trees and saw the guerrillas were trying to use the giant ank for cover, and the allosaurus was circling and snapping at them, while the panicked ank turned in circles.

* * *

"Watch out! Watch out!" Guitierrez shouted. He fired at the snapping toothy monster as it lunged and then dove under the ank's swinging tail club. The panicked ankylosaurus trumpeted, the sound huge.

"It won't die!" someone else screamed.

"It's bleeding, which means it can die," Domingo shouted, trying to keep the ank between him and the angry predator. Its face and chest were covered in blood even though the wounds didn't seem to be slowing it down.

The allosaurus darted to the side, trying to get around the ank so it could snag one of the men, and the frightened herbivore spun around faster than any of the men would have thought possible. There was a garbled scream as the ank knocked over one of the guerrillas with its leg and then stepped on him. He died instantly.

"Keep firing!" *El Tejón* shouted. He was twenty meters away, not having been able to run as fast as his men. He shoved a fresh magazine into his submachine gun and emptied it in one long burst at the back of the great beast. The animal turned at the pain and saw one of the small creatures out on its own, away from the ankylosaurus. It took a step toward *El Tejón*. Domingo saw what was happening and charged from behind the herbivore.

"*¡Aqui! ¡Aqui, cabron!*" he shouted, and emptied the entire magazine of his G3 into the side of the monster. The heavy bullets slapped into the animal's thick hide with loud meaty thuds.

The allosaurus roared at the pain and spun around in an instant with a coordinated snap of its head and tail. Domingo found himself staring it in the face with an empty rifle. The dinosaur lunged forward and bit down, then wrenched its head sideways as it pulled back. Domingo felt himself lifted into the air and then he was falling through drops of blood. He landed on his back and saw his left arm in the dinosaur's mouth.

* * *

"Oooh!" Seamus said, wincing as he watched the carnage through Leonidas' scope. "That's going to leave a mark."

"Damn," Corey muttered, watching through his own scope.

"What's happening?" Roger asked. He squinted and held a hand up to block the glare, but the action was taking place hundreds of yards away, and he couldn't make out any detail. Everything seemed to be happening around the huge ankylosaurus, and he could hear yelling and shooting.

The ankylosaurus bellowed, feinted, and swung its club tail wildly. One of the guerrillas went airborne and spun boots over head before landing thirty feet away.

"How about that? You see that?" Seamus asked. He was giddy. This was better than a front row seat at the World Cup.

Roger's mouth hung open. "I felt that."

* * *

He felt numb, with only a faint pain at the shoulder where his arm used to be attached. Domingo raised his head to look and saw the blood jetting from the wound in vibrant spurts. The animal had ripped his arm off, chewed it twice, then swallowed it as it ran after Guitierrez, who got away by rolling under the ankylosaurus. The man barely avoided being stomped.

Domingo snarled. His brachial artery was spurting blood across the grass in crimson jets. The brute had killed him, he knew that, but he wasn't dead yet. He struggled to a seated position.

The animal had moved a little ways off, snarling and roaring at his brothers who were running back and forth around the panicked ankylosaurus more than shooting. He couldn't reload his rifle with only one hand, at least not before he died, but there was one thing he could do to maybe save the rest of his unit. He dug into the magazine pouch on his chest and pulled out the *escaras'* grenade. He hooked its ring over the muzzle of his rifle and yanked the pin out that way.

"*¡Puta!*" he yelled at the frenzied, blood-soaked allosaurus. He waved his hand with the grenade in it until he got the carnivore's attention, then let the lever fly with a *ping!* "Come eat me *culero!*" He held his hand up, arm outstretched, as an offering. The animal roared and ran at him.

* * *

"**W**hat the hell was that?" Corey asked. The sound had been faint. "Was that an explosion?"

"He fed it a grenade," Seamus said, sitting back from his rifle. He was a bit stunned. "With his arm attached. Damn. That's a man who knew how to go out with style."

The allosaurus had taken the whole arm with a single bite. The grenade was at the back of its throat, just under its brain stem, when it detonated. At the muffled *thump!* the big predator, which had already been moving more sluggishly from the blood loss of over a hundred bullet wounds, straightened up then slowly keeled over sideways. It kicked a few times, then was still.

The explosion pushed the ankylosaurus into a blind panic, and it began running across the valley. Its huge feet thudded on the grass and sent clods into the air, and its departure left the remaining guerrillas dazed.

Seamus studied the scene through his scope. There were two guerrillas stumbling around, and he could see one more sitting on the ground rocking back and forth. The rest of them were dead or at least not moving. "Time to finish the job. How far away are they? Three hundred meters?" The four-power max magnification on his scope wasn't nearly as much as he wanted for that distance.

"Closer to four," Corey said, peering through the Ulfberht's scope. It was an adjustable magnification 5-25X scope and he had the power cranked up to 15X. He settled in behind the big rifle. "Let's see if this thing's still zeroed after the crash and all the running. G on the right, going for center chest. Shooter up."

Seamus found the man in his scope. "Spotter up. Send it." The guerrilla was simply standing there, unmoving, perhaps in shock, his rifle hanging forgotten in his hand.

Corey kept the crosshairs as steady as he could as he held his breath and squeezed the trigger. The rifle bucked with a huge boom that rolled across the valley. "Miss," Seamus calmly called out. "Four o'clock in the dirt just behind him, about half a meter low right."

"I don't know what the clicks are on the scope, so I'm just going to hold off," Corey said.

"Send it," Seamus told him, peering through his own scope.

* * *

Martin Guitierrez didn't hear the gunshot, or hear the bullet impact the ground behind him. After the battle with the dinosaur and all the shooting his ears were still ringing. The air around him smelled of blood and animal and gunpowder. His compatriots were scattered like dice, dead and dying or, like him, in shock and disbelief. Eight years fighting for *La*

Fuerza without a scratch, and he'd thought he'd seen everything, but now this. The men torn and shredded by an animal that wasn't even real. Damn American zoo monster. It had ripped off Domingo's arms! He didn't know whether to cry or laugh. So many dead, and for what? He looked around. The stupid truck-like dinosaur was still running away, even though the meat-eater was on the ground, dead. Domingo had sacrificed himself to save them. Or save what was left of them.

Mauricio was sitting on the ground nearby mumbling and shaking his head. "Mauricio!" he yelled at the dazed man. Then Guitierrez was on the ground, staring up at the sky, feeling intense pressure...then nothing. The big bullet hit him in his chest and left an exit wound the size of a fist in the center of his back. Martin Guitierrez heard the booming sound of the gunshot echoing down the valley, and had time to curse silently, then everything went black.

* * *

"Hit," Seamus called out. "He's down." He kept his voice flat. The other guerrilla on his feet saw what had happened and began running.

"Have any idea what the lead is?" Corey asked, shifting behind the Ulfberht.

"Not a clue. No wind, though."

It took the big .338 caliber bullet almost exactly a quarter of a second to travel that distance, and Corey had to guess how far in front of the running man he had to place the crosshairs to get a hit, then adjust even further for his hold-off as the rifle had lost zero and was hitting low right. It took him six shots to hit the sprinting terrified guerrilla, the booming gunfire echoing off the slopes, Seamus calling out his misses. The man had nearly made it to the line of trees along the stream when Corey got the lead right. When he was hit the man tumbled bonelessly to the grass and did not move again. A second later the meaty thud of the bullet strike reached their position.

"Do they have to?" Tina asked Hansen, a hand covering her mouth. What they were doing seemed no different than murder. The pilot was looking on, his face expressionless.

"They'll keep coming after us if we don't," he said gently. It looked like murder to him, too, but he was okay with that, after everything they'd been through.

The last guerrilla was still sitting on the grass and rocking back and forth when Corey swung the rifle back to him. He couldn't tell if the man was injured or in shock. Remembering his hold-off, he placed the crosshairs above and to the left of the man, took a breath, let it half out, and squeezed the trigger.

"And that, ladies and gentlemen," Seamus said, leaning back from his rifle's scope and rubbing his eyes, "is that." He looked around the group. "Everyone okay?"

"Apparently getting chased by a T. rex gives you enough of an adrenaline dump to numb any pain you've got," Roger told him. "But I think I'm going to need to lie down. Or throw up. Or both." Tina looked sick.

"That wasn't a T. rex," Mike told his father. "Wrong head."

Roger turned to him. "Like it matters?"

Mike looked down at his rifle and saw the bolt was locked back on an empty magazine. He started to retrieve a fresh magazine and his hands started to shake so badly he dropped it. "Oh my God," he whispered. He sat on the hillside, seeing the image of the nightmare beast charging straight at them. What was even worse was him shooting and shooting and shooting at it, and it kept coming, all giant teeth. It had been worse than shooting at the guerrillas on the hillside and seeing them die without ever having known he was there.

"We should put that thing in for a posthumous commendation," Seamus said. "It was brilliant."

"It tried to eat us," Roger growled at him.

Seamus shrugged, then told them, "I need to go back down there and retrieve the pack, it's still got a lot of water in it. Plus a few energy bars. And I should check the bodies. But let's give anybody still alive out there a chance to bleed out." He looked at Mike and the pilot. "Lead Roger and Rita up to the top of this slope while everybody's blood is still pumping. We'll meet you up there in a few and we can all take a rest."

"It's Tina!" she blurted in exasperation, in response to which he gave her another wink. She shook her head and cursed—so he *was* doing it on purpose.

"I need a new mag. Kid, Mike!" Corey said out of the corner of his mouth, still looking through the Ulfberht's scope. "You've got the mags and ammo for this thing, right? Don't walk off with them."

"Oh, yeah. Sorry."

"You want me on overwatch?" Corey asked Seamus, pulling his eye from the Ulfberht's scope. Nothing was moving in the valley that he could see.

Seamus smiled. "I thought you'd never ask."

* * *

Every breath was agony, wheezing in and out of his broken body. He knew he had broken ribs, knew at least one of his lungs was punctured, and he couldn't feel anything below the middle of his chest. He hadn't seen the dinosaur's giant tail club swinging toward him until too late, and then he was flying through the air, earth and sky spinning, fireworks of pain shooting through his body. A comedy, that's what it was. To be knocked through the air *como un piñata* by an animal that shouldn't exist. Except it wasn't candy spilling out of him now, it was life itself.

He heard the gunshots from a heavy caliber rifle, heard the heavy impacts. He knew what it meant. The *escaras* were finishing off his men. *Estaban terminados.*

El Tejón couldn't move his body, but he crawled his right hand out of the grass and searched through his pockets. He finally found it and brought the satellite phone up to where he could see it, since he couldn't seem to move his head. With shaking fingers he punched in the encryption code, then the number. It seemed to ring forever, and the sky above him appeared to darken as he waited.

"*¿Sí?*"

"General," he gasped.

"Who is this? I cannot hear you. Why are you whispering?"

"General. It is *Comandante* Daniel Chure," he said, fighting for each word.

"Yes? What is going on? Why are you whispering? Have you captured her?"

"We have failed. We have failed *La Fuerza*. I am sorry. The *escaras* have escaped with her. And we are all dead."

"You are not dead, I am talking to you on the phone. What is going on? *Comandante. Comandante! Comandante?*" The line was still open, but there was no longer anyone on the other end. General Aponte sat back in the overstuffed leather chair and stared at the satellite phone in his hand.

"Augusto," he called to one of his adjutants. "Find me Generals Ramos and Flores. Is Señor Sandoval still downstairs in the kitchen? Have them meet us there."

"*Si Señor.*"

The kitchen was on the ground floor of the hacienda. It was huge and done in pure white. Only the cooks and command staff were allowed in the kitchen, so the floor remained clean and the shelves remained stocked.

Ramos looked smug when he arrived, as if he knew what the news was. "You have news?" Aponte wanted to wipe the smirk off the man's face with a beer bottle but he kept his emotions in check. Flores arrived a moment later, and he too seemed to suspect what had occurred.

"*Comandante* Chure seems to have failed," Aponte announced. He waited until his fellow generals had arrived, but his news was first and foremost for his leader. Timotéo Sandoval nodded and took a sip of steaming coffee. He did not look angry, which was not in itself a good sign. He often did not look angry even when taking heads off with a machete or removing eyeballs with his pearl-handled knife. There it was in its sheath on the commander's belt, as always. He forced himself to look away. "While it was *our* plan," Aponte made sure to point out, "he was my man, so I take full responsibility for his failure."

"What happened?" Timotéo asked.

Aponte shook his head. "I do not know. He called me and said that they had failed, that all his men were dead. And then he died, or passed out, while I was talking to him." He had a map with him and unrolled it on the kitchen table.

"Did he say if she was still alive?"

Aponte nodded. "He said the *escaras* had escaped with her. But this was moments ago, and I have the GPS coordinates of his satphone." He put his finger on the map. "This valley is still nearly thirty kilometers from Victoria Base, and the *escaras* must still be close."

"We sent over two dozen men, correct? And they are all dead? Do we know if she has been rescued? Or has all this damage been done by the crew of the one helicopter?"

"I do not know, Señor."

Timotéo looked thoughtful and rubbed his beard for a bit. Then he looked at General Ramos. "Your 'Plan B' is still standing by?"

Ramos nodded rapidly. "*Si, Jefe.*"

"Then send them in. If Raven has rescued her she will be back at Victoria Base in minutes. But if not…..tell them not to kill anyone they don't have to. After what has happened, I want to know who's with her. I want to hear what happened to our men. And I want to make them pay." He moved a hand down and rested it on the handle of his knife.

"*Si, Señor.* With pleasure."

* * * * *

Chapter Nineteen

The slope was steep and a difficult climb due to all the rocks that wanted to turn underfoot. By the time they reached the top they were about spent.

Past the edge and a thick line of bushes was a large grassy clearing with a few young trees. Plateau was too grandiose a word for it, and perhaps not accurate as they could see taller ground to their east, but the nearly level clearing seemed isolated and sheltered. Seamus and Corey found the rest of their group collapsed on the ground not too far from the edge of the slope. Seamus was eating something.

"How long are we stopping?" Roger asked the two soldiers as they drew close. He was lying on his side, face screwed up in pain.

"Well, I hope that's the last of the bastards. Certainly nobody else showed up while I was looking the unlucky ones over." Seamus set the pack in the middle of the circle that had formed. "Top off with some water if you need it. I took some energy bars off the Gs, and some beef jerky." He held up a bit of it in his hand. "Eat up. I think we've earned it." He dug through a side pocket of the pack and handed Roger the last of the aspirin and ibuprofen. "Take these with your water; maybe they'll take the edge off." He then sat cross-legged on the ground with a grunt.

"What about me? I've got a broken arm you know," Hansen said. It ached, but not horribly, and he said it fighting back a smile.

"You worth three hundred million? I'm angling for a tip after all's said and done. Maybe Head of Security for Roger Rudd Enterprises when I retire."

Hansen laughed. "So that's how it is? You find any intelligence on them?"

"Such a loaded question." Seamus shook his head. "No. Did find a satphone, but it's encrypted and I can't even make a call without punching in a code, so it's useless. But I did find this." A wicked smile curled his face as he pulled a metal flask out of his cargo pocket. He unscrewed the cap and hoisted it. "May you be in heaven a full half hour before the devil knows you're dead." And he took a swig. He sighed in satisfaction.

"Tequila?" Corey asked.

"No, my son," Seamus said, handing over the flask. "The curse of the Irish, whiskey. Those men we killed today—with a little help from our big friend, may he rest in peace—at least had good taste in liquor."

Corey took a swig, and passed the flask on. It made its way around the circle as they opened energy bars with the crackle of wrappers and twisted open water bottles.

As much as Roger wanted to down what was left in the flask to help numb the pain in his back he only took one small gulp, then handed it to his son with a nod. Mike took the flask and stared at it, grinning, then took a sip. The whiskey made him cough, and everyone laughed.

"Would you prefer tequila, señorita?" Seamus asked Tina as she took the flask from the teen.

"Either is equally ugly on the tongue," she said, then smiled and took a drink. As the whiskey burned its way down her throat she coughed too.

"Couple of lightweights," Hansen scolded, taking the flask. After his sip he shook it. "Still about an inch in here," he told Seamus.

"Finish it you fairy. Maybe it'll stop you whining about your arm." Hansen smiled and hoisted the flask in thanks.

"How far are we from Victoria?" Roger asked, chewing an energy bar.

"Two days travel. But I can't imagine it'll take that long for a helicopter to spot us. We've already heard one this morning, and now that we're out of the fog it's only a matter of time. If there was anyone on the ground within a couple miles they heard the shooting."

"Do you really think we've seen the last of *La Fuerza?*" Tina asked.

Seamus shrugged. "I would hope so. Twenty men, four vehicles? This far north that's a big footprint on the ground for them. Last time that many of them came this far north was about six years ago. Then they were blowing up radio towers. But honestly, I don't know. These bloody bastards just won't give up. You insult their mother?" he asked Roger.

Tina had been struggling with her knowledge. Her father had told her for years that being related to a powerful man had just as many risks as rewards, and at first, she'd shaken her head at his paranoia. Then there were all the tabloid photos of her at their pool taken by *cabrones* who'd snuck onto their property, earning her the nickname *Chi-Chi Echevarria*. Not to mention the love letters and marriage proposals from *locos* she'd never met. She was sure her father and Beni never told her about the worst of them, trying to protect her. And it still seemed crazy to think that this had all been about her, instead of a rich American businessman. But she had to face the truth. Her father was a much more important man in Mexico than Roger Rudd. "I do not think they are after Mister Rudd," Tina said quietly. The comment almost went unnoticed.

"I admit they've done a piss poor job of it, but they're not exactly out here tinning for the Red Cross," Seamus said with a smile.

She shook her head, the guilt at what might be finally too much. "I think they are after me."

Mike was confused. "Why would they be after you?"

"I am Margarita Echevarria. My father is Eduardo Echevarria."

Seamus made a face and shrugged. "Should that mean something to me?"

But Roger blinked. "Your father is Gordito?" Roger asked. She nodded.

"Her father's a what?" Seamus asked. "A fat little boy?"

"Her father is the richest man in Mexico," Roger told him. "Actually, according to Forbes, I think he's the second or third richest man in the Western Hemisphere."

"Richer than you?" Corey said.

Roger nodded. "By a factor of ten at least."

Seamus did that math in his head. "Wait a—you mean he's a fooking billionaire?" Hansen coughed and tried not to spray the whiskey out his nose.

Roger nodded and looked at Tina, who seemed embarrassed. "And your mother's an actress of some kind too, right?"

Seamus held a hand up and stared at the young woman. "Wait, hold on, let me catch up. You mean to say your father's a billionaire, with a *B*? And your mum's an actress? Are you bleedin' royalty?"

"There's no royalty in Mexico," Tina said.

"If there was, you and your family'd be it," Roger said. He dug in his brain for details he'd picked up in news stories over the years. "Isn't one of your sisters married to the…." he snapped his fingers twice, trying to think of it.

"The Attorney General," she said quietly, making a face. The man was an arrogant ass. She'd punched him in the face once when he'd grabbed her chest. He'd told the newspapers he'd been hit by a racquetball.

"And you're just telling us this now?" Hansen said indignantly.

"Would it have made a difference?" She looked around the circle. "*La Fuerza*, well, maybe they don't even know I am here, maybe they are after Señor Rudd. But what would they have done differently if they were after me versus him? Him or me, what would you have done differently? Would you have spared those men you just shot?" She looked at Seamus and Corey in turn.

"I'd have flirted heavier if I'd known you were such a catch," Seamus said. "Daughter of a bleedin' billionaire who's smart and looks like you?" He shook his head. Then he huffed and stared at her, most of the humor leaving his voice. "I understand why you didn't say anything at first, but I think we're a bit beyond formalities now, don't you? Have been for a while."

"I am sorry," she said.

"And here I'm lugging your damn camera around all of God's creation." Seamus kicked the pack and took another bite of jerky. "I think you can afford a new one. Unless there's photos in there you need? Or, dear God, compromising selfies you'd like to share with the group? You should be able to pull the data card, right?"

"*Sí*, I guess I could, but I've never had to. The camera is Sirion Cloud-enabled so it uploads all the photos automatically."

Seamus opened his mouth, closed it, then cocked his head. "Even out here?"

"*Sí, claro*, it is digisat enabled."

Seamus and the pilot looked at each other.

"The EMP should have fried its chip," Hansen said.

Frowning, Seamus pulled the camera case out of the pack. In the sunlight it was an odd hue, a matte grayish brown. "This is Lattice," Seamus said. "Or whatever the trademark name is. Designed like a miniature Faraday cage, meant to block RFID signals so no one can hack the core, and tough as a nut. Expensive as all hell." He cracked open the case and pulled the camera out. There had to be twenty buttons on it. After a few seconds he found the Power switch. The camera's display immediately lit up. Seamus looked at the pilot, eyebrows climbing up his forehead.

"If it's satellite enabled that means it's got a GPS co-locator on it," Hansen said, his voice rising.

She frowned. "Maybe, I don't know."

"Wait...." Roger said, struggling to sit up. He was starting to get the picture.

"Do the photos you take have the GPS coordinates where they were taken embedded into the metadata?" Hansen asked her.

"Yes."

"Then it's got GPS. It may be passive, but it is in contact with satellites. Why didn't you mention this before?"

She frowned, not understanding their concern. "It's not a palm-pad or satphone, you can't call out on it. All I can do is upload photos to my cloud account. And nobody else has the password to that.

Only a few of my school friends even know about it." She looked at her camera in Seamus' hands. The Nikon looked a little dusty, but otherwise fine.

Seamus looked from Hansen to Roger Rudd, for once speechless. The businessman was shaking his head. He looked at her and said, "Don't be surprised if that's no longer the case. Daughter of the richest man in the country, one of the richest men in the world, missing in a war zone for days? I'd be shocked if they haven't already hacked into all of your email accounts in hopes of finding something, anything. Does it upload automatically every day, or only if you take new photos, or only if it's on?"

"Every day, but only new photos, and it has to be turned on. And out of the case."

"When was the last time you uploaded photos from that thing?"

"Well, it did it automatically right before I got on the helicopter with you, but I can do it manually. I think that's in the settings."

"Bloody hell. Please tell me the battery's still got some juice, I can't read this display."

She took the camera from him and studied the small screen. The battery was down to ten percent, but that was good for taking hundreds of pictures at least. "I've still got a little battery."

Seamus looked around the circle. "Anybody have some paper?"

"Check the backpack," Tina told him.

"Seriously? Didn't I tell you to empty it out of everything that—" Seamus stopped and shook his head. "My bloody fault for not checking the damn thing." He began to dig through it. "Wonder what else I've been toting up and down hill and dale. A tiara? Pumpkin that turns into a carriage? Any corned beef in here?"

* * *

"Well, I hate to break up our little picnic, but we haven't been rescued yet," Seamus said half an hour later as they all lay and sat on the grass, enjoying the warmth of the early afternoon sun. They'd finished the beef jerky and over half of the energy bars. "Best we get to walking again."

"You sure you don't want to wait here a little longer?" Roger asked him. He wasn't sure if that was the best course of action, but lying on soft grass hurt less than walking would. He couldn't remember what it was to not feel pain. Although the ibuprofen had started to work—now his back only hurt a lot. "They could be here any time."

"I've been thinking that for two days," Hansen said, unconsciously fiddling with the pink pony head hanging from his button. "But Seamus is right. The closer we get to Victoria, the greater the chances we'll be spotted by aircraft, even by accident."

Roger made a face, but accepted the decision. "Well, I'm going to need a hand up. Or two." Hansen and Corey helped him up as Seamus shrugged on the pack, and the group headed east across the big field at an easy pace. They all felt much more relaxed now that they were no longer being pursued by guerrillas. Mike hung back to talk to Tina.

"You get along with your dad?" he asked her. She caught the glance he threw in his own father's direction and smiled. She had to admit they had more in common that she had thought at first.

"No. I love him, he *es mi Papa*, but we fight all the time, about everything. My mother says that is because I am so much like him. Maybe she is right. I know I am nothing like my sisters. Do you and your father fight?"

"No, not really. He's so busy. I don't see him often."

"And your mother?"

"She died when I was young."

"Oh. I'm sorry."

Mike shrugged. "I barely remember her. But, without her, I guess Dad and I don't have much in common, you know?"

"Maybe after this that will change," she told him.

"Hold up!" Hansen called out. The pilot stopped and cocked his head.

"What is it?" The group was strung out in a ragged line, Corey in the lead.

Hansen slowly turned. When he was facing south he stopped, and then the rest of them could hear it as well.

"Well, speak of the devil," Seamus said as his ears picked up the helicopter. He began walking toward their pilot. "How far away is it? You see it?"

Hansen shook his head. "Getting a lot of bounce off all the slopes. Coming this way though."

"If you see it, call it out," Corey said. "And start waving."

"Took them bloody forever." His ears weren't as good as they used to be. "That's a heli, right? Not a drone?"

Hansen nodded as the sound grew louder. "Yes. Single rotor. Can't tell what it is, getting too much echo. Maybe a Blackhawk."

The noise of the helicopter grew louder and louder, until it sounded as though it was right on top of them. "Where the hell is it?" Corey asked. He'd drifted back to the rest of the group. They were looking in all directions, but even though the haze had burned off nobody had spotted the aircraft.

"Sounds like it's hovering," Hansen said. "Wonder if they spotted the bodies down below."

Then, with a roar, the helicopter popped over the ridge a hundred yards away. It had been skimming the valley floor below. It paused in the air a second, then the pilot spotted their group and the nose dipped as it headed in their direction.

"And I thought our helicopter sounded like shit," Roger said, listening to the vehicle's laboring engine.

It was a Blackhawk, but the engine had been rebuilt using scavenged parts, which was why Hansen hadn't recognized its sound. The bird had weathered Raven markings, and was a welcome sight.

Seamus waved the bird to an open spot in the clearing before them. The big craft came in closer, the chop from the rotors making the grass whip wildly, then it turned its nose away from them. Seamus' first solid clue that something was odd was the door gun on the right side of the bird. It looked like a PKM instead of a mini-gun. Then he saw the doorgunner, and the other men inside the bird.

"FRAP!" he yelled, lifting his rifle.

The doorgunner let loose a long burst as the group scattered. The man worked the burst up the grass and into Hansen as the man dove to the side. Blood sprayed everywhere as the pilot collided with Corey, and they both went down.

Seamus only fired one shot and then ran for Tina, tackling her as bullets whizzed by behind him.

"¡Manos arriba! Stop! ¡Basta! Put down your guns!" the doorgunner yelled above the sound of the rotor. He fired another long burst at the ground in front of the stunned people, spraying dirt into their faces. The men beside him fired warning shots from their AKs above their heads. Two *gringos* dropped their rifles. Two *escaras* were down and not moving.

Seamus rolled off Tina, grabbing at his rifle. She fought him for it. "No. No! They'll kill you!" she yelled in his face.

"Exactly!" he yelled back. He looked over his shoulder to see several guerrillas had jumped off the helicopter and were running toward them with rifles up. He turned back to her. "Trust me, you don't want to be captured," he yelled over the rotors. But she wouldn't let go of Leonidas. He let go and grabbed the Walther out of his thigh holster, but then a foot came down on his wrist, and he looked up in time to see the metal plate of a buttstock descending toward his face.

The guerrillas spread out and shoved the two *gringos*, a fat man and a teen, toward the helicopter. Two others dragged the unconscious *escara* off the girl and pulled him toward the salvaged helicopter they'd been hiding for just such an opportunity as this.

"Get up, *chica*," one of the guerrillas snarled, grabbing Tina by the hair and lifting her off the ground. She cried out in pain but he ignored it. He shoved her toward his *compadres* and then went to check the bodies. *El escara negro* had been torn apart by the doorgunner's bullets. The guerrilla pulled the pistol out of the dead man's hand. The other *escara* was under him, his face covered in blood. The guerrilla nudged him with his rifle muzzle and then shot him again in the chest just to make sure. He stripped the *escara* of his carbine and jogged back toward the helicopter with the extra weapon. Its blades had never stopped spinning.

"Search them for palmpads or satellite phones, any electronics," he reminded the men. "Anything the Army and *escaras* can track. Throw them out here. No mistakes now."

They had captured *la puta rica*, *un escara*, and *dos gringos mysterioso* for Timotéo without losing a single man. *El Jefe y los generales* would be very pleased.

* * *

When the elevator doors opened on the 65th floor lobby David Tejada nearly jumped through them. "I need to see Señor Echevarria immediately," he told the secretary.

Señor Echevarria had told her that if and when he returned he wanted to see Tejada immediately and without delay, so she briskly nodded down the hallway toward his office. David nearly ran down the hallway, personal tablet in hand, and knocked on the door frantically.

He nearly burst through the door when Echevarria opened it. "I have something," he told them as he set his tablet on the man's big desk and started tapping away. "She doesn't have another palm or phone number that I could find, but I did find another email account that seems to be her main one. The Estrella address she only uses to communicate with you, she uses the other one for everything else. But there's been no activity on it for three days. I also found her online storage and back-up account. Programs, downloads, music, but it also seems to be tied in with a camera she has. Quite regularly she uploads photos to it. Most of them seem to have to do with plants or animals, I'm guessing that's something to do with her schooling." He got into her account once more, access made easier by the 20G-equivalent speed of the building's wi-fi.

"*Si, si*, she is a graduate student in biology, working in the field," Senor Echevarria told him impatiently. "This helps us how?"

"She uploaded two photos a little over an hour ago," Tejada told them. When he'd stumbled across them he'd about wet himself. His fingers were a blur as he sped through the thousands of photos to the end. He tapped the second-to-last one and it went full screen, then he stepped back so her parents could see.

Rosita took two steps forward to see, then gasped and began crying. "My Rita," she sobbed.

Eduardo stared at the photo. It was a group shot of six people, all of them dirty, disheveled, and tired looking. Five were men, four of them were carrying rifles, and three of the men were in Raven camouflage uniforms. One of the *escaras* had his arm in a sling, and they all looked very serious, and capable. But the sixth, the sixth was his daughter. She was squinting in the bright sunlight, peering at the camera lens. She was dirty, her hair a mess, with many scratches on her legs. There might have been dried blood on her shirt. But her intense expression, as she stared at the camera, verifying that it was working properly and taking the photo, was painfully familiar. It was the expression she always had when she was arguing with him. Echevarria fought back a sob. It was the most beautiful thing he'd ever seen.

"You said this was taken an hour ago?"

"It was uploaded," David checked the clock on the nearby wall, "seventy-seven minutes ago. Along with this one." He flipped to the next photo, which was a much tighter shot of one of the Raven men holding up a piece of paper. Tejada zoomed in, and Echevarria was able to read what was written on it.

BEING PURSUED ON FOOT BY SMALL FORCE OF GUERRILLAS, HEADING SE FROM CRASH SITE TOWARD

VICTORIA BASE. ASSISTANCE WOULD BE APPRECIATED
YOU LAZY POOFS

"What's a poof?" Rosita asked.

"I don't know," David answered honestly. He said excitedly, "But the important thing is that these photos are geotagged."

"I don't know what that means," Echevarria said with a frown.

"There are GPS coordinates in the metadata, which is the background information of the photos." Fingers moving quickly he moved to an online mapping program he already had open and into which he'd already plugged the coordinates of the photos—he'd already verified that they were both taken at the same location.

A greenish brown splotch filled the tablet. David backed out and backed out until some sort of manmade construction was visible in the low right. "That's what I think they call Victoria Base," he told the Echevarrias. Between the pin of the GPS coordinates and the base there was nothing visible but greenish brown hilly terrain.

"They are so close," Rosita said.

"They're farther than it looks, that's probably twenty-five kilometers straight line," David told her. "And those are mountains. It would take days to walk, I'd guess."

Echevarria strode around his desk and started punching buttons on his communications console. "Give me those GPS coordinates," he told his tech. He hit the speaker button and ringing filled the room.

"*Si*, this is Beni." There was a constant mechanical noise in the background of the call.

"Beni, I don't have his number, are you still in contact with the Raven colonel who is directing the search?"

"*Si Senor.*"

"My girl, she is a smart one. Her camera uploads photos no matter where she is. She uploaded two an hour ago. With GPS coordinates."

"Hold on." He moved his palm away from his mouth. "I need something to write with," he yelled over the sound of the Peregrine in flight. Manny and Inspector Torres began patting their pockets. Torres found a pen and a scrap of paper and handed them to him. "Okay, go."

Echevarria read the numbers off the tablet to his man. "It is northwest of the Raven base at Victoria, in the mountains."

Beni stared at the coordinates on the scrap of paper on his knee. "The photos…she is unhurt?"

"She looks tired and dirty and irritated," Echevarria laughed, almost crying with relief. "Surrounded by *escaras* with guns. She looks ready to come home. Bring her home to me Beni. After all this, I only trust you to bring her home to me."

"*Si Señor.* We are on our way now."

Beni pulled his palm out from between his headset and his ear and moved the microphone down to his mouth. "*Capitán*, change of plans," he said over the intercom. "We need to head to Victoria Base."

"Something happen?" Ted Billings asked. They were most of the way to Mexico City, flying over brown and nearly empty country. To get to Victoria they'd need to turn around and head back northeast. Again.

"*Si*, we think we know where she is. I must call Raven now."

Billings and Chris Evers looked at each other. Billings shook his head, and Evers rolled her eyes. "Roger that," he said with a sigh, "but we're going to have to refuel." He switched channels and spoke only to Evers. "Pull up the map, see where the closest refueling point is before I alter course."

"Leon Base is behind us, and there's that smaller one up ahead." She couldn't remember the name of it and peered at the HUD map in front of her. "Cobalt Station, just east of Morelia. Don't know if I've ever actually been there." It would put them about a hundred miles northwest of Mexico City.

"Plot a course and get them on the radio. Let them know we'll be dropping in and have priority clearance. Which has been a complete waste of time and fuel for this taxi ride. I swear to God all we've done is fly in one big damn circle around this country. It's starting to piss me off."

"We're not going to Mexico City?" Torres said.

Beni shook his head. "Not right now. We have a location on *la señorita*, and Raven should have her by the time we get to Victoria. Senor Echevarria wants me to personally bring her back."

"I do have an actual job I need to get back to," Torres said. He looked as if he'd taken a bite of something sour.

"They said they had to stop to refuel, you can get off there. Maybe you can find a vehicle. Don't know that you'll get back to Mexico City any sooner than we will, however."

While Torres fumed, Beni dialed a number and wedged his palm back between his headset and his ear. "Kresge," he heard.

"Colonel, this is Beni Trujillo. Are you still searching northwest of Victoria Base?"

"Just got back on station after refueling. I've got nothing to report, yet."

Beni gave him the news about the girl, and the GPS coordinates, then handed them to the flight crew so they'd have them. Kresge relayed them to the co-pilot of his Blackhawk, who punched them into the system. The location popped up on the HUD and Kresge stared at it. "Shit, we're five minutes from there. That's where we're heading," he told the pilot, pointing, and the bird immediately tilted as it changed course. "I will call you back as soon as I've got news."

"More like ten minutes, sir," the pilot told him, eyeing the HUD.

Kresge was staring at the HUD map as well. "Five, ten, we're practically on top of them. We must have flown over that spot several times today ourselves. How the hell did we not spot them?"

The co-pilot squinted at the illuminated holographic map. "I think that's the big valley that was filled with fog this morning," she said. "Yesterday too, I think. Couldn't see shit. If I remember correctly a UAV or two spotted some animals on thermals, but no human silhouettes. Hopefully the fog's burned off now or touching down blind will be a mite exciting."

They approached from the southwest, soaring over the tall ridgeline that made the south wall. The valley floor dropped away beneath them, and the Blackhawk descended steeply. There were only wisps of fog remaining at the far north end of the L-shaped valley.

"What's that? There's something there," Kresge said, pointing at the valley floor about a kilometer away.

"There sure is," the pilot said. Three seconds later he calmly said into his microphone, "Gunners up, we've got bodies."

The five soldiers in the helicopter with Kresge were already alert, but at the announcement their rifles came to their shoulders and they started scanning. The doorgunner put his hands back on the minigun and double-checked it was ready to go.

The helicopter flared a hundred feet up and the soldiers stared down at the scene under the bird. "Holy shit," somebody said.

"Look at the size of that thing."

"I don't see any friendlies, these are all FRAP."

"Set 'er down," Kresge told the pilot.

"Sir, the GPS coordinates are actually about a kilometer north-east of here," he informed his commander.

"Yeah? Well, we've got to take a quick look at this first."

The grass and ground had been stomped and churned in a huge area around the bodies. His men jumped off the bird as it hovered off the ground and approached the still forms with their rifles up. Kresge was right behind them. The allosaurus was the biggest carnivore any of them had ever seen.

"Half these guys are shot, not chewed on."

"This guy looks like he was run over by a truck, he's a pancake. Look at these footprints, something else was here. Something huge."

"They shoot each other trying to hit it?"

"Even FRAP aren't that stupid."

"Sure they are."

"Look how many rounds this freaking beast took before it went down."

"They probably shot it while it was laying there."

Kresge looked around and saw an obvious trail of footprints heading east through the grass, in the direction of the GPS coordinates he'd been given. "Okay, back in the bird. We'll be back to check this out later. Friendlies are supposed to be a klick away."

They ran back to the bird which was hovering and barely touching the valley floor. It headed northeast, rising steadily to clear the steep slope in front of them. Beyond the next ridge was a big clearing, and it was the pilot who spotted the bodies first. "Sir," he said, pointing.

He saw they were wearing Raven uniforms, and Kresge's heart sank. "Goddammit. Put us down."

His men put up a defensive perimeter as he ran to the bodies. The co-pilot grabbed the bird's first aid kit and followed, wind from the Blackhawk's rotors buffeting both of them.

Kresge knew it was Hansen right away, even though he lay face down. He'd been the only black man on the downed helicopter. He'd been torn open by rifle rounds. With care, the colonel rolled him over. The man's eyes were closed, and he looked peaceful, in stark contrast to his bloody wounds.

The man underneath Hansen was on his back and covered in tacky half-dried blood from forehead to knees. There were bullet impact marks on his chest armor. His rifle was nowhere to be found, but he had a big knife clutched in one hand. As the co-pilot crouched over him he opened his eyes.

"Shit, you're still alive?" she said in surprise.

"It's not my blood," Corey told her through clenched teeth. "Well, most of it isn't."

"Where are you hurt?" she asked as Kresge squatted down next to the man. She began touching his body, looking for wounds.

Corey moved his head a bit and looked at the dead man beside him. "He died on his feet and fell on me. I don't know if he broke my knee going down, but it feels like it. And I took a round in the other leg. Not bad, just a through-and-through, but I couldn't get him off me. And I couldn't get my rifle out from under him as they were coming at me, so I played possum. One of the Gs put a few rounds into my chest armor to make sure I was dead. Idiot. I think he broke a couple of ribs, and I've got some frag in my arm. Other than that I'm fine," he joked. He didn't look happy about playing dead, but the move had saved his life.

"Corey. Where's the girl?"

The young soldier looked at the colonel squatting over him. "FRAP grabbed her. They showed up in an old Raven Blackhawk, surprised us. Didn't even get a shot off." He laid his head back on the grass. "Grabbed her and everybody but Hansen and me. I don't know how long ago."

The co-pilot found the bullet wound in his leg and applied a dressing. His other leg was bent oddly at the knee—definitely a break. She eyed the long knife in his hand. "What were you going to do with that?"

He shook his head. "Didn't know who or what might be showing up first, and I'm covered in blood." He waved the big knife weakly in a small circle. "Toothpick."

* * * * *

Chapter Twenty

Kresge stared at the palmpad they'd found in the grass away from the bodies, where it appeared a helicopter had touched down. It seemed to belong to a teenager from the apps and home screen wallpaper. It was the only electronic device they'd found at the location.

Satphone to his ear Kresge stomped away from his Blackhawk, which had powered down until he had a handle on the situation. The second bird was down in the valley, its crew taking a much more detailed look at the carnage there. He got Jeffers, the smart young communications tech who'd helped sort out the mess at China Base, on the line. "Jeffers, we've got a camera. A commercial Nikon. When you take a picture with it, it embeds the GPS coordinates of where you were when you took it into the data. And it then can automatically upload those photos to a cloud account using a satellite uplink. So it can at the very least communicate with the commercial GPS satellites. Does Raven have any way to locate that device in-country with the technology at our disposal? Triangulate its position?" While he talked he thumbed through the palmpad. He suspected it belonged to Michael Rudd and was looking to confirm that.

Jeffers sat and thought for about twenty seconds before he answered. "No sir. Not saying it's not technically possible, not at all, but we are not set up for that. Especially since it's a piece of commercial tech. We are military-centric. To do something like that you'd need resources usually only found in intelligence agencies."

"I was afraid of that." A lot of politicians loved to say Raven was a rogue military without a nation, but the truth of it was that Raven was but the sharp end of the stick and had very little intelligence capability. They provided highly trained bodies to their clients, and only had what equipment those clients—those governments—were willing to sell them. The governments who hired them always kept the best toys for themselves. The next call he had to make would be much less pleasant.

* * *

obalt Station was used solely for refueling. It appeared to originally have been a HyBridge commercial facility, and when the war broke out someone had simply switched all the signs from HyBridge to Raven. It was small, even compared to Norton Station in Juarez, with just two helipads, one hangar, and one small office building. The fuel was in trucks parked in a lot in back.

As he was smoking, Inspector Ramon Torres stood a good distance away from the ungainly aircraft while it was refueled. He was not happy, and he had already expressed the depth of his unhappiness to his supervisor Chief Inspector Abreu *al oficina del División de Inteligencia* in Mexico City during a short but unpleasant call.

"*¿Ramon, 'sta loco?* So you don't like the man. So he was a petty criminal twenty years ago. So you have other cases. So what? What is happening today is being watched at the highest levels of government. *La Fuerza* is chasing Gordito's daughter. You know how they will use her to their advantage if they catch her. How they would use her capture to recruit *muchos perros* to their cause. What they will do to her. You represent *El División de Inteligencia y los Federales total* in this matter and you will provide Señor Echevarria's people with whatever assistance they require. Am I being clear?" And he didn't wait for a response, he just ended the call.

So Torres stood apart from the others, smoking and fuming. It wasn't that any one aspect of it specifically bothered him—it was the whole situation. He had a daughter and knew how Echevarria must be feeling. With twenty-two years at *El División de Inteligencia,* he had unparalleled experience dealing with *La Fuerza* spies and informants, genius and idiot criminals, and the whole underground lawless society which operated in Mexico City. And none of it was doing a bit of good. The girl was still missing, *La Fuerza* was still after her. The problem was he felt powerless. He hadn't done anything. It was his men who had spotted Travers. It had been Trujillo who had interrogated the man—and, inexperienced interrogator or not, he'd gotten all there was to get out of the man, to Torres' chagrin. All he'd done was drive halfway across the country, then been flown back to almost where he started. And now another ride to pick the girl up, provided she was actually where they thought she was. He was not *un Inspector del División de Inteligencia*, he was a passenger in a flying bus.

He heard loud voices, then his name being called. Torres looked up and saw Beni and his partner waving at him from inside the Peregrine. The craft must be refueled, but as the rotors weren't spinning he took his time walking back to the aircraft, even though they kept waving at him to move faster.

"*¡Tortuga!*" Manuel quietly spat at him.

Beni waved the inspector onto the bird then turned back to the cockpit. "Colonel, I have Inspector Ramon Torres with the Intelligence Division of the *Federales conmigo*. Please repeat what you just now told me." Torres looked at Trujillo, wondering exactly what had happened to precipitate the call. The man appeared upset, and there was a vein pulsing in his forehead. The pilot and co-pilot were in their seats, and they looked stern.

Kresge's voice was a little distorted from the connection, but they had no problem understanding him. "The FRAP showed up in a helicopter, killed one of my men and captured the rest of the downed crew, including your girl, Miss Echevarria. This was perhaps an hour ago according to the man they left for dead. I am told they have her camera with them, the one that communicates with GPS satellites and can upload photos through a direct satellite connection." Kresge paused. "We have no satellites in the area, and have no idea where they took her, or even in which direction the helicopter departed. Raven has no tools available to us in-country to track or locate this camera. Do you?"

Torres stood there, for a second, staring at the controls in the cockpit but not seeing them as he thought. "Possibly. I need the type of camera, serial number, the account that it uploads the photos to, every bit of information that you have."

"I have none of that information," Kresge said flatly.

"Hold on," Beni said. He pulled out his palm and dialed a number, then hit speaker and adjusted the volume to maximum.

* * *

Echevarria removed a flavored water from the refrigerator in his office and gestured at David Tejada, who nodded. He brought a bottle to the tech, who was standing off to one side until he was needed again.

"She is with hard men, *sí?*" Rosita said, staring at the tablet and gnawing on her lip. Then she returned to pacing the room, biting her thumbnail.

Echevarria flipped to the last picture and stared at the man holding the note in the photo. An obvious professional soldier, lean and older than the other men in uniform. "Beni says that they have killed over fifteen of the guerrillas already. *Fifteen,* Rosita. And this one is smiling. Making a joke on the note." He'd looked up 'poofs.' "So *sí,* hard men."

His office line rang, and they all jumped. Echevarria saw it was Beni calling, and his heart jumped into his throat. He hit the speaker button. "*¿Sí, Beni?*"

"Señor Echevarria, you are on the line with Inspector Ramon Torres of *El División de Inteligencia Policia Federal* and Colonel Kresge of Raven. I will be brief. The colonel says that within the past hour *La Fuerza* attacked the crew escorting your daughter Margarita and kidnapped her. They escaped in a helicopter. It is believed she has her camera with her. The Inspector says *El División de Inteligencia* may be able to locate that camera, but he will need…." Beni looked at Torres.

Torres felt a bit out of his element, as he had since he'd taken the first call from Trujillo. Knowing that a Raven colonel and perhaps the most powerful man in Mexico short of the President were on the line had his heart hammering in his chest. "Make and model of the camera. Serial number. The account address where it uploads the photos. Any other information that you have on it or the account that it is tied to."

At the news that her daughter had been kidnapped Rosita bit back a shriek and covered her mouth. Tears burst from her eyes and ran down her cheeks and over her hands. Tejada nearly dove at his tablet and began frantically working with his fingers. He'd pulled up the information on the camera earlier, just in case. He grabbed a piece of paper and wrote down the account information, then flipped the tablet back to the page displaying the camera's serial number.

"I have that information, are you ready to write?" Echevarria asked. He was steadfastly refusing to think about his daughter and what might be happening to her. He needed to focus. One thing at a time. He tuned out his wife's weeping. Time to comfort her later.

The inspector's voice was clear as he gave a little nervous laugh and said, "Instead of that…I know the information that is needed if the camera is to be located. As for actually locating it, Señor Echevarria, perhaps you could stay on the line and connect me to, well, the most senior person you know in government who is aware of the situation with your daughter. I have a feeling your name will cut through the red tape much faster than my rank *con el Federales*."

After twenty-three minutes and four transfers, Inspector Torres found himself talking to a senior Signals Intelligence Analyst at *Centro de Investigación y Seguridad Nacional* (CISEN, Mexico's CIA) while the analyst's supervisor, Señor Echevarria, the Secretariat of the Interior, and the President of Mexico all listened in. Torres found his hands were shaking, and his shirt collar was soaked in sweat as he explained the situation to the analyst, knowing all the powerful ears listening in. *El Presidente…madre de Dios*. Echevarria's tech Tejada provided the serial number of the camera and the linked account information to the analyst.

Everyone waited and listened to the background hum of the call for the analyst to say something. "It will take me approximately twenty minutes to recalibrate our system to search for this kind of item," he told everyone listening. "The search itself…I don't know how long it might take. It depends if the camera is where our satellites can detect it, or ping it, and get a response. And I am unfamiliar with the specifications of these commercial cameras, but it may need to be powered on before we can successfully locate it. Does anyone know if it is on?"

The tech was faint, but Kresge heard the question. "There is no way for us to know that," he told all those listening.

"As soon as you have something, call me here on this direct number," Echevarria instructed the analyst.

The CISEN analyst cleared his throat and looked at his stone-faced supervisor standing across the desk from him. "Sir, I understand your concern in all this, but as these are classified systems I will not be able to provide any information I develop directly to you without—"

"Son," he was interrupted by the deepest voice on the conference call, "seeing as you are speaking *al Presidente de los Estados Unidos Mexicanos*, which would be me, and I am sitting here staring across my desk at the Secretariat of the Interior who is the very soul in charge of your agency…just do as the man says and call him with the information. As soon as you get it."

The analyst cleared his throat, feeling sweat pop out all over his body. "Yes Mister President."

* * *

When CISEN, the President's office and Raven were off the line, Echevarria leaned close to his speaker. "I will be calling you first," he told Beni.

"*Si Señor*," Beni said. "I will be ready."

Beni ended the call and looked around the Peregrine. "Done refueling? Get this thing in the air, and get us headed east as fast as it flies."

Billings and Evers traded a look and started hitting switches. The rotors started turning. "What if they can't locate the camera?" Ted Billings asked the man.

"They will," Beni told him. They had to.

* * *

Kresge stomped back toward his Blackhawk and waved at the pilot. "I can't even spin any goddamn satellites up overhead for another four hours. This and the other Blackhawk are the only birds I've got available right now within four hundred miles; they're throwing everything at Guadalajara. Let's get this thing in the air."

"Where are we going?"

"Where do you think? You know as soon as they lifted off they turned south, back to more friendly territory. I have no idea where they might be headed, or how far they're going, but maybe we can catch a break."

As he sat down Kresge found the photos in the palm and stared at the last one that had been taken. "Holy hell." He started flicking backwards through the photos until he found the first one taken in Mexico. It was of the Blackhawk crash site, from the ridge directly above.

"You okay, sir?" his lieutenant asked.

"Look at these." Kresge leaned over and started flipping through the photos. When he got to the first one of the ankylosaurus his lieutenant swore.

"Is that thing as big as it looks?"

"I think it's bigger. There, that's the last one. Taken just over an hour and a half ago, looks like." It was of the ankylosaurus, from the rear.

"That's not a photo, sir, that's a video. Hit that icon."

Kresge hit the icon and they watched the giant dinosaur slowly walk away, tail swinging sedately from side to side. Then there were several faint tinny cracks, and the video became blurred. Someone yelled "Guerrillas!" The screen of the palm went dark but the audio didn't cut off as it was shoved in a pocket. There was muffled frantic movement as the person with the palm ran, accompanied by yelling near and far. Then harsh breathing. Then more yelling, someone, maybe the boy, yelling "Stop!" over and over. More shooting, fast and furious, then a huge animal roar. Then the video ended.

"Was that roar from the dead dinosaur we found?"

"I don't know." Kresge was about to hand the palm to his lieutenant when it went dark in his hand. "Wait, what happened?"

"The battery died."

"Well, see if you can charge it up, and look through those photos and that video again. See if there's anything there that can help us."

* * *

Seamus wasn't sure how long he was out, but when he regained consciousness he found himself face down on the floor of the guerrillas' helicopter. His wrists and ankles were bound, probably with duct tape, as that was what he saw on the rest of his group. They lay nearby. He could see Tina's hair and Roger's back and feet that probably belonged to the boy. He couldn't see Corey or Hansen and had a bad feeling about them. Unfortunately, the guerrillas were smart enough to have bound everybody's wrists behind their back. There were at least three Gs sitting around them, all armed with rifles.

His head hurt so badly that it took him about a minute to realize there was a strip of duct tape over his mouth. He felt dried blood on his forehead. As Seamus tested his bonds he saw one of the guerrillas going through the pack he'd carried across half of Mexico.

The man passed around bottles of water to his fellows, as well as the rest of their energy bars. The camera he turned this way and that, finally figuring out how to turn it on. He had no use for it, but it looked valuable. Maybe he could trade it to one of the other guerrillas for a pistol, or tequila. He looked down at the sweaty fat American on the floor of the helicopter. "And who are you, *gordo?*" he asked, nudging him with a foot. The clothes he had on looked expensive, as did those on the teenage boy. But he didn't take the tape off the scared man's mouth to get an answer. Timotéo wanted to talk to them himself, and didn't want them trying to bribe the stupider men on the chopper, so he'd given strict instructions—gag them and bind them.

Tina was on her side, staring at nothing. One of the guerrillas stepped over to her and sat on her hip.

"*Buenos dias, señorita,*" he said with a big smile, pretending to tip his hat. All of the other guerrillas laughed. Tina glared at him, her breath huffing out her nose above the strip of duct tape over her mouth. "You are much trouble." He reached down and squeezed a handful of breast. Tina growled and struggled under his weight, but didn't have the strength or leverage to dislodge him.

The man laughed and pulled out a thin knife with an evil grin. "Let's see what you've got under there," he said, bringing the knife down to her cotton tank top. He began to cut.

"José, don't," one of the other men warned him.

The man stopped cutting just as he was getting to the good stuff. "Why?" he asked angrily.

"Do you have any doubt that Timotéo will be displeased if we bring her back raped? Look at her. She is not ugly poor trash. You know who she is, and you know how he is." Tina's heart was hammering in her chest but she took some comfort in the thought that the leader of *La Fuerza* had some decency. At least she did until the guerrilla's next comment.

"He'll let us have her after he's done with her; don't worry."

* * *

The helicopter did not sound healthy, but it stayed in the air. They had no way to judge the passage of time, but well over an hour passed before the helicopter descended. For ten minutes it flew nap of the earth, hugging the terrain so that it was harder to spot on radar. It felt much like riding a roller coaster, only being unable to see out the windows, many of the prisoners grew ill.

Finally the aircraft slowed, circled, and then settled to the ground in a swirling cloud of dust. One of the guerrillas pulled out a knife, but it was only to sever the tape binding their ankles. Then, one by one, they were pulled off the floor of the helicopter and yanked upright. They were marched across the open field where the heli had landed toward a large compound. The guerrillas laughed as they shoved them along.

Seamus looked around and caught Roger's eye. The older man was scared but forcing himself to be as calm as possible, because he knew the worst part was probably yet to come. Mike and Tina were both wide-eyed with fear. There was no sign of Corey or Hansen, and when Seamus paused to try to peer at the receding interior of the Blackhawk a guerrilla hit him in the back with the butt of his rifle. "Walk, *cabron*!" the man growled.

The air seemed thicker than it had in the mountains, but one look past the nearby trees showed him they were still in the foothills of a mountain range. The land was mostly green, with many trees. They left the grassy field and crossed a crushed gravel driveway that could have used some maintenance.

The massive hacienda had been constructed to resemble an old Spanish villa with tall adobe style walls painted white. The top of every door and entryway was arched, and all the roofs were covered in red clay tile. There was one large three-story main building and several smaller ones, with a lot of interconnected walls so that it resembled a much-stylized version of an old fort. The illusion was ruined by the satellite dishes on the roof and the detached six car garage. In addition to the half dozen men marching them from the helicopter, there were another dozen visible posted as guards or patrolling the grounds. The prisoners were marched to a door covered with an iron gate.

The gate opened before they got there, and the guerrilla leading the prisoners nodded at the man inside. "Grab as many men as you can and move that helicopter, get it out of sight immediately."

"Doing that right now," the man replied, and jogged toward the helicopter, followed by at least eight guerrillas. "Get the truck," he yelled, pointing toward the garage.

The prisoners were marched inside the massive residence. It was much cooler inside, and it took them a few seconds for their eyes to adjust as they were shoved down a wide echoing hallway with terra cotta tile. They were brought into a large, well-appointed room filled with expensive furniture. There were four men in the room, and they stood up as the prisoners arrived. Seamus' eyebrows went up as he saw the men—he recognized every single one of them. It was nearly the entire FRAP high command, in one room. This would not end well for him. He glanced at Tina to his left and the Rudds on his right. They were all sweating and panting, scared out of their minds. They were right to be.

"Only four?" General Aponte said. "How many *escaras* did you kill to capture these?"

"Two, sir."

General Martin Ramos smirked and looked at his fellow general. "And we have," he pointed in turn, "a fat old *gringo* who can't stand upright, a scared boy, *un solo escara*, and *la puta famosa*. Six people, only three of them Raven, and they managed to kill your entire team?" he mocked Aponte.

"*Our* entire team, filled with loyal men," Aponte growled.

"*Generales, por favor*," Timotéo said, pushing forward with a smile. He wasn't going to let their petty squabbling ruin his moment of triumph. He eyed the line of prisoners and couldn't help but smile. Finally. He stepped close and started with the oldest. He ripped the tape off Roger's mouth with a flourish.

"And who might you be?" he asked in perfect English.

"Roger Rudd." His lips had been dry and chapped from the desert air, and the tape had taken large chunks of flesh with it. His cracked lips began bleeding heavily.

Timotéo Sandoval eyed the man. He was obviously someone with money, or connections, or both, from the way he was dressed and the fact that he was on a Raven helicopter with Echevarria's daughter. "Are you injured?"

"My back, from the crash."

Timotéo nodded, feigning sympathy. "And Mister Roger Rudd, can you think of any reason why I shouldn't have my men feed you to wild dogs while they laugh?'

Roger blanched but said, "I'm worth over a hundred million dollars. I'm the CEO of the Pearl Sapphire hotel chain. You could get a lot of money if you ransom me."

One of Timoteo's eyebrows went up. He pursed his lips. "How much money?"

Roger had been thinking about it off and on ever since he'd learned the FRAP was trying to kidnap him. Which turned out not to be true, and still it had happened. Was that irony? A realistic ransom amount had been all he'd been thinking about on the helicopter. That, and how to get out of it alive, with Michael. "At least five million dollars. Probably more like ten. If I tell them to do it."

Timoteo leaned back, let his eyes drift over to Echevarria's daughter, then glanced back over his shoulder at his Generals. "It never rains but it pours," he laughed. Ramos pulled out his palm and began checking to see if this gringo was who he said he was. Timotéo turned back to the American and nodded his head at the teenage boy.

"And who is this?"

"My son."

That was what he'd suspected. The boy was but a younger, much less fat version of his father.

"They both carried rifles, *Jefe*," one of the guerrillas standing behind the prisoners said.

"Did they?" Timotéo grabbed a corner of the tape over Mike's mouth and ripped it off. The boy was scared, but he was also angry. "Did you shoot at any of my men?"

"No, we didn't, we had the rifles just in case," Roger answered for his son.

Timotéo punched Roger in the solar plexus, and the man doubled over, gasping. He then turned to the boy, who looked much less scared and much more angry. "Did. You. Shoot. My. Men."

"I did. He didn't," Mike said through clenched teeth.

The leader of *Fraternidad Progresista para un Mexico Nuevo* smiled at the angry teenager. "Brave," he observed. "Perhaps stupid, maybe honest, but definitely brave."

"Don't...hurt...him," Roger gasped, still on his knees. The guerrilla leader glanced down at him. He didn't need the boy, not really, and no one would pay a ransom for him, but getting the father to cooperate while arranging his own ransom would be much easier if they had the boy there as leverage. He would be much more valuable as insurance than he would as entertainment for his soldiers.

Timotéo looked at his men. "Take this *culazo* and his son down to the basement and lock them up. Post a guard."

Roger was hauled to his feet, and he and Mike were dragged off. Timotéo then pulled the duct tape from Seamus' mouth while barely glancing at him. "You...you killed many of my men I'd bet," he said, walking in a slow circle on the rug, studying his feet. Then he stopped and peered at the bloody *escara*.

Seamus smiled grimly. "Not enough."

One of the guerrillas behind Seamus punched him in the kidney, and he nearly fell over. They yanked him back upright. Timotéo smiled at him, then looked at the angry faces of his men. "He will be *El Chico's* entertainment for the afternoon. Take him downstairs and get him ready."

Seamus was dragged from the room by laughing guerrillas. Timotéo turned his attention to the remaining prisoner in the room. Her tank top had been cut down the front, revealing half a bra cup and a lot of cleavage. He switched to Spanish.

"I am debating as to whether I should even remove that tape from what I am sure is a pretty mouth. There is nothing you can say that I am interested in hearing. But…" with a theatrical sigh he grabbed the strip of duct tape and pulled it off. Tina glared at him. She was scared—no, terrified—but she refused to let him see it in her. She looked past him to the Generals and their ridiculous uniforms and shook her head.

"Your men are idiots and these 'generals' look like clowns," she told him. "I surely do not know how this war has lasted this long."

One of the Generals laughed. "And they say your mother is the actress," he said derisively.

Timotéo scowled. "I was wrong. Your mouth is not so pretty. But maybe I can fix that." He looked at the two soldiers standing on either side of her. "Take her upstairs to my bedroom and stay with her. I will be there shortly."

* * * * *

Chapter Twenty-One

Beni didn't know anything about flying but he could guess the crew had been taking it easy on the Peregrine's engines before, as the aircraft seemed to be making twice as much noise and vibrating much harder as they sped due east.

"If I get a call is there a way to plug my palm into the intercom so we can all talk using our headphones?" he asked the co-pilot.

"Yes, give it here." He handed it over and Evers plugged it into the brightly lit control panel in front of her.

"Where do you think they are taking her?" Manny asked him.

Beni shrugged. "I do not know."

"Somewhere they feel is safe," Torres said. "Whatever they plan to do with her; they do not want to be interrupted."

"Will they ransom her?" Manuel asked the inspector.

"That would be the best of all possible options." He stared at the two men soberly. "Forgive me for being blunt. They may want to ransom her, or they may ultimately plan to kill her, most likely on camera, but that will not happen for a long while. They have the daughter of *El Gordito*, and alive they can use her as a symbol of their success. After she is dead, she is much less useful. Simply one more dead girl in a war-torn country filled with them. A dead body is not nearly as effective theater as a weeping pretty girl, and if there is one thing we know *La Fuerza* is good at it, is propaganda."

422 | JAMES TARR

"They can do worse things to her than kill her," Beni said, his face dark.

Torres nodded. "Yes."

Several minutes later, Beni's palm lit up with Echevarria's number, and at his signal, Evers connected the call. "This is Beni," he said into his headset microphone.

"Beni, I've got *el CISEN analista* on the line with us. *Señor, diganos.*"

The analyst sounded nervous. "I have gotten some returns from her camera's digisat matrix. The returns are very weak, intermittent and brief. I'm not sure how reliable they are or the reason for it. Perhaps because of the nature of the device, or more likely, because it is moving. Each hit I've gotten off the device has been in a different location. It seems to be moving at a high rate of speed. South."

"She got put on a helicopter," Beni reminded the man.

"Give us the most recent coordinates, and then all the previous ones so we can try to plot a track," Evers jumped in.

The analyst read off a bunch of numbers while Beni and Manuel traded looks and Torres chewed at his lip nervously. Evers pulled up the HUD and began plotting the points on the holographic map. Glowing red dots appeared one by one, working their way northward as they went back in time.

"Four total?" the co-pilot asked the analyst.

"So far."

"Roger that," Billings said. "Keep giving us updated coordinates as soon as you get them. How long ago did you get that last location?"

"The device was at those coordinates twenty-two minutes ago. Nothing since then."

"Call us back as soon as you get another hit," Beni told the man. The analyst disconnected.

"How far away are you from that point?" Echevarria asked.

"Give me a wider view of that whole area, and compute a time on target," Billings told his co-pilot. She moved her hands rapidly and the map enlarged, the red dots moving closer together.

Billings nodded. "Those are the Orientals, right? That's smart. They're heading south-southeast, staying directly over the middle of the mountains. Fewer eyes to spot them, and no radar stations. He's tracked them across, what, close to two hundred miles? I didn't think they had the tech for that. Impressive."

"Where are we on this map?" Beni asked.

Evers backed the map out further and pointed. "Here. About seventy kilometers northwest of Mexico City, heading due east." The last return for the camera was over 150 kilometers northeast of their current location.

"So should we turn north?"

"If we want to head where they were twenty minutes ago. We can be there in half an hour. But my bet is they're still heading south," Billings said. "I say angle to intercept. But I'm just the guy driving this bus." He hadn't forgotten the last phone call had included the President of Mexico. These decisions were above his pay grade. Way above.

"Señor Echevarria?" Beni asked. "Turn north? Or continue east?"

"Where are they going? Are there any *La Fuerza* bases in that area?"

"Not that I know of," Billings said, "not for hundreds of miles further south, but the farther south they go, the friendlier the populace is to them."

Torres had a thought. "What's the range on their helicopter?"

Billings shook his head. "The guy left for dead said it was an old Blackhawk, right? Depending on how much weight it's lifting and extra fuel tanks, range could be well over a thousand miles."

"That could put them into Nicaragua," Torres said with a frown.

"Could explain why we've never been able to find their headquarters," Evers observed.

Beni was not happy. "And Kresge said there were no other aircraft in the area to search for this Blackhawk?"

Billings shook his head again. "They're all behind us." The Guadalajara offensive had turned into a real dust-up. The guerrillas had fielded much greater numbers than the Mexican Army had suspected, were more heavily armed, and were dug in. It was turning into the closest thing to a regular ground war the conflict had seen in ten years. "Maybe later today."

"That will be too late. I know it," Beni said.

"Lucille here is faster than that Blackhawk, but we're way behind the curve, trying to catch up. If we keep on our current course, maybe divert a little south, and they continue on theirs, we'll hit their track and come in maybe half an hour behind them." If the FRAP helicopter continued south over the mountains they would intercept its track in an hour.

"But they could change course at any time. They could swing east to the coast and get on a boat for all we know," Manny said with a frown.

"Continue east," Echevarria told them. "I don't think they have stopped yet. I don't know where they're going, but I know they won't want that helicopter up in the air any longer than necessary. Raven and the Army rule the skies."

"*Si Señor.*"

Echevarria disconnected. Evers contacted Kresge on the radio. "Colonel, the spooks came through. They've been able to track her camera, but it's a little hit or miss. Last ping was about twenty minutes ago." She gave him the coordinates. "That's about three hundred kilometers from your last location, and it's heading almost straight south. We are southwest of that point, trying for an intercept, but we're still a bit behind the curve."

"You're in a better position than we are. We are in pursuit, but we're at least a hundred and fifty miles north of that location, and you know they're still heading south, directly away from us. Plus your bird's faster. Godspeed, and call me as soon as you get another ping on that camera."

"Roger that."

Beni leaned forward into the cockpit. "Can you go any faster?"

Billings' eyes flicked to his computer video displays and analog dials. His RPMs were deep in the orange at 95% of recommended maximum. Engine temperature was good, hydraulics, electrical, every other system seemed to be solid. The CDU screen between the pilot and co-pilot was the primary alerting system for any problem with the bird, also visible to the crew behind the cockpit. Everything there was green. "Maybe a touch. Lucille hasn't stretched her legs in a while." He touched the throttle, edged it forward a bit. "C'mon, baby." Slowly the RPMs edged into the red until he was at 100% of the Raven recommended RPMs. It had been a while. He flicked his eyes over to the temperature gauge. It twitched, but that was it. He glanced over at his co-pilot. "And here I thought this was going to be a boring day."

* * *

Roger had to fight back screams of pain from his back as he was dragged down a flight of stairs into a basement. There was a door at the end of a short hallway, and one of the guerrillas threw it open. He was shoved into a storage room and with no hands free to help keep his balance fell down on the concrete floor. Mike was pushed in after him, then the wooden door was slammed shut and they heard a bolt slam home.

"Dad, you okay?" He could see all the blood on his father's lips and the pained expression on his face. He wasn't sure if his dad had been injured somehow or if the blood was from the tape being ripped off his face.

Roger's eyes were squeezed shut and his entire face was screwed up in pain. He couldn't even move at first. "Give...me...a...minute," he gasped, sweat dripping from his face.

It was closer to five, but finally he was able to breathe more or less normally. He lay on his side on the cool floor and looked around as well as he could without twisting his body. The storage room was maybe twelve by twelve and empty but for a few boxes and several chairs stacked in the corner.

"Dad, oh my God, I can't...." Mike was having a hard time not freaking out. He couldn't stand still. Getting chased by guys was one thing, but being the captive of a bunch guerrillas who wanted nothing more than to cut pieces off you with a dull knife was something else entirely.

"Just relax. We made it this far, and we're still alive. That Timo-téo is probably upstairs right now checking on me, and when he sees that I really do have money we should be okay. They may punch us around a bit, but they can't ignore the promise of that much money." Logically it made perfect sense. He wasn't sure how logical the guer-rillas were, but he didn't want his son worrying any more than he already was. He turned his head to see past his shoulder. Mike was there, pacing and panting. "Look, since I'm down here already, sit down on the floor behind me. So your hands are by mine."

"What? Okay." Mike sank down on the floor behind his father. "Why?"

"Use your fingers to feel for the end of the duct tape wrapped around my wrists. You should be able to unwrap me pretty easy."

"Dad, no! We'll get in trouble."

Roger forced out a laugh. "We're in trouble. We're already locked in here. And they didn't tell us not to."

"You sure they won't get mad?"

"What are they going to do, kidnap us?"

Mike began working. It was tough, doing everything by feel. "Co-rey and the pilot got shot, did you see that?"

Roger had. It had been horrible. With that much blood it was pretty clear they were both dead. "Yeah. I know it's terrible, but that's what they were paid to do. They're soldiers. And they killed a lot of FRAP before they got shot. It sucks, but there's nothing we can do about it now."

"I liked Corey. He wasn't much older than me." He looked over his shoulder at his dad. "What do you think they're going to do with Seamus?"

Roger didn't even want to think about that. "I don't know. But they could have already killed him and didn't, so take that as a good sign."

It took him almost five minutes, but finally Mike was able to unwrap the seeming yards of duct tape that had been wrapped around his father's wrists. With a grunt Roger pulled his arms in front of him and massaged his wrists.

"Okay, give me a few minutes to get upright, and I'll get yours," he told his son. Lying on the cold hard concrete wasn't doing his back any good, but getting into a seated position hurt a lot more. Breathing through the pain, Roger finally got off the floor and sat up as well as he could. He found he was listing to port like a freighter taking on water.

"Not quite the father-son bonding I was hoping for," he tried joking. He couldn't see the end of the duct tape around Mike's wrists, and started searching for it by feel.

"Dad," Mike said, shaking his head.

"The dinosaurs were amazing though. Even the one that tried to eat us." He found the end of the tape and began unwinding it from Michael's wrists.

"I'm sorry it got killed." He looked over his shoulder at his father. "Is that weird? Even though it tried to eat us? It was just hungry." He sighed. "I don't really want to shoot a dinosaur anymore, you know?"

Roger nodded. "Yeah, I know."

Mike's shoulders tensed. "That gunfight we had on the steep slope, the first time the guerrillas caught up to us? I was off to the side, away from you."

"Yeah?"

Mike's breath huffed through his nose. "I had to shoot some more of them. They were running right at me, and I had to. They never even heard me shooting because the Blackbird is so quiet."

"How many?" Roger asked quietly.

"Three or four. I can't remember exactly. I was pretty freaked out."

Roger struggled with what to say. "You think I'm going to yell at you for that, or that I'm upset? Don't be. I'm not. And don't beat yourself up over it. They would have shot you. It doesn't make you a bad person. I'm proud you're my son, and you did what you needed to do. If you ever start thinking about it, and it bothers you, you remember Corey and Hansen lying there covered in blood, you hear me? There, that's got it." He wadded up the used tape and tossed it away. "I'm going to sit here. You go see what's in those boxes."

Mike looked over at them. "Why?"

"Because you never know." *And because it will give you something to do other than sit and worry.*

Mike got up and walked over to the corner and started looking through the boxes. Roger looked around the room. Even though it was nearly bare, between the expensive light fixture and the textured paint on the stucco walls he could tell the last owners had spent some serious money decorating. He wondered where they were now, if they were even alive.

"This one's clothes." Mike moved that box aside and tried the next. "Magazines. Old ones, in Spanish." He pulled the last box close. "Shoes." He looked around. "Plus three crappy old wood chairs." He sat back down. "You think they'll feed us?"

"Yeah." Roger stared at the locked door, wondering if there was a guard on the other side. Wondering what was happening to the other people in the group. "Eventually." He thought he could hear a faint sound somewhere in the distance, almost like cheering, but couldn't quite make it out. "You hear that?"

* * *

Even though she knew it was futile Tina couldn't help but struggle against the hands of the two guerrillas as they marched her through the large residence. She thrashed like a child having a tantrum. They swore and yanked at her and eventually just grabbed her upper arms and simply carried her up two flights of stairs. The wide staircase was polished carved wood but its beauty was wasted on them as they sweated and strained.

Both the men took the opportunity to grope her as they wrestled her up the stairs, laughing the whole time. It made her angrier, but they were too strong; she couldn't break their grasp. And if she did, then what? She had no idea where they were, and the house and grounds were filled with men who she assumed were only the most trusted and loyal *La Fuerza* killers.

The third floor hallway was wide, with a carpet runner down the center of the expensive tile floor. The men took her to the right of the main staircase to white double doors. One of the men opened one of the doors, then they shoved her in.

Tina stumbled and turned around, swearing. The men stepped inside the open door and regarded her with evil smiles. She frowned, then looked around. She was in a large room; the centerpiece of it was a huge four-poster bed made of oak. She stared at it, then spun back around to look at the sneering men. They held their rifles carelessly, as if daring her to grab them. Their confidence in her helplessness made her quietly furious.

"Not so mouthy now, are you *puta?*"

The only thing she'd accomplished fighting with the men was getting herself even sweatier. But then she twisted her hands and found she could move them against the duct tape. "Don't even think about it, *puercos*. Your *Comandante* will have your heads if you touch me. You know how valuable I am to *La Fuerza*."

The men looked at each other and burst out laughing. "*La Fuerza* places no value on your honor. As long as your head is attached to your shoulders you'll ransom just the same. *El Comandante* will show you soon enough."

"And then we will too," the other guerrilla said and gave her a wink. Tina shuddered.

* * *

He never had any delusions about escaping, but Seamus fought with the guerrillas as well as he could on principle alone. As a group of them dragged him to the far end of the big house he kicked a knee that looked inviting, and the owner went down with a howl. When one of the men holding his bound arms yanked him up angrily Seamus hit him with a textbook headbutt in the nose. Seamus blinked away the pain of the blow and saw rich red blood flowing from the man's nose. Then another of the guerrillas hit him in the side of his head with the buttstock of his AK and Seamus' legs buckled from the pain. By the time he had most of his senses back he found he was on the floor of a room somewhere in the back of the house, with three men sitting on him and two more standing over him.

Seamus fought for breath as the men, who seemed to him to be far too cheerful, produced knives and began cutting off his uniform.

They were none too careful, and soon he was bleeding from several shallow cuts. One of the men shifted, and Seamus could finally catch his breath as they cut away his web gear, armor, uniform, and wicking underlayer. It appeared they were going to slice every article of clothing off of him.

"I understand there might be some confusion you nancies, what with my bloody Brit accent and all, but I am not into buggery," he tried to educate them. "I'm Irish. We prefer having relations with whiskey and angry women, in that order." He got a punch in the face for his trouble. They even cut the laces of his boots and pulled them off.

When he was naked as the day he was born and bleeding from a dozen cuts, two of the men left the room and started shouting, but he couldn't make out the words. The remaining guerrillas climbed off him, but he got a finger shoved in his face. "Stay on the floor," he was told, and kicked for good measure in the thigh. Then the men simply stood there. It appeared as if they were waiting for something.

Seamus grunted at the pain and with a little difficulty—as his hands were still bound behind him—got into a cross-legged seated position. The tile was hard and cold under him. He looked down at his naked body and shook his head.

"Ma always said I should be a podiatrist."

"Shut up," one of the guerrillas spat and kicked him with a boot.

Seamus grunted at the impact. "Absolutely."

He became aware of a growing sound outside, that of a crowd, as strange as that seemed. A lot of voices, and movement. The noise grew louder, and soon it was constant. If it wasn't a crowd it sounded like one. Finally, one of the guerrillas who'd run from the room returned. "Everybody is waiting," he said breathlessly. He looked at Seamus and smiled. It was not a friendly smile.

Guerrillas grabbed him under the arms and lifted him to his feet, then dragged him through a door and down a short hallway to a thick steel gate where a door used to be. Through the gate he could see dusty bare ground.

One of the guerrillas unlocked the gate, while another leaned in close behind Seamus.

"Run run run, little man," the guerrilla whispered in his ear, then gave him a shove. Seamus hit the gate and it opened outward. He stumbled out into the bright sunlight, the dirt warm under his feet, and the roar of a crowd rose up all around him. Squinting, he turned to see the guerrillas quickly grabbing the gate and slamming it shut behind him.

He found himself in a walled enclosure twenty meters wide by thirty long. It was the dimensions of a horse corral, but it had tall cement walls instead of a fence. Something about it seemed all wrong. The thick twelve-foot wall surrounded it on all sides, and dozens of guerrillas were peering over the walls at him, visible from the shoulders up, standing on planking put up for just that purpose. Some were pointing and laughing, calling out insults, while other faces seemed to be waiting expectantly. Many were yelling for *El Chico*. Seamus ignored the noise and took a good look around.

There was a little grass but most of the ground inside the walls was bare dirt. Near the middle of the space was an old vehicle lying on its roof. It had been crushed so it took him a second to identify it as a VW Beetle. It was while he was staring at the mangled car that he noticed the smell.

It was an animal smell; not quite barnyard, it was pungent and unpleasant. Under it was the hint of something rotting, maybe meat. Then Seamus noticed the deep shadow at the far end of the space, where two walls met. A wooden roof had been laid across the walls to provide shade. In the bright sunlight the shade under the roof was impenetrable.

He heard a deep sound, then something that might have been a huff. Then a darker shadow under the roof moved. Slowly the animal climbed to its feet and stepped into the sunlight, staring at Seamus across the length of the corral. The crowd of guerrillas roared in approval and anticipation.

While he was a little rusty on some of the more uncommon species, Seamus had no trouble recognizing a Tyrannosaurus Rex when he saw one. He looked down at his naked body, covered in fresh blood, then back up at the towering animal. Apparently this was *El Chico*.

"Shit."

* * * * *

Chapter Twenty-Two

"Hey." The pilot's voice came over the intercom. "Another call coming in on your palm."

"Connect it," Beni told him. He leaned forward between the seats and saw it was Echevarria. "*Si, digame.*"

"I've got another hit off that camera," the CISEN analyst announced without introduction. "Let me know when you're ready to copy and I'll give you the coordinates."

"Go," Evers barked, fingers at the ready.

The analyst read off the numbers, and Evers punched them into the nav system. A new glowing red dot appeared on the map, much farther south and east than the previous locations. "Bout a hundred and fifty klicks south-southeast of our last ping," Evers said. "Angling toward Veracruz and the coast but they're still over the mountains. That location is nearly off our nose, due east, eighty-two kilometers ahead."

"The device is not moving anymore," the analyst told them. "I have it at the same location for—" he paused to check his display, "seven minutes now. I do not know how long it was stationary before I could get satellite detection. Signal return remains strong and steady." Everyone on the Peregrine traded looks.

"They could have tossed the camera over the side."

"I do not think so, Manny," Beni told him.

"If they were going to do that, why wait until they'd flown hundreds of kilometers?" Torres said, shaking his head.

"I can have a satellite with visual imagery capability over that location in ninety-seven minutes," the analyst announced.

"ETA?" Billings asked his co-pilot.

She did a quick calculation. "At current airspeed, eleven minutes."

"Damn, sometimes it really is better to be lucky than good. Do it," the pilot told the CISEN analyst. "Couldn't hurt. Ten minutes to possible contact!" Billings said over the comm. "I want weapons check, commo check. Everyone make sure their gear is strapped down tight." He looked at Evers. "Get me Kresge."

"Call us if it starts moving again," Beni instructed the analyst. "*Señor*, I will call you as soon as I have news," Beni told Echevarria.

"*Si Beni.* I am counting on you."

The colonel was on the radio moments later. "Colonel, the camera is no longer moving, we think they may have landed."

"Where?"

Evers gave him the coordinates, peering back and forth between her illuminated nav system as well as a partially unfolded paper map in her lap. "It's in the southern foothills of the Orientals, hundred-fifty klicks northwest of Veracruz, hundred sixty northeast of Mexico City. Closest town on the map is Zaragoza, about eight kilometers away. Raven's got nothing in their database of interest in the area."

"What's your ETA?"

"Ten minutes at current speed," Billings told him. His eyes swept the gauges. RPMs still in the red, but no temperature spikes, no alarms.

"I'm at least an hour behind you."

"Roger that sir. You want me to coordinate arrival with your aircraft? Might be the camera's in the middle of an empty field. Then again it might not. CISEN will have an eye in the sky over those coordinates in about ninety minutes."

"Negative, do not wait for our arrival, or for that satellite. You get eyes on target ASAP and update me as the situation develops."

"Affirmative. Expect to hear from us soon."

Beni watched the two crewmen checking over their big gleaming Gatling guns and traded a look with Manuel. He pulled the bag he'd brought with him from the storage locker under the seats and laid it out on a seat, and Manny did the same. Both men took off their suitcoats and folded them. They were wearing pistols on their hips. They removed armored vests from their bags, worn most often when escorting the Echevarrias in high threat areas, and shrugged them over their shoulders.

"What do you think we will find?" Manny asked as he adjusted the straps around his chest. Beni just shook his head. He wasn't sure he wanted to think about it. All of the options were bad. "How many men were on the helicopter that grabbed her?"

"I think they said six?"

Torres looked at the two bodyguards arming up and then around the aircraft. The electric Gatling guns were huge. He hadn't had to point his pistol at anyone in months and hadn't had to pull the trigger in years. He dealt with criminals every day, but he wasn't a soldier. And here he was in a heliplane, or whatever they called it, that was bristling with guns, flying at breakneck speed toward what might be a bunch of heavily armed *La Fuerza*. He shook his head. That's what he got for complaining to his supervisor about riding around in a flying bus.

He stood and took off his suitcoat, then checked his duty pistol. It was a scuffed CZ P-09, a big pistol, but it had never failed him. He blew the lint out of its cracks, double-checked that the magazine was fully loaded and there was a round in the chamber, and put it back behind his hip.

Manuel pulled a vintage Heckler and Koch MP5K PDW from his bag and arranged its sling over his big shoulders. He loaded a magazine into the small submachine gun, chambered a round, and then checked the pockets in his armored vest to ensure there were spare magazines for the gun. Beni pulled a slightly larger weapon from his bag and worked its action a few times.

Torres stared. "Where did you get that?" Beni was holding a Tigre, a submachine gun made in Spain, chambered in the powerful but obscure 9x23 pistol cartridge. It was considered by many experts to be the finest submachine gun ever made, but because it was so expensive to produce and chambered in an odd caliber it had been manufactured only for a short period of time several decades past. They were hard to come by and highly prized by people who knew their weapons. It was accepted that a man with a Tigre was a serious and knowledgeable professional.

"Señor Echevarria is very resourceful."

Torres stared at Beni for a few seconds. "Hmm," he said finally. He dragged out his personal gear bag he'd taken from the trunk of the fleet car he'd driven to Juarez. After unzipping it he pulled out another Tigre and held it up.

Beni looked surprised. "Where did *you* get *that*?"

"Division armory. It was sitting in the back, dusty and unwanted, when I found it. They did not know what they had."

The two men looked at each other for a few seconds, and Beni nodded. They loaded the Tigres and hung them on their slings. Beni stuffed extra magazines into his vest and glanced at Torres, who had the SMG slung over his cotton button-down shirt. He had stuffed the end of his narrow black tie inside his shirt

"No body armor?" he asked Torres.

"In my office locker."

Beni hesitated, then asked, "Do you have enough magazines for your Tigre?"

The corner of Torres' mouth curled up. "Do you?"

"Five minutes!" the pilot called over the intercom.

* * *

Tina was so wrapped up in her thoughts and fighting to ignore the stares of the sweaty, sullen guerrillas standing guard by the door, hoping they didn't notice her working at the tape binding her wrists, that for long minutes she didn't notice the rising sound coming from outside.

"We're going to miss it because we're babysitting her," one of the men grumbled.

"You've seen it before."

Their exchange caught her attention, and she finally noticed the growing noise. She glanced at the sliding glass door, which led out onto a small balcony, but couldn't see anything but blue sky. But she heard cheering like there was a *fútbol* game outside.

She had a fleeting thought to step to the glass and look out, see what was happening, but then there was a sound by the door and she turned around. Timotéo was there, stepping in behind the two men.

"Go watch *la carnicería*," he told them. "I've got this."

"*¿Comandante, esta seguro?*"

He turned to look at them, one hand resting on the knife at his waist. "Yes. We will be fine, just the two of us. But for her *chichis* and mouth, she is tiny. Hardly seems possible she has given us so much trouble."

The two soldiers smiled and hurried off. Timotéo shut the door behind him while staring at her. She stared back, fighting hard not to show how nervous she was. She knew she should curb her normally sharp tongue, but she also knew that showing weakness would only embolden him. "Have you contacted my father?" she asked. It felt like one of her hands was ready to come free from the duct tape.

Timotéo Sandoval gave a little shrug and walked around her. She was tiny, only a few inches over five feet. While he was twice her age, he had eight inches and fifty pounds on her. "I don't care about your father right now."

"You should," she said nervously. "He's the only reason you wanted me."

He pursed his lips, very obviously dropped his gaze to her chest, brought his eyes back up and then raised his eyebrows. "Not the only reason." He sniffed. "You are dirty and smelly and I should wash you like a stray dog one picks up off the street. Maybe later." He stepped close. His face was blank, and he didn't make any overtly aggressive moves, but she could feel the danger and violence oozing off of him. His voice dropped low. "Many of my men died because of you," he growled, then abruptly slapped her.

The force of the blow caught her by surprise, and she shrieked in pain. She stumbled back and he gave her a helping push. She impacted the soft side of the bed. Tina pushed off the bed as fast as she could with her arms still bound, instinctively not wanting to be anywhere near it, and he slapped her with his other hand.

As her eyes teared up, he grabbed her shoulders and spun her around, then he shoved her forward and bent her down onto the bed. He stepped up close behind her. "No!" she shouted, fighting him. She twisted and yanked and then suddenly her hands came apart. She pushed up off the mattress and tried to kick back at him, but he clamped a hand around her neck.

She was no soft princess; she'd built up a lot of muscle working in the field, and she fought back against his tensed arm. Tina raised her torso off the bed and turned her head, screaming at him. She saw his face, crazed with lust and anger, as he tore at her belt. "*¡No! ¡Pinche cabron! ¡Puerco!* I will kill you!" She scratched at him, one of her dirty nails taking a hunk out of his cheek. She felt she was fighting for her life.

Timotéo slapped her hand out of the way and punched her in the side of the head. Tina took the pain of the blow with a grunt and swung her nails at his eyes. He grabbed her hand and struck her in the face with his forearm. She fell back onto the bed, stunned. Dazedly she was aware of him shoving her back onto her stomach and tugging down her shorts. He clamped one hand around the back of her neck. She heard a jingling, then a thump on the floor by her feet as his pants hit the carpet.

She tensed to yell and buck backward off the bed, but before she could, the sliding glass door exploded with a roar.

* * *

Seamus stared at the T. rex as it squatted in the dirt and focused on him. Compared to the allosaurus which had charged them in the valley, the T. rex was small, but solely because it was a juvenile and not yet fully grown. It still stood nine feet tall at the hip and was over twenty feet long, squatting over a tail that it twitched like a cat as it watched its new prey. There was a line of short fuzzy feathers from its shoulders down its spine to the tip of its tail, and other narrowing stripes of feathers running down the sides of its ribcage. The black feathers against its greenish gray skin gave it a camouflage pattern.

"Ha ha, funny mates, now open the bloody door," Seamus growled under his breath, looking sideways at the gate. Several of the guerrillas had their eager faces pressed up against the bars, ready for the show.

"*Adios,*" one of the men told him, smiling.

"Say hello to *El Chico* for us," said another.

The others at the gate laughed. The guerrillas crowded around the wall began chanting. "Chico! Chico! Chico!"

Seamus turned back to the T. rex, which had taken one step forward and cocked its head. He frantically twisted his hands back and forth, trying to free them from the duct tape cuffs. Except for his little covered sleeping area and the crushed car, the T. rex's playground was devoid of cover. Nothing to hide behind, no way to climb out. Even if he could get a purchase on the wall, somehow, and climb it, the guerrillas lining it would just knock him back down.

The T. rex's head was much larger, proportionately, than that of the allosaurus. This animal was only a teenager and its bulky head was already three feet long. Its jaws opened as it looked at Seamus, and he could see dozens of short sharp teeth. He remembered hearing somewhere once that the T. rex was thought to have the strongest bite force of any land animal.

"Go back to sleep, Sally, you're not hungry today," Seamus said to the dinosaur, his eyes darting this way and that, looking for an escape. There was no way out.

Suddenly, without making a sound, the Tyrannosaurus rex began running toward Seamus. As it weighed over three tons, it took a few steps to gather speed. The guerrillas watching cheered, and then shouted as Seamus took off running as well—straight toward the onrushing behemoth.

The dinosaur was faster, but Seamus' target was a little closer. He ran flat out toward the center of the corral as fast as he could with his hands tied behind his back, seeing the dinosaur closing on him quickly. At the last moment Seamus darted off to the side, toward the upended vehicle. It was the only cover in the dinosaur's playground and he was going to use it to stay alive as long as possible.

The T. rex lunged and snapped, but it was nowhere close enough to snag Seamus with its teeth as it went by. The animal stutter-stepped to a stop in the dirt as Seamus, panting, ran around the car to put it between him and the giant beast.

Irritated, the T. rex roared at him and came loping back to the vehicle. Seamus could feel each one of its steps trembling the hard-packed dirt under his bare feet. He backed away as the creature lunged over the car, jaws snapping the air a foot from his face to the roaring approval of the FRAP crowd. With the roof crushed, the VW Beetle was only three feet tall, but it still seemed a bit high for the dinosaur to jump over. It also didn't look solid enough to walk on. Seamus' main complaint was that the car was too bloody small to hide behind for long. All of the tires were flat and several of them appeared to have been chewed on.

The T. rex took two hopping steps to the side and tried a low end run around the car, but misjudged the angle and hit the car with its shoulder. The car spun on its crushed hood and a dented fender hit Seamus in the back of the knees as he tried to keep the car between them. He went down then rolled and popped right back up as the T. rex lunged again in the opposite direction. The big animal hit the car with its hip and it spun on its roof toward Seamus. He dove forward, rolled across the top of the spinning car, and fell facedown into the dirt on the far side. He scrambled backward, blindly at first, spitting out dust. The T. rex peered over the car and cocked its head like a bird, trying to figure out how to get to him. Its nostrils flared as it smelled the blood on him.

"Bugger off!" Seamus shouted at the animal, tearing at the duct tape which refused to yield.

The eyes of the animal were huge and locked on him. It straightened up, peering down at Seamus, then looked at the car before it. As it loudly sucked in air through its nostrils and seemed to crouch, Seamus finally managed to rip one hand free of the duct tape. Then the dinosaur was in the air, lead foot barely clearing the Volkswagen's undercarriage, open mouth shooting forward at Seamus' head.

He dove, aiming for the depression he'd spotted underneath the car when it had been spun about by the T. Rex's last lunge. The ground shook as the three-ton animal landed, and dust flew past Seamus as he scrambled underneath the car.

The depression under the car was barely a foot deep, much smaller than he'd thought it was. Half a second's thought, and he was crawling to get out from under it. If the dinosaur decided to climb onto the car with him beneath it, he'd be crushed into jelly. As he shoved his face into daylight on the far side, there was a huge roar above him, and something blotted out the sun.

* * *

The crew chief, Sweeney, made sure all of his passengers were secured by safety harnesses before hooking himself in, sliding open the door, and taking a position behind his M134D Dillon Aero electric Gatling gun. There were two vertical handles on the back of the weapon, with a paddle trigger in the center designed to be operated by either of the shooter's thumbs. He made sure the power was on to the weapon and a round chambered.

Why they called it a "minigun," he had no idea, as it was almost three feet long, had six barrels, and weighed eighty-five pounds, not including mount or ammo, which it went through at the rate of fifty rounds a second. Every fifth round was a tracer, visible as a red line flying from the barrel at three thousand feet per second, so when firing, it appeared to the operator as if there was a red laser beam shooting from the minigun. The effect of 3,000 rounds per minute was nearly the same as a laser beam, no matter the target.

Sweeney turned around and eyeballed Hatch, the other crewmember on the opposite side of the Peregrine. He was manning the second minigun and gave Sweeney a thumbs-up. "We're good to go back here," the crew chief announced over the intercom.

"Roger that. Two minutes," Billings said. He was flying at five hundred feet. He began a gentle descent and prepared to reduce speed as they wouldn't see anything flying by at 500 kph, but if there were guerrillas down there he didn't want to make Lucille too tempting of a target by flying low and slow. "Going to slow to two hundred kph, drop to three hundred feet for our first pass." Everyone on the aircraft could hear him in their headphones.

"Roger," Evers said, her voice tense.

In the distance he could see the Sierra Madre Orientals, jumbled green and brown hillsides rising away to the north. There were a few roads and small towns beneath them, divided by farmers' fields.

Evers looked up and down, back and forth between the nav system and the view out the windscreen. "Coordinates are right at the base of that first slope, maybe fifteen klicks, eight miles out," she said, pointing. She glanced back down at her paper map to double-check, then looked back up. It was then she noticed that her pointing hand was shaking. Badly.

Billings stared at her shaking hand, then at the other one vibrating in her lap. Then he looked her in the eye. "Be advised, Evers has the shakes," he announced over the intercom. Sweeney and Hatch looked at each other.

"How bad?" Sweeney asked. He looked worried.

Billings' eyes roamed over his panels as he keyed the radio. "Raven Command, this is Viking Three-Three, be advised we are one mike out from our destination."

"Viking Three-Three, roger that. Update us as possible. Be advised you've got a lot of big ears listening in to this one."

"Viking Three-Three copies that."

"Viking Three-Three, Raven Command, your co-pilot got any shakes yet?" The radio operator tried to play her comment off as a lighthearted question, but as an early warning system that had yet to be proven inaccurate, Evers' weird psychic ability was the stuff of legend at Raven, a good luck charm that most of the aviators scoffed at publicly while they privately kept begging her to join their crews.

"Worst I've ever seen," Billings said flatly. "Viking Three-Three out."

"Oh hell," Sweeney muttered.

Billings squinted. "What's that I'm looking at, all alone at the base of the slope?"

Evers shook her head. She'd clamped her hands into fists until the shaking had quieted to tiny shivers. "Some kind of compound. Maybe an estate. *Una hacienda.*"

Manuel was standing next to Sweeney. He covered his microphone with his hand and leaned close. "What do shakes mean?" he yelled at the crewman over the buffeting wind.

"Shakes mean FRAP, buddy," Sweeney said.

That didn't make much sense to Manuel, but he had a more important question to ask, making sure his microphone was still covered. "What about last night, when you said she liked girls as much as you. What did you mean?"

The crew chief looked over his shoulder, then covered his microphone with a fist. "I mean she's playing for the other team."

"*¿Como?*"

"She likes girls. Instead of guys. I saw you eyeballing her, we all did, but you don't need to waste your time."

"Thirty seconds!" Billings called out, pulling back on the throttle. The needle moved even farther back from the red line. The nacelles with their rotors tilted upward slightly.

"Airspeed two-eighty kph," Evers called out calmly. She checked the nav system, then peered back out the cockpit glass. "That's the coordinates, right there at that compound dead ahead."

Both Hatch and Sweeney put the visors of their helmets down and slid the side doors of the bird open all the way. The cabin filled with roaring air. They stuck their heads out the side of the aircraft to add two more pairs of eyes. The compound was still a mile ahead. They could see red roofs and a lot of white walls. "I've got a few people on foot, some civilian vehicles," Evers announced, examining the site through binoculars. They were still a little far out for her to make out much detail. She quickly stuffed the binos back into their compartment, as she needed both hands free. Her eyes flicked to the cockpit readouts. "Computer targeting does not pick out any military vehicle or heavy weapon silhouettes." From the cockpit they could fire the nose-mounted minigun and the small rockets stuffing the pod.

"Slowing to two hundred," Billings announced. It was coming up fast, a jumble of bright white buildings with red tile roofs and walls. "I think that's an estate; doesn't look commercial." They were roaring up on a big three story white residence, and as they flew over it, a hundred meters off the ground, the property on the far side of the hacienda came into view. There was a large walled off area, and suddenly there were dozens of figures in view, crowded around something.

"FRAP!" Sweeney yelled, spotting the mishmash of camouflage uniforms and rifles.

As the Peregrine roared by overhead the guerrillas stared upward in shock, then shouted and pointed. A few raised their rifles and began shooting.

"Son of a bitch," Billings swore, and turned Lucille hard. Beni, Manuel and Torres nearly lost their footing as the Peregrine rolled on its side.

Hatch found himself staring directly at two dozen guerrillas standing along a wall. Their faces followed the banking bird. He twisted the minigun and thumbed the trigger. The sound of God's chainsaw filled the cabin, and a four-foot flame erupted from the end of the minigun. A red beam of light ran along the guerrillas, and blood and concrete chunks flew as hundreds of bullets scissored across their ranks then up the side of the big building. Empty cases fountained out of the bottom of the minigun. Then they were past the estate, and Billings slewed the bird in the opposite direction.

Beni's mouth dropped open. The minigun didn't sound like a rifle—the noise it made was so far beyond gunshots as to not even be comparable, it was a constant explosion accompanied by a four-foot tongue of flame. It was a fire breathing dragon whose roar was death.

"Coming back around." Billings keyed the radio and spoke calmly. "Raven Command, be advised we have approximately fifty hostiles at this location and are taking heavy small arms fire. We could use reinforcements ASAP."

"Viking Three-Three, say again. Did you say fifty?"

"Roger that, five oh, we kicked an anthill."

"Holy shit, was that a T. rex?" Hatch swore. He'd only caught a glimpse of it in a big pen.

"Somebody was in there with it," Evers said with awe. "RPG!" she yelled out, pointing. A guerrilla had climbed atop a small shed and fired a rocket-propelled grenade at the bird, but it flew harmlessly past as Billings banked Lucille away from the contrail. Sweeney ran a long burst from his minigun across the ground and into the man, who toppled backward.

"Viking Three-Three, Raven Command. Did you just say T. rex?"

Guerrillas began to appear on foot, running in every direction, and the crew chief fired bursts as the Peregrine flew back in. Evers spotted a helicopter concealed by camouflage netting beneath some trees, tagged it with their targeting computer, and fired a rocket even as they turned away. The guided rocket curved back and impacted the tail of the parked Blackhawk, which blew apart. A vehicle sped off along a gravel drive, a dust cloud blooming behind it. Sweeney poured tracer fire into it until it exploded in a ball of flame and drove into a wall, which crumbled.

"Try not to shoot the main house, that is likely where she is being held," Beni yelled at him.

"If she's still alive," Evers said flatly, hands flying over the controls. Beni shot her a dirty look and shuffled forward as well as he could on the bucking floor of the aircraft.

"Put us down there!" Beni yelled, pointing at the ground.

"I'm a little busy right now," Billings spat through clenched teeth. He put Lucille's nose on a guerrilla trying to aim an RPG and triggered a burst from the minigun in the nose, then banked the Peregrine in a sharp turn. Beni realized he could see the ground through the side window of the cockpit. There were dull thunks as incoming guerrilla bullets found the fuselage.

Hatch let loose with burst after burst from his minigun as they buzzed the compound on his side. The T. rex was running flat out and he stared at it for a second, then went back to firing at guerrillas. Hundreds of spent casings rolled around the floor of the Peregrine. Guerrillas died running, died shooting at the aircraft as the crewmen turned the snouts of their fire-breathing miniguns this way and that. The high rpm of the Peregrine's miniguns cut men in half, blew holes in adobe walls and sprayed chunks of concrete into the air. It was a bloody madhouse.

Manuel fired burst after burst from his subgun at *La Fuerza*, then t was empty. Beni raised his Tigre and fired at several running guerrillas, then had to grab hold of a strap to keep from falling as the aircraft banked hard again. "We are not here to kill FRAP, this is a rescue. Get us down!" he shouted at the pilot.

* * * * *

Chapter Twenty-Three

Seamus lay on his back in the dirt, half under the car, and blinked at the shadow blotting out the sun. Then as the roar of straining engines hit his ears he recognized the silhouette of a Peregrine, and someone on the bird let loose with a minigun.

The roar of the gun was unmistakable. He could hear bullets hitting everywhere as he scrambled out from beneath the car, and pieces of flying concrete pinged against the VW. Empty brass cases fell past him. The spectating FRAP started shouting and shooting and screaming in pain.

"Bout bloody time," he panted, and looked around for Chico. The dinosaur had been distracted first by the loud aircraft, then by the guerrillas firing wildly. It swung its head this way and that, disturbed by the noise, then spotted Seamus out from underneath the car and roared its irritation at him.

"Shag off to your flat," Seamus yelled at the T. rex, unwinding the duct tape from his wrists. With his hands free he had a little better mobility, for what good that did him.

The T. rex growled and snapped at him over the car, then turned its head at the sound of more shooting. The guerrillas' rifle fire increased in volume, and then the Peregrine roared by again, miniguns thundering. There was an explosion nearby, and he saw a ball of fire over the top of the wall. Then the wall burst apart in chunks of concrete as a flaming car punched halfway through. The dinosaur jumped back in surprise, snarling.

Several FRAP guerrillas fell into the enclosure as the wall collapsed. They got up, stumbling, forgetting where they were. The disoriented T. rex snapped at one of the stumbling men, then charged another and bit down on his head and shoulders. The man's scream deep in the animal's mouth was muffled. The T. rex shook the guerrilla like a dog with a chew toy and then tossed him to the side. He flew twenty feet and landed hard.

Seamus dove over the VW and ran for the pile of rubble and the break in the wall. A woozy guerrilla popped up in front of him and Seamus collided with the man. They landed hard. Seamus ripped the AK out of the guerrilla's hands and hit him across the face with it, then some sixth sense made him turn and he saw the T. rex charging. He shouldered the rifle and fired. The AK-47 was on full auto and Seamus put a ten-round burst into the attacking dinosaur's chest, then the magazine ran dry.

The piercing pain was a foreign sensation to the huge creature, and it slowed down slightly. Seamus grabbed the guerrilla whose rifle he'd stolen and shoved the man at the snapping dinosaur, then dove out of the way. He heard crunching bone and screaming as he rolled in the dirt. A glance at the gap between the wall and the car showed him it was currently full of flames from the burning vehicle. No exit there.

Seamus spotted another body on the ground, half buried by rubble. He jumped and slid to it and tugged at the man's rifle, but it was pinned under a table-sized piece of broken concrete. The ground shook as something ran toward him, and in desperation, Seamus grabbed the machete sheathed at the man's waist and yanked it out, spinning with the blade up. The dinosaur pulled up in a cloud of dust mere feet in front of Seamus. The pain of being shot made it hesitant, and the explosion and noise and fire were disorienting, but the smell of blood all around was too much to ignore. It opened its mouth hugely, long rows of bloody teeth gleaming, and roared in Seamus' face.

Seamus roared back at the monster, a primal scream, and waved the machete. "Come on then, you bastard! I came into this world naked and covered in blood and have no problem going out the same way!"

The T. rex stared at him, huffed, and then lunged. With a wordless shout Seamus swung the machete in two hands with all his might and buried the middle of the blade between the beast's nostrils. His hands stung at the impact, and he felt hot breath against his knuckles. The dinosaur reared back at the unexpected pain, lifting Seamus into the air before jerking the machete right out of his hands.

The animal bellowed and its eyes crossed as it tried to look at the blade embedded in its snout. It roared, as much in confusion as hurt, and shook its head to try to dislodge the object. Seamus spotted a body a distance away—the guerrilla the dinosaur had tossed through the air—and he ran for it. There was a rifle under the man's legs. Behind him the dinosaur was making confused, wounded noises.

Seamus snagged the rifle at a full run and directly in front of him was the gate leading into the house. He fired a burst at the concrete next to the lock, disintegrating it, and yanked the gate open. Then he charged into the dark hallway, leaving the roaring T. rex behind him.

* * *

Mike stared up at the ceiling. "I think that's cheering." It was muffled and distant, through the walls and floors of the house.

"Yeah, but at what?" Roger wasn't sure he wanted to know the answer to that. It probably wasn't good. He was still sitting on the floor, because it would hurt too much to get up and his back wouldn't hurt any less.

There was more faint cheering, then what might have been a distant roar. The hair rose on the back of Roger's neck and he had flashbacks of the allosaurus charging them. "Was that—" Then there was a much larger roar, and they felt the floor shudder. "What the hell?"

There was shouting outside their door, running feet. They could hear gunfire, and yelling. "What's going on?" Mike asked. They were both staring at the ceiling of their basement room as if by concentrating hard enough they'd be able to see through it.

They both heard a slow building noise, and Roger identified it as some kind of aircraft. Then the thunder of a massive gun firing over and over. "It's Raven!" Mike said. "It's a rescue!"

"I don't know."

"What else could it be?"

Roger didn't have an answer for him. All they could hear was muffled shooting and yelling. There was staccato thudding which he thought might have been bullets hitting the house. He looked around, and pointed at the chairs. "Break some legs off one of those."

Mike frowned. "What for?"

"If it is Raven, the FRAP may want to come down here and kill us rather than let us be rescued."

"Oh." Mike glanced at the locked door. It had sounded as if their guard ran away from his post, but they couldn't be sure. And busting apart a chair would make some noise. But what did he have to lose?

He grabbed the top chair off the stack and set it on the floor, then stomped on one of the legs. It cracked loudly, and with another stomp it came free from the chair. Mike kicked it over to his father. There was cursing outside the door, and they heard fumbling with the lock.

A guerrilla threw open the door and stared at them. "*Pinches grin-gos,*" he swore as there was a loud explosion just above. They all ducked instinctively, then the guerrilla recovered, scowled, and start-ed to raise his rifle. Roger threw his chair leg at the man's head, and as the guerrilla ducked Mike charged him with a yell, chair in front of him like he was a lion tamer.

Mike crashed into the man as his rifle went off, and the chair splintered between them. The guerrilla bounced off the door frame and fell backward, Mike on top of him. There was shouting and Mike jerked his head up to see several more guerrillas down the hallway running in their direction.

"Michael!" Roger yelled.

In slow motion Mike looked down and saw the angry face of the guerrilla beneath him, struggling to get up. His arms were pinned by the fractured chair and Mike's weight atop that. Mike punched him hard in the face, twice, the man's face bouncing off the concrete floor, then he ripped the rifle out of the man's hands. Mike fell backward into the room, firing the rifle, and the two running guerril-las stumbled and fell at his feet, nearly on top of the guard.

"Michael!" Roger yelled again. "Are you okay?"

Panting and wide-eyed, Mike backed away from the groaning pile of bodies, keeping the rifle up. "*Hijo de puta,*" one of the men growled, bloody trembling hand reaching for a knife. Another guer-rilla was trying to get up. Mike looked from them to his father, un-armed and crawling as fast as he could to the back corner of the room away from the door and the men, then back at the injured guerrillas. He fired a long burst across all the men on the floor, the sound of the rifle huge in the enclosed space. Blood flew, and their struggles ceased. He stared at what he'd done, then ducked as bullets flew over his head and blew chunks out of the door frame. There was a guerrilla running down the hall at him, firing from the hip.

Mike raised the rifle and fired a short burst, then the hammer clicked on an empty chamber. The man stumbled and fell face down, not moving.

Roger swore, scooting back from the door, the bullets, and the bodies. Mike tossed away the rifle and grabbed another, a big G3, from the pile of bodies in front of him. He peeked past the door frame. There was a long hallway directly in front of them, and a short one to the right ending at stairs. He heard a long burst of rifle fire nearby.

"Can you get up? We've got to get out of here!" he yelled to his father, hearing blown out by the gunfire.

"I'll try," Roger gasped.

"Lad? Laddie!"

"Seamus?" Mike peered around the door frame again and there was Seamus, halfway down the stairs, rifle in hand. He was covered in blood... and nothing else. "You okay?" Mike stared at the man and his lack of clothing, eyes wide. Seamus sounded as though he was hyperventilating; his veins were sticking out all over his neck and face, and his eyes were bugging out of his head.

"Peachy." Seamus took in the picture, blood spray all over the walls and half a dozen booted feet sticking out the doorway past the lad's anxious face. "You?" he panted, coming the rest of the way down the stairs. One of his eyelids was twitching and there was a tic in his neck.

"So far."

Seamus looked around the corner and saw Roger struggling to stand. He then stared the other way down the hallway and observed it was empty but for a body halfway down.

"What's going on?" Roger asked.

"The cavalry arrived, finally. You see Rita?"

Mike shook his head. "I don't think she's down here. Let's get the hell out of here."

Seamus put a hand on his shoulder. "No. Trust me, you don't want to go upstairs, not yet. And don't go outside, whatever you do." At that the Peregrine made another roaring pass, miniguns sounding like giant zippers, and an explosion vibrated the walls. "Not safe. You'll be better off down here. I'm going to go find the girl. You stay here until help arrives." He patted Mike on the shoulder, and nodded at the bodies. "Looks like you've got this well in hand." Then he sprinted back up the stairs.

"Was he naked?" Roger asked.

* * *

Seamus ran back up the stairs and found himself off the main entryway, the only men present the three he'd killed before heading into the basement. The main house was a madhouse, with guerrillas running in every direction, shouting and cursing, shooting out every window. The Peregrine made passes overhead, miniguns ripping death, men screaming, and the T. rex roaring.

He grabbed a spare magazine for the AK in his hands and held it against the rifle's handguard as he was temporarily short of pockets. "Rita!" he yelled, jogging down main hallway. "Rita!" The noise was tremendous, and he wasn't confident she'd be able to hear him unless he was close.

He ran into the room where he'd met Timotéo. It was empty but for a guerrilla in one corner, peering out a window. Seamus shot him in the back and kept moving. "Rita!" Past the big room the hallway didn't end as he thought but rather took a sharp right. As he turned the corner he came across two guerrillas uncrating an RPG launcher. They stared in surprise at the naked man in front of them and didn't think to reach for their rifles before Seamus gunned them down and did a mag change over their bodies. He then grabbed a new spare from the mag pouch of the man beneath him.

"Rita! Rita!" A guerrilla stuck his head out of a doorway at the far end of the hallway, wondering what the shouting was about. Seamus shot him in the face, then cursed. The house was even larger than he'd thought. *So where would they have taken her? Probably Timotéo's private quarters, the bastard, wherever those were.* He glanced up. *Top floor. The egotistical bastard would have taken a bedroom on the top floor, no way he'd suffer one of his men sleeping above him.*

Seamus sprinted back toward the stairway he'd passed and took the steps two at a time. At the second floor landing he literally ran right into a group of guerrillas heading for the ground floor. They froze in shock at the bloody naked apparition running up the stairs at them, and Seamus screamed at them for good measure, and then bowled two of the men over. He rolled and came up shooting, killed two of them before they could react, then his rifle jammed. One of the men fired wildly at Seamus, who was already moving, and hit one of his compatriots by mistake. Seamus broke his rifle's wooden buttstock on the shooter's face and kicked another down the stairs, then tackled the last man standing

"Fucking. Had. Enough. Of. You. Evil. Bastards," he spat, hitting the man in the face with his broken rifle with every syllable, until he felt bone crunching.

Grunting, he rolled off the man and grabbed a short-barreled CZ 805 off the floor. He shot anybody on the floor still moving, then stood up and put the rifle's stock against his shoulder and peered down the staircase. When the man he'd kicked down the stairs started trying to get up Seamus shot him in the top of his head, then turned to look up and down the second-floor hallway. "Rita! Rita!"

He waited a second for a response, then continued his charge up the stairs.

* * *

"Raven Command, Viking Three-Three, make that in excess of one hundred enemy dismounts, one-zero-zero, although maybe half that are KIA now," Billings spat, slewing the Peregrine sideways. Lucille was getting stitched up pretty badly; he had half a dozen hits on the armored cockpit glass in front of him already, but she was still going strong.

"Copy that Viking Three-Three, I'm moving Heaven and Earth, but closest reinforcements are at least forty minutes out. It's all you until then."

"Roger." It would be all over one way or the other long before that. "Take out the rest of those parked cars with rockets on our next pass," he told Evers.

"Sweeney's down! Sweeney's been hit," Hatch called out. The crew chief was hanging limp from his harness behind his minigun, bright red arterial blood running from beneath his helmet where a lucky round had hit him in the throat. The Peregrine was gyrating too violently for anyone to even attempt first aid.

"Dammit!" Evers cursed.

"Señor," Beni growled.

"Yeah, yeah," Billings said, hitting the throttle and spinning the bird in place. "RPG," he said calmly, triggering another rocket. He was starting to run low on rockets. So much for a boring taxi run. The man had run out from behind a barn with his RPG and went cartwheeling through the air as the Peregrine's rocket exploded at his feet. "I'm not hovering or landing, this area's too hot," Billings snarled at Beni. Hatch's minigun roared behind him as counterpoint.

"I'll swing low and slow over the roof, if you want to jump," he told Beni. "How you get down from there is on you."

"*Sí*, do it!" Beni yelled. He looked to Manny and Torres for confirmation, and they nodded.

"Ten seconds," Billings told the three of them. They unclipped their harnesses and hung onto the hand straps. He swung Lucille wide over the big enclosure on the north side of the hacienda. Evers triggered three rockets which impacted the vehicles parked in the garage and exploded. The guerrillas were scattered. While a few had run away, most of them were still fighting, shooting up at the aircraft, although there didn't seem to be any organization on the ground.

"Get ready, go!" The Peregrine slid sideways through the air, and suddenly the expansive L-shaped roof of the hacienda was below them.

Beni leapt without hesitation. He landed hard on the red clay tiles, the wind from the aircraft's rotors a hurricane. Several tiles broke under him and went sliding off the roof, and for half a second he thought he was going to follow them down. Torres was right behind him but landed a dozen feet away as the bird never stopped moving. Manuel was the last out the open door, but as he planted his foot to leap there were empty shell casings rolling on the floor and his leg shot out from underneath him. He seemed to fall in slow motion out of the aircraft, and twisted his body in midair to absorb the impact. Manuel tucked his arms and head and hit hard in the center of his back six feet from Torres—then the roof collapsed under the impact of his heavy weight. Torres was caught off balance as the roof tilted wildly, and he fell through the hole after Manny.

They hit with one grunt, the air filled with dust and falling pieces of tile. Torres found himself on his back atop Manny, whom he'd landed on. They were in a small room which seemed dim after the bright sunlight on the roof. There were two guerrillas right in front of him. They'd been shooting out the window at the passing Peregrine and turned in surprise as the ceiling imploded behind them. The whole room was filled with dust, and they squinted to try to see through it.

His Tigre nowhere to be found, Torres rolled to his side and pulled his pistol from his hip holster. He fired and fired at the two startled men until they fell, then rolled off Manny. He discovered they'd landed on a bed. No wonder his ribs weren't broken.

"Manny!" Beni yelled from the roof.

"*¡Claro!*" Torres shouted back. Manny was still trying to fill his lungs with air as Beni jumped down through the ragged hole. Torres looked all over for his Tigre, then realized it was hanging from its sling behind his back. He holstered his pistol and grabbed his SMG as Beni pulled Manny off the bed.

Manny glowered at the inspector. "I am glad you are skinny," he said, still struggling to breathe.

"Let's go," Beni said impatiently. He opened the door leading into the hacienda, Tigre leading the way. They found themselves in a short well-appointed hallway with small decorative tables against the brightly painted walls. The tile floor was covered with a carpet runner.

There was a narrow staircase a few feet away and Torres peered over the low wall at the top, only to see guerrillas charging up the stairs. They'd seen the Peregrine drop men on the roof of the main house. They shouted when they saw him and raised their rifles. Torres fired back and Manny joined him, trading fire with the guerrillas below with stuttering bursts from their submachine guns. As they were firing a nearby door opened up and Beni found himself face to face with a bearded guerrilla. The man blinked in surprise, then gave a wordless cry and tackled Beni. They went down hard.

Beni grunted as he hit, then twisted and shoved the guerrilla away from him. He got up on one knee and struck the *Fuerza* across the face with his elbow, then the man's partner who had been behind him in the room darted out and kicked Beni in the ribs. Beni grunted again, falling to the side, the armored vest absorbing most of the blow. He got the Tigre into his hands and fired at the man diving on him. Past the man he caught a snapshot of Torres and Manny side by side, frantically shooting on full auto, jerking the flaming muzzles of their subguns back and forth as they fired down a staircase shoulder-to-shoulder with guerrillas, the air in front of them dense with gunsmoke and empty cases and exploding plaster. Then the guerrilla hit Beni with his full weight.

* * *

As the sliding glass door exploded and sprayed glittering shards across the room, a shadow ran over the balcony and then they heard the roar of a large aircraft going by. Timotéo cursed and punched Tina in the back of the head in frustration and anger, bouncing her face off the bed.

"¡Hombres! ¿Que paso? ¿Raven?" he shouted, making his way to the door and opening it. Several guerrillas were running through the hall outside. One skidded to a stop.

"Si, escaras. Un grande helicoptero."

"Fight them! Kill them like the dogs they are. I will join you in moments." Then he slammed the bedroom door and turned, ready to vent his rage on Echevarria's bitch daughter.

As Timotéo pulled away from her on the bed, Tina pushed up on her hands, shaking her head to clear the pain. Glass shards fell from her hair. She turned and there he was, at the door, looking out, his back to her.

Tina went to charge him and fell to the floor, her feet twisted up in her shorts around her ankles. As she went down she saw Timotéo had his pants around his ankles as well. On the floor on all fours, she reached for his belt as he took a half step and turned toward her.

When Timotéo spun around, the girl was nowhere to be seen, then he looked down and saw her on the floor at his feet, groveling. He snarled at her and reached down. He grabbed a fistful of her black hair and pulled her upright, and with a scream, she drove his knife, the pearl-handled one he kept in a sheath at his belt, into his belly.

His eyes bugged out in pain, and in a fury he wrapped his free hand around her throat. Tina stabbed him again and again as he shook her, cursing. Then his strength faded, and his grip weakened. Tina shoved him back against the door and stabbed him in the throat, screaming in rage and crying. Timotéo reached up both hands to his neck as blood spurted over his chest, joining the gouts running down his belly. He stared at her in disbelief, then fell sideways to the floor. Tina collapsed onto the floor, knife still in her fist, unable to take her eyes off the man as he gurgled and gasped and soaked the carpet beneath him with blood as he slowly died.

She had no idea how long she sat there, staring at him, but slowly she became aware of the shooting and yelling going on everywhere, the roar of an aircraft back and forth over the house, and the explosions made her flinch and duck. She pulled her underwear and shorts back up and buckled her belt, then grabbed the knife again. It was her only weapon. Gunfire ebbed and flowed through house like waves on a beach.

The knob of the door rattled, and the door shook as someone tried it. Timotéo's dead weight kept it shut. "¡Jefe! ¡Jefe!" The man trying the door sounded panicked. The door shook violently, then there was a burst of gunfire and a thud.

She heard a voice, faint at first. "Rita! Rita!"

"Seamus?" She climbed to her feet and put both hands on the knob. She pulled with all her weight and Timotéo fell onto his face, enough for her to get the door open six inches. Just outside the door was a dead guerrilla. Beyond him was a stretch of hallway, then a bloody nightmare holding a rifle.

"Seamus! Seamus?" He ran toward her and she realized that under all the blood and dirt he was totally naked. As he stepped over the dead man in the hallway and shoved open the door she asked, "What happened to you?" He smelled like fresh raw meat.

Seamus saw the bloody knife in her fist, then looked down at the body at her feet. "You weren't watching? Then have I got a story for you that you won't believe." He looked around the bedroom, tossed his rifle onto the bed, then grabbed the body under the armpits and dragged it out of the way. "Looks like you've got one of your own." He picked his rifle up, then did a doubletake as he saw who the dead man was. "Holy hell, is that Timotéo?"

"*Sí*."

Seamus heard her tone and glanced at her, then back at the dead man. For the first time he realized Timotéo's pants were around his ankles. "Are you…okay?" He took a position at the door, rifle up and ready.

"I'm…" she started, her voice quivering, then gulped and nodded. "*Sí*, I am unhurt."

The third floor seemed mostly quiet, with most of the shooting going on elsewhere. The Peregrine roared by overhead, minigun chainsawing away, and the walls shook. Seamus cracked the door and peered out, then closed it again. He eyed Timotéo's half naked corpse, then met Tina's eye. "Of course you're fine." He nodded at the body. "I'm not sure what he thought he could do with that little thing other than hurt your feelings."

She didn't know how to react at first, then burst out in a harsh laugh that almost immediately turned into a sob. She fought the tears back then looked him up and down. "Why are you naked?"

"Apparently I taste better that way."

"*¿Como?*" Then she blinked, and stared. With a hesitant hand she reached out and plucked a broken tooth from the half-dried blood coating his neck. She held it up for him to see.

"Sorry I was late. Took a bit of work to get here," he told her flatly. They traded a long look.

There was a lot of shooting nearby, and the thud of bodies, then more shooting and yelling. The battle was fierce but brief. Then more shouting and running feet. "*¡Margarita! ¡Margarita!*"

Tina stared at Seamus, her brow furrowed. "Beni? Beni!" she shouted. "I know him," she told Seamus, gesturing at the door. "He is one of *mis padres hermanos*, my father's men."

Seamus cracked the door. He could hear men approaching. "Beni!" Tina yelled again. Seamus stuck his head out and saw three dusty armed men, one of them in a dress shirt and tie. No bloody way he was FRAP in that outfit. They saw him and started to raise their weapons, then Tina stuck her head out next to Seamus.'

"Margarita!"

They rushed into the room, and Tina threw her arms around Beni, then Manuel. They crouched in the center of the room. Seamus knelt by the cracked door, keeping an eye out. "Anybody else on the ground besides you three?"

"No, it's just us and the Peregrine," Manny told the obvious *escara*, then did a double-take when he realized the man was naked underneath all the blood and dust. He opened his mouth, closed it, then asked in awe, "*¿El hombre pelean con el tyrannosaur?*"

"Tyrannosaur?" Tina asked.

"Told you I had a story," Seamus said with a wink.

"This is Inspector Torres, *un Federale*," Beni told her, but Torres wasn't paying any attention to them.

"Is that Timotéo Sandoval?" Torres moved to examine the body.

"The one and only," Seamus said. He glanced at Tina, but didn't say anything further. The knife was on the carpet next to the body. "How far out are the other birds?"

"At least half an hour."

"Seriously? That pilot just went balls-in here all by his lonesome? Remind me to buy him a bottle of something nice if he lives. Even if they stop getting incoming they're probably not going to land until reinforcements show up. We should stay in here. With only one way in it's as defensible a spot as we're going to find."

"What about Roger and Michael?" Tina asked.

"In the basement, last I saw, safe as can be expected. The lad was stacking up bodies at the door. Anybody have a palm?"

Manny handed his over and took over door duty. Seamus stared at the device's display. Three bars of service. "Look at that. Civilization. Anybody know the call sign of the Peregrine up top?"

"Viking Three-Three," Torres told him. Seamus punched in a number by memory and listened to it ring.

"Communications."

"Hello luv. Can you please connect me to the pilot of Viking Three-Three?"

"Negative. That aircraft is on priority tasking—"

"I know that, I'm in the building he's been bloody shooting up for the last ten minutes. Perhaps you can hear the explosions and screaming behind me? This is Sergeant Seamus O'Malley." He rattled off his Raven ID number. There was a pause on the other end of the line.

"Stand by."

* * *

"Viking Three-Three, Raven Command, stand by for communication, possible ground unit in your area. Go ahead."

"Viking Three-Three, this is Sergeant Seamus O'Malley, Raven. I am with a group of friendlies on the third floor, center of the big building you are currently circling. There are more friendlies in the basement on the west end. Everyone else in this structure is a hostile, do you copy?"

"Copy that," Billings' tense voice came over the line. "I dropped off three at that location, did they make it to you?"

"Roger that, with me now."

"What about the package they were trying to secure?"

Seamus eyed her. "Here as well, safe and sound. We will remain at this position until you can get boots on the ground to secure the site, over. Raven Command, please connect me to whoever is in charge of this hooley."

"O'Malley, Colonel Kresge, just got linked in. We are the next closest bird but we're still half an hour out if we don't blow our engines getting there."

"Colonel! Lovely to hear your voice. Take your time, no rush, just be aware that we've got three generals from the FRAP command staff running around out here. Ramos and Flores are the two names I remember."

"O'Malley, repeat, did you say FRAP Generals Ramos and Flores were at your location?"

"Yes sir and one more, can't remember his name. Ugly bald fellow with a pug nose. Have not seen them since the shooting started. Oh, and did I mention Timotéo joined us for the festivities?" Seamus smiled.

"You saw him?" Kresge said. "You saw Timotéo Sandoval there?"

"I'm looking at him right now. Mark him KIA if you please." Seamus traded a look with Tina.

"O'Malley, you…" Kresge didn't even know what to say. "Raven Command, on my authority retask any aircraft with the fuel reserves not in active combat within a five hundred klick radius to Viking Three-Three's location to help secure the area, with as many trigger pullers as they can carry."

Seamus jumped in. "Raven Command, you capture this number when I called?"

"We have it."

"Good. We will remain in place. Call me if there's anything I need to know." Seamus disconnected the call and found the camera in the palm's menu. He waved Torres out of the way and then took several photos of Timotéo's pantsless body.

"What are you doing?" Beni asked him, vaguely offended.

"Never underestimate the value of propaganda," Seamus explained. "How upset do you think the macho FRAP are going to be when they find out that they were being led by a guy hung like a chipmunk?" He turned around and took a selfie of himself smiling and giving a big thumbs-up, Timotéo slumped in the background. "Okay, now how do I send that to myself?"

* * * * *

Chapter Twenty-Four

For nearly ten minutes the house shuddered from repeated bursts of the Peregrine's miniguns as the crew was given the green light to engage targets as they appeared in the windows and doorways, avoiding known locations of friendlies.

Tina stared at Timotéo's body. She'd been so angry, so furious with him for what he'd done, what he'd tried to do to her, yes, but also what he had done to her country. Him and all the men like him, *Los Generales Fuerzan*, destroying the lives of millions of people in their own quest for power. But she had killed him with her own hands. Already it didn't seem real, a dream instead of a memory, even though she was staring right at his body. And now she felt...nothing. She wasn't sorry she'd done it. She supposed she was in shock and would have a breakdown of some sort later, but as she stared at his bloody corpse all she felt was tired.

Gradually the firing tapered off, until it had been minutes since they'd heard any, either from the air or the ground. The sound of the Peregrine grew distant as it ascended to a safer altitude. They crouched in the bedroom silently, waiting. Then, finally, Manuel's palm vibrated with an incoming call. Seamus grabbed it and recognized the number.

"O'Malley."

"Sergeant, have you moved from your previous location in the house?"

"Negative."

"Okay. We've got more birds two minutes out. Stay put." Then she was gone.

"Two minutes," Seamus told them, handing the palm back to Manuel, who was on the door. He knelt down next to Tina in the middle of the room. Beni was on the far side of her, and caught his eye. Beni nodded at Timotéo questioningly. Seamus gave a little shake of his head, glanced at the girl without saying a word, then went back to staring at the door. Beni looked thoughtful.

Not long after that they heard the sound of approaching aircraft, and Torres moved to peer out the window, his shoes crunching through glass.

"Two helicopters," he announced. He kept watch as the sound grew louder. "They've both landed, and a number of *escaras* jumped off."

"I'll take the door, these are my blokes," Seamus told Manny. They heard nothing for a while, then a flurry of gunshots somewhere below them and shouting. Eye to the cracked door, Seamus finally heard thudding boots, and Raven troops appeared at the top of the main staircase in full armor, complete with helmets, carbines up.

"Raven!" one of them yelled.

"Down here," Seamus yelled back, and opened the door. He waved a hand and the team headed quickly in his direction. They crowded into the bedroom, suddenly making it seem small.

The lead soldier saw a number of hard Mexican men in the room protectively circling a pretty woman, as well as a naked bloody former hostage with a liberated rifle.

"Sir, you can put the rifle down and relax, we've got you now," he told the man.

The dirty man looked up at him. "Piss off, Carter, you're late as usual."

"Seamus? Is that you?" He flipped up his armored visor. "Why are you naked? Wait, never mind, I don't want to know." One of the soldiers took a lookout spot at the window, and two others took up positions at the door. The rest spread around the room.

Carter keyed his helmet mike. "Raven Command, this is Whiskey team. We are with the package, awaiting transport. Gonna need boots on the ground to clear the rest of this building before we move, there are still tangos in the area."

"Whiskey team?" Seamus asked.

Carter smiled. "Well, we heard you were here. Glad you're still alive. Could have done without seeing your junk, though."

"Don't be jealous, luv. I'm sure you measure up."

Carter shook his head. "How much of that blood is yours?"

"Enough."

"We need to hunker down here," Carter told the group. "Ran into a couple FRAP on the way up, and we need more troops to secure the building." He nodded at Tina. "We've got a bird inbound specially for her. Take her wherever she wants to go. All of ours here are near bingo fuel."

"*Sí*," Beni said.

Carter looked at Seamus. "Just about blew our engine up getting here, and it's still all over before we show up. Looks like you had a hell of a party." He cocked his head. "Weren't you supposed to be on vacation this week?"

Seamus shrugged. "Wasn't I?" He pointed at the body slumped against the wall. "You should leave someone here, to secure his body."

"That's Timotéo?" Carter then noticed that the man's pants were down, and eyed the multiple stab wounds. "Couldn't have happened to a nicer asshole. Who got him?"

"I did," Seamus said quickly, looking directly at Tina. She blinked, then looked away.

"Well you'll never have to buy a beer again. No, hold on, you get that bounty that was on his head, you lucky bastard, you can buy all of us beers. Okay, Shelby, you stay here when we move, this is one body we do not want to lose."

Twenty minutes later the air itself vibrated with all the aircraft inbound, and shortly thereafter the hacienda was flooded with Raven soldiers. They heard shouting, and the occasional gunshots, which after a few minutes tapered off. Carter took the door and signaled the second wave of contractors as they reached the third floor hallway. They cleared all the other rooms on the floor, then gave an all clear.

Carter keyed his mike again. "Whiskey team, on the move." He looked at the hard Mexicans surrounding the girl. "We'll take front and rear, you stay on her." They nodded. "Moving!"

The house was a ruin, with glass and wood splinters covering every square inch of floor. Whole sections of walls were blown out from minigun bursts. Uniformed and armored contractors were checking bodies and looking for intelligence, picking through the rubble. The Raven team hustled her through the house and out a side door into the sunlight. Before them half a dozen helicopters sat in the brown field, half of their rotors turning. More circled in the sky

bove. The Peregrine which had come to their rescue had finally
anded, smoking heavily.

"Which is ours?" Beni asked from the center of the moving pack.

"That one right there," Carter said, pointing.

"No! Not yet," Tina said, darting to the side. She caught all the
men unawares as she ran up to a Blackhawk helicopter. Roger was
on a stretcher inside, and Mike stood next to him holding a rifle, his
face splattered with blood. "You're alive!" she exclaimed and hugged
Mike. She let go of him and backed off. She saw the blood. "You are
injured?"

Mike smiled seeing her. He looked down at his bloody shirt, then
back up. "I'm fine," he told her, sounding exhausted. He'd refused to
put down the rifle even with Raven on the scene in numbers. Since
they weren't quite sure who he was, and they knew there were VIPs
on scene, they didn't insist. Plus, the team who'd found the Rudds
had seen the bodies piled up by the door and filling the basement
hallway. There'd been a hell of a fight down there. He'd earned the
right to keep the rifle.

She hugged him again, fighting back tears, and looked at Roger
on the stretcher. "You are hurt?"

"Just my damn back, still," he told her. He smiled wide, then lifted a hand and she clasped it. "But they've given me some serious
painkillers, so I'm *goooood*." The Raven medic was sitting on a seat
behind him, and she smiled.

Tina laughed in relief, and sniffled and wiped at her nose.

"Are you injured?" the medic asked.

Tina sobered immediately at the thought of what Timoteo had
tried to do, what he had done, and her anger flared white hot again.
She was furious, but physically injured? "No, I am unhurt."

Roger nodded at the armed men clustered behind her. "You heading home?"

Tina glanced behind her at the impatient men. "*Si*. I must go."

"Me or you, it didn't make a difference who they were after."

She smiled at the man. "Maybe not."

Mike shifted the rifle in his hands. "Can I call you?" he asked her. "I'd like to talk. When things are a bit more normal."

She looked up into his face and smiled warmly. Then she hugged him again. "*Si*, I'd like that."

"Rita, looks like this is where the medic is, so I'm going to take my leave of you as well," Seamus told her. She turned to him and without regard for his lack of clothes or the tacky blood covering his body, hugged him fiercely then kissed him. Beni and Manuel turned away, embarrassed.

"You are a good man, Señor O'Malley, and I owe you my life many times," she said.

"Just cos I'm naked, don't get any ideas," he told her. "I'm too old for you."

She laughed and hugged him again, then hugged Michael as well. She waved at Roger, then was whisked off by her escorts.

"Crap, I forgot to get her number," Mike said, staring after her.

"I don't think that will be a problem," Roger told him. "I'd actually like to talk to her father about a business deal."

"Dad, seriously?"

Roger started laughing, then hissed as his back clenched.

Seamus studied Michael. Both he and the Fire Snake in his hands were splattered with blood, which didn't happen unless you were shooting someone right in your face. Seamus caught the boy's eye and nodded, then patted him on the shoulder.

Grunting painfully, Seamus climbed into the Blackhawk past the Rudds and sat on one of the seats. He set his rifle down and started pulling glass slivers out of his feet. The medic eyed his body. "You been rolling around in dirt? I'm going to have to wash you off before I can work on those cuts."

"I'm too tired for foreplay, luv. You would not believe the day I've had. Just get to it. If I start snoring please don't take it personally."

Surrounded by the Raven security team, Beni saw they were heading past the Peregrine he'd flown in and jumped from. It was in the middle of the gravel road and in such bad shape he wondered how it had stayed in the air. There didn't seem to be a section of hull larger than a palm that wasn't dimpled or pierced by bullet holes, and the cockpit glass was nearly opaque from impacts. It smelled of burning oil and rubber, although he only saw one faint wisp of smoke. The crew was standing beside the bird, clustered around a body. As they drew close Beni caught the eye of the pilot and nodded his thanks at the man.

Billings eyed the girl with him, and nodded back. Then he looked down once more at the body of Sweeney, his crew chief. "Anybody know if he's got family beyond the ex-wife?" He was more tired than he could ever remember.

"I don't think so," Hatch said. "But I'll find out. Tell them what happened if they want to know." He looked up at the aircraft. "Hell of a job, keeping her in the air. I don't know how you did it. You had Lucille dancing up there."

"Gonna take days of repairs just to get her back up in the air."

Evers was staring after the group escorting the VIP toward a nearby helicopter. She turned back and shrugged. "We're going to be here for a while. You know we had the whole head of the snake here, right? Timotéo and over half the generals on his command staff. They'll be searching the compound and the countryside all around for days at least."

"They get away? Or don't we know yet?"

"Timotéo's dead for sure. Bought it in the house. I heard the sergeant you were talking to on the radio gutted him. They better give him a freaking medal; we've been after that bastard for twenty years. And they're pretty sure the guy driving that car," she pointed at a burned out husk half buried in a wall, "is wearing a FRAP general's uniform."

"Sweeney tagged that one," Hatch told them. "Pretty early on in the fight."

"Yeah?" Billings said. He looked at the still smoking car, then down at this crew chief's body. "Good."

* * *

The helicopter looked brand new. It wasn't a Blackhawk or a Peregrine; that's all Beni knew. He helped Tina up, then climbed into it himself. Manny jumped up and sat next to him, followed by Torres. There were four heavily armed *escaras* in back, with a minigun aimed out each door. Beni was comforted to see them—the *escaras* and the miniguns. The men escorting them peeled off and headed back toward the hacienda.

"Mexico City, right?" the pilot asked, as he started the aircraft's engine.

"Yes," Beni told him. He set the Tigre on his lap and rubbed his eyes, then looked across at Manny. His friend was obviously exhausted. "*¿Esta bien?*"

He was pretty sure he had a cracked rib from when Torres had fallen on him, but at the moment that pain didn't matter. Manny looked at Tina, sitting nearby on the seat. She was dirty, smelly, haggard, and spent, but she was alive and whole. He smiled at Beni. "*Sí. I am good. I am very good.*"

"Shouldn't be much more than an hour in the air," the pilot said.

"Hey!"

They looked down out of the open door of the helicopter and saw Chris Evers standing on the ground. The Peregrine co-pilot was looking up at Manny.

"You get back home big guy, get things sorted out and calmed down, you look me up." She nearly had to shout to be heard over the engine. "Never had anyone fall head over heels for me before, and you never know what might happen. Life's too short." She smirked, and Manny realized she was talking about him falling out of the Peregrine. But he was confused.

"*Pero, el hombre,* he said...." Manny looked around, embarrassed to be having this conversation in front of everyone. Both Beni and Señorita Echevarria were paying close attention. His neck got hot. "You liked girls," he finished lamely.

Evers smiled widely. "Relationships with coworkers are always a bad idea. If they think you like girls, nobody gets upset when you say 'No.' Or they just don't ask." She stared up at him, the accelerating rotors making her strawberry blonde hair fly around her face. "But you're not Raven." She knocked on the floor of the helicopter and walked off with a wave. "And I like men just fine," she shouted over her shoulder.

Manny leaned back in his seat, a stupid smile on his face. He traded a look with Beni, who rolled his eyes.

Torres sat next to Manny, working his head around, trying to unknot his neck. He had a bad bruise on the side of it and couldn't hear out of one ear, but he was alive. He huffed at the ridiculousness of it all. He'd spent the morning complaining about being leashed to a flying bus and ended up in the middle of the war, on phone calls with the President. God definitely had a sense of humor.

Beni caught his eye. "Thank you," he told the inspector sincerely. Torres stared back at him, then nodded.

Beni pulled out his palm as the rotors of the helicopter began gaining some real speed and punched in a number. He then handed it to Tina without saying a word.

She put it up to her ear and listened to it ring.

"*Si, digame.*" The words were terse.

"*Hola, Papa,*" she said and burst into tears.

* * *

The lieutenant held up a tablet on which five faces were displayed. Some of the photos were grainy. "And you're sure it was these three generals? Aponte, Ramos, and Flores?" he asked, pointing at the photos on the screen. Kresge stood beside him.

"Aponte, that's his name. I couldn't remember. Yes it was those three, in their stupid clown uniforms." Seamus had a fuzzy baby blue blanket wrapped around his waist. It was so damn hot in the Blackhawk he was thinking of taking it off and going starkers again.

Kresge looked at his lieutenant. "We identify any of their bodies?"

"Only Aponte, tentatively; he was the one in that burned car."

"That's a carbeque, how did we ID him?"

"General's uniform, plus his wallet, if you can believe it. It's a preliminary ID only, until we do DNA. If we have any DNA samples from him or his family to compare to. There are a lot of bodies out here, Colonel, and some of them are burnt and blown up. Need dental or DNA to make positive identification for those. Ramos and Flores could be out there. Or on the run."

"Hopefully that Peregrine pounded them too. They were about four pulls of the trigger from being out of ammo when we showed up. Make sure you get facial photos of each and every body and DNA samples as well." Kresge looked at Seamus. "You need to come with me, I've got someone who needs to talk to you."

"Yes sir."

"You be careful, don't pull open any of those wounds, that glue only does so much," the medic told him.

"Yes, Mother." Wrapping the blanket tight around his waist, Seamus carefully climbed down from the helicopter and slowly limped behind Kresge to another Blackhawk. The ends of the blanket dragged in the brown grass. There was a stretcher inside the other helicopter. Kresge simply pointed and walked away.

"Nice skirt."

"Corey? You bastard, you're not dead?" Seamus beamed with delight. "I thought you got lit up."

"Hansen took most of that for me, although I caught one in the thigh. Broke a knee, got some spall in my arm. Looks like I got it worse than you did, just a few tiny cuts on you. Lucky bastard."

"God loves the Irish."

"He must." Corey laid his head back down on the stretcher and closed his eyes. "Shit, I need a few days off."

"You and me both, laddie. I think we've earned it. Hansen dead?"

"Yeah. Before he hit the ground. He's in one of the other Black hawks. I think he's got a wife and a little girl."

Seamus nodded. "I'll talk to Rudd. I don't think he'll have any problems helping them out with a little cash, maybe a trust fund for the girl."

"Tina's father might want to get in on that action as well. I hear everybody else made it?"

Seamus nodded. "With a few scars for their trouble."

"No doubt." Corey lifted up his head. "Watch out, incoming officer." He dropped his head back down. He was still exhausted from the past two days.

"Sergeant, there you are." Kresge's lieutenant walked up to him, typing on his Raven tablet. "We'll need an After Action Report of course, no rush on that, but can you tell me roughly how many guerrillas you engaged at this location?"

"Wasn't engaged to any of them. I killed fifteen to twenty."

The lieutenant's eyebrows went up. "Seriously?"

"That's inside the hacienda. None in the basement, first floor or up. Doesn't count the FRAP I fed to the T. rex out in the yard."

Corey, eyes closed, chuckled. The lieutenant stared at Seamus, then shook his head and walked off. Was the man ever serious? You couldn't believe half the stuff that came out of his mouth some days. Not that the sergeant hadn't been through the grinder, but still.

The lieutenant returned ten minutes later, the strange expression on his face unreadable.

"Sergeant, how many men did you say you killed inside the hacienda?"

"Twenty, give or take." He was too tired to joke about it, and it appeared the lieutenant believed him this time. Seamus guessed they'd had time to do a body count.

"And you did not engage any hostiles in the lower level, the basement?"

"No. Why? How many bodies did you find down there?"

"We counted nine."

Seamus' eyebrows went up. "Did you now? Hmm." He thought of something. "I've got a rifle out here somewhere. FRAP bastards took it off of me. Pistol too. A Walther. Hoping to get those back, if they weren't destroyed."

"I know they're collecting all the recovered small arms in a pile outside the main building. I can send someone to look for yours. A Walther pistol?"

"A P99. And a rifle."

"What kind of rifle?"

"You'll know it when you see it. It's one of a kind, just like me."

The lieutenant put his hand up to his ear, listening to his comm. "Sergeant, could you come with me please?"

"I'll catch up with you later," Seamus told Corey. He followed the officer over to the Peregrine which had given the guerrillas so much trouble. It looked like it had been through three wars. There was a small crowd of Raven men gathered inside the bird, in and around the cockpit, talking loudly. They gave him a lot of looks as he limped up, and grew quiet.

"O'Malley!" Colonel Kresge waved at him. "Get over here. Look at this." He pointed at one of the computer screens in the cockpit. It showed a still image, a freeze frame from one of the Peregrine's gun cameras. While a bit blurry and distant, Seamus clearly stood naked and streaked with blood, brandishing a machete, screaming in the face of a roaring Tyrannosaurus rex which dwarfed him. "Mister, what am I looking at here?"

Seamus studied the image for a long while before answering. "I'm not sure what in that picture could be confusing to you, sir."

Kresge blinked, swore under his breath and shook his head. "So what the hell happened?"

Seamus straightened up. "I fucking kicked its arse, didn't I?" He hid a shudder as he stared at the T. rex, then said loudly, "Can I get a print of that to hang on me wall?"

Kresge sighed. Jesus, he'd been a pain to deal with before he killed Timotéo and went face to face with a T. rex. Naked. Now he'd be insufferable. And probably demand a raise. Over the laughing, Kresge said loudly, "Yeah, well, Sergeant, I have another question for you. Where is it?"

"What do you mean?"

"I mean—"Kresge waved a hand around the destroyed hacienda "—do you see a T. rex anywhere around here? Because he's not in that pen they were keeping him in. And there's no body. I think we'd have noticed a T. rex corpse."

Seamus peered out the open door of the Peregrine at the T. rex enclosure in the distance. There were several breaches in its walls from explosions and minigun fire. Then he looked all around. Black-hawks, Peregrines, two Copperheads, even a Krait, over a dozen aircraft in the air and on the ground, and close to a hundred Raven men moving about with more arriving every minute. But no Tyrannosaur to be seen.

"Hmm. Good for him."

* * * * *

Epilogue

Andy Brady awoke to the gentle hum of Hybridge machinery all around him. The bunk room was so dark, the sound of the machinery so gentle and familiar, it was a bit like being back in the womb. However, whoever had designed the bunk rooms in most of the pumping stations had never slept in one, Andy was sure of it. If he (or she) had, they would have known to put in another light source.

There was a ceiling light, sure, with a switch by the door, but once you shut that off, the room was black as a tomb. No windows in any of the buildings. Getting to your bunk from the light switch—or back—could cost you some skin as there were a lot of sharp edges on the bunks and metal shelving units covering the floor space not occupied by bunks. Because the bunk rooms were the storage rooms, or vice versa. Typical HyBacon efficiency.

He turned his head. As usual they'd cracked the door of the room about six inches, and the monitoring lights on the control panels in the next room were just enough to see by. He heard heavy breathing and looked over. Gabe was a darker shadow on his bunk, still deep asleep.

Andy held up his watch and checked the luminous hands. Ten minutes before six. Still early. He always woke before his alarm out in the field, especially after that run-in with the squad of Raven contractors several months back. He didn't sleep well at all in the field anymore, waking at any sound. Not that he could usually hear much past the hum of the machinery, but the faintest clank or buzz from the equipment now woke him up. That never used to happen.

He and Gabe tried to be up by seven and working by seven-thirty. The sooner they started the job, the sooner it was over, but the real reason was the brutal heat. The siesta had been invented for a reason, but he still refused to shave his beard.

This time, they were working the Veracruz Main line. This particular pumping station...he wracked his brain...number 266, only needed its yearly inspection. It was on the main pipeline between Veracruz and the Tula Refinery north of Mexico City. Mexico's most productive oil field, the Ku-Maloob-Zaap, lay offshore Veracruz in the Gulf of Mexico, and a lot of the crude went straight to Veracruz and then on to Tula. Over three-quarters of a million barrels a day came out of that field, with Upper Paleocene, Cretaceous, and Middle Eocene-producing formations. The pipeline had been blown up once during the war, years before. Hopefully that was all over now.

Veracruz Main ran northwest from the coastal city through the southern end of the Sierra Madre Orientals. The engineers picked the most level path for the pipeline as possible, dynamiting a few ridges here and there, as elevation changes made it much harder on the pumps. Pumping Station 266 was about halfway between Veracruz and Tula, a mile north of Highway 140D near El Salado Lake, almost on the border between the states of Veracruz and Puebla. They were less than five miles from what he'd heard was a fabulous archeological site at Cantona, a huge Mayan temple if he remembered correctly, and he wanted to finish early enough to check it out.

He wasn't going to fall back asleep; there was no chance of that. He pushed his blanket down to his feet and carefully sat up on the unk, fighting back a groan. The pumping station bunks had never een comfortable as a real bed, and he wasn't getting any younger.

His boots were right below the cot, and he slid his feet into them hen stood up and stretched. His back popped, and he worked his eck. He'd fallen asleep reading and was still wearing his HyBridge work shirt, which was now one giant wrinkle. It hung down past his oxers, which were so old they were gray, having started off white.

Andy shuffled out of the room and blinked in the faint glow of he control room indicator lights. He could see at a glance that every-hing was in the green. Barring any unforeseen complications, the nspection should go by the numbers, and they'd be finished and ack on the road in four hours.

He jumped a little at a sudden sound, then realized the coffee naker had turned on and started brewing. The first field teams, which were running the pipelines long before he was out of school, had made it a point to equip every pumping station with a coffee naker. They got used so infrequently, perhaps three times a year at most, the machines seemed to last forever, but coffee itself was an-ther matter. Andy and Gabe traveled with their own supply, a nice trong Ethiopian mix. Half the world's coffee came from Ethiopia, which was a weird fact that had been stuck in his head for years. And ver since he'd learned that it took a coffee plant a whole year to roduce what—dry roasted—became but a single pound of beans, ie had appreciated his coffee even more. He liked his coffee black, ut Gabe stuffed sugar and powdered creamer into his tool kit. The nan liked a little coffee with his cream and sugar.

Moving to the outside door Andy disabled the alarm and opened t. Cool moist air rolled in over his bare legs, and he waved his arm utside the door to pop on the motion activated security lights. They flashed on, momentarily blinding him. The security lights lit up the entire interior of the compound, but a thick fog had rolled in and the area outside the door looked eerie. The truck was only thirty feet away and its outlines were fuzzy, the fog was so thick. After a few seconds standing in the doorway he closed the door and shuffled back into the bunk room. He grabbed the AK leaning against the wall between their bunks.

HyBridge didn't want any employees but those on their security teams armed, but being out in the field in a country nominally at war, Andy and Gabe had always brought a pistol along, just in case. They'd never needed to even pull it out, and it had seemed more than enough protection until that night outside Chicontepec. That episode was unforgettable as the pack of dinosaurs attacked the guerrillas, and the Raven men listened and watched it happen on their computer screen. He could still hear the faint screaming. He'd had nightmares.

Leave it to HyBridge to forget to mention there were man-eating monsters roaming the countryside in addition to the communist guerrillas. Dinosaurs? Seriously? And nobody told them? Both he and Gabe had brought it up to management, but they'd acted as if both of them were crazy. "All the dinosaurs were killed when the park was attacked," they were told over and over. Gabe was incensed, but Andy knew the reason for it—if HyBridge officially admitted the problem existed, they would have to do something about it. Something that cost money, such as sending out security teams with their pipeline engineers. Better to ignore it and hope nothing ever happened. So far nothing had.

Still, he and Gabe had had a long and serious talk. Sure, the chances of something like that happening were slim, but they were out on their own, usually in sparsely populated areas. No one could guarantee their safety. So Gabe had talked to his cousin, who was in the Army, and a few weeks later, they had an AK-47 hidden in the truck. And it came into the pump stations with them overnight, unless there were other HyBridge employees present. In which case the pistol, hidden in one of their toolboxes, was nearby.

Andy wasn't even sure they needed the rifle anymore. Two weeks before there'd been a big Raven attack on the hidden FRAP headquarters, some thirty or forty kilometers north of where he was now, killing most of its leaders. The fact that the headquarters was so close to the Veracruz Main, and this pump station, was in itself sobering. However, ever since then, the guerrilla army had reportedly been in disarray. Plus, Chicontepec was over a hundred and fifty kilometers to the north, so there was no way that dinosaur pack was anywhere nearby. Still, better safe than sorry.

There was enough coffee in the pot now, and Andy filled a cup with the black stuff, just the smell of it making him feel better. With the AK in one hand and the coffee cup in the other, he awkwardly opened the front door again and headed down the metal steps, which were wet with dew. The fog was so thick it felt like breathing liquid. So early in the day, it was barely more than sixty degrees and felt cool, but he knew that unless the fog burned off, the afternoon would be a nightmare of heat and humidity.

Boots crunching across the gravel, the sound echoing oddly in the fog, he walked around the truck, which appeared to be as they'd left it. He then headed for the perimeter fencing on the east side. The security lights combined with the pea soup fog made him feel as if he was walking through milk. The rifle felt heavy in his hand. He'd fired it, once, to make sure it worked. He had no idea if he'd even be able to shoot anyone or anything if push came to shove. He had to admit to himself the rifle was more a security blanket than anything else—having it made him feel safer. Whether or not it actually made him safe...

The chain link fence was ten feet tall and topped with razor wire. He stopped a step away and peered through the fence. If the sun was lighting up the sky in the east, the fog was too thick to see it. Even though he couldn't see more than twenty feet past the fence he knew the land in front of him was mostly flat for about half a mile, before climbing into hills, with a small farmer's house off to the south. Half a mile past the house was Highway 140D, but there was nothing moving on it at that hour. The security lights faded in front of him, the white fog turning gray.

The machinery made a faint hum behind him, but otherwise there was no sound in the cool early morning air. His coffee cup gave off a thick head of steam to compete with the fog. He sipped and stared off into the distance, rifle hanging nearly forgotten from one hand, enjoying the stillness and quiet of the pre-dawn.

From somewhere, perhaps in front of him, he heard a faint sound. It snapped him out of his haze. He couldn't say what the sound had been, only that it hadn't been mechanical. He knew the sounds of the pumping stations by heart. Andy heard it again, something soft and subtle, maybe a boot on dry grass. He squinted, and in front of him at the very edge of the spotlights was a faint silhouette.

"Hello?" He didn't know who might up at this hour, maybe the nearby farmer.

The fuzzy silhouette was barely darker than the gray fog. It grew larger as whoever it was approached the sound of his voice. For some reason Andy wasn't scared; he had the fence in front of him and a rifle in his hand. This was no terrorist attack, this was one person, one silhouette. Maybe somebody lost in the fog, drawn to the bright lights of the pumping station. Yeah, that was probably it.

"*Amigo*, you lost? *¿Ustedes* losto?" Crap, what was lost in Spanish? "Um...*peligro*, no, *perdido*?" he asked as the silhouette grew larger. He was pretty sure that was right, *perdido*. Of course Gabe, with his fluent Spanish, was asleep. Andy took another sip of coffee as his visitor came closer, feet making soft crunching sounds on the brown grass outside the fence. Then he was standing in front of Andy, peering through the fence.

Andy's mouth dropped open as the tyrannosaur dipped its head and sniffed at the chain link, then raised an eye to peer at the shiny coils of razor wire running along the top of the fence line. It chuffed and ducked its head back down, staring at Andy.

He couldn't move, frozen by the sight of the huge animal. Its head was as big as Andy's body, and it appeared to have recently been in a battle with something even bigger. There was a long healing vertical cut on its snout. There were a number of wounds on its chest clotted with dried blood. A cloud of buzzing flies surrounded the wounds.

Andy could hear the breath chugging in and out of the tyrannosaur's lungs. It took half a step forward and cocked its head, regarding him with one huge eye, then straightened its neck enough to press its snout against the chain link. The fence jingled, then Andy heard a groan of straining metal. The eye swiveled around, then stared down, seemingly looking at the forgotten rifle in his hand. For the space of several heartbeats they stood there, face to face, neither one of them moving. Faint wisps of fog swirled around the chain link as the animal sniffed at him with its huge nostrils.

Finally, the giant beast grunted and stepped away. With one look back at him, it turned and began walking southward, angling away from the fence. The animal was remarkably quiet for its size. The fog swirled around it, blurring its shape. In a few seconds, it was a dark shadow against a gray background. Then it disappeared into the fog as if it had only been a dream.

# # # # #

Author's Note

Being born and raised in the American Midwest, my grasp of ritish idioms and army slang is not exactly encyclopedic, so I ached out to Iain Harrison. Current editor of Recoil magazine, eason One winner of the History Channel show Top Shot, and ritish Army veteran, Iain vowed to help make Seamus O'Malley's alogue accurate and "as colorful as a St. George's day vomit." I still ave no idea what that means. I'm not sure I want to.

As for my *Español*, I was pretty darn fluent after four years of gh school Spanish and numerous trips to Mexico…but that was ack in a previous century. Alfredo Rico, who is an artist, profes- onal photographer, and avid mountain biker among other things, d his best to correct any mistakes I made. And thanks go out to a rtain overworked magazine editor (2000 pages of edit a year!) who ffered to copy edit the rough draft of this manuscript but didn't ant to be mentioned by name. She did her best to trim my exces- ve adjectives.

Richard Venola, former editor of Guns & Ammo and one of the ost interesting men in the world, came up with the character name arne Anders for a completely unrelated work. I borrowed it for this ovel, and after reading Bestiarii, Venola gave me his blessing.

Technical expert David M. Fortier stepped into the role of futur- t, trying to help me envision what firearms and military technology ould look like a few decades from now.

My son Barrett gave the rough draft a read-through and spotted veral of those hard-to-see typos that frustrate authors and editors e world over.

I also want to specifically thank Adam Blalock, CEO of Walther rms. Before I ever typed one word of Bestiarii, I was having dinner ith him in Germany, talking writing, and told him of the somewhat ffbeat plotline of this novel. He was nothing but encouraging and ought it sounded like a great read. Adam, hope you like it.

While I have no knowledge of a valley so deep in the Sierra Ma- re Orientals it has its own micro climate (file that under literary ense), in every other way I strived for the utmost in accuracy in is novel—including having the dinosaurs act like real animals as pposed to comic-book villains, which is a particular pet peeve of ine. From geography to oil pumping stations to paleobotany, every detail in Bestiarii is accurate according to current scientific thinking. Including feathered dinosaurs. Any mistakes, of course, are mine.

While most people might assume that the inspiration for this novel came from the late great Michael Crichton's Jurassic Park, people of all ages love dinosaurs and have since they were first discovered. Boys especially—I'm pretty sure it's genetic. Way back in 1912, Sir Arthur Conan Doyle wrote The Lost World in which members of an expedition to South America discover a number of prehistoric animals, including dinosaurs, on a plateau in the Amazon basin.

We all stand on the shoulders of great men, and while I took inspiration from Jurassic Park, that novel's idea of obtaining dinosaur DNA from the blood of mosquitoes trapped in amber actually came from Charles Pellegrino, a darn good author himself (check out his apocalyptic novel DUST).

While in the early stages of this novel I happened to visit the Children's Museum of Indianapolis with my two boys. You can't turn around in there without seeing a photo or sculpture or diorama or actual fossilized remains of a dinosaur, and it touched the twelve-year-old boy in me. I spoke to several paleontologists there in-between their lectures to the actual biological children around me and they recommended two books, both of which I used extensively doing research for this novel.

The first is The Complete Book of Dinosaurs by Dougal Dixon. This book is a great one-stop-shop for everything you might want to know about dinosaurs, and it's great for all ages—if your kids are too young to read it themselves, read it to them one dinosaur at a time. There are full-color pictures on every page. The second book is actually a three volume set: Dinosaurs, The Encyclopedia by Donald F. Glut. This is a very technical piece of work but indispensable when you need to get the final word on gigantothermy, the K-T boundary or T-rex tooth length. I quite often used it as the final word when other reference material of dubious veracity (such as Wikipedia) gave me conflicting information.

While I am no paleontologist I did my best to ensure that the science portrayed in this book is as accurate as possible. Laboratories have been extracting genetic material from fossilized dinosaur bone for years, and at our current rate of progress in genetics it seems safe to conclude that within a couple of decades it will be possible to cre

ate animals which at least look like dinosaurs, even if their DNA is a
bit muddled.

I, for one, can hardly wait.

* * * * *

About the Author

James Tarr is a regular contributor to numerous outdoor publications and has appeared on or hosted numerous shows on The Sportsman Channel cable network. He is also the author of several books, including **Failure Drill**, **Whorl**, and **Carnivore** (with Dillard Johnson), which was featured on The O'Reilly Factor. He lives in Michigan with his fiancée, two sons, and a dog named Fish.

* * * * *

The following is an

Excerpt from Book One of the Lunar Free State:

The Moon and Beyond

John E. Siers

Available from Theogony Books

eBook, Audio, and Paperback

Excerpt from "The Moon and Beyond:"

"So, what have we got?" The chief had no patience for inter-agency squabbles.

The FBI man turned to him with a scowl. "We've got some abandoned buildings, a lot of abandoned stuff—none of which has anything to do with spaceships—and about a hundred and sixty scientists, maintenance people, and dependents left behind, all of whom claim they knew nothing at all about what was really going on until today. Oh, yeah, and we have some stripped computer hardware with all memory and processor sections removed. I mean physically taken out, not a chip left, nothing for the techies to work with. And not a scrap of paper around that will give us any more information...at least, not that we've found so far. My people are still looking."

"What about that underground complex on the other side of the hill?"

"That place is wiped out. It looks like somebody set off a *nuke* in there. The concrete walls are partly fused! The floor is still too hot to walk on. Our people say they aren't sure how you could even *do* something like that. They're working on it, but I doubt they're going to find anything."

"What about our man inside, the guy who set up the computer tap?"

"Not a trace, chief," one of the NSA men said. "Either he managed to keep his cover and stayed with them, or they're holding him prisoner, or else..." The agent shrugged.

"You think they terminated him?" The chief lifted an eyebrow. "A bunch of rocket scientists?"

"Wouldn't put it past them. Look at what Homeland Security ran into. Those motion-sensing chain guns are *nasty*, and the area between the inner and outer perimeter fence is mined! Of course, they posted warning signs, even marked the fire zones for the guns. Nobody would have gotten hurt if the troops had taken the signs seriously."

501

The Homeland Security colonel favored the NSA man with an icy look. "That's bullshit. How did we know they weren't bluffing? You'd feel pretty stupid if we'd played it safe and then found out there were no defenses, just a bunch of signs!"

"Forget it!" snarled the chief. "Their whole purpose was to delay us, and it worked. What about the Air Force?"

"It might as well have been a UFO sighting as far as they're concerned. Two of their F-25s went after that spaceship, or whatever it was we saw leaving. The damned thing went straight up, over eighty thousand meters per minute, they say. That's nearly Mach Two, in a *vertical climb*. No aircraft in *anybody's* arsenal can sustain a climb like that. Thirty seconds after they picked it up, it was well above their service ceiling and still accelerating. Ordinary ground radar couldn't find it, but NORAD *thinks* they might have caught a short glimpse with one of their satellite-watch systems, a hundred miles up and still going."

"So where did they go?"

"Well, chief, if we believe what those leftover scientists are telling us, I guess they went to the Moon."

* * * * *

Get "The Moon and Beyond" here:
https://www.amazon.com/dp/B097QMN7PJ.

Find out more about John E. Siers at:
https://chriskennedypublishing.com.

* * * * *

The following is an

Excerpt from Book One of Abner Fortis, ISMC:

Cherry Drop

P.A. Piatt

Available from Theogony Books

eBook, Audio, and Paperback

xcerpt from "Cherry Drop:"

"Here they come!"

A low, throbbing buzz rose from the trees and the undergrowth ook. Thousands of bugs exploded out of the jungle, and Fortis' eath caught in his throat. The insects tumbled over each other in a lling, skittering mass that engulfed everything in its path.

The Space Marines didn't need an order to open fire. Rifles cked and the grenade launcher thumped over and over as they ed to stem the tide of bugs. Grenades tore holes in the ranks of the gs and well-aimed rifle fire dropped many more. Still, the bugs vanced.

Hawkins' voice boomed in Fortis' ear. "LT, fall back behind the hting position, clear the way for the heavy weapons."

Fortis looked over his shoulder and saw the fighting holes bris- g with Marines who couldn't fire for fear of hitting their own mrades. He thumped Thorsen on the shoulder.

"Fall back!" he ordered. "Take up positions behind the fighting les."

Thorsen stopped firing and moved among the other Marines, re- ing Fortis' order. One by one, the Marines stopped firing and de for the rear. As the gunfire slacked off, the bugs closed ranks d continued forward.

After the last Marine had fallen back, Fortis motioned to Thor- .

"Let's go!"

Thorsen turned and let out a blood-chilling scream. A bug had roached unnoticed and buried its stinger deep in Thorsen's calf. e stricken Marine fell to the ground and began to convulse as the rotoxin entered his bloodstream.

"Holy shit!" Fortis drew his kukri, ran over, and chopped at t[h]e insect stinger. The injured bug made a high-pitched shrieking nois[e] which Fortis cut short with another stroke of his knife.

Viscous, black goo oozed from the hole in Thorsen's armor a[nd] his convulsions ceased.

"Get the hell out of there!"

Hawkins was shouting in his ear, and Abner looked up. The li[ne] of bugs was ten meters away. For a split second he almost turn[ed] and ran, but the urge vanished as quickly as it appeared. He grabb[ed] Thorsen under the arms and dragged the injured Marine along wi[th] him, pursued by the inexorable tide of gaping pincers and drippi[ng] stingers.

Fortis pulled Thorsen as fast as he could, straining with all [his] might against the substantial Pada-Pada gravity. Thorsen convuls[ed] and slipped from Abner's grip and the young officer fell backwa[rd.] When he sat up, he saw the bugs were almost on them.

* * * * *

Get "Cherry Drop" now at:
https://www.amazon.com/dp/B09B14VBK2

Find out more about P.A. Piatt at:
https://chriskennedypublishing.com

* * * * *

The following is an

Excerpt from Book One of This Fine Crew:

The Signal Out of Space

Mike Jack Stoumbos

Now Available from Theogony Books

eBook and Paperback

Excerpt from "The Signal Out of Space:"

Day 4 of Training, Olympus Mons Academy

I want to make something clear from square one: we were winning.

More importantly, *I* was winning. Sure, the whole thing was meant to be a "team effort," and I'd never say this to an academy instructor, but the fact of the matter is this: it was a race and I was in the driver's seat. Like hell I was going to let any other team beat us, experimental squad or not.

At our velocity, even the low planetary grav didn't temper the impact of each ice mogul on the glistening red terrain. We rocketed up, plummeted down, and cut new trails in the geo-formations, spraying orange ice and surface rust in our wake. So much of the red planet was still like a fresh sheet of snow, and I was eager to carve every inch of it.

Checking on the rest of the crew, I thought our tactical cadet was going to lose her lunch. I had no idea how the rest of the group was managing, different species being what they are.

Of our complement of five souls, sans AI-assist or anything else that cadets should learn to live without, Shin and I were the only Humans. The communications cadet was a Teek—all exoskeleton and antennae, but the closest to familiar. He sat in the copilot seat, ready to take the controls if I had to tap out. His two primary arms were busy with the scanning equipment, but one of his secondary hands hovered over the E-brake, which made me more anxious than assured.

I could hear the reptile humming in the seat behind me, in what I registered as "thrill," each time I overcame a terrain obstacle with even greater speed, rather than erring on the side of caution.

Rushing along the ice hills of Mars on six beautifully balanced wheels was a giant step up from the simulator. The design of the Red Terrain Vehicle was pristine, but academy-contrived obstacles mixed with natural formations bumped up the challenge factor. The dummy fire sounds from our sensors and our mounted cannon only added to the sense of adventure. The whole thing was like fulfilling a fantasy, greater than my first jet around good ol' Luna. If the camera evidence had survived, I bet I would have been grinning like an idiot right up until the Teek got the bogey signal.

"Cadet Lidstrom," the Teek said, fast but formal through his clicking mandibles, "unidentified signal fifteen degrees right of heading." His large eyes pulsed with green luminescence, bright enough for me to see in the corner of my vision. It was an eerie way to express emotion, which I imagined would make them terrible at poker.

I hardly had a chance to look at the data while maintaining breakneck KPH, but in the distance, it appeared to be one of our surface vehicles, all six wheels turned up to the stars.

The lizard hummed a different note and spoke in strongly accented English, "Do we have time to check?"

The big furry one at the rear gruffed in reply, but not in any language I could understand.

"Maybe it's part of the test," I suggested. "Like a bonus. Paul, was it hard to find?"

The Teek, who went by Paul, clicked to himself and considered the question. His exoskeletal fingers worked furiously for maybe a second before he informed us, "It is obscured by interference."

"Sounds like a bonus to me," Shin said. Then she asked me just the right question: "Lidstrom, can you get us close without losing our lead?"

The Arteevee would have answered for me if it could, casting an arc of red debris as I swerved. I admit, I did not run any mental calculations, but a quick glance at my rear sensors assured me. "Hell yeah! I got this."

In the mirror, I saw our large, hairy squadmate, the P'rukktah, transitioning to the grappler interface, in case we needed to pick something up when we got there. Shin, on tactical, laid down some cannon fire behind us—tiny, non-lethal silicon scattershot—to kick up enough dust that even the closest pursuer would lose our visual eading for a few seconds at least. I did not get a chance to find out hat the reptile was doing as we neared the overturned vehicle.

I had maybe another half-k to go when Paul's eyes suddenly ifted to shallow blue and his jaw clicked wildly. He only managed ne English word: "Peculiar!"

Before I could ask, I was overcome with a sound, a voice, a shrill reech. I shut my eyes for an instant, then opened them to see here I was driving and the rest of my squad, but everything was ash in some kind of blue light. If I thought it would do any good, night have tried to plug my ears.

Paul didn't have the luxury of closing his compound eyes, but his imary arms tried to block them. His hands instinctively guarded his tennae.

Shin half fell from the pivoting cannon rig, both palms cupping r ears, which told me the sound wasn't just in my head.

The reptile bared teeth in a manner too predatory to be a smile d a rattling hum escaped her throat, dissonant to the sound.

Only the P'rukktah weathered this unexpected cacophony with ce. She stretched out clearly muscled arms and grabbed anchor ints on either side of the vehicle. In blocky computer-generated rds, her translator pulsed out, "What—Is—That?"

Facing forward again, I was able to see the signs of wreckage ead and of distressed ground. I think I was about to ask if I should n away when the choice was taken from me.

An explosion beneath our vehicle heaved us upward, nose first. ough nearly bucked out of my seat, I was prepared to recover our ding or even to stop and assess what had felt like a bomb.

A second blast, larger than the first, pushed us from behind, bably just off my right rear wheel, spraying more particulates and ng us again.

One screech was replaced with another. Where the first had been ost organic, this new one was clearly the sound of tearing metal.

The safety belt caught my collarbone hard as my body tried to que out of the seat. Keeping my eyes open, I saw one of our tires—maybe two thirds of a tire—whip off into the distance on strange trajectory, made even stranger by the fact that the horizc was spinning.

The red planet came at the windshield and the vehicle w wrenched enough to break a seal. I barely noticed the sudden escap of air; I was too busy trying, futilely, to drive the now upside-dov craft…

* * * * *

Get "The Signal Out of Space" now at:
https://www.amazon.com/dp/B09N8VHGFP.

Find out more about Mike Jack Stoumbos and "The Signal Out Space" at: https://chriskennedypublishing.com.

* * * * *

Made in the USA
Las Vegas, NV
11 September 2022

55106259R00282